A

The old man watched the water as the sun sank behind him on the landward horizon and turned the expanse of the iron-grey Atlantic into molten gold. He was alone but for the forlorn cries of the gulls and the thunder of the sea below. He stood stock-still on the edge of the high causeway path, the great rocky mass of Kingsport Head at his back, dragging in the sea air in steady, deliberate breaths as the waves pounded in vain fury far beneath him. It was all he could do to purge the smell of blood and cordite from his head.

The vision had come to him unbidden, as many had before, in dreams.

Unwanted and unlooked for as it was, he desired to be rid of it. Its actors were unfamiliar, its battle and loss carrying no novelty for one such as he—for one who had lived as long and unforgivable a life as he had. Behind it lay something darker, a falling shadow, something terrible he wanted no part of.

An

ARKHAM HORROR™

Novel

Dance of the Damned

Book One of the Lord of Nightmares Trilogy

by Alan Bligh

Fantasy Flight Publishing, Inc.

For my late father, John Francis Bligh, who wrapped me up in stories.

Cover illustration by Anders Finér.

This is a work of fiction. The characters, incidents, and dialogue are
drawn from the author's imagination and are not to be construed as real.
Any resemblance to actual events or persons, living or dead, is entirely coincidental.

ISBN: 978-1-58994-970-6

Fantasy Flight Publishing, Inc.
1975 West County Road B2
Roseville, MN 55113
USA

Find out more about Fantasy Flight Games
and our many exciting worlds at

www.FantasyFlightGames.com

Dance of the Damned

PROLOGUE

The world died screaming.

The girl stumbled forward, her vision swimming, the corridor sliding erratically to the side, breaking apart like the grains inside the Kaleidoscope her brother had brought her for her birthday.

She had been walking for a long time; her dolls had fallen by the wayside some time back, choked with cobwebs and dust, she couldn't remember where.

She looked down at her shiny leather shoes with their silver side buckles, then beneath them to the light and dark tiles of the floor. The white shone like moonlit snow, the black fell away, falling forever.

Step on a crack, break your mother's back.

She walked-stumbled-tumbled-crawled. The screaming grew louder.

Where is father? I must tell him; why doesn't he come back? I have a fever; he must send for the doctor to make the medicine.

Empty pictures stared down from the walls, all the people in them stolen away.

Coming down with fever; couldn't play the stupid parlor game, but he promised, promised, Michael promised. I wasn't bad!

Half a face looked up at her, familiar, painted red; a hand grasped frantically at her stocking-clad shin, leaving crimson stains as the fingers failed to find purchase.

Lottie, is it Lottie?—She cannot be the one screaming; she has no mouth.

The maid was gone, sucked away into the narrow black tile like she had never been.

Stepped on a crack.

Onward and onward, she placed one foot in front of the other as the Kaleidoscope turned, the screams sounding a song without words, insistent, calling to her, louder, ever louder.

I'm not listening.

She turned away from the staircase where the shadows curled like ink in water, vines of thorns and mouths, slavering, the woodwork burning away to ash in a fire whose flames she could not see, but burned so very cold.

Not looking.

To the wide window she crept and ran, slid, and stood still.

Perhaps my father is coming, coming up the drive in his big motorcar; perhaps he has medicine for my fever.

The sky over the valley was violet and black; the trees thrashed in a hurricane without sound, splintering, falling. Down in the town, the houses toppled and dissolved in fires the girl could not see, and, in place of smoke, the screams of the people rose to the tortured skies. Only the blackened church steeple still stood high, but soon its pinnacle cross would crack and crumble to splinters as the ants swarmed around it, dying.

Kingdom come.

Something shapeless and vast swooped by, and on the driveway below, a running figure—she didn't have time to tell who—came apart in ribbons, their screams caught, trapped in the air long after the ribbons fell to the ground and soaked the gravel red.

I don't want to see!

But closing her eyes made no difference.

Darkness rose up behind her; its shadow blackened the glass.

Father! She turned.

It was not her father.

CHAPTER ONE

In a private reading room, deep within the Miskatonic University's Orne Library, all was stillness and dusty quiet. The brown and green shadows of its bookcase lined walls were deep and somber, and the pervading gloom was lengthened into premature dusk by the overcast day. Soft rain pattered at the tall, arched windows, offering the merest suggestion of sound.

Daisy Walker was a solitary figure perched at the great desk which occupied the reading room's center, her head propped up on her hand, and her artless golden-blond hair shading her eyes as she focused her unwavering attention on the pages before her.

The square-paneled door behind her swung open loudly on less than well-greased hinges, but Daisy did not stir.

"Miss Walker?... Excuse me?... Daisy?" the incomer asked tentatively after she had gone unnoticed for almost a minute by the room's occupant.

"Oh, Carol...what is it?" Daisy said, pulling her eyes away from the stack of puritan tracts she'd been fruitlessly trying to catalogue for the last three hours. "I didn't see you there, or hear you come in for that matter." She smiled in apology.

"Um," Carol said uncomfortably as Daisy's attention focused on her. She fidgeted a moment in silence.

Daisy smiled again and considered her colleague as she waited patiently for her to speak. With a habitually pinched expression, and her hair pulled back in a bun so tight it made Daisy wince thinking about it, Carol was just about everybody's idea of a bookish spinster—at least on the surface. Daisy, however, knew better than to let her colleague's appearance deceive her, and had long come to terms with the fact that Carol's prim exterior hid a riot of conflicting fancies, a string of broken hearts, and an absent-minded streak wide enough to mislay a battleship in.

The silence dragged on, and finally Carol spoke. "Any luck?" she asked, first nodding to the wide jumble of loose ivory-colored pages in front of Daisy, then peering at them suspiciously over her half-moon spectacles.

"Not much," Daisy replied, after a pause in which she struggled to work out why Carol was there. "While it was good of the Derby estate to donate these," Daisy continued, filling the awkward silence between them. "I do wish that whichever of the Derby patriarchs who collected them hadn't sliced them up and folioed them by subject, rather than date or authorship. It's proving a devil to sort out."

Carol nodded in commiseration, then just stood there waiting for Daisy to continue.

At twenty-six, Daisy was more than ten years Carol's junior; she was also a full Librarian—a tenured reader and researcher at Miskatonic University, with authority over Carol—making the relationship between them often strained. Carol was somewhat uncomfortable with the fact that Daisy had been so favored, and was also dubious of her relative youth and short time with the faculty. The two of them had, nevertheless, settled into an acceptable pattern of work together, despite Carol's foibles, and had even edged into a kind of tentative friendship. Sadly, Daisy knew that some days a gulf just seemed to yawn between them, in which neither knew quite how to deal with the other. Today, it seemed, was destined to be one of those times.

"Carol?" Daisy asked with a familiar exasperation.

"Yes?"

"You wanted something?" she smiled.

"What?… Oh, yes!" Carol said, suddenly producing an envelope from her jacket pocket. "This arrived for you earlier; it's marked personal—all the way from New York City by the stamp—forwarded through from Kingsport."

Daisy took the slightly battered looking letter from her. Carol hadn't been wrong; it had been sent to her at her old address at the Hall School in Kingsport. Whoever had sent it clearly hadn't realized she'd taken a new position here at the university in Arkham nearly three years ago.

"Have you ever been to New York City?" Carol asked. "I never have… I'd love to see Broadway, though…see the lights and catch a show," Carol, suddenly animated, went on in an impatient, gossipy tone, "I've been to Boston, of course…but it's not the same."

"Once, when I was in college, my whole class went on a tour of the museums. We stayed three nights," Daisy answered absently, carefully smoothing down the letter on her desk blotter.

She didn't recognize the penmanship on the address, precisely, but it was a familiar style of hand and one not unlike her own. For someone with Daisy's naturally analytical mind, it didn't take much reasoning to narrow down a list of possible senders.

"Aren't you going to open it?" Carol prompted, a little too eagerly for Daisy's taste.

"Later," Daisy replied, forcing a smile and tucking the letter into her desk drawer. "I'm afraid I've a date with some eighteenth century firebrands first."

Carol, clearly a little put out by this development, but knowing that once Daisy set her mind to something it was more than Carol could do to budge her, turned away and wandered off with a sniff, closing the reading room door behind her with a loud clunk.

Daisy sighed. Knowing Carol, she was already fermenting fantasies of torrid love letters from secret Manhattan beaus in her mind, but Daisy didn't much care; she had her fiancé Ted—even if he was a couple hundred miles north for the next few months. Despite Carol's daydreaming—she'd do that anyway, even without encouragement—Daisy was content.

Such talk could be bad for a working woman's reputation, but Daisy didn't worry; over-imaginative as she was, Carol knew better than to spread those daydreams too far. The dean notoriously took a very dim view of idle speculation, either from or about his staff. But then again, such an attitude was not uncommon in these parts, and Daisy found that Arkham was a town full of secrets well-kept.

As for the letter from New York, innocent as it might seem, just touching it made her uneasy, as if it carried an impending sense of tragedy—although Daisy couldn't for the life of her imagine what such news could possibly be. She wasn't overly keen to find out just now, and for a moment, she had the startling urge to light a match and consign the letter to ashes unread, but the strange desire left her as swiftly it came.

The letter could wait till later, Daisy decided, much later.

* * *

Annabel pulled the fur collar of her dark woolen overcoat close, and stepped out over the intersection and into the rain, weaving between the stalled traffic. She had lived in New York City for over a year now, but had never felt more a stranger to its bustling, narrow canyons of weathered concrete and soot-stained brick.

Heartsick and afraid as she was, everything that had once

seemed familiar about her way home had become sinister and alien. The faces that came out of the rain around her seemed furtive, ugly, and leering, and, a few feet beyond her, a host of empty, shadowed shapes came and went chaotically like an army of ghosts on the city streets.

Annabel was afraid. It wasn't an emotion she was used to, and it was galling. She was proud of the fact she was a modern, independent woman, but she wasn't stupid either. Annabel knew she had just cause to fear for her life—her life and something yet more dear to her heart.

Her boots clicking with quick syncopation on the wet-slick paving slabs, Annabel dodged quickly forming puddles of rank water and refuse as she turned off the main avenue and onto the cross-street. The wind and rain cut away as if a door had been shut.

Two blocks, just two blocks more.

The cross-street, dotted with small thrift stores and anonymous nickel-and-dime businesses, was unusually busy with people hunkering down out of the rain, and Annabel drew more than a few lingering glances as she hurried by. Somehow, she didn't hear the screaming until she was almost blocked in by the crowd that had gathered ahead of her. The pitiful, inhuman wails slowed her in her tracks far more effectively than the milling backs of the human vultures that had been drawn in to watch.

Annabel wanted only to be through the press of bodies and gone on her way, but the screaming continued and she was torn between pressing on and turning back. However, she knew if she retreated now, she'd be another half an hour at least in working her way around, and the rain, which had already started to soak through her hat and coat, would drench her through to the skin. She picked her way forward, eyeing the eager faces around her with dread as she tried to make her way around the crowd.

Before her, the bulk of a vagrant, his form misshapen by layer after layer of uneven, soiled clothing, shifted sideways and the crowd suddenly parted to show her the cause of the carrion attraction.

A heavy, wet thrashing sound was accompanied by a short burst of fresh wailing as a badly wounded draft horse tried to pull itself off the ground, still tangled up in its harness, one of its forelegs twisted horribly out of shape. Dark blood pumped into the street gutter foaming the running rainwater red as it swept downstream into the sewers. A small motor Sedan was pulled up against the opposite curbside from the stricken beast's milk wagon, its nearside headlamp shattered and wheel-cover mangled from the impact. The man who appeared to be the driver, hawk-featured and sharp-suited, was in heated argument with a stocky, mustachioed teamster, finger stabbing the air viciously as the teamster's fingers curled and his color visibly rose. Violence and blood was heavy in the moist, oppressive air. Onlookers on all sides were beginning to shout and harangue both the arguing men and each other, and scuffles began to break out.

Annabel looked on appalled; she knew such things happened—much of the trade in the city was still horse-drawn, and the ever increasing number of motorcars made such things a tragic inevitability—but she had never seen an accident such as this one up close.

Why is no one helping? she thought desperately.

Annabel's ill-defined fear was suddenly given definite shape as a waspish older man was sent stumbling into her by a careless elbow. He turned on her suddenly, a curse on his lips, his hand raised to strike. Adrenalin flooded her veins, and she felt her own gloved hand clench reflexively as she backpedaled away from him, her eyes blazing with defiance.

A shudder ran through the crowd like an electric charge as a new voice entered the fray and the confrontation between Annabel and the stranger was instantly broken. The older man was suddenly left blinking in confusion, visibly shocked by what he had nearly done, leaving Annabel with a sick feeling in her stomach.

"Fools!" the voice shouted. "You see them not, but they are among you! As a foulness shall you know them, and in suffering they are exalted!"

Annabel stared up to where a ragged, scarecrow-like man had clambered up on the back of the stranded wagon, one spidery hand spryly clutching at the tall steel milk pails for support.

The man looked frail, dirty, and ill-shaven, and with the rainwater glistening on his bald dome, he should have made a fragile, perhaps even pitiable figure, but his booming voice, startling in its power and heavy with the sonorous cadences of the Deep South, echoed across the narrow street. Even from some yards away, Annabel could see his eyes, shining like two chips of polished tin as they swept through the crowd.

The horse screamed anew, and somewhere in the crowd a woman broke down in tears, while others, suddenly silenced, trembled as if about to bolt and run, or renewed their arguments with even greater hostility as if trying to drown out the ragged man's voice, but some few she saw, looked up at the street preacher—for preacher she now saw he was from his stained white-and-black collar—as if transfixed.

"As lambs to the knife shall you be, and with death they are in agreement! When their hour comes 'round once more, you will find no solace in lies, but shudder and perish as children cast to the serpent's lair! But rejoice, for there is salvation and rapture for those strong enough to find the way!"

Four blue-coated policemen in sodden caps barged their way through the thick of the growing melee, and proceeded to try to break the crowd up with commanding shouts and brandished nightsticks as the ragged preacher laughed and a brawl broke out at last between the teamster and the car driver.

Annabel seized her chance and dove across the space that opened up, almost breaking into a run.

"You cannot escape him! He comes, he comes for you!" The ragged preacher's voice seemed to follow her as she broke free of the crowd and away, her escape punctuated by a single pistol shot behind her, her tears lost in the rain.

* * *

The cell was as cold and black as the grave, and there was nothing but Morgan's own dark thoughts to keep him company.

His friend, Ray Thorpe, was dead.

He forced himself to see the man's jovial, flushed, Irish face, his overcoat looking like he'd slept in it, that battered hat at that off-kilter angle like he always wore it, the way he snapped his cheeks after taking a belt of whiskey, the wife and daughter he never saw but were always on the tip of his tongue.

Janice? That was her name, wasn't it?

Widowed now—no more alimony checks from her washed-out private eye husband…another ripple in the water.

Would she cry? Of course she would. *What a stupid question to ask…*

In his mind, he had known Ray had no realistic chance of living long enough to catch sight of an ambulance, gut-shot and dying on that forlorn stretch of Staten Island beach, but Morgan had tried anyway. He'd scrambled, ran, half-fallen down to the caretaker's shack the rum runners that owned the place used, and smashed his way in, bargaining they'd have a working phone. He'd been amazed when he'd managed to get a line on the cracked Bakelite handset.

Despite his effort, Ray had bled out minutes after he'd gotten back from the shack. They'd picked him up soon after, but Morgan couldn't bring himself to regret the call.

Tony, Tony I'm cold. Ray's dying voice rang unbidden in Morgan's memory.

He had held Ray like a baby as he had started to shudder just before the end. It was the least he could have done. After all, Ray Thorpe had been a friend of sorts—one of the few Morgan had made since coming to the city—and more than that, his "partner," as the Yanks would have said, and that ought to count for something.

The spirals of guilt and consequence in his brain were cut short when the cell door cranked open and a pair of flashlights shone in, scattering vermin and forcing him to squint against the sudden glare.

"Get up. Come with us. No talking. Put a foot outta line, and we'll break you in half."

The orders were issued in a cold, firm tone—not the bark he might have expected—and as Morgan pulled himself to his feet and held his hands out for the shackles, he realized it was still full night outside. And there were four guards—bad news.

He was led by flashlight through cold, benighted corridors away from solitary, through anonymous now-empty workshops and holding pens that stank of moldering cement and human suffering, and then out, up steel companionways and over cell blocks where only the weeping of the fresh meat and the occasional howls of the broken interrupted the heavy silence.

He'd been in custody before, and moreover, he'd put a lot of other men there, so he knew by what was going down that he was in deep and sinking fast. Lawmen the world over never made themselves work more than they needed to, and moonlight prisoner transfers on rainy nights spelled trouble of the worst kind, particularly for the prisoner, and particularly when the guards were making every effort to pass with him unnoticed.

Morgan knew he hadn't exactly cooperated; he'd stuck to the truth, which unfortunately wasn't what they'd wanted to hear. He'd already taken a couple of beatings for doing so, but they had been more an effort to soften him up than to do real damage. After all, as they told him, he had a grand jury appearance to keep. Had they changed their minds? Would this long walk end in a dead-end corridor and some real punishment, or was he about to have a more serious "accident" and save them the trouble of the trial?

Morgan weighed his chances, and they were about non-existent. Not that he wouldn't fight back; he wasn't the surrendering kind.

A corner and a narrow flight of stairs, and they were suddenly in a part of the prison that had seen paint in the last decade, somewhere high up. His guards became even more furtive when the lights came on, as if they were children sneaking around the house after dark.

Stranger and stranger, Morgan thought.

A door, a wooden paneled one, not a cell door, he noticed, was thrust open and he was pushed through.

"Anthony Percival Morgan," a coarse, deep voice said as soon as the guards had dumped him in a chair and departed. His name had been spoken as a statement rather than a question, and issued from a bear of a man wrapped in a shapeless overcoat, sitting behind what looked to be a senior warden's desk. Morgan had seen the warden on his arrival, and this wasn't him.

"Yes." It was the first word Morgan had spoken aloud in he didn't know how many days.

Well, it's not a bullet in the back…not yet, Morgan thought, taking in the room: the faded print of Washington on the wall, rusting filing cabinets, prison clock reading quarter-to-four in the morning.

"You American or English, Morgan?" The waiting man casually indicated a file on the desk beside him with a fist full of thick, blunt fingers that looked like they could have gouged brick without effort. "Says here, 'dual nationality by blood'—don't see too much of that. Father took off from here to the Far East before you were born, eh? What, about 1894-1895?"

It seemed an incongruous question to be dragged out of a cell for in the dead of night, and Morgan said nothing in reply. He waited. He was being sized up and he knew it.

"Quite a mouthful," the man continued, "your name I mean, but you limeys love your long-winded names, huh?"

Morgan just looked at him silently, taking in the details of his inquisitor. He was a big man, a good few inches taller than Morgan's six feet, with a face like a slab of chipped granite, deep set eyes, iron-grey hair close cut, the wrong side of fifty—but still powerful. He wore a lifetime of violence around him like a second coat. All in all, a hard man to cross.

"I guess I'll just call you 'Killer,' huh? I'm sure Joe Luca and his pals would attest to that?"

Morgan remained silent and unreadable as he stared at the older man behind the desk, watching as the man's big battered hands flexed slowly in the light from the green glass-shaded desk lamp. His interrogator was trying to intimidate him, just to see which way he would jump. He was looking for a reaction, and after long seconds passed without one, the slab-like man just nodded slightly and changed tack.

"You in the War, Killer? You look about old enough. What are you thirty, thirty-three?"

Morgan flexed his painfully stiff shoulders. Whatever was happening, he needed to make sense of it, and if they were going to kill him, they were damn well taking their time about it. Either way, it was time to put aside his natural inclination to give them nothing, and try and get some information in return. "You got my file—Singapore—I volunteered after the mutiny," Morgan replied, seeing no reason to lie about his war record.

"Huh, it speaks!" the man said with mock surprise. "At least you lost most of the limey accent somewhere on your travels. Volunteered—I figured it was something like that. At least you missed the trenches out in France, lucky damn you." He lit a cigarette.

Morgan was growing impatient; the handcuffs on his wrists were heavy, and he never slept well in cages. "Detective…?" he offered.

"Captain Grissom," the big man replied, smiling unpleasantly as if he'd scored a point in some kind of one-sided game he was playing.

"Captain Grissom," Morgan continued, "you've hauled me out of my cell before the crack of dawn, insulted me some, and established that we are both old soldiers. Now, do you mind getting to the point of whatever it is you're after?"

Grissom laughed, "My, you got vinegar; I'll give you that, Killer. All of a sudden I'm glad we got those bracelets on you, eh? What I'm after? Maybe I just wanted to see you in the flesh—how about that?"

"Why?" Morgan asked, looking Grissom in the eye, neither breaking their stare.

"You walked out of a gunfight leaving five dead hoods," Grissom offered, "all with bullets from your guns stuck in them, they tell me. Five ventilated scum and one very dead drunkard—a former beat cop, later drunken deadbeat P.I."

"Ray Thorpe," Morgan said.

"Ray Thorpe, yeah," Grissom returned with a nod. "He was the only one you didn't kill, but then again, he was meant to be on your side."

Grissom paused and studied Morgan, as if looking for a hidden truth he could find if he just stared long enough and intently enough. "Maybe I just wanted to see what kind of lucky man comes through that kinda storm without a mark on him, and calls the damn cops himself, and stands around and waits for them to scrape the carcasses off the pier…"

Grissom reached behind him, tossed a paper-wrapped bundle onto the desk between them, and tore it open. Inside were Morgan's clothes and Grissom pulled out the grey jacket, still stained in dark patches with other men's blood, and pushed one blocky finger through a bullet hole in the fabric to make his point.

"Got pretty close, though, didn't they?"

"As you say, I'm lucky," Morgan replied, but the words tasted ashen in his mouth. "Ray...he wasn't."

"Lucky," Grissom muttered, almost as if he were weighing the word. "Well, I guess you're gonna find out if that's true or not— *Killer*."

"Just what's going on here, *Captain* Grissom?" Morgan demanded, emphasizing the man's rank scornfully.

Morgan didn't know if Grissom was mocking him or just expressing some personal loathing...or if there was some hidden meaning to what Grissom was saying he just wasn't getting.

"Again, I ask you, why am I here, now, with you? You want to put me on trial, put me on trial. You want to bounce me down a few flights of stairs, go right ahead—you've got the muscle, and I'm not going to be able to stop you!" Morgan said, raising his shackles and shaking them. "Just cut to the damn chase and tell me: what the hell is going on?" Frustration was making him bolder than he meant to be.

"You don't get it, do you, Killer?" Grissom laughed. "You haven't a clue why I'm here." Grissom leaned back and lit another cigarette, clearly satisfied in some way by what he'd heard.

"Why, I'm here to send you off on a little ride, Killer. That's the long and the short of it. There's a man wants to meet you downtown—he's a real fan, and you'd best put these on," he said, prodding the bloodied clothes. "Though, maybe not the jacket... Don't want to frighten his receptionist," Grissom chuckled.

Morgan shook his head. "You wanted me face-to-face at four in the morning just so you could send me somewhere else?" he asked incredulously.

"Oh, I wasn't lying; I wanted to look you in the eye, see just what kind of man you are. You are a rare fish, my friend. You should be looking at a damn noose," Grissom said with a croco-dile smile, "and instead it looks like you're gonna walk away, not even stand trial. Now, ask yourself: why?"

Grissom kicked back his chair and went to leave. Pausing in the open doorway, he turned, saying, "Be seeing you around, Killer, and maybe when I do, you can tell me if you'd have picked the rope instead."

Morgan was left in stunned silence as a pair of plainclothes cops—not the black uniformed prison bulls he'd been expecting—came and stood guard over him as he changed from his prison overalls into what was left of his blood-stained, unkempt clothes, including the bullet-holed jacket. They looked straight through him whenever Morgan met their eyes, as if he were already a ghost.

He didn't see Grissom again as he was led out into the main yard and into a waiting van with grim, high, steel-barred slats for windows—a Black Maria; in fact, Morgan didn't see anyone but the silent detectives, and they stayed gingerly at arm's length as if he was a plague-carrier.

The journey from the unknown jail began before dawn, and carried on into the morning. The van went straight over ill-kept roads, hard-rimmed tires bouncing and rattling over every pot-hole as if the whole thing was going to fall to pieces at any moment. Through the thin, barred slots that passed for windows in the steel box, came the chill night air, and soon he was shivering. But to Morgan, shackled to his bench and unable to see out, the clean bite of the cold was a blessed taste of a wider world.

The journey dragged on into hours without pause, and the van turned and turned again before finally halting. But then they rocked gently on a ferry for some time, the tainted oil-and-salt tang of the harbor spray unmistakable.

They started moving again, and no one came to check on him. He heard no murmur of conversation from the cab. Only the intermittent clang from a trolley car now and again let him know he was now inside the city bounds somewhere. It was almost as if they had been driving in circles, water-crossing notwithstanding, and perhaps they had been.

The Black Maria shuddered to a stop at last, and the doors swung open, letting the feeble light of an overcast day into the van, focusing his drifting mind firmly on the present.

Standing there between Morgan and the bustling city beyond were two nearly interchangeable men he didn't recognize, and whose allegiance he couldn't guess at. Both were broad-shouldered and heavy-set, with expressionless, bland faces, neatly dressed in fashionable and expensive-looking brown woolen herringbone suits, and sporting trilby hats. They certainly weren't cops; instead, they looked like stevedores dressed up as lawyers.

"Mr. Morgan," the first said in a curiously flat voice as he held up the key to Morgan's shackles, "if you'd come with us, Mr. Shawcross is expecting you."

* * *

Annabel looked around her studio apartment for what she knew in her heart-of-hearts was likely to be the last time. She could see no way of avoiding leaving now, however much she regretted it; the city had become a prison to her, a place of fear—perhaps even a death-trap—and even if she stayed, what then? She knew her frayed nerves could take little more of the cat-and-mouse game of dread and suspicion her life had devolved into; the horrible encounter with the injured horse and the street brawl the previous morning had proven that much.

And if I stay and I'm right…, she let the thought trail off unfinished. *No backing out now. I have to go.*

She had to leave her things, her possessions—bits and pieces of her past strewn with memories, her dresses and paintings most of all—and travel light. In her mind, she also knew that leaving the place looking like she intended to return might do her some good in the long run, but here and now, doing rather than thinking about it had proven an unexpectedly painful wrench to her heart.

She knew why: it maybe wasn't much, but it had been hers and hers alone—the bedroom-cum-studio-cum-kitchen-cum-sitting room, the walk-in closet, the tiny tiled bathroom—her very own chunk of the world. From the pictures on the wall, many her own work, to the dozens of trinkets and curios collected on her travels, to the old ornate clock she'd picked up in the market for a nickel with the Chinese characters on it that never worked right—it was all hers, and she hated abandoning it all. It had been her home for nearly a year, and it represented the longest she'd stayed in any one place since she'd been old enough, and moneyed enough, to be independent.

It was a place where she'd tried to put down roots after years adrift, a place of memories, some happy, others not. But now she was running, skipping town, and she had little chance of avoiding pursuit if she took her time and packed up like some sodbuster piling his worldly possessions on the back of a truck. She needed to be swift, and at least give the illusion of maybe returning soon. Her first move was to head to Grand Central, catch the Boston line sleeper, and get the hell out of New York before whatever stalked her reached out and dragged her down. After that, well, she wasn't so very sure.

I hope I'm doing the right thing, she fretted, not for the first time that morning.

There was a sick fear in her stomach, but its chief focus was not for herself.

Run away, run, Annabel. He's gone; no use in staying now.

The apartment door swung open suddenly and she nearly jumped out of her skin.

"Miss Ryan, ya taxi's waitin'," a gravel-rough voice barked.

The mousy figure in the doorway was Mrs. Fawn, her landlady, cigarette cocked insolently in her mouth as always, her narrow shrewish face pinched as if she had just tasted something sour. Not for the first time, Annabel recalled that counting dollar bills had been the only time she'd ever seen Mrs. Fawn remotely happy.

Quickly recovering her poise, Annabel drew herself up and peered down on the older woman—quite literally, as Annabel was a full head taller, even without her heels—with all the considerable studied disdain her New England breeding allowed, just because she knew the mean old souse hated it when she did so.

"I take it still no telegram, Mrs. Fawn. Any letters?"

"No, nodda peep, and the mailman's been and gone. You expectin' a stay of execution?"

Annabel fixed her with a withering stare. "I'm sure I don't know what you mean. You're paid to the end of next month. See to it the room's not disturbed."

Mrs. Fawn sniffed indignantly but made nothing more of it. Truth-be-told, Annabel Ryan did intimidate her, not that Elma Fawn would ever admit it. The young woman—with her picture perfect looks, fashionable clothes, lean and lithe stature, and old-money accent—seemed part of a world she had little grasp on. Her tenant was the real thing, too, not just putting on the airs and graces like some did; she'd managed a women's lodging house since before the War, seen them come and go, and been around the block enough times to know the difference. Yes, Miss Annabel Ryan was too good for her joint, and maybe that spelled trouble she didn't need, but the Ryan girl always paid up in full, which, given the sliding state of the world, wasn't something to be scorned.

"If anyone calls, where shall I say you've gone?" Mrs. Fawn muttered grudgingly, stepping out of the striding young woman's path as she picked up her valise and a small portfolio bound up with leather book straps and made it through the door.

Annabel paused suddenly, scanning both sides of the corridor before heading toward the elevator doors at speed. "You won't!" Annabel's shout drifted back as the cage doors slammed shut.

Tutting to herself, Mrs. Fawn backed out of the room and locked the door with her passkey. Turning to leave, her breath caught suddenly in her throat and she nearly fainted, catching herself on the doorknob to stop herself from falling.

She blinked rapidly just to make sure it was gone. At the far end of the corridor was a high window. It did little more than let the light in, usually, with no view to speak of but the blank wall of the building opposite, but as she'd turned, just for a second, she would have sworn there was something *there*, outside the glass.

She couldn't quite work out what she had seen: something huge and rippling, flabby, or shrouded in cloth? She couldn't bring to mind just what it had really looked like, and after a second or so realized she didn't want to, but she knew it had been terrible somehow, and her stomach knotted just thinking of it.

Mrs. Elma Fawn turned her back to the window and shuffled as swiftly as her arthritic knees would take her in the direction of the stairs, focusing her mind on Annabel Ryan's folded bills tucked in her apron pocket, and the half bottle of bathtub gin she had stashed in a planter in the front parlor; just a nip she needed, to steady her nerves and put it out of her mind.

She never saw the thin rime of sudden frost ascending the window pane at unwonted speed.

* * *

The receptionist had a chill, too-perfect beauty that was somehow at odds with the stifling heat in the office building. Morgan flexed his hands—the cuffs had come off once inside the building—and now he relaxed, enjoying the surprisingly visceral pleasure of the reception area's deep leather sofa after the police van's battered bench seat.

He studied the girl, and ignored the two brown-suits who flanked the brass-framed elevator door which guarded access to the ground floor, and with it, the outside world. After weeks of cells and shadows, the girl offered a much better prospect to the eye.

Although covered primly from neck to heels in curiously old-fashioned and very proper clothes, they fitted her form perfectly and suggested, rather than concealed, a figure better-suited to a Greek goddess than an office worker. Caught at some inde-terminate point between youth and maturity, her wine-dark hair was frozen in a perfect Marcel Wave, and the little silver half-moon glasses she wore—as her hands effortlessly stroked an unbroken rhythm on her typewriter—rather than humanizing her, only drew attention to her perfectly symmetrical and flaw-less features.

Beautiful, yes, Morgan thought, *but so is a tiger.*

Had Grissom known? He'd said something about "upset-ting the receptionist," Morgan recalled, and at the time it had sounded like a line, but now he wasn't so sure. The old bear of a policeman had also said the whole deal stunk, and Morgan was inclined to agree with him.

She hadn't batted an eyelid at his blood-stained clothes as he had been led in, merely looked him squarely in the eye and said in an even and accentless voice, "Mr. Shawcross is regrettably occupied at the moment, and cannot be disturbed. He begs your indulgence and apologizes for the delay. Please take a seat."

And so he had. He'd sat and started to sweat. Somewhere be-low, he thought, a large furnace must be working overtime be-cause it was both bone dry and sweltering hot inside the office building. Morgan had known cooler summer days on the Cape than this. Just sitting here, quite still, a sheen of perspiration had already formed on his brow. After ten minutes, even the brown-suits were looking rumpled and uncomfortable, but not the girl

behind the big oak desk—oh no—she remained blissfully unaf-
fected: as prim and coolly serene as a Victorian funeral.

Morgan was at once wary and more than a little intrigued.

A chime sounded from the small electric bell on the wall, and
the cold beauty looked calmly up at him with those strangely
colorless eyes of hers.

"You may go in now. Mr. Shawcross and Mr. Dane will join
you momentarily," she said, and indicated one of the three equally imposing doors leading off the reception area.

Feeling like a lamb asked politely to place his head on the
butcher's block, Morgan rose, unconsciously straightened his
ravaged shirt and jacket, and walked to the door, half expecting
the brown-suits to follow behind him; but they stayed still at
their post.

Inside was a small conference room, dominated by a central
table topped in black marble. Mahogany bookcases to shoulder height flanked two of the walls, and high arched windows
dominated the far side of the room, glass frosted halfway up
their height, with clear lettering flowing across them. His brain
worked on the inverse letters for a second, *C-O-P-P-E-R-H...
Copperhead.*

As if he'd called on a genie by thinking the word, part of the
left hand bookcase proved itself to be a door as it swung open and
two very different men entered the room, one young and athlet-
ic-looking, the other slight and grey. The grey man took a seat
at the head of the table without a word, while the younger one
came over with a politician's practiced, empty smile and offered
his hand. Morgan ignored it, and as he expected, the newcomer
launched into a cheerful, almost companionable spiel regardless.

"Good morning, Mr. Morgan. My name's David Dane, I'm
with the District Attorney's office. Thank you for joining us
here—"

"Where is here, precisely?" Morgan interrupted in a hard voice that cut through the young lawyer's patter like a falling axe, fixing Dane with a bleak stare that had reduced better men to quivering. He was in no mood to be soft-soaped.

"Well, hey now, ah…," Dane spluttered.

"These are the New York offices of Copperhead Industries, Mr. Morgan," the grey man at the end of the table spoke, silencing Dane's bluster. "I am Walter Shawcross. I have brought you here. Dane, get Mr. Morgan some water and do not speak until I require you to."

Dane's bravado was unexpectedly blasted away, and, to Morgan's eyes, the man looked suddenly vulnerable and very little as he backed away like a scolded schoolboy.

Morgan sat, unbidden, across from the grey man. As Dane put down a cut-glass tumbler filled with clear water, Morgan caught how his hands were trembling out of the corner of his eye, although the man sitting at the other end of the black reflective marble slab held most of Morgan's attention.

It had been a calculated display of power, Morgan knew, all of it: from his pre-dawn extraction from prison to the seemingly aimless ride in the Black Maria to the wait outside and to Dane, a representative of the vaunted DA's office, cowering like a child afraid of a drunken father's belt. It was all a message driven home with little subtlety and undisguised force. *Witness my power; I can pluck you up and set you down where I will. The law is mine to make dance as I please and so are you; your life is in my hands and there's nothing you can do about it.* That was about the sum of it.

The unnatural heat of the place, however, didn't seem part of the pattern; it was just damn strange, and this Shawcross, like "Queen Hera" at the reception desk, was not visibly troubled by a bead of sweat.

Shawcross's skin was an unhealthy grey pallor, not unlike dampened newspaper; his old-fashioned pinstripe suit was grey, and even the silk tie he wore was grey. He was quite bald and his arms and face were almost shiny from a lack of hair, his eyebrows no more than a suggestion of shadow, but Morgan didn't have to guess what color his hair would be if the small man had any.

Shawcross waited as Morgan drank the water and held his tumbler out for Dane to refill, which the lawyer did with slavish urgency. Whatever the game was, Morgan, even battered and bone-tired, had nothing in him that inclined him to bend the knee to anyone, least of all bullies and tyrants...even when they had a gun to his head.

"Why am I here, Mr. Shawcross?" Morgan asked, coldly civil, drawing on old reservoirs of cold comportment and discipline, instilled in him from a young age in dark and dangerous territories.

Shawcross smiled as if he had to remember just how to do so, and didn't quite get it right. "You are a direct man, Mr. Morgan. Anthony Percival Morgan—that is your name?"

"Why is it that strangers keep asking me who I am; are you all so unsure?" Morgan replied with some scorn. "I can't imagine you're about to tell me there's been a terrible mistake with the filing and I can go home now. Or perhaps I'm a cleverly disguised vaudeville act pretending to be me and I've actually escaped already?"

A shadow momentarily crossed over the grey man's face like a passing cloud, and then was gone, and Morgan suddenly realized that his earlier interview with Grissom was something this Shawcross knew nothing of. *Circles within circles.* Games were being played here; he was the piece being moved across the board, and he didn't even damn well know who the players were yet.

"Levity," Shawcross uttered flatly, "has no place here. You must answer my questions truthfully, even though you have given the answers to the authorities no doubt many times since your arrest. I must hear them from your own lips."

The slight crawling sensation Morgan had felt since the small grey man had entered the room—in fact since Morgan had entered the building to some degree—intensified markedly. Every instinct he had screamed *Fight clear, and run!* and behind that was something else, a whispering reflex born of a life of fighting in the back of his brain that just wanted Shawcross, Dane, the two brown-suited torpedoes, even the cut-glass perfect receptionist, very, very dead.

"I am Tony Morgan," he made himself say it evenly, his hands flat on the marble tabletop, which felt blessedly cool despite the oppressive heat of the room.

"Dual United States and British nationality; American father, English mother; born in Macau 1896; privately educated in England; formerly of Singapore, Rhodesia, and the West Indies; no spouse, no children; entered the United States in May of 1924 via Seattle; resident in New York for the last six months, and before that, first Chicago and then Nevada, and in the latter state you were deputized for a time?" Shawcross reeled off without taking his eyes from Morgan.

"Correct," Morgan replied. They'd done their homework. Much of it they must have gleaned from his immigration records and his British passport; they'd both left out what he'd wanted left out—the Colonial Office had owed him that much.

"For the last four months, you have worked…intermittently, in partnership with one Raymond Thorpe, now deceased, a private investigator of dubious repute out of Brooklyn, New York."

"Also correct."

"In what capacity, exactly?" the grey man demanded.

"He had formerly been focused on matrimonial work and serving minor warrants, lower paying jobs," Morgan replied. "He was branching out into higher paying cases which carried an increased amount of danger, particularly in a city like this one. He needed assistance and protection. I provided that," Morgan stated as plainly as he could, leaving out Thorpe's driving financial problems and the badly frayed nerves that had ended Thorpe's police career and sent him to the bottom of one bottle after another.

"Were you his hired gun or bodyguard, then?"

"Not exactly. If I was his bodyguard, I failed, didn't I—he's dead."

"Just as those men on the pier are also dead, Mr. Morgan, dead by your hand."

Shawcross pointed to where Dane stood sweating in the corner of the room. The young lawyer stepped forward, taking a file from a bookcase drawer and laying out a typewritten report with stark black-and-whites pinned to them: photographs of contorted bodies in black pools of blood, white-coated coroners pointing at gunshot wounds with measuring rods, bullet casings in chalk circles.

"The evidence of your guilt is damning: fingerprints on the guns you used, the guns matched to the bullets from the bodies by use of a microscope, all very modern—our age of progress at work, quite fascinating. If you go to court, you will hang," Shawcross pronounced.

Morgan's sense of déjà vu only worsened. "This leaves out, of course, the fact that those men were armed and attacked the two of us first, ambushed us. They were killed in self-defense."

Shawcross said nothing in reply and Morgan continued, "Thorpe and I had tracked down Joe Luca—a known racketeer and bootlegger who faked his own death to dodge a murder rap, and even had the temerity to falsely claim on his own life insurance via an alias. This was where Thorpe and I came into the bloody mess: Thorpe had gotten the job of checking out whether he was alive or dead for the insurance company.

"Luca was hiding out at a bootlegger dock on Staten Island. He wasn't so hard to find, but he'd been tipped off somehow, and was waiting for us with a pack of hired guns."

Morgan somehow knew the argument would be pointless, his protestations irrelevant, but the truth was the truth.

"You were ambushed, you say?" Shawcross almost whispered.

"Yes."

"Ambushed by five hardened and well-armed criminals?"

"Yes. I'm tired of going through this."

"And yet you lived and they died, and not a scratch on you, Mr. Morgan. Despite, as you say, that they had the advantage over you and your companion in all respects."

"I was lucky," Morgan said through gritted teeth. It had been brought up time and again in his interrogation, the question sometimes punctuated by a fist, and now again today, first by Grissom and then by this bloodless, bone-dry snake.

Shawcross's smile was more genuine this time, but even less pleasant. "And even without the marvels of science, what jury would believe that?"

Shawcross let the question hang unanswered, while outside the rain began to patter against the windows. Morgan imagined the droplets steaming and hissing as they hit the glass as if dropping on a hot stove. It felt like hell in the conference room, and he guessed the devil was about to outline the contract.

He wasn't disappointed.

Dane was dismissed, taking the police file with him, before Shawcross outlined his proposal.

"You undersell yourself, Mr. Morgan. You have been trained to be a particular kind of 'Son of Empire' the British find very useful—the kind with blood on their boots and starch in their buttoned-up collars—and you have since found a place for yourself here, in America, as a hired bounty hunter.

"You are a creature of violence, Mr. Morgan, adaptable and hardened to the suffering of the world. You have a talent for bloodshed and are an able hunter of men. You also have the added bonus of being relatively well-educated and well-traveled; you have seen much of the world. You have no ties to speak of, and no dependents. Moreover, you are a survivor. It is, in fact, what you are best at—and I would like to employ your talents."

"Really," Morgan replied, unable to hide the scorn in his voice.

"There is a man we want you to find," Shawcross began, unperturbed by Morgan's tone.

As if on cue, lightning flashed, and thunder rattled the windows as the dry, grey man explained the price of freedom.

* * *

After receiving the unexpected letter, Daisy spent the rest of the day at the library with the distinct sense that something had gone awry. She hated to think the letter's arrival had so thrown her off-balance, but afterward, her research and cataloguing steadfastly refused to bend itself to her efforts, and she ended up feeling as if she had actually made herself more work than she had started with.

Later, when she had covered for Carol on the withdrawals desk for her break in the afternoon, she had snapped at the supercilious and presumptuous attitude of one of the more socially inept postgraduate students. Daisy almost had him hysterical by the time she finished tearing strips off the young man in low, formal tones, and had him begging not to have his lending rights revoked. That he'd been so badly upbraided by an attractive woman who was also younger than him had only worsened matters for the fragile ego of the would-be scholar, who had fled almost in tears.

Afterward, she'd been slightly shocked at her own actions, and almost regretted what she'd done—although for his attitude on this and a dozen other occasions he'd more than deserved it—so, she almost regretted it…*almost*.

Once Carol returned, and after making sure the rain had passed, Daisy had put on her muffler and coat and taken a walk around the university grounds to clear her mind. Savoring the chill of the early fall day in a way that recalled her childhood in northern Maine, and taking an odd comfort from the rhythmic crushing of the gravel underfoot, she trod the well-worn pathways of the sprawling campus. As always, she mentally remarked on her surroundings and the eccentricities of the campus, its dotted buildings having grown up almost haphazardly over time, as wealthy benefactors came and went, each leaving their own mark on what had once been the old Arkham town commons.

A few heads nodded to her as she passed, most of those she encountered hurrying to get to one class or another and out of the damp air, and more than a few she knew likely thought of her as a fellow student, imagining her familiar face belonging in one of the tiered seats of their lecture halls, not behind the library desk.

Still, despite her walk and the benefits of fresh air about her, she could not shake a sense that something was wrong—that the world had somehow slid slightly and all but imperceptibly out-of-joint—and the small comfort her walk brought her could not quite dispel the sense of impending sorrow that edged upon her mind.

It was as she paused beside the imposing and thoroughly modernist-looking façade of the Science building, rebuilt after a fire, or some such, years before she had arrived, that she suddenly felt quite faint and had to sit down. Resting a moment on one of the benches that fronted the marble plinths that flanked the building's wide steps, she recovered herself.

The strange, dizzying sensation that had taken her had been fleeting, but momentous—a shudder that came and went unseen in the blink of an eye, leaving her upset in its wake, like a small fishing boat nearly capsized by a warship's passage in the night.

"So that's what they mean when they talk about somebody 'walking over your grave,' then," she muttered as she steadied herself. "Come on, old girl, you're much too sensible for a fit of the vapors."

Looking up, Daisy smiled to see she was seated at the base of one of her favorite of the many disparate marbles scattered around the campus, this one a suitably heraldic-looking gryphon sitting on its haunches in an attitude of fierce vigilance. It was not a particularly large or imposing piece, being no greater in size than a large mastiff, but it was old and somehow careworn, and although it was not her field exactly, she'd have laid odds of the statue being a good deal older than the university it currently graced, and no doubt originally had been some donation or import from an older situation. Still, she liked it, and did not puzzle over the placement of a mythical beast in front of an institution dedicated to science, as some she knew might. The gryphon had ever been a guardian of secrets and treasures, not least of all that of immortality to the medieval alchemists, and what was science but the pursuit of secrets? No doubt whoever placed the gryphon there knew that just as well as she did, even if most of the students that streamed by under its watchful stone gaze over the years were content in their ignorance of the statue's significance.

My, but I am maudlin all of a sudden!

Shaking off her train of thought, she reached up and patted the wet stone claw affectionately before walking away, feeling somewhat better.

It was only as the gothic bulk of the Orne Library reared up in front of her that, quite unbidden, another, older part of the gryphon's myth trailed into her thoughts. To the Persians of the Bronze Age, there had been no more sovereign remedy against witchcraft and the eye of dark forces than the gryphon, although the beast had its own price, as she recalled. *Now*, she thought, *what put that into my head?*

* * *

Morgan walked free from the Copperhead building at a little after noon. The hard rain soaked him and he reveled in it, holding up his arms like a "born again" Christian at a baptism as the sky rumbled above the city. Passersby looked at him askance as they hurried about their business under the cover of their umbrellas, and a battered-looking Ford full of college kids honked its horn raucously at him in the street as it chugged by, but he didn't care.

Still in his blood-stained suit, the soaking also had the added bonus—he privately conceded—of making him look rain-swept and bedraggled, rather than like a cast extra from a particularly murderous Jacobean play.

He'd agreed to Shawcross's proposal—how could he not? They'd been right about that. And after all that sinister import and naked display of power, it had been no more than a single fugitive they wanted found—not even killed or captured, just found—along with what he had stolen.

It would not be that simple, of course. Morgan was not so stupid as to believe that, or why would they have needed him when they so clearly had resources of their own, not to mention the law in their pocket, to do their bidding?

Why me?

No, it would not be that simple, but it would be a start.

He'd given his word on the matter, and somehow that dusty viper Shawcross had known implicitly that, once given, he would keep it as best he could—that Morgan's word was one of the few things that meant a damn to him.

So, when they cut him loose with an envelope stuffed with six hundred dollars cash, his returned passport, a concealed weapon permit, and a phone number to call when he had news, he did not do what he knew almost any sane, rational man would do and flee for the hills, or better yet for the harbor and the first ship out. Instead, he'd started working on the contract.

His first action had been to get to a telephone and place a call to the closest thing to a friend he had left in the city: Greta. This required him to swallow down a few unpleasant facts, and arrange a meeting with her for the following day after she'd done a little job for him. The second, was to flag down a ride home.

The taxi driver, who he'd had to heavily tip to allow him even to sit in the back of the cab as wet as he was, had trouble finding the anonymous apartment-cum-office he had rented above a half-disused hardware store for his last few months in the city. The police, however, had clearly suffered no such difficulty, as he'd obviously had a number of flat-footed visitors in his absence.

The place had been roughly turned upside down and dismantled with the thorough and callous indifference of men not looking for anything in particular, just looking for something. Most of what he owned was scattered on the floor, the guts of the mattress opened up and spilled out in clumps.

As soon as he made it through the door, the weight of his exhaustion caught up, and every ache and fading bruise he had hit him like an oncoming train, nearly toppling him where he stood. Groaning as he bent down, Morgan nevertheless took the time to pick up a few scattered books off the floor and shelve them properly. He was a man of few and transitory possessions—a habit picked up over years of wandering—but he had been raised in a house where the condition of printed matter was as sacrosanct as godly prayer in the house of an ardent pastor, and he couldn't stand to see his second-hand copies of Swift and Voltaire spread-eagled and boot-printed on the floorboards. This small victory against chaos achieved, he at last went through to what was left of his bedroom, undressed, and collapsed on the murdered bed.

Janice. Damn! Ray Thorpe's wife.

He'd meant to call her—swore that he would if he'd ever made it out of jail alive. Morgan had been told she'd tried to see him once, but they hadn't let him in. She deserved—*What? An explanation, a word?*—something from him, and she'd fallen out of his mind silently and almost completely, just as Ray had in the short span of time since his trip from the jail. *Another dead soldier.*

He considered hauling himself out of bed and calling her, but was caught by the cold thought that the last thing she needed was a call from a man who, at the very least, had let her husband get himself killed. *What is there to say anyway? What words will make it all better?* He'd lost friends before, comrades, it never got any better, and he always vowed after each one to never put himself through it again, but he did.

He decided to put some money in an envelope tomorrow and mail it to her, no name, no forwarding address—a coward's way to salve a conscience maybe, but practical, and given his current situation he could hardly do much else. Besides, thanks to Shaw-cross, money was one thing he was no longer short of.

Shawcross, Copperhead, Grissom, and one other.

"Maxwell Cormac," he tried the name aloud, rolled it around in his head awhile before giving in to the bone-deep wariness he felt.

Missing geologists and pacts with ice-blooded devils can wait until tomorrow, he thought dimly, and sank into oblivion.

* * *

Cole Patch shivered in the cold, damp air of the untamed woods outside Arkham. The sun was sinking below the horizon as he picked his way through the undergrowth that cluttered the path. He muttered and cursed both the old cardboard he'd wedged in his shoes, which was failing to keep the wet out, and his so-called friend Pete, who'd warned him against coming here, but he wasn't afraid. Cole was no stranger to the night outdoors, and he'd spent half his life sleeping on roofs, or elsewhere he wasn't supposed to, one way or another.

Thin and frail, with a coarse stubble dotting his chin unevenly and a twitchy, jerky way of moving, a casual observer, if they had bothered to notice him at all, would likely have marked him as living through a declining middle age, when in fact he wasn't yet thirty.

A drifter, a thief when the opportunity arose, and a drunk when he could manage it, Cole Patch was born and raised on the streets of Chicago, and when he was old enough to realize he was neither strong, smart, nor vicious enough to prosper in the slums, he lit out on the railroad and had been human driftwood ever since. Nursing a long-born grudge against the cruelty and injustice of the world, he walked through life like a ghost, leaving no trace of his passing.

Arkham had been an unplanned stop; he tried to stay away from the smaller towns, he'd taken too many beatings from fat lawmen and sullen hicks in places where vagrants and strangers were too easy to spot. To his surprise, though, the New England varsity town had turned out to be larger than he'd expected, and a place where people seemed unusually inclined to "mind their own beeswax," as he thought of it, which suited Cole fine, except they locked their doors more than most, as well.

He'd met Pete by the river, picking for loose coal shed by the colliery barge, and he'd seemed a good guy, war veteran maybe. Cole had met the type before—even shared some chicken scraps and a pan of beans with him and his dog, all friendly like. But when Cole had asked him the lay of the land here 'bouts, the man had just gotten strange: rambled on about his nightmares, about things he'd seen, and started to reel off a list of places Cole shouldn't go. That's when Cole tumbled him. Pete wasn't a crazy like he pretended; he was just playing it smart, keeping away the "competition" from the best pickings—*some friend.*

Cole pulled up short where the overgrown path forked deeper into the woods, and hawked and spat while he considered which path to take. Pete had already averred that there were bootleggers set up in a glade out here, back from the regular bridle-path, and to Cole that meant a mess of drink and provisions, not to mention maybe a hand-out or two, even a look-out job—he'd done it before—and a sloppy camp he could maybe scavenge from if nothing else. He wasn't particularly afraid; after all, what was he to anyone? And as for Pete going on about "monsters in the woods"—what a pack of lies! Did he really expect him to believe that?

"Do a' look that stupid?" he mumbled out loud with a sneer.

It was then he smelled something. He couldn't identify it at first, but when he did his mouth watered and his stomach flipped over in a pang of hunger—it was meat, roasting meat.

"Hog," he muttered, slobbering suddenly, "I bet that's hog, whole hog on the spit an' turnin'."

He set off at a shuffling run down the left hand fork in the path, his eagerness getting the better of his sense until a branch scraped his leg hard enough to draw blood, but still he hobbled on, a slow chant of "bootlegger hog" tumbling from his lips.

He broke into the small clearing quite unexpectedly, a cold wind suddenly snapping him to his senses.

"What the…where's the hog…," he muttered dumbly, looking around in shock.

There was no fire, the smell of meat had gone completely, replaced by a cold, squalling wind that smelled of rotten, damp earth and stagnant water. There was no bootlegger camp, no stills, no heavy smell of fermenting mash or hops—as he knew there ought to be now he was suddenly thinking straighter than he had been moments ago—no trucks or barrels, and no people, just a single tent, black against the night.

Still more curious than afraid, Cole walked a few more steps forward into the glade. The tent wasn't a camper, but a big, high-pitched, square job, near the size of a barn, held down with guide-ropes and stout stakes—it was more like a revival tent or a traveling mission than anything else that came to mind. *But where are the folks?*

He edged forward, torn between the idea of calling out and running away. The tent flap snapped suddenly in the wind startling him. There was a faint light inside, almost too weak to be seen, but there was no other sound or movement, nothing.

Perhaps they all left and are coming back tomorrow. There couldn't be nothing sleeping in there? Cole's thoughts ran on, and he slowly drew closer to the tent flap and peered within.

There was a single candle stub burned down almost to extinction at the far end of the tent's cavernous space. It stood on a square, upright object that might have been a lectern, before an isle of over-trodden ground, either side of which he could barely make out a mismatch of shapes in the darkness. *Are they chairs, or sleeping people?* He couldn't tell. The stench hit him and he gagged, immediately transported by a flash of unwelcome memory of an old hobo named Jakes who'd lost his footing and fallen beneath two railroad freight cars and gotten caught up and torn to pieces. The old tramp hadn't suffered—it had been too quick—but Cole and two other men in the railcar had. The train hadn't stopped, the driver hadn't known, and Cole had been forced to stay in the freight car behind the poor bastard's corpse in the sweltering hot June sun. The black tent stank of gutted human.

Cole turned and ran, but as one foot pushed in front of the other, something slammed into the back of his head and white exploded in front of his eyes. He lay face down in the cold, stinking mud, helpless and blinded, but mercilessly still aware of what was going on. Rough fingers felt at his neck.

"He ain't dead. Will he do, there ain't much to him?" a rough voice growled.

"Yes, I think he shall do very well," another voice replied, cultured and precise, but somehow strained near breaking point. "Another lost soul. Bring him."

Cole felt fingers like steel pincers fasten around his ankles and he was dragged along, face-down like butchered game, through the clearing and into the wood. Coughing and moaning as the underbrush snapped at him, it was all his feeble struggling could do to keep himself from choking on the mud.

He was thrown down and then there were other voices around him, dozens of them, chanting in feverish tones words he could not understand that turned his stomach and made him clasp his hands over his ears as he wept and moaned like a child. The voices grew louder, more distorted, and were joined by an awful keening sound that cut through him like glass.

A brutal hand grabbed him by the hair and yanked him off the floor and his hands windmilled helplessly as he cried out in pain.

"Look!" the strained voice screamed, and powerless to resist, Cole's eyes snapped open at the command. "Let there be dark!"

He was in the center of another clearing, this one a fetid hollow around which the trees were curled and distorted like figures of half-melted black wax. In the center of the clearing, head-height in the air, was an impossible, boiling blackness, spinning in place like a caged thunderhead. It swallowed in light and heat like a hungry leech, the night air rushing into its maw, leaving numbing cold in its wake.

"Behold!" the voice behind him exulted, and with mounting horror, Cole saw something was coming, impossibly deep in the black, hurtling faster, closing on him with terrifying speed, and with each second, his brain refused the full terror of what it could not comprehend.

Cole screamed. He screamed and screamed again; he screamed so loud and raw that he did not feel the blade slither across his throat until it had done its work.

CHAPTER TWO

Morgan occupied a window seat booth in a busy diner on Madison Avenue and worked his way methodically through a plate piled high with steak burnt-to-order and griddled eggs. Clean-shaven again, and dressed in a respectable, if somber, charcoal-black suit and an ivory-white double-breasted waistcoat, he would not be taken at a glance for the man who had been dragged from a cell a day before.

Despite his more genteel appearance, he radiated sufficient desire to remain undisturbed that, although the lunchtime rush was in full swing and the other booths were packed with loud knots of gossiping secretaries, somber office clerks, scruffy typesetters, louche day traders, and more besides jostled at the counter for elbow room, not one of them intruded on the empty three seats at Morgan's table. Morgan, cooped up as he had been in a cell for so long, found the experience at once refreshing and a little claustrophobic. Even with room at his table, the crowd from his angle looked like little more than a sea of grey suits, slouched hats, high-collared herringbone coats, clicking heels, and cigarette smoke.

The decision to come to the diner had been a more or less spur of the moment one. After returning to his apartment the previous afternoon, Morgan had slept for nigh-on thirteen straight hours before hauling himself headlong into a very busy morning, and it had been nearly noon before he realized he was ravenously hungry. He'd decided to kill two birds with one stone and telegrammed Greta to meet him at the diner.

Having demolished his steak and eggs, Morgan looked out through the cloud of cigarette smoke that hung thick across the room and caught the eye of the exhausted-looking waitress. After she cleared away his plate and refilled his coffee, he caught her elbow again, ordering a second cup when he saw Greta walk in, the lunch crowd parting before her like a bow wave before a clipper ship in full sail.

Greta Thorsen was a striking, rather than attractive, woman in her late thirties, strong featured and somewhat hawkish, and with her fur-trimmed herringbone wool coat and the jade brooch pinning up her chestnut locks, she was far too upmarket for this joint. Morgan had liked her ever since their first meeting, back when she'd been a prospective employer. He liked her strength and her intelligence, and after he'd cleaned up a nasty spot of blackmail for her, they'd kept up a strictly platonic acquaintance.

For his part, her job as a freelance journalist of independent means with connections with several of the city papers was an asset for a stranger in town in his line of work. For her, he was a useful man to keep on the right side of, not to mention a source for first-hand stories about places and peoples a world away from the city's concrete and brick canyons—stories he kept carefully edited, of course. They were friends, after a fashion, with no danger of romantic entanglements on either side for entirely different and unspoken reasons of their own.

She sat down unceremoniously, casting her furled umbrella into the corner, and with a boyish grin said, "I thought you'd look like hell—if I ever got to look at you again, I mean. But you don't even look like you lost weight!"

"I can't say I'd recommend the accommodations," he replied wryly as the waitress poured Greta a coffee.

"Did you find anything out for me?" he asked, serious again, knowing that he didn't really have the time for their usual slightly grim banter.

Her face fell somewhat into a concerned expression. She took a notebook from inside her coat and flipped through pages of cramped shorthand to the entries she was after. "Some—you didn't give me much time, you know."

"I know, but time is not something I suspect I have in great supply."

She nodded, her eyes not leaving the notebook. "What would you like first?"

"Let's try Copperhead."

"Well, I hit the library stacks and the *Post*'s clipping archive, and most of it's a stone wall—a real cold stone wall. As far as I can tell, it's a big mining outfit like you said—metals mostly—Mexico and Brazil is where they're based, some interests here in the US, mainly Nevada and North Dakota. All I can tell you for sure, is that they have a lot of money, a lot of clout, and their stock isn't traded on the markets. That, and the financials writers I tapped up for information clammed up far too quickly when your man Shawcross was mentioned, on or off the record. I got the feeling they were scared of him. Like I said: lots of clout," she gave a lopsided smile.

"That I can believe. Keep digging, but don't push too far. Your silent friends may well be right to keep their mouths shut from what I've seen. What about Cormac?"

"*That's* where it starts *really* getting juicy, not to mention more than a little weird," Greta said teasingly, taking a sip from her coffee and staring at him fixedly over the steaming brim.

"Well, Greta, as you're fond of saying: spill it."

"Fine, when you asked me to check into some missing geologist, I wasn't expecting much, you know? I'd imagined some dusty middle-aged bald type with leather patches on his jacket elbows, but boy was I wrong."

She reached into her purse and took out a folded photograph which she opened to show a crowded night club scene in full swing, and one with a fairly classy clientele, at least as far as Morgan could make out. The picture had been cut from a cheap plate, and from the flash and the slight blur, the cameraman either hadn't been the best at his trade to begin with, or had been a little worse for the wear when the shot had been taken. A little off to one side of the mass of the crowd, and caught mid-revel at the center of the image, was a tall young man whose side-profile had been circled on the print in blue pencil.

"That's your man, right there?"

Morgan stared for a moment and compared it with the image in his mind's eye of the stiff formal portrait he'd been given by Dane at Shawcross's office. "That's him," he affirmed.

"Handsome guy—if you go for that type. Looks like he ought to be out boating on some crystal blue New England lake, not digging up rocks in the dirt, doesn't he?" Greta mused.

"I'm more interested in where I can maybe find him, than whether he's missed his calling," Morgan prompted.

"Don't be a bear, Tony, I'm getting to that," she admonished him lightly, letting her nerves show a little.

He made himself relax and lean back, nodding an apology. There was no sense in letting his stress out on Greta.

"Maxwell Cormac, golden boy," she began portentously glancing down again at her notebook. "The edited highlights: Old Yankee blue blood, educated at Yale, graduated just before the War with honors in geology and chemistry, unmarried.

"Family long dead; sold up hearth and home back in some

out-of-the-way mill town his folks more or less owned once upon a time, and went off to make his way in the world. From what I can tell, he's also sitting on a nest egg big enough that going to work as a field geologist had to be a choice, because he sure didn't need the dough—we are talking maybe seven figures here, my dear. Added to the good looks, breeding, and cash, he's also a rising star in the field of digging in the dirt, apparently. I say 'apparently,' because he turns up mentioned in periodicals whose gist I can only just read."

She traced a line in her notebook with an immaculately manicured fingernail. "Here we go: *'Young Mr. Cormac, in his recent endeavors at Sultan Lode, which even the most crook-backed dredgers of the old school had long given up as all played out, showed what some say is an eye for the color unseen in anyone this side of Hearst back in the great days, and struck deep and wide for his marker,'*—which deathless prose, I'm guessing, means he was good at whatever he did."

Morgan nodded thoughtfully, knowing about enough to decode what she had just read out. "It means he found gold, and a hell of a lot of it, for whomever was his employer."

"Which," she carried on, "back then, was an outfit called Hale and Sons. It looks like Copperhead made him an offer and poached him right out from under them back in '26. Quite the coup from what I can tell. After that, he seems to have done a stint for Copperhead in Mexico, then Central America, and started bouncing back between there and here for the last year or two."

"By 'here' I take it you mean New York."

"Attaboy, yes, I mean New York, the big bad city. That's where it gets juicier, but I'm guessing you know that already?"

"Some maybe, but as you have no doubt already calculated in that first-rate brain of yours, Greta, I don't exactly trust my sources. And anyway, I'd lay money down on a roulette wheel that you've already found out more than I've been told."

She flashed Morgan a sparkling glance, "You always did have me figured as to how to butter me up, Tony; most don't, it's one of the reasons I like you. Yes, well, first up, no one seems to know where he is. He's not currently 'missing' as such, just 'away'— which, given all the trips abroad, is no surprise, I suppose.

"But, when he was in town, our golden boy seems to have liked the high life, which is where he gets into my professional territory. He shows up on the guest list for some very important parties, and some very private ones, string of It girls and flappers on his arm; he's a habitué of a half dozen or so of the more upmarket speakeasies and card joints. No different than any other young rake with a big old bankroll, and New York's got more than its fair share of those you might say, at least on the surface."

"And?" Morgan prompted, knowing full well that the dramatic reveal was part of the deal with Greta; it was a trifle indulgent perhaps, but a small price to pay.

"And…there's the rumors, of course, the kind of story that never sees print in the society columns, even the scandal sheets."

"What do you mean exactly?"

"You know—but then again maybe you don't. You see, Tony: John and Jane Public have a taste for scandal, vicarious thrills, and the dirty goings on of the dirty rich. It fills up column inches and it sells copy…but there are limits.

"Some of those limits are self-imposed by the reporters themselves depending on what they have the stomach for; the more ironclad limits are enforced by hot-tempered editors, and ultimately come in the form of late night telegrams from paperbarons that will get a hack on the skids so fast their head'll spin if they try and go too far in giving the public what they most want.

"Most times, though, it comes down to good old-fashioned

self-interest. You—if you're a reporter, I mean—if you damage the wrong people, you end up shut out of the circle, behind a glass wall looking in—a pariah no one will give the time of day to, no more invites, no more back-door privileges, no more gossip, finished. But that's not all, because sometimes, just sometimes, you say the wrong thing about the real-wrong people and they end up fishing you outta the river.

"All of which adds up to the fact that some things—stories, rumors, whatever—they never see print, no matter how lurid or low rent the paper," Greta said.

"And just what didn't see print about our missing geologist friend?" Morgan pressed.

"Bad company, in short," Greta said after a pause, "the kind that gets you 'option three' on my little list. Said company rumored to include one very nasty piece of work named Milo Laski."

"I've heard of him, I think—some sort of syndicate heavy-hitter," Morgan replied, searching his memory. As a rule he'd steered clear of the major league mob since coming to New York, but it paid to know who was who.

Greta shrugged languidly at that. "I'll take your word for it, not my patch, but that sounds about right. Anyway, on top of that, there's talk of your golden boy in attendance at the kind of parties where the guest list is very, very select, and there's more goes on than bathtub gin and a touch of Bolivian sugar in the cocktails."

Morgan leaned back in his chair, a number of possibilities now circling in his head; money troubles sounded unlikely as a motivation for the theft and disappearance Cormac was involved in; blackmail seemed a far more likely candidate.

"There's some strange stuff, as well," Greta continued, "stuff that doesn't seem to fit, stories of our boy on the fringe of the black velvet drapes and tarot card crowd. I talked to an old acquaintance of mine who spends her time messing around with crystal balls and whatnot between frittering away a trust fund—she's my usual insider on the ingénue witch set, such as it is in fashion. She's a bit scatter-brained, but usually reliable. Anyway, turns out she'd met him at some party or other, and she said he had a 'fell aura'—whatever that means—and she'd 'never have allowed him to darken one of her rites,' or some other such nonsense. I got the impression under the mumbo-jumbo that she'd gotten the hint Cormac was maybe into something a league or two worse than half-cut séances and excuses to get a little naughty while some incense burns and call it an occult mystery. Take that for whatever it might mean to you."

Morgan waved for more coffee and sighed. More questions than answers, smoke and mirrors and no solid leads. He picked the photograph up from the table and looked at it properly again, searching for something to spark his mind.

The picture had been taken in a big, decked out speakeasy that looked more like an old theatre than a gin joint, and an up-market one by the tuxes and bow ties on the men and the strings of pearls on the short-skirted girls with the long feathers in their headbands. Prohibition was in full swing, and the contents of every martini glass and champagne flute illegal, at least in theory, but from this you'd never have guessed. Here they were posed for a photograph red-handed in crime—the great, the good, and the bad—but Morgan doubted this party was going to end abruptly; no police raid was going to come crashing through the doors on these particular revelers.

One law for the rich and another for the poor; wherever he'd been in the world, from Calcutta to Providence, it had been the same.

"Where was this taken?" he asked suddenly, holding up the picture to her.

She smiled. "I was wondering when you would get to that. I had to wheedle it out myself, it's a juice-joint called the 'Falling Angel' uptown, very swanky, very select, popular with the upmarket tarot card crowd, as well." Greta smiled again. "One of Laski's, in fact, or so they tell me—oh, and the picture's no more than a month or so old."

"Wait a minute, you're sure of that?" he asked urgently.

She nodded, her smile widening. "Sure as sure, I tracked down the shutterbug that took it himself, cost me a double sawbuck to establish the time it was taken within a week. More than that… well, let's say our snapper's nights get a little hazy."

"Shawcross was right: Cormac did come back here afterward, but why?" Morgan muttered, his mind running through the new implications of what he'd just learned.

"After what? From where?" Greta asked a little testily, clearly wanting to know what this whole mess was about—which was more than Morgan had told her so far.

"The photographer," he said, ignoring her question, "I'd like to speak with him."

"Mason? No chance, I'm afraid; he's already skipped out of town 'on assignment,' he said. More likely taken a few too many candid shots of the daughters of liberty in compromising positions again, if you ask me, and needed to split till the heat dies down. It won't be the first time, or the third. If he hadn't needed the cash, I'd never have gotten him to sit still long enough to give me the skinny on this snap. The man's incorrigible, and the crowd at the Angel gave him the creeps."

Morgan just nodded and went on staring at the picture.

"Level with me, Morgan, what's this all about? You said this runaway digger went on the lam about two months back 'somewhere' south of the border, so why'd he come back where he's going to be looked for first? What did he do, anyway, to get Copperhead all riled up? By the state of his pocketbook, he had no need to run away with the day's takings…"

Morgan shifted in his seat, unsure of whether to tell Greta

more, not that he knew much more himself in truth. He knew, too, that he may be putting her in danger by dragging her into the whole mess, but in short order, she'd found out more than he could have hoped to pounding the streets for weeks. What was more, it seemed Greta's enviable web of connections had discovered things about their employee's personal life than Copperhead had known, or had bothered to discover.

"Cormac stole something—an antiquity I suppose you'd call it—from Copperhead's offices in Campeche, Mexico," Morgan said carefully. "A 'small fragment of a bas-relief' as it was described to me, about the size and thickness of a Sunday bible when put together, made from five chunks of blue-black volcanic rock-glass and with characters carved on all sides."

"All this for some chunks of rock-glass? Truly? Not diamonds or emeralds or gold?"

Morgan shook his head in reply.

"It's got to be valuable somehow…"

"It is to Copperhead. Oh, they want him, as well, but they want the rocks, or their whereabouts, first, foremost, and soon. There were accomplices, as well, down in Mexico I believe, and men were killed while taking the rocks from Copperhead's offices. I don't know the full details, but they are certain only Cormac got away from them. They are equally sure he made it out of the country somehow, and they believed he came back to New York, despite the danger of being spotted here, which you have just confirmed."

"But what if he's dumped the rocks by now, or sold them on or whatever?"

"Then they want to know all about it, and Shawcross made it plain he didn't care how I found out or who from, and that any mess I made along the way would be cleaned up. This is entirely sub rosa and under the table, no official investigation stateside or down south."

Greta leaned back against the booth and let out a slow whistle before saying, "And for this they pull you out from under a murder frame, and walk you straight out of jail."

"So it would seem."

"But this is crazy! Don't get me wrong, Tony: I'm glad the next time I saw you was here—not in a little grey room before they threw the big bad switch—but this is just plain crazy!"

Morgan sighed, "It's the hand I've been dealt, and I don't see any way but to play it out."

She said something uncharacteristically unladylike in reply, and they sat in silence for a while, the both of them wrapped up in what they had learned from each other.

"What are you going to do?" she asked after a time.

"Follow what leads I have, which aren't much. Cormac's house first—he kept a place over on Long Island. Shawcross's people have already quietly turned it over, but I'm going to head on out there and see if I can turn up something they missed, try and get a feel for the man perhaps. After that, the Falling Angel tonight or tomorrow night; that's one more decent lead than I started out with before meeting you, so thanks for that."

He reached over casually and slipped a tight wedge of folded bills under her hand as if holding it demurely.

"You don't have to. I owe you, you know, more than—"

"You are taking it—you've more than earned it—and they are paying me very well for this blind scavenger hunt they've put me on."

"I'll keep at it," she demurred. "None of this adds up. There has to be some thread to pull I haven't found yet," she offered softly.

"Be careful," he insisted, squeezing her hand. "Don't expose yourself, and play it safe. It isn't worth your skin; remember that."

She met his eyes with hers and winked slowly. "Yes, daddy," she purred mockingly, and got up from the table, sweeping her notebook into her purse.

Morgan was far from the only man in the steadily emptying diner that watched her swaying hips as she left, but after he folded the photograph away in his jacket, he kept on staring after her into the blur of traffic beyond the glass-plate door. He gazed out into that space until the dregs of his coffee had turned cold and the lunchtime rush was long over.

* * *

Bull Devlin looked up from his solo game of hearts with some annoyance, feeling a sense of unease he couldn't account for. Getting to his feet, he first looked out the grimy windows onto the street, and then glanced sidewise out the open cabin door down to the enclosed yard below. Rain was starting to fall outside, darkening the Manhattan skyline, and under the corrugated tin roof that covered the warehouse yard in which his cabin-office perched on its timber scaffold, the shadows around the packing crates and barrels swallowed much of the floor in darkness as deep as night.

Marty hadn't turned on the lights, despite the drawing darkness, and Devlin almost didn't notice the figure standing by the open loading doors next to his Packard at the edge of the yard. Nonplussed, and unsure for a moment it wasn't Marty or another of the boys come 'round, he peered closer; the man was a stranger, bulked up in a dirty black coat that had clearly been expensive once. The man was not especially tall but quite broad, and he had a shapeless black hat jammed down tight on his head and some kind of funny scarf wrapped around his face.

Whoever he was, he had no right to be standing there.

"Hey, hey yous!" Devlin called out.

The man turned slowly, not his head, but his whole body stiffly at once, and walked a few paces closer to the wooden steps up to the cabin-office.

At once, Devlin saw it wasn't a scarf he was wearing, but

strange, shiny bandages wrapped around his whole head, leaving only a shadowy gap for his eyes and the suggestion of a slit for his mouth.

Devlin swore under his breath and threw down the cards he had in his hand. He hated minding the store down here on the docks—long hours of boredom or trouble, that was all you got, and this looked like the latter. Still, it was better than riding shotgun on the beer trucks hurtling through the countryside in the dead of night, or freezing in the chill of the harbor waiting for a boat to make a drop.

"Is this the Emile Brothers Trading Company?" the bandaged figure asked, and to Devlin his voice sounded wrong, foreign maybe, but also, somehow wet.

Trouble, definitely trouble.

"We're closed pal, get out of here," Devlin shouted down the steps as threateningly as he could manage.

"Might I ask who you are, sir?" The stranger's voice sounded more strained with each word, as if speaking was progressively painful to him.

Devlin inched his hand toward the scattergun that lay beside him on the card table; the gun was placed where he knew nobody down below could see it, and him reaching for it should have been a last resort, but the guy was giving him the creeps just standing there.

"That don't matter none," Devlin barked. "I said we're closed, see? Now, get out before things get rough." His fingers brushed the cut-down walnut gunstock.

Where the hell's Marty got to? Can't he hear me shouting back there?

The stranger coughed, an unwholesome sucking sound that put Devlin in mind of the dying men he'd shared a field hospital with in the War—men who had caught a lung full of gas, and went out of the world one painful breath at a time.

"I have traveled…traveled a long way to be here, and things would be so much simpler if we could remain…civil; now answer my questions…please," the man said, an even more sinister note of barely restrained anger creeping into his ravaged voice.

Devlin was getting itchy and cold, the kind of bad itch he often got before either his or someone else's blood got spilled.

A man like Devlin made few friends and a lot of enemies in his life, and possibilities quickly started bounding around his thick skull and were discarded: there was no chance the man was with the law—he was too damn weird—and if it was another gang making a move, why hadn't he cut up already? Where were the rest of them? Added to which, the warehouse was between shipments; nothing to steal or bust up but plywood crates and straw.

The cold itch got worse as the man just stood there waiting for his answer, and, quite unbidden, old spook stories that he'd heard over the years came flooding back to Devlin. Crazy, whispered rumors and dockside gin-fables, the kind of tales ruthless men told each other during long nights spent waiting in the dark to end some poor mug's life. Stories of thieves whose greed got the better of them and took on some shunned house and never came out again whole, of bodies screaming out strange languages after they'd been pulled dead from the black waters of the harbor, of crazy burned-out drunks, half-poisoned by bad liquor, staggering out of the night with an axe in hand for the bootlegger that had sold them the bottle that had blinded their best girl or killed their curious kid.

With grim certainty, Devlin knew that was what was looking up at him with shadowed eyes: something from a murder's whispered myth.

Get a grip, Bull, get a grip! It's just some freak out wandering where he shouldn't, he told himself.

Bull Devlin was well past his prime, he knew, but he still considered himself a dangerous man and knew others did the same.

He'd boxed in the Marines in his youth, and worked over more saps for the syndicate than he could remember—and he'd killed when he'd needed to. Right up until now, he'd have said he was no coward to any man that asked, and backed those words up with blood if needed. But now he knew he wouldn't walk down the stairs toward that stranger if somebody handed him a diamond the size of his fist for his trouble. Instead, he let out a shrill, high whistle using his free hand to make a "V" before his lips.

"Marty! Marty!" he shouted. "Get out here you lug, we got some garbage off the street here that needs the bum's rush!"

Better that dumb lug gets out here to deal with this freak than me.

"Ah," the bandaged man spoke more, it seemed, to himself than Devlin, "two of you, better in some ways, worse in others."

Devlin almost laughed aloud when he heard Marty muttering as the big longshoreman barged his way onto the scene from the warehouse that backed on to the yard. Devlin's relief was short-lived, though, as the bandaged man reached inside his coat with a gloved hand.

Devlin clumsily snatched up the scattergun and brought its double-barreled snout to bear on the stranger, but instead of looking down the barrel of a pistol as he had feared, the bandaged man was holding a strange ochre colored stick in his gloved hand. No, not a stick, but a flute—a strange, uneven flute that looked for all the world as if it was made out of honeycomb.

Confused and uncertain, Devlin could only watch as the man seemed oblivious to Marty's hulking form reaching out to grab him from behind. The bandaged man put the strange flute to his lips, and Devlin knew with a terrible, crushing certainty that he should have fired when he had the chance. He hadn't pulled the scattergun's trigger, and now he was done, just done.

The bandaged man pushed the strange flute into the slit where his mouth should have been but no sound came, no sound at least that the human ear could register.

The world shuddered and rippled with a sickening pulse, and Devlin fell to his knees; he felt as if he were screaming, but could hear nothing at all, only an all-consuming, horrific silence crashing down on him like he was being buried under a tide of numbing snow.

His trigger-finger obeying him far too late, the scattergun fired; Devlin felt the gun buck in his hands and saw the bright flash as it discharged uselessly upward, but still heard nothing as he slumped backward over the table. Helpless and without strength, the scattergun slipped from hands too weak to hold onto it, as he slid to the floor and lay there helplessly.

Devlin could have been sprawled there for mere moments, or hours for all he knew, as the dreadful silence ate into him, gnawing relentlessly away at his reason and his senses until iron-fingered hands plucked him off the floor and dumped him unceremoniously on his back on top of the card table.

The bandaged man loomed over Devlin, and pulled his head up lifelessly with one hand, as with the other he held before him a ragged square of torn packing canvas. On the shred of cloth was a faded ink stamp where the legend "Emile Brothers Trading Co., New York" was just legible.

The iron-fingered grip pressed across his forehead, clamping down like a vice, and now he heard words and saw strange and unfamiliar images flash in his mind. *"Where is he?"* the words roared louder than any sound Devlin had ever heard—every syllable a screaming agony in his brain.

Again and again he was questioned, questions for which he had no answer, and on and on the agony of sound came until Bull Devlin tried to pray for the first time in thirty years; he tried to pray to die.

"Who is your employer?" came the deafening voice in his head, with a note of angry exasperation.

Through the shattering pain, Devlin's mind flickered in recognition, and the sneering face of his boss swam before his recollection.

"Ah, progress," thundered the voice, and Devlin squirmed helplessly as the fingers sunk bloodlessly through his skull without a sound.

* * *

One look at Cormac's house told Morgan that Greta hadn't been wrong in her assessment of the missing man's finances.

It was modest perhaps in size, but only in comparison to some of the mansions and manses that dotted the peaceful countryside around it. Morgan had never been here before, and it seemed a world away from the noise and grime of the city, though it had taken Morgan less than an hour to reach it in his newly rented Ford touring car. No, this kind of genteel peace came with a fairly hefty price tag, and Greta's digging around made it out to be owned outright by Cormac, along with the two or three acres of lightly wooded grounds it sat on.

The house was a compact blue-brick affair, not too old and very self-contained. It was barely visible from the road, thanks to a screen of well-kept trees; as he walked up to the front door, Morgan got the impression the house didn't so much command the grounds, but rather concealed itself in them, out of sight and earshot from the rest of the world.

The brand new key he'd been given at Copperhead's offices fit the old lock snuggly and he had no trouble getting in. The first thing that greeted him was a sense of emptiness, and he was immediately given the impression of a place unlived in and abandoned. It was sparsely but well-furnished, from what he could see as he made his way quietly through the ground floor, through the reception room and dining room, through to the kitchen out back. In fact, the only incongruity at all was the sense that much of the furniture had been moved ever so slightly out of place, no doubt because it had already been thoroughly and diligently searched, and he had to hand it to whoever Copperhead had used to carry out the job—they'd made a good effort at not making a mess, very professional.

Indeed, the furnishings seemed to match almost too well, as if the place was a show-house of some kind, lacking any trace of personality, as dead as the empty kitchen cupboards, with a dining set in the drawers—the various cutlery still individually wrapped in the wax paper in which it had been delivered. "Not one for entertaining, were we?" Morgan said aloud, breaking the silence.

The whole place was just plain *wrong*. It was as if Cormac had been a ghost, barely touching the world in which he lived. It just didn't add up. Where were the personal touches, the knick-knacks and curios from years spent crisscrossing the back of beyond, even the expensive toys and trinkets that a man of Cormac's wealth and standing picked up along the way like fleas on a skid row bum?

The upper floors were in some ways worse: rooms with a thin layer of dust, barely disturbed, that gave the impression they'd been laid out and never so much as walked in until recently (again he likely had Copperhead's lackeys to thank for that one). The closets were full of neatly hung and laid out clothes, some with the tailor's tags still attached.

It was only in the highest room in the house—a gable end study with a wide picture window looking out over the sweep of the country around toward the barely visible sea—that he found the slightest trace of personality at all. The books that lined the walls were fairly pedestrian affairs: leather-bound compilations of *Harper's* alongside manly-looking octavos of Hawthorne and Scott. Their spines cracked when he opened them—never before read. There was also a long case of books related to Cormac's profession—geological tracts, manuscript-bound site maps, works on mineralogy and chemistry, and histories of mining—but those too seemed equally unloved.

The great teak desk that sat with its back to the window was bare of anything but a writing set and paper, but as Morgan sat behind it he was struck by the painting that faced him on the opposite wall. It was by no means a grand affair, or particularly incongruous at first glance, but of the few pictures he had seen in the house, it was the only one he did not recognize as a high quality reproduction of some bland, if famous, work. Instead it was an original work and unfamiliar. He could see the textured heavy strokes of the paint on the canvas. The style was rough, deliberately so, almost primitive and very modern, and its palette consisted only of deep midnight blues, sable blacks, and caustic whites. The scene depicted a huddled, half-seen costal village or town concealed under cover of night, the dark so heavy about it as to blot any sense of time or place. Above the buildings rose a high black cliff, and out to sea on jagged rocks, a dagger-like spar of a lighthouse was set, the brilliant white beam of its light slicing through the scene like a scythe blade, revealing in its passage the echoes of strange shapes that the eye couldn't quite fathom. The effect was of a picture that grew more uncertain, somehow, in subject the more Morgan studied it, and the vague shapes in the passing of the beam made him uneasy in a way he couldn't put his finger on.

He got up to look more closely for a signature, and his foot kicked something small and solid which clattered against the desk. Bending down he picked up the battered fob watch his boot had found, or what was left of one at least. The casing seemed unremarkable, other than the fact the metal was partly scorched black and left no trace of soot on his fingers; it had reached its sorry fate a long time ago. Remarkably, the glass, although discolored at the edges, was un-cracked, but the two hands on the face inside were no more than corroded streaks of verdigris marking a time of six minutes to eleven, the cipher *E.M.* engraved on the dial.

Morgan pocketed the old watch, sighing and more than a little frustrated.

"Who are you, Cormac? This may well have been your house, but you sure as hell didn't live here," Morgan asked aloud in the empty room.

More than once in his life, Morgan had found that "nothing" could mean "something" all on its own, and he got that feeling now loud and clear. The house was a lie, what else could it be? An expensive deception to paint Cormac as a wealthy, established bachelor with an enviable life, a long-term ruse that was starting to ring all kinds of alarm bells in Morgan's mind about just how deep that lie went, and just what it might conceal.

As he locked Cormac's front door behind him and headed toward his motor, he didn't spare a glance backward to the mute, lifeless house.

* * *

"Why the hell am I here?" Burke Haskell demanded as he stepped in out of the rain, doffing his fedora, tipping water from the brim to splatter on the dirty cement floor of the enclosed yard.

Overweight, pushing forty, and his prime rotted on the vine with too much rotgut and bad living, Haskell lived in a perpetual foul mood, which was only worsened when his job with the New York Police Department's Bureau of Detectives demanded he put his neck on the line, and everything about the call to come here had reeked of bad times ahead.

Haskell already knew the answer to his shouted question, or at least part of it; this was his patch more or less, and Emile Brothers Trading belonged to Milo Laski, and Milo Laski filled Haskell's pockets with enough greenbacks to keep him copacetic when anything "unhappy" (as the gang boss called it), occurred. And, from the look on the face of the waiting patrolman, something very unhappy had happened indeed.

Haskell had never been here before in person, but knew the rough layout: warehouse, yard, and office, just one of a score of all alike little outfits on the edge of the wharfs. It was fully dark inside the yard, night having fallen some hours ago, and the patrolman, a young cop that Haskell dimly remembered as being named "Meeks" or "Weeks" or some such, was waving his flashlight around with a helpless look and mouthing something Haskell couldn't quite make out.

The flashlight's beam flickered over the corpse at the foot of the set of wooden stairs leading up to a raised cabin. Whoever it was had been a big man, such that Haskell could tell at a glance, but he seemed curiously contorted, like a broken puppet caught up in its own strings. Haskell walked over the dozen or so steps to the body, passing the patrolmen who just stood there as if he didn't have a damn clue about what he was doing. Close up, he caught sight of the glittering black stain of blood under the dead man's head, blood which appeared to have gushed thick and heavy from ears that looked like they had been split open with pickaxe blows.

"What the—," Haskell began before being interrupted by a shout from the office above.

"Haskell, that you down there?"

The voice had a thick, nasal New Jersey accent with a rough edge like ground glass he recognized immediately.

"Malloy, that you?" he responded, looking up at the office cabin raised above the floor of the tin-roofed warehouse yard. The soft light of a paraffin lamp shone within the square wood-slatted structure, outlining a stocky, thick-waisted figure in a police cap in its open doorway. Yes, it was Malloy, the senior sergeant for the district, and that fact also answered the question of who had phoned in the garbled message for dispatch that had sent him down here; Malloy was no stranger to Laski's generosity either.

"Yeah," Malloy replied, "Gitup here, willya, there's a body!"

"I hate to break it to you Malloy, but you missed one down here, as well!" Haskell growled back, already angered by the turn this was taking; if Laski's boys had taken a hit, this was going to be trouble all around.

When Malloy refused to bite and turned silently back into the office, Haskell stepped over the corpse and headed up the rickety stairs with a barrage of invective ready to broadside the beat sergeant with, but as he stepped into the open doorway, the words died unsaid on his lips.

The office smelled like a charnel house, and the shadows at the edges of the room were as thick as ink stains. There was, as Malloy had said, a body. It lay slung over a card table in the center of the room, what was left of the head hung down backward facing the doorway, at least it would have if it had a face. Instead, there was a delicate array of grey-white bones and thick yellowish gristle with two dirty half-circles of teeth uppermost, a scruffy halo of hair hanging down, and most incongruously off all, two perfectly around and featureless eyes the color of goose fat gazing blindly out from the horror to give it meaning and form. Of skin and meat and blood, there was none.

Haskell fought to keep from vomiting, his gut clenching and unclenching in spasms. He dragged his dirty cuff across his mouth to take away the taste of his own bile, speechless.

"Hav'ya, hav'ya ever seen anything like it Haskell, hav'ya?" Malloy's guttural voice was torn halfway between disbelief and anger, and he had to repeat himself several times before Haskell realized he wanted an answer.

Involuntarily, Haskell's mind drenched up a dozen bad memories, the aftermaths of murders for fun and profit, bloody accidents, and messy suicides. He thought he'd seen it all; he had been wrong.

"No, no I haven't," he muttered, unable to take his eyes away from the nightmarish mess before him.

"Once I seen an old boy that'd slipped and dumped his head in a fish fryer over at Parkhurst Reformatory," Malloy muttered, "but it wasn't like this. I don't know *what* did this."

Haskell realized that Malloy was maybe half right, the head looked like a chicken carcass boiled off for broth, the flesh sloughed off the bone. Haskell turned and bolted out onto the stairwell and threw up violently over the side.

The patrolman's flashlight spilled over him until he swore loudly at the beat cop and the beam was turned aside again to play about the reaches of the dark space below.

After a minute to steel himself, Haskell walked back inside the tiny cabin, took a swig from his hip flask of bootleg rye, and offered it to Malloy who took it and drank, returning it without a word as if nothing had happened.

Something small and swift moved in the thick darkness at the edge of the room and Haskell twitched his head toward it but there was nothing there.

"Who'dya think he was?" Malloy uttered.

Gritting his teeth in response, Haskell leaned in, and with his skin crawling, he reached out and picked gingerly at the faceless body's clothing. It was a fruitless ordeal: no billfold, no gun, nothing. He pulled back cursing when a glint in the lamplight drew his eyes to one of the body's shirt cuffs. With queasy trepidation—he hadn't felt around a corpse for more than twenty years—Haskell picked up the wrist and revealed a gilt-edged cuf-flink in the shape of a bull's head, enameled in red.

"Damn," Haskell swore, "there's going to be hell to pay."

"Who is it?" Malloy asked.

"Bull Devlin."

"Mother Mary."

"Yeah, he may have been getting long in the tooth, but he was tight with Laski, real tight," Haskell shook his head, dropping the corpse's wrist, and cursed himself for letting his mouth run on. "Where the hell's the coroner's wagon? Where're the rest of your boys?"

Malloy started defensively, "Down by pier thirty, they got a boatload of dead sailors or something, typhoid or poison or what the hell do I know."

"Get this place sealed up, and get some damn lights on!" Haskell's own anger was riding down his fear and shock now.

"Fuse is gone…it was like that when we got here."

"What, who set up the oil lamp?"

"I don't know," Malloy muttered, deflated.

Haskell shook his head; this was just getting worse, if it could possibly get any worse.

"When? Who placed the call? How long ago did this happen?"

"I don't know."

"Damn it, Malloy, what you don't know might be worth enough rope to hang with when Laski gets wind of this, you understand?" Haskell blazed.

Malloy flinched as if struck, and it was only then that Haskell noticed how sickly and close to tears the big man appeared, but instead of pity he felt nothing but disgust.

Haskell looked again around the office and was struck by the momentary impression that the inky shadows were actually growing thicker, inching closer across the crooked floorboards, around the battered filing cabinets that lined the far wall, caressing the back of Malloy's deflated frame.

Haskell found himself stepping backward out of the office without realizing he'd intended to, swearing again violently. "Don't you dare move until the medical examiner's got here, and touch nothing! No one in or out, understand!" he shouted as he took the unsteady stairs two at a time, and didn't stop until he was out in the rain and up the street to his parked car, practically knocking down two reeking vagrants wrapped in blankets and old coats who stood defiantly in his path, as if oblivious to him or the rain.

At the wheel of his roadster, Haskell calmed his nerves with another belt from his half-empty hip flask, and waited for his heart to calm down as he listened to the rain patter against the canvas soft top. He had no radio in his car, but he wasn't going to stop at a call box until he was well away from this place. He needed to speak to the precinct house and the examiner's office, but first he needed to speak with Milo Laski.

He'd been right the first time: there would be hell to pay.

* * *

Daisy Walker woke up sodden with sweat, her nightdress clinging to her skin like it wanted to strangle the life out of her. She flung back the coverlet and collapsed sideways onto the rug beside her bed, gasping as if she had broken free of an attacker, hand groping out for the switch of the electric lamp, heart pounding.

The flare of white light banished away the tendrils of black at the edges of her mind, and as her breathing calmed, she shrugged the nightdress off over her head and struggled back on top of her covers, lying unceremoniously naked across the bed with her arm flung over her eyes, savoring the cool silk on her bare skin.

The nightmare had been a bad one. She couldn't remember the details, of course—she never did—but she could still feel its aftermath acutely. Her inability to remember or put a face and name to the terrors that came to her by night sometimes vexed her awfully, but for the most part, she thought likely her inability to remember might well be a blessing, given the state they left her in. She was feeling, like usual, as though she'd run a marathon with the jaws of hell snapping at her heels, joints aching, sickly, and exhausted, her skin hot enough for steam to rise from her in the cool night air.

Daisy's thoughts jumbled. She considered her plight as she had many times before. The nightmares had started two, three years ago? She wasn't sure, but it had been sometime not long after she'd netted her position with the university library, her skills as a philologist proving the trump card over her age and gender with the stuffier members of the faculty. That, and of course they knew they could pay her a deal less than an equally erudite male counterpart, *damn them,* no matter how "progressive" they congratulated themselves on being.

Turning on her side, she glanced absently at the carriage clock on her nightstand next to her perennial companion copy of Poe. It was a quarter to four in the morning, barely halfway till the Wednesday morning alarm was due to wake her for work, *damn and double damn*. It just wasn't fair, but what could she do?

Her eyes lingered on the gold print on the blue legend on the spine of *Tales of the Grotesque and Arabesque*, and she wondered without much conviction, *Is it all my own doing?*

She'd always been interested in the literature of the strange, and she supposed what some would consider the morbid; indeed Poe, Le Fanu, and Rymer had accompanied her adolescent years when other girls were more interested in Louisa May Alcott and the like. Her books had been her refuge, her way of coping with the things that she abhorred in a world seemingly gone mad. But of late she'd lost her taste for them in a way she couldn't explain. They seemed now to conceal more than she could fathom, and offer mute accusation where they had once brought her solace and escape.

She knew, vaguely, that it had to do with something that had happened not long after her arrival in Arkham. She had been told it had been a case of influenza, and she had been lucky to live through it. In her mind, all became a dull white emptiness when she thought back to that time, like a part of her memory blanketed in silent, secret snow. In these dark moments of the night, she was sure that there was more to it than she had been told. There was an incident of some sort whose shape she couldn't make out, something before waking under her doctor's care, worried faces hovering by her bedside. One morning, sometime after the blankness, it was as if her usually excellent recall had just "started up" again, and she had a distinct recollection of a few days sequestered in bed, a hired nurse from the hospital clucking around her before she was up and about again, almost as if nothing had happened—almost.

Not long after, she had met Ted, and sweetheart that he was, he'd have married her then and there she knew, but it would have been false so soon, almost like duress, or folly rushed into after a tangle with the reaper, and she didn't want that. A further complication to their romantic entanglement had been that she'd studiously avoided any mention of her nightmares between them, and being a conventional sort of girl in most ways, Ted thus far had never had the opportunity to find out about them firsthand.

It was so strange as she considered it, here and now in the dark of the night, but she barely gave the gap in her past life a thought during her days, her life folding around the incident as if it had never happened; the rest of the world seemed content to forget it as well, to steam right on regardless.

It was only when the nameless dreams came, sometimes weeks apart, that the awful emptiness welled up and she felt the nagging sensation of dreadful loss, just as now the fear of the shape of truth she was missing rushed in on her with oppressive force.

No, that's not strictly true, she admitted to herself, there were other moments as well, when it was as if her mind skirted the recollection of something and she would shudder at the most incongruous of things: a patch of fresh paint in a back room corridor that didn't quite match the aged blue of the surrounding wall, the heavy thud of a book falling from a precarious shelf, a bloody patch of feathers left by the predations of the bursar's cat, the sensation of a cold hand on her soul when walking on a rainy afternoon. Foolish things with no meaning of their own, but which found a dark echo in her mind.

She screwed the balls of her thumbs into her eyes.

Daisy, Daisy, maybe you are going mad, bottled up, frustrated, and lonely. So many lonely castles, premature burials, and maidens forlorn running 'round your head you've decided to join in and caterwaul at the moon.

No, she knew what had triggered the bad dream if anything had: that letter with handwriting so like her own on the envelope. It lay in her study, unopened still after three days, nagging at her like a sore tooth.

Fighting against her mental inertia, and both calmer and cooler, she forced herself up. She flung her yellow silk kimono around her shoulders and went padding barefoot across the rugs of her little one story brick cottage across the road from campus grounds, and plunked herself unceremoniously down before her study desk. With a deep intake of breath, she slashed open the letter with her scrimshaw-hilted knife—one of Ted's gifts from an Alaskan expedition—and unfolded the page within.

'Dear Spook,' it began, *'I know I've been a perfectly awful friend and completely failed to keep in touch these last few years, but I hope you can forgive me and find it in your heart to help an old school pal out…'*

"Annabel," she whispered, half in expectation and half in shock. There was nobody else who ever called her "Spook" except Annabel, back when they shared a three-bed senior's dormitory room at the Hall School in Kingsport: Annabel Ryan, Daisy Walker, and Claudia Cabot made three, brought together by chance and time.

Old friend, maybe, but they'd never been close since school. But that was Annabel, wild, inconstant, and deep, very deep, and this bolt from the blue was just like her, just as she herself had been studious and enraptured in her books even then, and

Claudia haughty and proper as always. A tableau of a little part of the graduating class of 1921, little more than eight years ago but it seemed like forever.

And there it was again, the chill of missing memory, the dark echo in her soul, tragedy on the wind.

Annabel, oh Annabel, what trouble have you got yourself into now?

CHAPTER THREE

Arkham's Northside Station was wreathed in a cloying blanket of mist, worsened steadily by the grey smoke that fumed from the steam locomotives that labored and rumbled intermittently through its blackened, red-brick platforms. A fine sheet of moisture glistened on the wrought-iron spear tips and frozen vines of its ossified Victorian grandeur and gave it an unusually morbid and unwholesome air.

All in all, Daisy mused to herself, not for the first time, *there are quite a number of other places I would prefer to spend a morning.* She'd listed a few of them, grumbling to herself for the hour or so she'd been sitting on the old bench under the wide canopy of the waiting area, next to the almost fortified-looking blockhouse that doubled as the ticket booth and porter's office.

The damp air was thick in her lungs, and she quietly lamented that just about everything she was wearing would now smell of mildew and wet soot for the foreseeable future. Bill Washington, the stationmaster-cum-head-porter, whom she had known vaguely thanks to getting shipments routed to the university, had been very solicitous, at least, during her enforced wait, even bringing her a cup of hot tea, asking, with charming embarrassment, for her to "not be telling anyone, Miss Walker. The Boston to Maine will have my guts for garters you see—not company policy to provide free refreshment."

It was a particularly grim day, even for someone raised in northern Maine and well-used to bleak spells and freezing fogs from childhood as she was, and aside from herself and the handful of half-seen porters and guards bustling about distantly along the platform's edges, she felt quite alone. The world had been swallowed up by a mist that had risen up before dawn from the Miskatonic River which cut the town in two, and the mist's fingers had stayed wrapped about old, gambrel-roofed Arkham all through the morning like a miser coveting his horde. Today, the well-to-do varsity town looked every inch the myth-haunted cauldron of wickedness and puritan excess spoken of in New England folklore.

But as an intimate of the area, having been a resident now for nearly three years, she knew that mists like this were not commonplace; in fact, they were better-suited to her memories of spring and autumn in Kingsport down where this very river met the sea. The fogs and mists of Kingsport were part of the coastal town's well-established mystique, along with its picturesque history, and the so-called Kingsport fugue: the dreamlike state its panoramic harbor was said to inspire in artists and other sensitive types. Its mists, however, were justly famous and infamous in equal measure, and the irony of them putting in an appearance today was not lost on her.

The eleven o'clock train from Boston was, of course, late.

Some sort of accident had occurred on the line, she'd been told; livestock had inexplicably panicked and broken through onto the cutting near Dean's Corners, where they soon after lost the argument with a freight loco from Bangor. As a result, things were out of kilter in both directions while the carnage was cleared, and the whole network was suffering stalls and delays. It was another cheerless thought in an entirely cheerless day as far as Daisy was concerned.

She was still unsure why she was doing this at all.

A steam whistle sounded sharply in the mist, startling her out of her reverie, and she watched Bill Washington almost jump out of the office in his shiny flat-topped cap and wave green and yellow flags as a looming black iron beast rumbled through on the opposite side of the line, followed by a clanking trail of empty coal carriages dragging in its wake. He turned to her afterward on her lonely bench, as if suddenly remembering she was there, and spoke with almost child-like enthusiasm.

"Not long now, Miss Walker. They got the junction cleared. We just heard it through on the telegraph. The Boston Local should be right on up in a quarter of an hour now, no more."

"Oh, thank you, Mr. Washington, that is good news," she managed to smile.

It was only after she spoke that she realized how still she'd been up to that point, her mind turned inward, and now she rubbed together her gloved fingers and stamped her feet a little to get her blood going again and drive out the chill.

So, here it was: despite her misgivings, the point of decision had already passed, but this would make the matter real—a face from the past back in her life. Annabel's letter and then her telegram from the Boston hotel had both been short on detail and heavy on implication, and Daisy knew they hadn't told the whole story. Even without the full facts, there had been enough for her to know Annabel had gotten herself into trouble and was being hunted, or *haunted* perhaps might be a better word, and she had turned to Daisy for help. Of course, Annabel had believed her still to be in Kingsport, which it seemed would still be her ultimate destination, and the question remained unanswered: would

Daisy accompany her back there when she went? In truth, she didn't quite know herself.

Annabel was afraid, something Daisy found hard to imagine based on her memories of the precocious, utterly self-confident girl she had known in her own youth. The Hall School had been a disciplined, though not overly harsh, environment: a combination of finishing school and junior college for girls, with a reputation that brought in students from old families from as far afield as Lynn and Newburyport, as well as the old towns along the Miskatonic's run. It also quietly specialized in educating young people who had been either left bereft of family, as Annabel had been, or whose people were at the very least distant like Daisy's, and family lawyers and trustees visited the place as often as parents, and often with considerably more real interest.

Daisy, of course, had really come to know these facts concretely only afterward with an adult's hindsight, and her time at the Hall School had been golden for her in retrospect. She'd loved the old building, bequeathed at the school's founding; it had once been the grand house of Eben Hall after the Revolutionary War and was every inch a display of ostentatious wealth and power. Its soaring spiral staircases and high-domed ceilings with their bacchanalian frescos had seemed to her like something out of a fairy tale kingdom, and its private library had been equally as wonderful, with vaulted cases stretching from floor to ceiling and stacked to bursting point with a treasure trove of literature and learning from around the world.

These were her happy memories from an otherwise unhappy time in her life, bundled away to school after her mother lost her long fight with sickness and her father buried himself in his missionary work. *Eight years ago,* she marveled to herself, but the line of memory between then and now was broken, with nothing but a hazed, menacing blackness in between like a crack in a porcelain vase that hinted at something foul hidden within.

That division had occurred long after Daisy had graduated and gotten on with her life, long after she had last seen Annabel, and yet there was something about the letter that tugged at that break with quiet force. The feeling that the idea of meeting Annabel again seemed somehow the important thing to do, that it might shake something loose—or maybe it was just the idea of her taking charge of herself again, doing something other than burying her head in her work. That, on reflection, was what she deeply desired to do.

It had been with that reasoning that she had invited Annabel to stay with her for a few days, to rest and think things through in the safety of an old friend's company just as she had asked to do. But as for Daisy's own motives for agreeing—those she'd kept silent, and intended to keep so, just as she would not say anything about the timbre of dread that had settled in her soul like a precognition of what was to come. The fear she felt was not something she could easily define, nor was her own willingness to accept it as real.

Another steam whistle shrilled and shrilled again, this time in the expected direction, snapping Daisy out of her somber thoughts, and the thunderous bronze and black iron serpent came into view wreathed in the smoke spitting forth from its stack funnel, its headlamps blazing like dragon's eyes in the fog-induced twilight. Washington and the porters hurried to be ready with particular eagerness, the Boston Local ignominiously late.

Daisy got to her feet, the backs of her knees painfully stiff. *A hot bath and a whiskey in my coffee tonight, or I'll be in no fit state for guests,* she thought, forcibly quelling a slight moment of panic by focusing on the mundane around her, as the carriage doors along the shrouded train clattered open forcefully and a smattering of passengers scattered out like prisoners on license.

Wrapped up tight in a charcoal grey overcoat with a high sable collar, Annabel Ryan made an unmistakable sight: tall, beautiful, and classically proportioned, with her pageboy hair as black as a raven's wing and a depth to her gaze that could stop you from across a crowded street. She looked as if she ought to be stepping out onto a platform in Paris or Vienna in her high button-hooked boots—not a branch line junction in a provincial town in New England, no matter how prosperous or ill-famed.

Arkham doesn't know what's hit it, Daisy mused with a smile, her foreboding momentarily forgotten as she went to greet her old friend.

Annabel stood expectantly for a moment, and, catching on quickly, Bill Washington and his porters fussed around her, all but knocking each other over to trolley her baggage, which Daisy noted seemed limited to a single case and a valise hardly warranting the attention.

So much for a low profile, Daisy walked forward and held out her hand to her friend.

"Jehoshaphat, girl!" Annabel beamed with relief. "Look at you, Spook!" Brushing past the porters, she grabbed Daisy's gloved hand in her own and pulled Daisy toward her, kissing both her cold cheeks.

Despite herself, Daisy laughed. "Welcome to Arkham! It's good to see you, too, Annabel. I hope the journey wasn't too trying?"

"Hellish!" Annabel's voice cracked just for a second, but long enough for Daisy to notice and wonder at the emotion caught in the word before Annabel continued. "You are a sight! When did you get so grown up, and well, *womanly*? You used to be such a mouse—now you look positively serene."

"Nonsense," Daisy said amicably. "I've a motorcar outside. Let's get out of this confounded mist and get us both in the warm before we catch our deaths."

The motorcar, in truth, was Ted's worn-down old Model T, but Daisy had free reign of it while he was away, and even though it still had half-a-ton of rock-climbing gear rattling around in the trunk that he insisted live there, it was far better than nothing.

Matters of substance would wait, and the two women walked arm in arm down the platform, swapping further pleasantries as Bill Washington himself pulled the baggage trolley behind them.

But for all their outward bonhomie, Daisy could not help but notice just how fiercely her old friend clung to her arm, as if frightened to let go, and how her eyes darted left and right, as if hunting for something in the mist.

* * *

The bandage-faced man cast the half-eaten sandwich down on the passenger seat beside him, next to the scattergun, noting with passing distain the crimson smears around the tentative bite marks he had made in the bread. He knew that he needed to eat—that doing so might slow the progress of his condition somewhat, although of course there were no guarantees. He could taste nothing, however, which may have been a blessing, and had not felt hungry or thirsty at all for some time; there was pain in chewing, and of that, at least, he had had enough for a time.

He leaned back into the cab of the stolen Packard truck as a small group of coal-stained workmen in brown overalls and flat caps ambled by the entrance to the alleyway in which he was parked.

He cursed his unfamiliarity with the great city and its ways, cursed his condition and his state, and cursed yet more the treachery that had brought him here. The truck he had stolen from the warehouse proved a blessing, but not one he could over-rely on, as surely it would be reported missing soon, not that its use hadn't presented problems of its own—driving motor vehicles, as he had discovered, was something of a different matter in New York than it had been in Cairo or Merida. His first choice would have been to remain in the shadows, blend in as but one of the many beggars he saw, but quickly he had seen the peril in doing so, for there a trap had been laid, although perhaps not for him particularly, and he must be circumspect.

On the other side of the road, the side door of a garment wholesaler's opened and three men in dark suits and raincoats trailed out. One, older and perhaps more disheveled than the rest, turned and pointed his finger, seeming to argue with the other two who looked on impassively.

Haskell, Detective Haskell, he dredged up the fragment of stolen memory from the quagmire of his mind and identified the arguing figure.

The bandage-faced man flinched back suddenly as if stung—something dark and huge, traveling fast, flickered between sky and glass. Again, the shudder and the speed, and again, a flash like black summer lightning. Quickly, painfully, he wormed as low as he could into the Packard's seat well, his breathing ragged and rasping. Regaining his composure, he scrambled one hand up and brought the scattergun down from the seat and clutched it to him. He knew it was little protection, but he would take what little he could get.

They didn't see it? Of course not, if they did I would hear them scream.

He must tread very carefully indeed.

* * *

"There was a shadow over the tracks," Annabel broke the silence quite unexpectedly in a soft, halting voice.

"What was that Annabel?" Daisy asked, matching her companion's low tone.

"You asked—at that beastly, mist-shrouded station—you asked what my journey had been like and I said, 'Hellish,' do you remember?"

"Yes," Daisy replied, her attention focused, as she put down her novel and slipped off her half-moon reading glasses.

Daisy had been waiting for the last several hours for Annabel to start an honest conversation about what had brought her back, even prompted her visitor a little as she began to grow impatient despite herself, but to no avail, until now.

The rest of the dismal afternoon had been spent in getting Annabel settled in Daisy's spare room, freshened up, and fed. The whole time, Annabel had been disturbingly skittish, talking about everything and nothing in a show of good companionship, but checking for herself that the doors were bolted and the windows firmly latched when she believed Daisy was too busy preparing dinner to notice.

Now, after their meal, as a dank night gripped Arkham, they were in Daisy's small parlor together, the various books, papers, and curios that commonly littered it marshaled temporarily into the corners for the rare occasion of a house guest, the fire in the small grate warming the room. Soft Strasbourg waltzes murmured from the phonograph in the corner as Daisy read *The Face in the Abyss* and Annabel leafed through magazines without really seeing them, sherry in hand, and the evening began to pass. Daisy had patiently waited for her friend to bring up the subject of her visit, and at last she had.

"You see, I was being a bit more literal when I said that than I would have liked," Annabel continued with a self-deprecating smile, drawing herself closer to the fire before continuing.

"I've been followed, shadowed—is that the word?—ever since New York, and I thought in Boston I'd outrun them, given them the slip—you see it was just people then, but looking back now, I'm not so sure—I even relaxed a little; I thought 'what's a few days in town to settle my nerves, a little spell of room service won't hurt!' but I was wrong—there was an incident in the hotel."

"What kind of incident?" Daisy asked, confused and wary.

"Oh, Daisy," Annabel said, somewhat theatrically, "as soon as I get through telling you all of this, you're going to think I'm stark raving crazy and throw me right out on my ear. That or telegram for the men with the butterfly nets to come collect me, I don't know…" Annabel's words trailed off as she stared into the fire.

"Annabel," Daisy began softly but firmly, "I'm not going to judge you like that, whatever happens. But what is this about? I know from your letter that there's a man involved, a man you care for who's disappeared, but I've no idea how the rest fits in, or what you mean by a 'shadow.'"

Annabel turned her face to Daisy and, for a brief moment, she looked on the verge of something close to panic. "I don't think I quite know where to start."

"Speaking as something of an expert on stories," Daisy smiled with genuine warmth, "I often find the beginning is best."

"Well, here goes, my dear—you'll just have to make what you can of it. After graduation, a chunk of my inheritance came through, do you remember?"

"Yes, you bought me a goodbye present, a copy of the *Castle of Otranto* you found in that little shop by the wharf," Daisy replied. She was not the sort to forget a kindness, even after the passage of years.

"Oh yes, I'd quite forgotten—I did, didn't I?" Annabel smiled briefly. "Well, with that chunk of money, I wanted to go on the grand adventure I'd always dreamed of, freed of the prim and proper shackles of the fussy old Hall School," she said with something that almost sounded like regret. "So, I decided to travel a bit—squandered the money, mostly. I ended up on a slow tour of the Mediterranean: a season in Provence, then Florence, a winter in Cairo, Milan, and so on. The War had started to become a memory already along the Med, and I soon found a few dollars went far. I never stopped anywhere for too long, and wasn't so stupid as to stray too far from the beaten track."

Like quicksilver, Annabel's mood changed again, from remembrance to a slight, smirking pride. "I don't regret it, you understand," she said, "I enjoyed what there was to enjoy: parties, regattas, the wonderful ancient world laid out before me with a cocktail glass in my hand. There were suitors, of course, and less than serious boyfriends along the way, but they didn't mean much in the end, none of it did. It was all a little hollow—champagne bubbles gone in moments and leaving nothing behind. I was too clever to see the flatterers and the gold diggers for more than what they were, and maybe a little too vain to not enjoy the attention anyway; I needed more than all tomorrow's parties it seemed after all."

Annabel paused and sipped at her small glass of sherry, her eyes, far, far away and burning deep in the flicker from the fire. Daisy watched silently and reflected on the change in her, enough to make her a stranger with a familiar face. Oh, Annabel had always been beautiful, and more than a little wild, for her life at the school had been stifling, and even before she'd blossomed into her full looks and grace, she'd turned heads, and not artlessly. But, the woman who sat in her parlor now was much more than that precocious girl; she was self-possessed, her manner and poise effortless and honed to perfection—*devastating,* Daisy guessed, when wielded against the opposite sex, and intimidating as hell to her own when she wanted. Even stranger was the self-reflection and self-awareness she now displayed, quite alien to the girl Daisy had known who would hare off at the slightest chance to break her boredom, regardless of the consequences.

But then, Daisy thought, *I'm hardly who I was then, either—the person I'm pretending to be now—am I?*

Annabel continued, "I started to get this nagging feeling to come back to the States and do *something*—and I know how sappy this sounds—but something a bit more meaningful with my life. Like there was something I just had to do."

That one raised Daisy's eyebrow. "What did you do?" she asked when Annabel paused, as if waiting deliberately for the question.

"I came to New York, settled down for the first time—well,

since school in Kingsport to tell you the truth—lived a little more frugally on my private income, which I'd pretty much hammered up till then. You'll never believe it, but I took up painting again, and it…it helped."

Daisy did remember then: Annabel's artistic flowering at the Hall School had been brief and quickly stifled and Daisy recalled she'd gotten into trouble over it. Kingsport had always been a mecca for artists in a quiet way. They were attracted to its vistas and dreamlike atmosphere. Annabel's teachers had thought, however—not without some reason—that she had been attracted to the "wrong company" and the matter was quickly halted by the school. But, there had been something else, too, something about what she had painted being "unsuitable for a young lady," but Daisy couldn't quite remember why, or even if Daisy had seen the work in question.

Daisy refilled Annabel's sherry glass from the old dusty bottle she'd rescued from the cellar and opened for the occasion as she went on with her story. "Well, of course I was completely rusty and really quite awful. It had been years since I'd taken a brush to anything except face powder, so I enrolled in college and I got better. It really felt like I was on the right track somehow. And, well, I've never been a wallflower, or one to stay on the shelf, so when I was invited out with the art crowd, I started to hit the town a little. I think they thought me quite exotic, you know, quite the prize guest—the mysterious heiress artist who'd sipped wines in the near orient or some such—and I couldn't stay cooped up forever!" Annabel ventured with a roll of her eyes.

"I bet you loved that," Daisy said and not harshly—Annabel had always needed people around her; that had been one way in which they had been very different.

"You're quite right, I did," she replied, smiling a little again, "and that's when I met him."

"'Him'?"

"Maxwell Cormac," she sighed with deliberate drama, "'the one.'"

"You fell in love with him at first sight?"

"Oh yes, I was smitten, like a little girl with her first crush; being a woman of the world, of course, I tried to hide the fact and feign seductive disinterest," she laughed, "but I'm not sure it worked."

"Where did you meet him?"

"At a very decadent nightspot called the Falling Angel in Manhattan—oh, about a year ago now. Would you believe, I saw him across the darkened floor and that was it. I just had to sidle over and put myself in his way like a landmine—don't be shocked." She smiled again, warming at least to this part of her story.

"We do get the newspapers, Annabel," Daisy chided gently. "I do know what a speakeasy is, and we're not above a little bootleg brandy at the faculty socials, you know, just as long as the Dean of Divinities is elsewhere." She winked at her friend.

"Why, Daisy, I think you're teasing me!"

"Just a little," she replied, "but go on, tell me about him."

"Well, he's very handsome, of course, but that wasn't it, not really, I mean, he's hardly the first good-looking man to ever cross my path, after all. No, there is something about him, a sense of something deeper than the superficial. He was so clever, interested in everything—science, art, philosophy, the occult, oh, he was never boring. There was fire and wit in him, and a melancholy, too, I suppose. Sometimes you would catch a briefest glimpse of something unutterably sad and poignant about him, as if all the world was just window dressing and he was the only real thing in it and quite alone. And the strangest thing—and I know it sounds so cliché—but I would have sworn I'd met him before, known him all my life in a way, but of course I hadn't."

Daisy sat up in her chair. "Did he have a white charger, as well?" she asked, a little more pointedly than she intended.

"Well I suppose that all sounds total rot," Annabel replied, shooting her a rebuking glance, "but it was quite true, and here I was completely head-over-heels for him after our first meeting, and I think he was just the same in his own way, but he was the perfect gentlemen—as if I was delicate porcelain and he didn't dare risk anything going wrong between us. Well, we started seeing each other regularly, whenever we could. He would take me out dancing and to the theatre, but it wasn't as easy as all that. There was, well, a darkness over us right from the start."

Annabel trailed off in reflection, her mood shifting once more, and Daisy waited intently for her to continue again.

"He was—*is*—a geologist you see, and a very good one, I think, and he'd traveled all over the world working for mining companies and governments and he loved what he did. He used to say 'the Earth talked to him,' whispered its secrets and let him uncover its wonders—it sounds foolish when I say it, but from him, it was like poetry. It was his calling, I suppose you'd say, and sometimes he said it could blind him to what was going on around him."

Dark memory passed like a shadow across Annabel's face.

"What happened, Annabel?" Daisy prompted.

"He would go away with work for weeks," she began again in a troubled voice, "sometimes months at a time, down in Central America somewhere, and every time he returned, he seemed more fatigued, troubled, like a pall was cast over him. Oh, after a time he would laugh and smile, being with me 'lightened his soul,' he said, but it was always there, driven away but never entirely dispelled. I could never get him to talk about it, not right up until he, well…until he disappeared."

"Do you mean he went missing, or…left?" Daisy asked as tactfully as she could.

Annabel shook her head. "The last time he returned to New York, which was, I suppose, about a month ago now, he was in a terrible state, my poor darling; he looked exhausted, almost on the point of collapse. But despite that, he insisted on holding a party at the Falling Angel. He spared no expense, invited all the old crowd we used to go around with, and had me invite people from college. It was a great smash, but also strangely terrible, like we were 'whistling in a grave yard,' making pretend some disaster wasn't about to swallow us all."

Daisy, despite the cozy room and its normality, felt something of that same feeling now, that same sense of tragedy she had felt before. "Go on," she made herself say.

Annabel drew in a heavy breath. "I didn't know why until that very night after the party. He took me aside and he said he had to flee for his life, that he was fleeing something, something dreadful, and that the party had been nothing more than a diversion, a show to cover his escape. I was mortified, frightened, and disappointed all at once; I didn't know what to believe."

"You'd hoped he was going to propose—marriage, I mean. You'd hoped that was what the party was about…didn't you?" Daisy interposed quietly.

Annabel's eyes welled up a little but she quickly regained her composure, dabbing them with a tiny lace handkerchief. "Clever Spook. Yes, I suppose I did, at least, hoped as much. I did love him—*do* love him—you see."

"Why did he have to escape? Who from?" Daisy asked.

"He said it was the people he was working for—Copperhead Industries, or the people that owned the company at any rate. He hadn't known when he had started working for them, but they were very bad people. He said they were responsible for terrible things in the world, but kept them hidden in backward places where nobody cared what they did, or where the tin-pot governments were so corrupt they could be paid off to turn a blind eye to anything, no matter how monstrous. Copperhead was after finding things, things hidden in the ground, 'secrets better left buried,' he said, terrible secrets he said some people would call lurid superstitions and opium nightmares—but that were *real*. That's why they caught him in their web, you see, because he was the one the Earth shared its secrets with...," Annabel said with a sad smile. "Oh, I don't pretend to understand what he meant—not really—and I know how it sounds: it's crazy! I've been turning it over in my own mind for weeks and it's crazy whichever way you look at it. But, I know he was terrified, terrified for his life."

Daisy shivered. She felt suddenly cold, and reached out for her own sherry glass and took a long drink of the warming liquid to cover her sudden reaction to Annabel's words.

Annabel waited again for Daisy to gainsay her, but her old friend remained silent for a time, instead asking, "Why didn't he just resign, or the two of you just go away and not come back? Forgive me for saying so, but it doesn't seem like money was an issue for either of you."

Annabel demurred, "It wasn't that simple. You see, he had suspected for some time that something was terribly wrong with the people he worked for, but couldn't bring himself to truly believe until he had seen with his own eyes—until he had proof. After that, he secretly sought out people, people in New York who could help him understand what he'd experienced, what he called 'the real awful truth of things.' He hoped maybe he could even find somebody to help him stop Copperhead from going further—but that only got him into even more danger, and attracted even more unwelcome attention. He found out that Copperhead wasn't the only one, you see: they had rivals just as bad as they were in search of the same kinds of secrets."

"You couldn't go to the police?" Daisy asked. She was having the strangest feeling of something that wasn't exactly déjà vu, but something like it, and definitely unsettling.

"They'd have just called him crazy," Annabel said, and shook her head. "He was trapped, backed into a corner, and so he had to act for himself. He stole something from them, something they needed, and brought it back to New York with him that last time. He had found it for them in the first place, you see, and so he couldn't escape responsibility for what they would do with it. Even though it put his own life in mortal jeopardy, he had to act."

"That sounds as if it was a very brave and honorable thing to do," Daisy said.

"Yes." Annabel smiled with pride, despite her grave manner.

"What was it he stole…was it a book?" Daisy heard the dread in her own voice, asking the question without consciously forming it first. *Now,* Daisy thought, *why ever did I ask that?*

"Oh, you mean like a chemical formula or some secret manuscript in code? Oh no, nothing like that, at least I don't think so…quite the opposite: it was a small, broken block of blackish-greenish quartz or something, mineral, about the size of a chopping board. It had little spidery lines on it, but I think they were just decorations, not writing as such; they may even have been natural."

Daisy's heart was beating faster, and the sensation of being on the edge of something supremely threatening, something terrible glimpsed at the corner of her eye, intensified, but she struggled to keep any unnamed fears from entering her demeanor. "What did he do with it—the block or whatever it was he stole?" she asked.

Annabel sighed and clumsily refilled her sherry glass from the decanter. "I asked him why he couldn't just smash the thing into dust with a hammer, but he said 'it just didn't work that way' and he 'had to be sure'—oh, I don't know. But he had to go that night, and I was to try and carry on as if nothing had happened to give him time to get away before Copperhead realized what he had done. After that, nobody could be trusted, least of all anyone at the club…

"I wanted to go with him, begged, but he insisted it was far too dangerous. It was the only time he ever lost his temper with me when I wouldn't take no for an answer—it was quite sweet, really."

"Surely that couldn't have been all of his plan?" Daisy asked.

"Once he knew he had gotten away safely, he would send me a telegram with a certain phrase in it so I knew that it really was from him, and that everything was all right, and then we would meet up and put all this behind us."

"You mean run away together?"

"Yes—a fresh start, new names, and a new country even. We were both accustomed to travel, and we would have each other. But…," Annabel's voice gave way a little, "the days passed, then weeks, and nothing came. I was worried sick, but I tried not to show it, just carried on. I went to class, went out to a few parties, but it was all a sham. It was at a gallery exhibition opening that it started. I noticed someone looking at me, following me, a man—someone that didn't belong there, but I'd seen him before."

"Who was he?"

"I didn't know him personally, but I recognized him from the Falling Angel, name of Haskell. He'd been pointed out to me as someone to avoid, a corrupt police detective with an eye for pretty girls, a 'bagman' I suppose you'd call him. The rumor was, as well as carrying a badge for the police department, he was also in the pocket of a very nasty piece of work, a hood named Laski or Lesko or something like that. It was this mobster who I think owned the club—and here he was, following me."

"What did you do?"

"I'm not ashamed to say, I bolted out of the gallery like a frightened rabbit. But that was just the start of it. Afterward, I was jumping at shadows; I was being followed on the street, and taxis I took were tailed. I started to get secondhand reports from friends, of strangers asking after my business at the college, at the bank, everywhere.

"Up to then—and I know this will sound foolish—it didn't seem real somehow, more like I was part of an adventure in a book, utterly silly really," Annabel's face fell, "but then I was afraid, really truly afraid for the first time.

"I was sure I was being watched, but whoever it was always stayed just out of sight after the gallery. They never approached me, never came too near, but I'd catch glimpses of them. I could hardly call the police; I didn't know what to do or who to turn to. I started to get paranoid. I even thought that the bums on the corner of my block were watching my every move—silly, I know. It was getting to me and I don't mind saying so… I started waking up in cold sweats, absolutely certain that there was something hideous crouching at my windowsill watching me—three stories up! I just had to get out. Go somewhere."

Brave. Brave and headstrong, Annabel has always been both, Daisy thought as she digested what she heard, and wondered just how many people she knew who would have been able to deal with what had happened to her as well as Annabel had; few, she decided, of either sex. Annabel had fallen in love, and for that love would risk death and who knows what else without a second thought, and not blindly but with resolve.

"And that's when you first wrote to me?" Daisy asked with a calm she didn't feel.

"Yes, I wanted, *needed* a friend, someone outside New York. Look, I know I had no right to involve you in any of this, but I was getting desperate."

"Was Kingsport where you'd agreed to meet Maxwell once he'd contacted you?"

"Yes, yes it was…however did you guess?" Annabel replied, honestly shocked.

Daisy demurred, "It just makes sense—I'm not all that clever, I just read a lot."

Annabel snorted derisively at that bit of self-deprecation before continuing, "Well I'd talked about it often, Kingsport, I mean—and he liked to hear of my time there. He said he was sure he had summered there once as a child from my descriptions of the old town, but he was too young to remember it properly. I used to wonder if he was just humoring me a little. But when he had to go, he said Kingsport was not that far from where he had to go anyway—to get rid of the block properly."

Daisy's brain tried to fit the story together. It made sense at least as far as it went, but there were so many unanswered questions, not least of all: What was the block of glass? How was it so dangerous?

Annabel continued, the story clearly pent up for weeks from stress and fear now coming out in a rush. "The strange thing was that Kingsport had been on my mind, as well. I'd even dreamed of it a few times since coming back to America, before I met Max, and it's such a beautiful and out-of-the-way place. I wanted to see it again, before we left. Even after…after I didn't hear from Max and began to think something terrible had happened to him, I thought I'd go to Kingsport and maybe see if I could find him. It was as if I was drawn there. It's utterly foolish I know, but I started to wonder if perhaps he was laying injured there, or…or I don't know what—all kinds of nonsense was going through my head.

"I thought, if I go there and wait, it would get me out of New York if nothing else, and at least I would be there waiting if he somehow made it back. Then I thought you were still there after you got your job in the Hall Library."

Daisy's own heart and mind were in turmoil. Consciously, she knew she should laugh the whole thing off as preposterous, or at least get her friend to seek medical help, but much to her own surprise, she believed Annabel utterly and completely.

"I'm terribly selfish, I know, involving you," Annabel added listlessly, seeming to have run out of emotion, "but I needed somebody to talk to; I've been going out of my mind. But I've ended up here in Arkham first, and if I'm honest, I'm afraid to go to Kingsport alone."

Daisy drew herself up in her chair, got her own feelings under control, and considered the matter. Annabel seemed in earnest, not to mention on the last threads of her strength, but what she had said jarred in Daisy's mind. The Annabel she had known couldn't wait to get away from Kingsport. Over her years at school, Annabel had grown to see it as provincial, stifled, and macabre— not "beautiful" or anywhere she'd considered "home"...

The evening had drawn late, and heavy rain began to batter at the windowpanes of Daisy's sturdy little cottage. The embers collapsed in the hearth, the wood all but spent.

After a spell of silence, Annabel said suddenly, "Oh but what a mess I am! I haven't even told you about Boston and the train..."

"You're exhausted Annabel, and it's been quite a day. We should both go to bed." Daisy put an edge to her voice that declined refusal, deep down wanting a little time on her own to think through what she had been told. "Don't worry; I'm not going to send for the men with butterfly nets any time soon. I'm not saying I understand any of what's happened to you, but I can see you're at your wits' end. You're welcome to stay with me a while, and if you want, I'll swing some leave from the faculty and go with you to Kingsport for a few days, take a look around," Daisy offered with as bright a smile as she could muster.

"Thank you." It was all Annabel could bring herself to say for a while.

"Tell me the rest in the morning," Daisy said, adding *in the daylight*, silently to herself.

Daisy got up, closed the fire grate, ushered her troubled guest to her room, and retired for the night.

Alone in Daisy's comfortable little spare room with its haphazardly shelved books and framed arabesque prints, Annabel, still dressed, sat in silence in the near darkness on the edge of her bed. She waited for the light that glimmered under the doorway to be extinguished and the sounds of Daisy settling down in the room next door to cease. She let a few minutes pass in stillness with nothing but the sound of the rain before letting out a long, low breath. Reaching down, she pulled up the hem of her skirt and one by one began to undo the buttonhooks on her almost knee-high calfskin boots with quick, practiced movements. She let out an audible moan of relief when the leather parted, freeing her well-toned calf, and a slender object popped out into her waiting hand.

It was a hard, wedge-shaped object, deep black in the semi-darkness, no more than a half inch at the widest point and around four inches in length. *The smallest piece,* entrusted to her by the man she loved.

Annabel tucked the shard under her pillow and with jerky, tired movements continued to undress.

Outside the window, despite the heavy rain, the trailing ivy which garnished the wooden frame withered quickly, as if taken by a hellish frost.

* * *

Getting into the Falling Angel had turned out to be easier than Morgan had feared, but proved not without its hazards.

After his trip out to Cormac's place, he had spent an afternoon brooding, and most of the following day and a half doing leg work, checking hospital records, hitting newspaper morgues, and chasing down a few scant leads around town to no real good result. Cormac was long gone, and the list of people that knew him as anything but an acquaintance or a name they'd maybe heard was almost non-existent, which meant he was either chasing a phantom, or the right people to ask were themselves deep in the shadows, which alone only added to his growing suspicions about the man.

The Falling Angel was his best bet as far as locating Cormac was concerned, but he'd no intention of blindly walking into the unknown, and wanted the lay of the land first. His last port of call, then, had been to an old friend of his dead partner in the pawnbroking game named Selby—a money-grubbing spider who could be counted on to know the movers and shakers in the rackets, play-by-play. He'd looked at Morgan as if he'd been Banquo's ghost, and more than a few bills had been needed before the wily old man had overcome his suspicions and given up a little intelligence on Milo Laski and his crowd. The mobster had a bad reputation—even for someone in his line of business—as a vain and violent man, and while the smuggling and bootleg liquor distribution for the syndicate made up his bread and butter, the Falling Angel seemed to be the icing on the cake for him and his outfit—a "real money spinner" that catered to a "strange trade"—all confirming what Greta had told him.

Forewarned and forearmed, Morgan had decided on his plan of approach, and headed back for a few hours' sleep in preparation for a long night ahead of him.

He'd lit out in a battered old tux which had seen better days and an open-collared dress shirt under his overcoat. Thanks to Selby, the pawnbroker, and his gunsmith connections earlier in the day, Morgan had also picked up a couple of revolvers and a few boxes of shells to replace the guns the police had cleaned him out of during his spell in jail; he selected the smallest of the two, a .32 snub-nose, and tucked it away in an ankle holster to see him by for the night. It wasn't much of a cannon to be sure, but it was far less likely to draw the wrong kind of attention in the places he was heading.

When he ventured out, it was Friday night going on Saturday morning in Midtown Manhattan, and between flashes of rain, the town was roaring; indeed, if you'd stepped off a ship from overseas, you'd never have guessed Prohibition was anything but a distasteful rumor. The street cops in their dripping flat caps and bluebottle overcoats may as well have been blind and deaf, and yellow cabs packed with revelers young and old zipped past in pulses of headlamp flare and stolen snatches of drunken noise. Morgan spent a few hours making the rounds and getting his bearings again, listening for who was up and who was out, who'd made a score recently and who'd taken a one-way trip to the Island. The night city was a whirlpool in which the unwary could easily drown, and Morgan may have been many things, but unwary wasn't one of them.

Morgan had never seen New York before Prohibition, but they said more drink flowed and more money was made in supplying it now than before the Volstead Act had been passed, and he well believed it. Nightclubs and speakeasies, good time gals and mobsters, the idle rich and scum of the sewers: it was an ever-shifting quagmire of fortunes good and bad, broken allegiances, and still-born notoriety to an extent anyone who wasn't part of it could never truly understand. For most, the false drama of the newsreels and gossip columns was more than enough, and the cops and the "respectable businessmen" between them made sure blood was washed off the sidewalks before morning.

He'd made a slow circuit through the bars and joints along the way to his destination, played a hand or two of cards at Whitey's, and went dodging through pools of sidewalk rainwater to the sound of car horns blearing and slow jazz slithering out into the streets from open windows and closed doors, his grey fedora set against a chill wind that blew through the concrete canyons of the city.

There was also an unfamiliar raw edge of violence to the night, more than he'd remembered, and Morgan couldn't quite put it down to the shadow that had fallen over his life lending the world a darker edge to his perception. Thus far, he'd seen a pair of cops drag apart two men who'd half-beaten each other to death while their jittery girlfriends looked on hissing like vipers, a drunk getting hard-rolled by kids by a bus stop, and the local meat wagon blurring by twice, bells clattering fit to wake the dead.

He'd also almost had to resort to violence himself to get past a trio of reeking homeless men with feverish eyes that had cornered him and a few other passersby exiting a pool hall. The three had come out of nowhere, grinning slackly and pressing poorly printed fly bills on them for some revivalist church or other. He'd taken one himself and stuffed it in his pocket in order to get by them without causing a scene—there'd been no sense in getting rousted by the cops or attracting undue attention brawling with tramps on street corners.

The Falling Angel, Morgan had discovered, occupied the upper stories of a sprawling and otherwise thoroughly respectable antiques business in Midtown, the building itself a former townhouse for some Victorian magnate with a taste for Doric columns and florid Italian marbles. The illegal nightclub, it turned out, wasn't exactly on the beaten track as far as Manhattan's half-shadowed nightlife was concerned—and as speakeasies went it was neither as famous as places like the 21 Club or as big as the Lyle Tiger, which took up the entire three-level basement of an old factory in the garment district—but it had gained some notoriety because it catered in part to a fairly special crowd.

Access, it turned out, was by the rear fire escape stairs in a busy back alley that also led away to a number of other late-night venues, and Morgan had simply attached himself to a party of very well-to-do fraternity boys with pretensions to culture and simpering co-eds in fur mufflers—all too merry to notice a cuckoo in their midst. He sailed past the doormen without so much as being patted down, although from the searching expressions on their meaty faces as he'd passed over his five dollar door fee and taken his hat and coat, they knew full well he didn't fit. Most likely this was the kind of place where more than a few sharks swam in search of new fish on which to dine, and as long as he caused no overt trouble, the management was content to stay clear.

Inside, emerald shadows and flickering flame awaited him.

The grainy photograph hadn't nearly done the place justice. The wide central room was almost in total darkness, lit only by a few candles couched in lanterns tucked away in the booth tables and hanging above the bar, while two great braziers of burning coals flanked the raised dais of the stage, softening its green-shaded footlights. What the flickering illuminations revealed—or more accurately hinted at—was a setting more akin to a nocturnal Venetian palace than a rowdy city gin-mill, set as it was with looming statuary and bedecked in green velvet hangings that further swallowed sight and distorted sound. The conversation was muted, and the clientele select for the most part; it was busy, but not bustling, and certainly nowhere near as crowded as the night the photograph had been taken.

A band hidden somewhere on an all-but-unseen mezzanine above undercut the murmur of voices with slow, sonorous notes to which a dozen or so well-heeled couples danced slow and loose in the emerald gloom. Beneath the haze of tobacco smoke and the sharp tang of cologne and perfume, there was a faint hint of another odor, something cloying and sickly sweet Morgan knew from half a world away—opium, and that alone told him the kind of games the bored rich came to play at the Falling Angel.

Morgan cruised easily to the farthest bar, taking in the details. In truth, it all made him far more uncomfortable that he let show; there was an undercurrent of malice to the place that the average gin joint just didn't have, no matter how raucous, or what racketeer sat overhead in a small room counting the greenbacks. Morgan had set foot in a great many very bad places before, and this one felt like it ranked alongside the worst. The sheltering darkness harbored death far too easily, the fat-cats leered over pale girls half their age, the gaunt young men in crumpled evening dress lounged half-insensate like lizards, and the ones clearly out of their depths were even worse, with their borrowed finery and their brave, terrified smiles—little fishes swimming with sharks, waiting to be gobbled up.

You're letting it get to you, jumping at shadows. It's no more dangerous than half of the other joints you've been in tonight, just a different kind of dangerous, he told himself, and while his mind accepted the truth of that, there were a lot of shadows to jump at in the Falling Angel.

The barman looked just like what he was, an ex-con in an ill-fitting white dinner jacket that didn't vaguely manage to conceal the gun he was packing from anyone who bothered to look. Morgan immediately felt on firmer ground as he parked himself on a leather-covered stool in front of the bartender and tried to affect the air of a man with a slow thirst to quench.

"What'll it be?" the man growled.

"Bourbon," Morgan replied easily, making sure to smooth out his accent and dropping a five spot on the bar, "and one for yourself."

"I don't mind if I do." The barkeep smiled as if it was an offer he seldom heard and poured them both stiff shots from a bottle under the bar, rather than those racked behind the counter.

"Hey, do you know a guy named Mason, drinks around here sometimes, shutterbug, round face, glasses?" Morgan asked; it was his opening gambit.

The barkeep's face froze into a blank expression. "He a friend of yours?"

Morgan felt a twitch in his spine, *dangerous waters.* "Not exactly—a pal of mine wants a word or two with him, maybe a word he don't want to hear."

The barkeep sized Morgan up for a second before his features softened and he knocked back his drink. "I ain't seen him in here in a while, always getting into trouble, though, with that camera of his, riling up some big shot or some slumming dame that don't want to be snapped."

"So I gather, from you and half the other bartenders here 'bouts." Morgan sighed and picked up his shot glass. "Well, so much for business. Thanks, friend," he said and toasted the barkeep, who in turn nodded sagely and went on to the next customer.

The bourbon was expensive, but tasted close enough to the real thing for Morgan not to care.

Well, I'm definitely on the right track, but the ground's rough going.

Morgan took to watching the crowd and the staff in equal measure, getting a feel for the place, and soon, a tall, willowy girl with skin the color of cinnamon and a dress of gossamer-printed ivy took to the stage and began to sing slow Creole jazz as the Falling Angel continued to fill up. It was a syndicate joint, all right, too well-run and well-protected to be anything else—although they were sensible enough to rake in the cash, keep themselves out of their customers' hair, and do their own socializing elsewhere—even if the security seemed on the heavy side. There were no familiar faces to speak of, making any accurate tally of the crowd impossible, however, and the more Morgan checked off the faces in the photograph he held in his head against the shadowed haunts that passed by, the more he grew to doubt the efficacy of trying to find someone who matched, and decided to change tack.

The man who'd taken the photograph, Mason, was a side show; he'd have been good to talk to about the photograph, but he hadn't really expected him to be here—Greta wasn't usually wrong. Cormac, however, was the main event; it was Cormac he needed a line on, as all else was showing up dead ends and more damn questions and no answers. This was hardly Morgan's first time at table, so to speak, and that cold-blooded lizard Shaw-cross was right: he was a more-than-able hunter. Long ago, he'd worked out that sometimes, when seeking information, the real trick was not to ask "everyone" but just the "right one."

Before his second refill had disappeared, he'd decided the best bet lay with the staff, rather than the regular clientele, the latter more than likely to be tight-lipped to an outsider rather than helpful. The barkeep and the other discrete heavies that patrolled the place withstanding, the hired help seemed a much better prospect, and gave his jaded eye the impression of being worn out, wary, and distrustful of the effete and hungry crowd whose glasses they kept filled.

Morgan bided his time until the bar staff was busy before making his play. He hadn't long to wait, as soon half the place was in cheers of uproar, and the white-coated bar staff scurried to charge the crowd's glasses with something in bottles that may have even been champagne, all in order to toast a moon-pale woman wearing very little silk and a lot of sparkling stones who was being hoisted up on the shoulders of some wolfish suitors in disarrayed tailcoats. Half the place seemed enraptured at the celebration, while the rest retreated even deeper into the darkness.

Just as the third cheer went up, Morgan signaled over to the cigarette girl he'd seen circling the edge of the crowd. She was a redhead caught up in a Halloween outfit halfway between a gypsy princess and an underdressed bellhop, but he'd watched her negotiate the crowd with ease, steering well clear of certain darkened booths with practiced ignorance; her glance missed little. She sashayed over with a ready smile which never reached her eyes and Morgan ordered a book of matches from the white tray suspended from a golden cord around her neck.

He paid with a twenty and she demurred for change until he said, "Keep it."

Her eyes narrowed, but the smile stayed. "Mister, I'm sorry; you seem like a swell guy, but all that's on offer you can see in the tray, you know?"

"Do I really look that bad? You've hurt my feelings—my intentions are strictly honorable," he replied with a chuckle and got a more genuine smile in return. "Not that you aren't a good-look-ing girl…?" he continued, letting the question hang in the air.

"Jenny," she let slip ruefully. She looked at him hard for a moment, making up her mind before saying, "This crowd kinda thinks everybody without a house in the Hamptons is for sale cheap, you know?"

"And I'm not part of 'this crowd,' you reckon?" he asked.

"I'm not sure what you are, mister, but I'm giving you the benefit of the doubt, maybe. Well, just what are your 'honorable' intentions?" She grinned.

"Well," he echoed, "I was thinking more of a penny for your thoughts?"

Her posture relaxed, but her expression grew thoughtful. "That's more than a penny, mister, so just what thoughts did you have in mind?"

"I'm looking for someone, or at least some information about him. He is, or was, one of your regulars here." That might have been pushing the truth a bit far, but he hoped it was so; had the photo been merely an aberrant visit on Cormac's part, it didn't matter a damn anyway.

"You got a name?" she asked, glancing around. "I know most of the regular marks that slide around the dark here, whether they know I do or not."

Morgan leaned in. "Cormac, Maxwell Cormac."

She pulled back suddenly and laughed, setting the cigarette tray to quiver. She'd almost been fast enough for him to miss the sharp panic in her eyes.

"You suicidal, buddy?" she whispered through a wide smile. "You can't have asked anyone else here or you'd already be dead—that greenback just bought you your life, pally, now scram."

Jenny disappeared into the crowd as it broke up from around the *fatéd* woman—her adoration, it seemed, now complete—and was gone.

He gave it another ten minutes before sliding away, forewarned that he was unexpectedly on enemy territory, the Falling Angel all of a sudden a far less healthy place to be. The syndicate, it seemed, wanted Cormac dead, and if that was the case, any dumb fool asking after him was likely to become of interest as well, and Morgan wanted that kind of attention only on his own terms.

He knew he was being followed no more than five minutes after leaving the Falling Angel. *Well, this just gets better and better,* he thought, not without a little self-indulgent resentment.

There were two, maybe three, of them keeping pace behind him maybe twenty or thirty yards back, shadowing him through the alleyways and across the main streets and the sleepless city traffic. Morgan never turned to look at them square on, but he knew they were there, marking their distance. He hadn't lived so long without being able to feel such things, letting the cold certainty of pursuit settle into his bones. After ten minutes or so of leading them in a dance to follow, he tempted fate and ducked into a darkened side street he knew would be all but empty and dark enough to make for an easy murder, but they didn't close in; it was a tail then, not a hit or roughhouse job—someone wanted to know who he was and where he was headed.

His watch showed it was just past three in the morning, and while across the bulk of the city the well and rush of New York was finally sound asleep, here, traffic was just thinning down, and it would be another hour or so before the joints around the main drag would start to empty out. It was time to lose them if he was able.

Taking advantage of a sharp turn at a junction on the edge of the bright lights of the avenue, Morgan ducked back into the leeway behind a shuttered newsstand and the darkened office building behind it. Here, he swiftly transferred his .32 to his overcoat pocket as pure insurance; then, he folded into the blackness and waited, as still and silent as a stone.

The first to pass by his hiding place was a middle-aged couple muffled up in furs, staggering along and unsuccessfully trying to hail a cab as they went. Soon, they were followed by a running man in what looked like a military uniform, huffing and panting and moving too fast to even spare a glance in Morgan's direction if he'd wanted to.

There was a pause, then, before the hulking figure of a street dere-lict, bulked out in layers of mismatched overcoats and ragged scarves, walked slowly into view. For a second, Morgan dismissed him as well, but it was as the tattered man stopped stock-still and began to stare about intently, the flash of surprised recognition went off in Morgan's head. It was one of the trio from earlier that had accosted him as he left Whitey's bar. Yes, the size of him, the ragged mane of greasy black hair, and beard were the same; the sodium-yellow street light wasn't good enough to make out the feverish eyes, but Morgan would have laid money on it being the same man.

The derelict stayed where he was, curiously still except for his head which swung slowly left and right like a searchlight. There was a strange, unnerving purposefulness to him, lacking any of the haunt or tremor you might expect from someone reduced to living on hand-outs, prey to foully cold nights, and seek-ing oblivion with the worst the city's stills turned out. Morgan quelled his natural urge to withdraw further into the dark gap behind him, knowing that the movement would likely do more harm than good. The derelict's face turned to look straight at him—the eyes black pits in the half-light—paused for a long moment, and then moved on.

A heavy, lumpy form ran over Morgan's boot, tiny claws scratching against the leather, but he didn't flinch or let his own gaze flicker from the searcher.

The first derelict was joined by a second of his ilk, this one Morgan didn't recognize from the earlier encounter he was sure; this newcomer seemed all but collapsed in on himself like a hollowed-out shell. Wordless gestured communication passed between the two and they quickly hurried off in separate directions along the junction.

He'd been tailed all right, but not by whom he'd thought.

Morgan waited soundlessly for a minute more and looked down to where a barely visible form was worrying at some discarded object wedged under the stand, no doubt the remnant of someone's dinner. He'd seen rats in Bombay that made New York's look like church mice, and with the sudden force of unwanted recollection, the image came to mind of a carrion-filled, fly-haunted street shrine intended to keep the beasts appeased and slum children safe in their cribs from the gnawing, ever-hungry things that plagued the ancient port city. It seldom worked.

Morgan kicked the squealing, fat body out of the way and strode swiftly out of the gap, the stench of rotting meat suddenly overpowering to him.

Stepping out into the street, he forced a taxi cab to break rather than risk hitting him, and threw himself inside before the driver could finish his string of curses. He felt sick and tired as the adrenaline started to fade, and reeled off his home address to the driver without thinking in a brutal tone that brooked no further conversation.

It was not until he was back behind his own door, with the pistol beside him and the kettle whistling, that it struck him to go through his overcoat pockets for the fly bill the derelicts had pressed on him earlier in the night, and, as he did so, another square of neatly folded pressed white paper came out with it. Intrigued, he opened that first and read the brief line of swift pencil writing in the middle of the notepaper:

Bring a lot more than a penny, Nite Bird Café, 5 am.

"Jenny, you resourceful girl!" he exclaimed aloud with an unforced smile, brought on by what was maybe the first good break he'd had all day. She must have slipped the note into his overcoat in the cloakroom before he'd left. He glanced at his watch. An hour and a quarter to go, a few belts of strong coffee and the phone book to find the place; it couldn't be too far from the Falling Angel, but just as far as she could make it to avoid prying eyes.

His mind flickered to the derelicts that had searched for him, and that strange cold feeling returned in earnest.

Beside the note, he smoothed out the fly bill; it was crudely printed on nearly transparent yellow paper as cheap as you could buy. At first glance, it looked just like any other bill for one of the numerous mission halls and churches that catered to the dead ends and ghettos of the city, and there were many.

"Join the Legion of Rapture!" scanned the banner line wavering on an uneven pennant ribbon down the center of the page, *"Salvation, Joy, and an End to Suffering"* tagged like an afterthought across the bottom.

Set behind the words was what looked like a cross surrounded by what was meant, perhaps, to be the rays of the sun or shafts of glory. But on closer inspection, the upper bar of the cross was actually more of a stylized oval and not connected to the *T*, and the rays, while at first taken for merely being badly drawn, were perhaps instead deliberately overly sinuous in shape, almost snake-like. The fever-eyed faces of the vagrants came again to mind. *If that was salvation, you can keep it.*

Morgan turned the paper over in his hands and it rustled like dead leaves. *Stranger and stranger,* he thought. Nowhere on it was to be found an address, let alone a schedule of services or sermons or a pastor's name, not even an admonition to "give generously"—nothing. It was a declaration of faith, but with no grounding in place, denomination, or time.

More questions to add to the ever-growing stack, but perhaps a few answers at last would come at his appointment with Jenny.

CHAPTER FOUR

The old man watched the water as the sun sank behind him on the landward horizon and turned the expanse of the iron-grey Atlantic into molten gold. He was alone but for the forlorn cries of the gulls and the thunder of the sea below. He stood stock-still on the edge of the high causeway path, the great rocky mass of Kingsport Head at his back, dragging in the sea air in steady, deliberate breaths as the waves pounded in vain fury far beneath him. It was all he could do to purge the smell of blood and cordite from his head.

The vision had come to him unbidden, as many had before, in dreams.

Unwanted and unlooked for as it was, he desired to be rid of it. Its actors were unfamiliar, its battle and loss carrying no novelty for one such as he—for one who had lived as long and unforgivable a life as he had. Behind it lay something darker, a falling shadow, something terrible he wanted no part of.

As he had done many times before, the old man had waited till dusk, until the dying of the day, before leaving behind his timeworn, decrepit cottage on Water Street, with its chiming bottles of colored glass and tree-darkened garden, and walked alone the narrow, tangled roads of the fearful town, his twisted driftwood stick tapping rhythmically against the flagstones and cobbles.

Shunned and friendless, those few he met in walking slinked by without meeting his eye or offering any greeting; although, that was as expected, so old was he now that hardly any lived that knew his name, though all feared him. Leaving the town behind, the old man had made his way up the steep and winding path of the causeway, here to the edge of the world, here to cast one more secret to sink with the many in the deep.

The old man closed his eyes, feeling a familiar numb emptiness inside, a sense of unnatural calm at the border of which, like a shadow caught at the corner of sight, was the chaos and disorder of the hungry, mindless beyond.

It was not enough that we hung him, scattered his kin, so long ago. Others have come, far worse yet, to pick over the spoils.

A dark time approached, keeping pace with the storm, perhaps the last time, perhaps the end of all times. It was dim yet, but as a hurricane far off over the horizon bestirred the sea and winds before ever it was sighted, so did this dark hour herald its coming with signs and portents to set the jackals howling. Blood already was spilt in the water, calling the beasts from the deep.

Tired, he felt so tired.

Bitter victory, blood and ashes, emptiness—I have lived too long, seen too much.

* * *

The Nite Bird Café proved to be an unexpectedly nice little place on the edge of the West Village, and at this time of the morning, frequented only by a few listless bohemian types, a pair of grey-bearded nocturnal chess players, and a huddle of beat cops trying to stay out of the rain.

It was a good choice for a meet on Jenny's part, Morgan reflected on entering, as it was maybe not the last place in the city any of Milo Laski's crew would be seen frequenting, but way down on the list for sure. As for him, he knew this meeting was the best chance he'd come across so far for getting some straight answers.

The girl from the club sat in a booth toward the back, prettier by far outside the darkness of the Falling Angel, and a little older, with white skin dusted with freckles that spoke of more than a touch of old Ireland running through her veins. She was also a deal more sensibly attired out of work in a dark printed dress and a tweed jacket.

"I was beginning to think you wouldn't show," Jenny stated a little reproachfully as Morgan sat down across from her.

"I very nearly didn't find the note in time. Mind if I order?"

"Be my guest. You're a cocky S-O-B, aren't you?" she laughed, taking the sting out of her words as she said them.

"Just hungry, hungry and running against a clock," he replied, waving over the waitress and ordering eggs, bacon, and coffee.

They were silent as he ate, and she alternated between studying him with uncomfortable intensity and staring distantly out of the rain-slick windows. Morgan judged she was making her mind up about something, most likely just how much to tell him, and so waited for her to start in her own time.

"Let's get down to cases," she said not long after he pushed his empty plate aside, gathering herself and looking him straight in the eye. "This conversation we're having isn't free. I'm putting my life in jeopardy just by speaking to you, and not just from my boss, who, let me tell you, has a habit of taking an ice pick to the teeth of people that rile him, just as the warm up act. So what're you offering?"

Morgan drew in his breath. She didn't look desperate, just a little scared, but the fear never reached her eyes, and lurking beneath her measured husky tones was the snarl of the ghetto just clawing at the edges to be heard. She knew exactly what she was risking and wouldn't settle for less than she imagined her price tag carried. Hell, Copperhead would be footing the bill anyway.

Morgan took three fifties from inside his coat pocket without a word and laid them on the table beside his plate, but didn't take his finger off them. It was no small amount of money to her, and her eyes focused in on the green bills with an earnest desire.

"Maxwell Cormac," she said hurriedly, "youngish guy, early thirties, real handsome in that blue-blood kind of way, sandy blond hair, cool eyes that look right through you, rich, well-connected, works in the gold business they say. Hits the Falling Angel once in a while to get fawned on by the North Avenue crowd, that and toy with the Shebas on the lookout for a sugar daddy."

Morgan nodded at her flowery, but apt, take on his quarry, "That's the man, now tell me something I might not know."

"Bad juju, as they say in Harlem. Some real strange folks circling him like vultures. A couple of the girls that catch his eye, well, they don't get seen again at the club. I hear they don't get seen again. Period."

Morgan pushed one of the bills forward an inch from the others. "Go on, details."

Jenny chuckled, "I got nothing to take before a grand jury, mister, just what I see and what I don't see, what I hear that maybe I shouldn't.

"Look, I may be telling you what you already know, but the Falling Angel gets a strange crowd, always has; it's not like the other places I've worked. Apart from the usual lushes and marks, all the freaks hook up away from prying eyes, and they pay for the privilege like you wouldn't believe. Rich dope heads, ten-cent swamis, dragon-chasers, table-rappers, you name it."

Morgan nodded, just about keeping up with the girl's barrage of slang, all of which confirmed what Greta had told him and more.

Jenny paused and looked around a little nervously before she continued, "Don't get me wrong, the pay's twice the going rate and the tips are good, and you get pawed at a lot less than working some clip joint on the skids, but every so often, well, maybe a girl doesn't show up for work ever again, or maybe washes up at low tide, and little men in grey suits from city hall come looking hungry and leave with heavy pockets and blind eyes. Maybe now and then some irate brother or father or boyfriend barges in shooting their mouth off about somebody missing, or missing limbs, or just plain dead, and Laski's boys make sure they don't bother the customers too much, understand? And everything just goes right on rolling.

"This isn't a sob story, mister, and I'm no saint. I get paid and I look the other way, just like the rest. I'm just telling you like it is so you know what I'm saying and why I'm saying it."

"Bad company" indeed, Morgan thought, *Greta didn't guess the half of it.*

"So, what's changed? And what's Cormac got to do with it?" Morgan prompted, guessing he'd hit the crux of things. "Why are you here talking to me?"

"It's the boss, Laski, he was always a piece of work, but now…" She shook her head almost involuntarily. "He's gone crazy, and that Cormac fella's the cause of it. And when a dog's gone rabid, you get bit or get out of its way."

"And you're looking to get out of the way," Morgan cut in, the pieces falling into place, at least where she was concerned.

"Sure, why not? I saved every other cent I took from that place; I can up and go when I want. I'm nobody to him, Laski I mean, just window dressing. If I don't steal nothing on the way out the door, he'll just shrug his shoulders and get another girl with the right 'assets' to fill that stupid getup. Inside a week, he won't even remember I was ever there.

"I stay, I got a chance that, the next time he loses it, I happen to be the first pretty thing he sees and wind up being a lot less pretty when he's done—if I don't end up as dog food, just because."

"Sounds like a charming fellow, your boss. What happened with Cormac that's pushed him over the edge?"

"They had some kind of deal going, but it went sour, real sour. Look, Laski's got more on the table than the Angel and the dozen other joints he looks after. His real business is import-export for the syndicate, but he only takes a cut, not the whole dime. Laski's in tight down at Red Hook and the Liberty Docks: booze, guns, cocaine, you name it he moves it. He wants to make some real money, he needs bread upfront to cut his deals, you know, cash-flow, and swells like Cormac, they don't ask no questions like the bank, and don't take a piece of the action like the bosses… at least, that's the idea. But with Cormac, I think Laski got more than he bargained for."

Inside Morgan's head, a few more pieces started to slot together. "You say he runs contraband. How about, maybe, people, as well?"

"Sure, why not? I heard he's sent a few fugitives down south when the heat was on: easy money."

And boats travel both ways, no questions asked, which gives us how our friend made it back to the States with Copperhead tearing up half of Central America to find him—he just sailed away with the rest of the freight. Simple, Morgan thought.

"So what happened with this deal? When did it sour?"

"That's the crazy part: I don't know for sure, or just how, no-body does 'cept Laski. One day, maybe a month back, Cormac turns back up at the Angel, after nobody's seen him in forever—but he comes and he goes—so what? But this time it's like he's a different guy—scary, real scary, like he's laughing at some nasty joke you ain't heard, and you're the punch line.

"Anyhow, now he's lording it over everybody, holding big blow-out parties for four, five nights running, all on the house. All of a sudden Laski's acting like I've never seen him: like he's the chump and Cormac's running the show, and Laski's having his boys bend over backward to do whatever Cormac wants. Then, no warning, Cormac was just gone—again! Then it starts getting really weird. Some of the regulars, well they maybe aren't so regular anymore, people that do business with Laski, turn up dead or vanish, and suddenly the Angel's swarming with dumb muscle packing guns pretending to tend bar…"

"Yeah," Morgan nodded, "that much I spotted."

"Right, well not long after this hits the fan, then we—the girls at the Angel I mean—are all taken under instruction: Cormac's never to be allowed back in the joint, his name is never to be spoken, and anybody that asks after him is to be pointed straight to the boss's 'personal' attention."

"And I show up asking fool questions," Morgan chuckled.

"You show up, mister, acting all nice as pie, asking fool questions," she smiled, with a glint in her eye that belied her years.

"What about this?" Morgan asked, avoiding where that remark was heading, and taking out the folded photograph that Greta had given him and passing it to Jenny.

"That was one of Cormac's last blow outs," she nodded in confirmation. "Everybody in the joint had a real swell time. Well, not all of us…the girls, I mean—waitresses and singers you know—we hadn't got a clue what was going on…but the, I don't know, *fear*, I suppose you'd call it, backstage…it was like an undercurrent running through everything. It was, I don't know, infectious…" She looked down at the picture. "That girl, the real looker, genuine class…" Jenny tapped her fingernail on the picture.

Morgan leaned over and looked. Just to the right of Cormac in the picture was a striking, beautiful, patrician-looking young woman in a silver and black dress with her dark hair cut in a Louise Brooks style pageboy bob. "What about her?" he asked.

"Well, she knew him *real* good."

"You mean she was one of his…hangers on…weird friends?"

"No…at least I don't think so, not like you'd think." Jenny

paused thoughtfully. "Like I said before, plenty of girls fell for him or just wanted to latch on to him for a sugar daddy, more fool them; I reckon he got his kicks having them compete for his attention, and a few of those girls, well, they just dropped right out of view, afterward—you know what I mean? *Right-out-of-view.*" Jenny ran her fingernail in circles around the image of the woman's face. "But this one, she was different, she seemed to know him, I don't know, from somewhere else." She shrugged. "And he was always the perfect gentleman with her—real sweet, not like he was with the others, and he didn't stand for any nonsense near her... Like that film with John Barrymore—*Real Jackline*...oh, you know the one?"

"*Jekyll and Hyde?*" Morgan offered.

"Yeah, that's it," she nodded.

"Do you know her name?"

Jenny smiled coldly and Morgan pushed the other two bills forward. "Do you know a woman named Greta by any chance?" he asked wryly.

"What's that?" she replied, evidently confused.

"I think you'd get on like a house on fire. Never mind. Who is she, this one here in the picture, do you know her name?"

"Ryan, Annabel Ryan I think she's called. Real classy, but not so much a stuck up... Well, you know what I mean... Not as bad as some of them. She looked me in the eye—more than most of them do.

"I think she was an artist or had dough herself. She certainly didn't need a sugar daddy, and she paid her own way mostly. To hear her talk, she'd been right the way 'round the world—London, Paris—all those places you read about in magazines." Jenny appraised him coolly and licked her lips. "She has an apartment down near Barnard Hall, I can't remember the address, but I heard her get a cab sent for more than once. My guess is a clever guy like you won't have much trouble finding her." She shrugged.

"And that's all that's fit to print."

Jenny stood up and collected the money on the table, scooping it into her purse.

"You're a sharp girl, Jenny, 'window dressing' be damned. Something tells me you're going to go far," Morgan said as she started to walk away.

She stopped and looked down. "Far from here, at least; I got a six o'clock bus to catch. I'm deserting the ship before it sinks. Goodbye, mister. Oh, and my name's not Jenny," she quipped over her shoulder, and she was gone.

Morgan slumped slightly in his seat as she went, the long night catching up with him at last.

"Like I said, sharp girl," he muttered.

It had been a long, hard day of cold alleyways, sour liquor, darkened spaces filled with faceless people, and smart women taking his money and walking out on him it seemed, but at least he was starting to get some answers, no matter how vague.

Now he had a new name to chase, but that was fine; one name lead to another and another, all links in a chain that sooner or later would lead him to the increasingly sinister-sounding Mr. Maxwell Cormac.

Was he a thief, a betrayer? Patron to a mobster? It seemed pretty certain so, not to mention that by Jenny's reckoning Cormac was the bane of a string of out-of-their-depth, vapid young women who couldn't look beyond the Ivy League charm, and paid the price.

Sharp, young Jenny had seen right through him, of course—past the money and the looks—didn't know just why, but knew right off he was a wolf. But then again, Jenny likely had no illusions to start with, he guessed—she was probably brought up the hard way with her eyes wide open and a stone heart to see her through the pitfalls of the world.

Cormac had something on Laski, too. Not just a loan marker,

that much made sense, something that had Laski all shaken up, and, by reputation, the hood wasn't the kind of man to get rattled easily—that bore consideration all on its own.

As for this Annabel Ryan: here, at least, was a fresh link in the chain, a lead that felt hot instead of cold. Time would tell just how important this particular line would be, but his gut—his gut was telling him she would be the key, and maybe, just maybe, she was what Cormac had come back for.

* * *

The sallow-skinned man stood at the head of the alleyway; behind him, other vagabonds and homeless derelicts crowded around the smoking ashcan of their night fire. Once, he had had a name, an empty thing, but now he just called himself Vigil, for that was his assigned task. The others feared him, for he was not like them, and that he found pleasing. They would have fled, scurrying away to other bolt-holes, other fires, but he had ordered them to stay, and they had obeyed, vermin as they were.

His flesh burned despite the cold air; clammy and taut, he stood as still as a statue, his vigil uninterrupted as he looked out across the busy intersection toward the door of the woman's apartment building. Soon, dawn would come, creeping into the city, and then others would come to him, and he would speak of what he had seen and abase himself and perhaps be rewarded.

A smile dragged his lips open like a wound at the prospect, blood-specked froth teasing down his chin unnoticed. He yearned to be rewarded, to know joy, to once again see!

Soon, the rapture would fade and he would be again like those filthy vermin who crowded around their pitiable fire—broken, purposeless, crawling, hurting, and lost.

But when the gate opened—the gate whose key was blood and whose pathway was darkness—and he looked within, all of that burned away, all the dim, pathetic memories that tormented him—the failures and the scorn, the long cold nights huddled in doorways, the dimly remembered face of the woman that had been his wife, the gambling, the drink—all gone, all swept away in burning bliss searing him to the bone.

Running footsteps scattered the trash behind him, and he turned with a grimace, his neck creaking with tension. *The meat had run away: why?*

Behind him stood a heavy figure in a dark overcoat and wide brimmed hat, his face heavily bandaged, the eyes two dark rips in the fabric that glinted like polished tin.

Suddenly, he was falling, the world tilting madly on its axis, his blood spilling out into the trash and dust of the alleyway like a river. He wanted to howl, to scream, but his voice was gone.

The bandaged face bent low over the dying man and whispered, "Spider you may be, friend, but scorpion, am I." Intoning under his breath dark words, older than man, that dripped like poisonous venom, the sorcerer pushed his fingers into the dying man's face as if it were wet putty and, with labored steps, dragged him further out of sight.

* * *

Morgan had flat out lied his way into the apartment building—after the day and a half it had taken to track it down, he was in no mood to wait on the niceties. It was a decent enough place, somewhere between down-at-the-heel and first rate, certainly respectable and close enough to several colleges to attract a clientele of self-supporting female students and office workers without fear of compromising their reputations or attracting the wrong sort of attention.

The elderly doorman, with his Spanish-American War medals displayed proudly on a tan greatcoat that had seen better days, hadn't been inclined to stop him anyway, but his more than passable card identifying him as an investigator for the DA's office had been needed to sooth the suspicions of the wretched soak of a woman that passed for building manager and allow him across the threshold.

Both the manager and the doorkeeper had been on edge; he hadn't needed any particular skills to garner that. From the woman, he had quickly learned that "Miss Ryan" was out of town. The manager's unprompted refusal to follow him up to the floor where Annabel Ryan's room could be found had caught him off guard for a moment. Instead, he was handed a passkey and told that the Ryan woman had "paid up in advance" before the manager went to ground as fast as her stumbling gait could take her, audibly slamming and locking her own door behind her—no inquiry about why he was there or what he was after.

Fear filled the place like fetid breath in a nailed down coffin.

Morgan prided himself on being nobody's fool, and a thorough investigator when the need arose, but knew full well that it was his instincts that kept him alive. No sooner had he pulled open the lift cage door onto Annabel Ryan's floor, than those instincts went into high gear, and he found himself loosening the revolver in his shoulder holster even though nothing, not even dust, stirred in the drab hallway.

Inside the apartment, he worked swiftly and methodically, the atmosphere of menace that seemed to hang over the place lending speed to his search. He quickly found enough photographs, matchbooks, and correspondence to be sure this was the woman he was after and link her to the Falling Angel, at least as an occasional customer. Unlike Cormac's almost sterile house, Annabel Ryan's apartment was very much well-lived in, filled with more small curios and detritus than most people's lives swept along in their wake, which told him that, if nothing else, she was well-traveled, and exotic odds and ends spoke of memories and emotional attachments he had no access to. It was like encountering a library whose books were written in a foreign and unknown language. She was also clearly literate and educated, artistic, and with a genuine sense and taste for the finer things in life, even if the apartment told him the means no longer quite matched the style, she wasn't exactly brushing Skid Row either. There were clothes and a few personal items missing, but not much, and the echo of disturbance and leave-taking rushed through. There was some effort to conceal the facts, but Morgan was a professional and wasn't deceived—she'd skipped town, traveling light.

Frustration and the corrosive fear in the place welled up in him as sudden anger, and he fought the urge to snap every piece of furniture in the place to kindling and pound his fists into the wall until the plaster cracked. It wasn't like him, he knew, to run so close to the edge like this, but it was getting to him. He could feel death breathing down his neck, and him running around like a rat in a blind maze with his quarry just out of sight. No matter what new leads he found, they just seemed to bring more questions, and everybody, but *everybody*, he came across was afraid. Shawcross's face floated up unbidden in his mind's eye and brought with it the memory of dry heat. Well, perhaps not everyone.

There has to be something here…just look at the place! She left in a hurry, she'll have left a sign, a clue; they always do. Look at the details, he told himself, *look for what's there, but you don't usually see.*

Forcing himself to slow down, he went over the place again. It wasn't a particularly big apartment, and was made up of a studio room with a kitchenette in one corner and a painted Victorian screen folded up by the bed in the other, with two small, white-painted doors leading to a closet and a shoebox bathroom, respectively.

The walls were covered in pictures of all shapes and sizes: photographs, prints, mixed in with some charcoals and painted studies that had the look of the same artist's hand. There were landscapes, still lifes, human forms, abstracts, even a watercolor of the Manhattan skyline. Then it caught his eye, tacked up by

the side of the window, no bigger than a page from a legal pad—
a heavy black charcoal sketch so deeply ingrained and smudged
over it seemed at first glance like nothing more than an angular
dark mass in the center of the paper. But it was a lighthouse, and
Morgan had seen it before.

He carefully plucked it down and placed it on the bed and
studied it. *It's the same!*

He went to the closet and dragged out the battered portfolio
case he'd seen there earlier and dismissed. It was jammed with
odds and ends of sketches and half-finished studies, pages torn
from magazines and pages from old books. Morgan dragged it
into the studio room and started to rifle through them one thing
at a time, separating out anything that looked like it had bearing on what he was after. After a few minutes, he was sitting on
the edge of the bed with more than a dozen various pictures and
papers laid out whose subject and nature seemed singular and
disquieting in a way he couldn't quite put his figure on. Many
were variations on a theme, inconsistent and dreamlike. At the
center of them was an unfinished composition, but half-formed
as it was, it was undeniably the prototype for the striking picture
he had seen in Cormac's study. Next to it was a faded and spotted
plate reproduction photograph razor-cut from some unknown
book depicting a small and very picturesque coastal town nestled
in the shadow of a huge headland cliff, out in the bay from which
lay what he was sure was the very same lighthouse Annabel Ryan
had drawn and painted over and over again. It was real.

"*Kingsport Head and the North Point Lighthouse, Kingsport,
Mass. 1881 (reconstructed, after the Great Storm of 1781, the lighthouse at its centenary)*" ran the header.

There were other pictures, as well, that she had drawn, or attempted to: dark shapes rendered in heavy strokes of paint and
black charcoal, suggestive and somehow misbegotten, and something that might be a crater-like rim or valley dotted with smashed

houses lit with strange green marsh fires. At the very bottom of the portfolio, rolled up and tied with ribbon, was a scrap of heavy canvas, what must have been part of a larger work that had been torn up, but this part, it seemed, had been rescued and hidden. Again was depicted the familiar benighted lighthouse in part, but at the center of the fragment was a terribly thin, tall figure, passing along the crest of a storm swell's waves. All but featureless, the figure was nevertheless utterly disquieting in some way, and its action in walking across water, which might have seemed foolish or even messianic, instead gave the impression of something appalling in its breaking of the natural order of things, something that echoed with wanton misrule and breathed darkness.

Morgan stared at the images for long minutes in silence, trying to get his mind to encompass the importance he somehow knew they portended, feeling on the edge of some revelation he couldn't quite grasp.

With a soft rattle, the handle of the apartment door turned and caught against the latch.

In a moment, he was fully alert, and acutely conscious that he'd been sitting too long in one spot in reverie and nearly paid for it with his life, and might even do so yet. He'd been saved only because he'd dropped the latch on the door after he'd come in, a prudent habit from long ago after a certain night in a Singapore plantation house had left him with an eighth-inch bolo scar on his thigh to remember it by.

Morgan got to his feet almost silently, barely disturbing the stacks of paper on the bed, and assessed his options, his mind and instincts in high gear. The studio apartment left very little space in which to hide, especially if he wanted to keep his options open as to what he would do next. Deciding that sometimes the old ones were the best, he quickly but calmly crossed the room to the wall where the door would open. He calculated there was just enough room to escape the door smashing into the wall if it was slammed open, but he'd be out of immediate eye-line of whoever entered. If he was lucky, the pictures laid out on the bed or the half-open closet door might give him a few seconds distraction, as well. If not...

There was silence as the door handle was still for a moment, and in the pause Morgan barely breathed; the familiar cold, inward calm that came over him when it came time to fight for his life folded over him now, his perceptions sharpened down to a razor's edge.

A faint ticking-scratch, metal against metal.

They're picking the lock. Subtlety then, was the order of the day—more chips stacked in his favor, maybe.

Morgan reached with glacial slowness inside his coat and withdrew the larger of the two revolvers he was carrying, but, for fear of giving himself away with the sound, he didn't pull back the hammer.

A sharp click heralded the door giving up its defense against the intruder. A pause again followed before the handle was turned, and, with almost no force at all, the door was nudged slowly open.

Damn, Morgan thought. Whoever was on the other side was being cautious. They'd let the door swing, but not entered in with it.

Seconds passed and there was slow movement, Morgan watched as a boxy, blued-steel barrel of a .45 automatic led the way into the apartment, followed by a black-gloved hand, then a thick, leather-clad arm.

Out of time, Morgan heard himself think, almost as if the voice in his head was that of a stranger. It was now or never: attack or wait for the gunman to get a clear sweep of the room. If there were more behind him, he might as well be signing his own death warrant. *To hell with it!*

Morgan launched himself at the half-open door with all the bodily force he could muster from a standing start, his shoulder impacting the upper door panels with a dull bang, his weight slamming it into the intruder with rattling force.

The door vibrated heavily, hinges splintering from the frame as Morgan stumbled but kept his feet, ignoring the spreading numbness in his shoulder; he felt as much as heard the intruder crash down to his knees with a loud grunt, and joy hit him as the big automatic tumbled heavily across the floorboards.

The elation was short-lived as the intruder hauled himself off the floor with something akin to a guttural roar and slammed the door back at Morgan, but he was already circling around to press the attack and it missed him by inches, slamming back into the wall. Morgan had a brief instant to take his enemy in: ruddy-faced and pig-eyed, a shade under Morgan's own height, but bull-shouldered and strong, a cheap suit and a heavy leather overcoat, fedora already spilled off his broad, bullet-thick head. He came on with his shoulders hunched and his blunt fingers spread like talons—a wrestler's stance that meant to grapple him close and tear him apart.

Morgan timed his own assault as the grunting man made a grab for him, lunging in and grabbing his attacker's left wrist in his open hand. Morgan braced himself and sharply turned around, throwing his full weight smoothly into the move, yanking the already off-balance gunman forward and sending him staggering into the room. Careening off the closet door, the gunman turned again, recovering quickly, but was met abruptly by a crushing downward blow by Morgan's revolver butt to the side of his head.

The gunman collapsed like a sack of coal and was still. Morgan spun around and raised his pistol at the doorway, but the hallway was empty and there was quiet except for the sound of his own heavy breathing.

After a second's pause Morgan collected the automatic from the floor and checked the corridor. It was empty—nothing and nobody stirred, despite the commotion the fight had made, and somehow he wasn't surprised. He pulled the door to the apartment shut, not that it fit squarely in the frame anymore, and checked on his attacker. The hood was a tough customer—despite a blow that would have split most men open to the skull bone, he was breathing regularly and there was little sign of damage except for a blooming bruise and a trickle of blood from a forehead already thick with scar tissue. Morgan rifled his pockets, then dragged him over to the wall, grunting with effort, and, taking a pair of horse-shoe handcuffs from the back of his belt, fastened him to the radiator.

After a moment's breather, he walked into the tiny bathroom and poured himself a glass of slightly rusty-looking water and sank it in a single long swallow, then poured a second, and threw it over the hood's face.

The battered man spluttered and stirred fitfully, wincing as he came around, rattled the cuffs, and, looking up at Morgan, swore long and inventively in pure guttural Bronx.

"Charming," Morgan said, sitting back on the bed, the .45 held openly in his hand, the message clear: it was time for some answers.

"You gonna kill me? Get on with it, Morgan, you limey bastard!" the man attached to the radiator growled.

Despite himself, Morgan smiled. Whoever the hood was, he was as tough as nails all the way down, and Morgan could respect that at least.

"It's funny," Morgan said, "the English call me a Yank, and the Yankees call me a limey—guess that leaves me stranded somewhere in the Atlantic doesn't it?"

The hood looked up at him sullenly, saying nothing.

Morgan looked him in the eye and said, "Get this straight, friend: if I wanted you dead, you'd already be cold and still, understand me?"

The hood nodded slowly.

Morgan flipped open the tattered gator skin wallet he'd taken from the man and flipped to the driver's license. "Salvatore Finney," he read aloud from the small printed card, "well, there's a meeting of nations right there. 'Sal,' I'm guessing, unless this is a fake?"

He slowly nodded again, his piggy eyes sizing Morgan up visibly, and from his expression not liking what he saw.

"Well, Sal, we've now been formally introduced, and while I don't have a mind to kill you, I'm not in a good mood and don't like people coming at me from behind with a cannon like this, so I advise you to drop the tight-lipped routine or this is going to get ugly."

Sal shifted on the floor, drawing himself up into a more comfortable sitting position. "So ask," he grunted resentfully.

"Let's start with who the hell you work for, and what you're doing here after me?"

"Laski, Milo Laski," Sal offered forcefully as if hoping to get a reaction. When it didn't, he carried on in a more subdued tone. "I ain't here after you. We was watching the joint and eyeballed you coming in. We waited, but you didn't come out, so we figured you'd given us the slip, and I came in to see what you'd been up to."

"Wait a minute," Morgan interrupted, "who's we? And what do you mean waited; you're a bit quick off the mark, aren't you?"

"I got a partner, if you can call him that—no good bastard wouldn't step foot in here with me. He's watching the front." Sal's forehead knotted for a second. "I ain't 'quick off the mark,' neither; you been messing around in here a full two hours, buddy."

Morgan glanced at his wristwatch and realized with faint alarm the gunman was right, it was past three p.m., and it had been a little after midday when he'd lied his way through the lobby. Somehow he'd lost more than an hour in Annabel Ryan's apartment.

The gunman muttered something under his breath that sounded like a curse that Morgan couldn't quite catch, but he was sure the words "freak show" had been part of it.

"Spill it, now," Morgan said with iron in his voice, pulling back the hammer on the automatic, readying it to fire. He wanted to be very much gone from this place as soon as possible.

The gunman took the hint, unnerved by the cold that had come over Morgan's features. "Look, the boss wants the girl who lives here; she's tied up in some mess that's giving him real grief— some heebie-jeebie bull I don't understand. You—you I know 'cause you were ratted out; one of the dames at the club heard you asking questions about that freak show Cormac. She recognized you from the papers and put the finger on you. The boss got your picture from the *Herald*. Says you're a stone killer—took out a bootlegger crew one-handed or some such, so I wasn't taking any chances, understand?"

Jenny, oh you are a sharp girl all right. It made sense: she'd recognized him right off and angled for a payoff from both sides; sharp indeed, and braver than even he'd credited her for.

"What's Cormac to your boss, Sal?" Morgan pressed.

The gunman turned his head in reply. "I wouldn't tell you if I knew, pally, I ain't part of that club deal. I look after shipments and deliveries. I shouldn't even be here…"

Then it came together in Morgan's head like a puzzle box opening: *the lock picks and hard muscle, Sal isn't the kind of guy you put on a tail or a stakeout, he's too damn noticeable—he's a racketeer and torpedo, not a bagman or sneak thief—and then there's the fear Jenny had spoken of, the barely contained violence at the club, the thugs dressed up like waiters, Sal walking into what he thought should be an empty room with a gun drawn, ready to shoot first, and ask questions afterward, fragments coming together, making…*

"How many men has Laski lost, Sal? Just how many of your crew is down?" Morgan asked suddenly.

Sal shifted nervously, startled. "I dunno, plenty, I suppose," he said grudgingly.

"And he doesn't know who or what's coming at him, does he? But he suspects the beef with Cormac has something to do with it, doesn't he? That's why the heat? That's why he's got you watching this girl's place?"

Sal's obvious discomfort was all the answer Morgan needed.

Morgan considered for a moment and came to a decision, clearing the pistol's breach before releasing the magazine, popping it into his pocket, wiping the other gun with the bed sheet, and tossing it on the pillow.

"Tell your boss I'm not the one putting his staff on ice. I'm looking for Cormac, not working for him," Morgan said as he stood up. "Tell him we should talk, if he's in a mood to be civil. Maybe we could help each other out. But if he's uncivil, I'll be uncivil back. I'm sure he can work out where to find me."

Sal looked up at him in surprise as Morgan placed the handcuff key on Annabel's nightstand. "Here, for when your partner gets his act together or when you pull loose of that radiator," Morgan said, and was out of the apartment before Sal could overcome his shock and reply.

* * *

"Haskell, your call!" the tired cop on the night desk shouted, holding up the receiver and handset and waving it unceremoniously over the edge of the counter.

"All right, all right, I'm coming!" he barked back, spitting a half-burnt cigarette into a cup of stale coffee at his side and stomping his way out of the detective bullpen.

He ran his hands over his face to wake himself up a little and snarled at the desk cop to scram while he took the call. With a look that came from nothing but scorn, the duty officer complied, heading off downstairs. The floor of the precinct house was empty, and so it should have been, the monstrous old gothic clock behind the back wall—which precinct legend had it dated back to a long-forgotten Tammany Hall donation and chimed thirteen when an honest councilman walked by—showed a quarter to one in the morning.

Haskell put the greasy, bell-shaped earpiece to the side of his head and held the candlestick receiver in front of him, drawing in a breath to half-shout, "This is Detective Haskell."

"This is Corby," the static-thick voice replied, "I have the preliminary results for you."

"Spill it, doc," Haskell said.

"This is highly irregular, you understand…" The rest was lost in static hiss.

"Say again, doc," Haskell spat.

"…a combination of simultaneous pressure force and exsanguination… I really don't wish to say anymore; I shouldn't even be talking to you."

"What? Say again and imagine I ain't got no medical degree!"

"Crushed and bled, Detective Haskell, he was crushed and bled," the voice on the suddenly clear line affirmed in no uncertain terms. "It was as if somebody flattened him under a cement pile while pumping his blood out cleanly at the same time, and no, I have no idea what caused it, nor am I willing to speculate on what did."

"Look, doc… Hello…hello?" The line had clicked dead.

Eddie Green, real name Eduardo Verde, small-time hood and con-man—card tricks and a well-oiled gypsy routine to bilk the old maids out of their savings and the young ones out of their virtue—had been a handsome guy, but not anymore. Found on a roof three stories up, crushed flat and bled dry four blocks from where Haskell now stood, and nobody saw or heard a thing. If it hadn't been for a tattoo on his forearm, they'd never have known him. But Haskell had known him; he'd pulled him in once or twice, and drank and gambled with him a couple of times around the town. He had been one of Laski's boys, and that kind of association was looking increasingly unlucky.

Dropping behind his desk, he reached for his hip flask and swore when he found it empty. He wanted to sleep, but there was too much awfulness mounting up behind him to make that a wise idea. Instead, he put his head in his hands and stared down at the blurred gibberish of papers strewn around his desk: files, photographs, typewritten beat reports and witness statements that made even the usual New York faire of robberies, shootings, and arsons seem like a provincial tea party in comparison. Most of these reports were never going to see the light of day, let alone a courtroom: nightmarish murders, together with a huge up-swing in disappearances, reports of weird prowlers, unprovoked assaults, bloody suicides, mental breakdowns, and even a slew of dead pets. It wasn't a crime wave, it was a damn biblical plague, and the only reason no one that mattered had spotted it—yet— was because it was all happening on the wrong side of the tracks. It was like the whole borough had gone mad. Half the force was talking about it under their breaths, but the official word was there was nothing going on, just the same-old, same-old. The heat was coming down from on high like Haskell had never seen it, and the first cop that opened his mouth where the press could hear would wish the ocean had rolled over him instead.

Haskell, however, was starting to see a pattern in some of the latest reports, and was praying it wasn't him that was going to drown. He had to do something about it, but he was sure as hell going to wait till broad daylight, so he sank back in his chair and pulled his hat over his eyes.

CHAPTER FIVE

Annabel sat, poised like a painter's study, on the edge of the huge mahogany desk in Daisy's customary private reading room hidden deep in the hulking mass of the Orne Library building. One booted foot kicking slowly in the air like a child on a swing, Annabel leafed casually through a large folio in the manner of an indulgent mother about to say, "It's lovely, darling, but what is it?"

Daisy looked up from where she was seated juggling papers in her high-backed leather chair, and couldn't help but smile at her guest's attitude, asking, "Still nothing you recognize as being similar to the marks you remember seeing on the fragments Maxwell showed you?"

Annabel snapped shut the folio and gave an exaggerated frown of disappointment and apology. "No, sorry, I'm not being a lot of help am I?"

"If it's not there—it's not there," Daisy mused. "You want the next one?"

"You mean there's more?" Annabel's eyes widened.

Daisy laughed. "Oh yes, this happens to be one of North America's foremost anthropological and philological libraries, don't you know?" she said with mock primness. "This may not be Harvard, but when it comes to the dead, dusty, and downright obscure, we can't be beaten!"

Annabel sighed and held out her hand palm up. Daisy smirked and dropped a small, overstuffed tome bound in what looked like threadbare lizard skin into her waiting grasp.

As Daisy watched as Annabel began to pick through the book with a look of slight distaste and definite concentration, one perfectly sculpted eyebrow arching up quizzically, she was lost for a moment in contemplation of the character of this half-stranger from her past and the events of the last few days.

It had been almost a week since Annabel had stepped off the platform at Northside Station into a mist-shrouded Arkham, and the time had passed at speed, with Annabel quickly recovering her easy charm and somewhat mysterious demeanor, particularly in the company of strangers. Daisy, however, knew that underneath, the fear and tension Annabel felt had not left her, only receded from view, as the sometimes frightened dream-cries she heard from her guest's room in the dead of night attested, but as one who was no stranger to such intangible terrors herself, Daisy left that particular matter well enough alone, and carried on with the intent to bring what normality she could to her old friend's stay. Outwardly, though, none would have guessed the strain Annabel was under, or the fears that beset her. Indeed, Annabel had caused quite a stir in the orderly world Daisy inhabited, particularly today.

Daisy had "introduced" her friend at one of the often dull recital evenings held in the main hall to unsettling effect, and afterward, when Annabel had accompanied Daisy to the university, it seemed to trigger a spate of unusually random library visitors. Both faculty members and undergraduates had all found some excuse to make their way into the two young women's proximity, often on the somewhat dubious pretext of borrowing or returning some book or other.

Daisy had found herself more amused than bothered by the sudden attention Annabel garnered, and had been more than a little surprised, truth be told, at the spell Annabel seemed to cast. Although Daisy had never been short of suitors to rebuff, particularly when she had first started work at the largely insular and stuffy male domain of the university—and of course she'd netted Ted when he'd arrived almost by accident—but Daisy had never courted such attention herself, and flirting never really occurred to her—it just wasn't in her character. Annabel, however, had been a headstrong beauty who'd always attracted admirers like bees to honey, and in the intervening years, Annabel, it seemed, had honed her looks, charm, and force of character to devastating effect, and now effortlessly had half the university smitten without reproachable effort or encouragement on her part.

To put it simply, Annabel Ryan was more *glamour* than Miskatonic University knew what to do with.

After the initial flood of her story, Annabel had grown more reticent to talk, but Daisy had slowly pried out some of the stranger facets of her experiences, and was now utterly convinced that there was something far worse going on than a mere missing beau who may well have led Annabel on and vanished under some darkly suggestive cover story. It was peculiar, but the more bizarre Annabel's story became, the more Daisy was certain she was telling the truth; the events she described were at once strange and distressing, and at the same time, they had the ring of something familiar. So much so, that Daisy began to doubt her own motivations in the matter, and had to admit with a thread of worry that her own mind was attaching importance where perhaps there was none. Was she so desperate to fill in the numb blankness in her own memory that she had latched on to Annabel as a means of doing so, right or wrong? She didn't know, but there was other, more tangible evidence to back up Annabel's tale, evidence that perhaps ought to disturb Daisy more than it did.

As Annabel worked her way through the curious old book, Daisy put the sequence of events Annabel had described together in her mind again, as she had done dozens of times over the last few days, ever searching for a pattern or meaning she had not considered before. There were gaps and inconsistencies in the story, of course, but Daisy was smart enough to know that did not lessen the likelihood of the story's truth, quite the contrary. Were Annabel's weird experiences too complete, too coherent, it would have aroused suspicions in Daisy of fabrication, conscious or otherwise.

Out from under the direct threat and observation she had experienced in New York, Annabel had broken her lengthy train journey in Boston, and checked into the Grand Hotel for a day or two's break to rest and spend a little money to calm her nerves before she carried on, and for a day and a night she had been free. The second night, she had been troubled again by nightmares and the hideous impression something unholy gazed at her through the arched windows of her sixth floor room. She awoke to find frost shrouding the window glass, and the fresh flowers that adorned the suite withered and dead.

Steeling herself against the terror that grew within her, Annabel had once again telegrammed Daisy for aid, now begging to join her in Arkham as soon as possible. She had forced herself to go out and tour the city while she waited for a reply, and the day slipped slowly away, staying always in public places and never without the feeling that something dark and terrible watched her every move. Daisy's positive reply had brought with it the promise of hope, but Annabel had no way of escaping before the morning train, and viewed the approaching night with dread. By Annabel's own admission, she had tipped the house manager outrageously and obtained a bottle of bootleg gin and drank herself into a stupor even before dusk had fallen, determined to be well out of things come what may. The night had passed in blessed oblivion, for Annabel at least, and aside from a hangover that made her teeth ache, she had been in good spirits for her journey…at least until she had passed the white-sheeted body being stretchered out of the hotel in the lobby.

The man, a guest, had been a banker of some sort—middle-aged and florid, in town to seal some deal or other. "Heart attack, sadly it happens every now and then, nothing to be concerned about," she'd been told. She would have been able to dismiss it as such—after all, such things did indeed happen—if not for one overheard detail from one of the hotel busboys—the man, in dying, had dragged down the heavy curtain from the window rail and "clutched it to his chin like a kid with a sick blanket" and died staring out into the dark beyond the glass.

Sick and afraid, Annabel had left the hotel in a heavy rain-storm and started a troubled journey to Arkham; at her wits' end, she had sat alone in an all but empty Pullman carriage and fretted on her own sanity as the smoggy, rust-brown industrial wasteland of the sprawling city gave way to the autumnal woods and rolling fields of the countryside, broken by glimpses of the sea as the line veered to and from the coast as it made its way northward.

It was a journey Daisy herself had made by train more than once, traveling to Boston on university business, and she could easily picture the shadow of the train against the patchy green and hardscrabble spoil of the railroad cuttings, and, beyond those the drab boundaries of worked fields already gouged clean of their harvest; Annabel supplied the details of a faint drizzle of rain and the weak morning sun of an overcast fall day.

Annabel had told Daisy that she had dosed a little, lulled by the dull rhythmic thunder of the train, but as she woke, she slowly and with creeping horror became aware of something odd, so that at first she thought it a fragment of a lingering nightmare.

Annabel's description had been such that it seemed as if Daisy had seen through her friend's eyes: the shadow of the train was a dark, regular serpent, trailed by the fainter pale cast of the dispersing smoke from the engine. But as Annabel watched, something detached from the train's shadow—another shapeless form, uncertain and wavering—casting over the parallel railroad tracks and looming over the cutting. Whatever it was, Annabel had said it seemed "heavy," "coiling," a thing "changing and seething," but which nevertheless somehow kept pace with the speeding train as it clattered along the track. Annabel had described the feeling of horror she felt at seeing the dark shadow drift wide and elongate, and Daisy had seen how still and pale her friend had become as the recollection had taken her. Despite Daisy's careful prompting, she could ascribe to the shape no firm characteristics or even guess at its true size, but of all things, Annabel was sure the shadow could have been only cast by something in the air above the train.

When asked by Daisy if she had actually seen any part of whatever the thing was that had cast the shadow, Annabel had declared a shuddering, "No, thank God," and said that such dread the thing inspired that she could not have opened the carriage window and leaned out to look up if her life had depended on doing so.

Of the only two other passengers in the carriage, a sleeping businessman and an elderly woman engrossed in knitting a shawl, neither saw what she did, and Annabel could not bring herself to call on them, or risk losing herself to a hysteria she was only just keeping under control.

Minutes or tens of minutes later, Annabel hadn't known which, her ordeal had ended as the shadow on the track dwindled and disappeared, a reddish-black smear coating her window seconds before it departed, soon diluted by the rain. Not long after, the

train had ground shuddering and screeching to a halt, with livestock on the track ahead blamed.

Annabel frowned again and put the book down with some
caution, as if it was somehow dirty and likely to stain anything it
touched, and Daisy remembered vividly Annabel's words as she
had closed her story: *The waiting, the waiting was almost worse,
stuck there with nothing but rain and black mud to either side, and
the sky turned so grey. It was as if the world was over and gone and
here I was just waiting for everything to decay around me. As if it
had already started and there was nothing beyond the mist and rain,
nothing at all, and every bit it inched closer was another piece of
the world eaten away, and the other people in the carriage paper-
faced dolls with nothing inside but rotten meat. It was awful, I just
wanted to scream, scream and run, but I had nowhere to go!*

Daisy knew some would use hysteria and delusion to easily
explain away Annabel's story, happy to dismiss it as "woman's
weakness" or some other such rubbish, but she knew better. Oh,
Annabel was under great stress, certainly, but she was no hys-
teric. Annabel was strong, very strong, and Daisy doubted many
people would have kept their self-control given the same events
and influences, and wondered if she herself would have…and
then there were the roses outside the window of the guest room
where Annabel slept, now quite dead and withered…

Beyond her own sphere, she had heard that John Clancy's yard
dog from three streets over had been found headless and gutted,
the chain that held him down shorn through the morning before
last, and then Carol's whispered rumors that the old, inward-
looking families in the ramshackle tenements on the far side of
French Hill had seen corpse-lights flickering in the attic windows
of the old derelict "witch house," which had brought a sudden
stir of gossip and ill-omen to the town—all of which Daisy had
kept from her old friend, telling herself it was "best not to upset
her unduly." Her full reasons for keeping quiet she would not

admit even to herself.

Why am I suddenly so credulous, so willing to believe? And why am I so un-shocked by it all? And just what am I planning to do if it is all true?

"Spook, Spook…Daisy, calling all ships at sea, Daisy?" Annabel chided.

Daisy blinked rapidly and came back. "Oh, sorry lost in thought there for a time. I have gotten into a bad habit of doing that while I sit here. It's usually Carol who comes barging in and snaps me out of it."

"Well, not to decry your chosen calling, old girl, but I'm surprised you can stay awake for more than ten minutes at a stretch in this place; it's all dim corridors, dark bookshelves, dust and cobwebs. This joint has about as much life as a cemetery in a slow spell," Annabel replied smiling.

"Hush now," Daisy shot back playfully. "It's not that bad, and it's nothing like a cemetery," and then added under her breath, "even if some of the faculty members appear to have been embalmed already…"

Annabel started giggling just as Mr. Tompkins, one of the administrators, gave a short knock, opened the door, and edged into the room somewhat shamefacedly—white-haired, pushing seventy, and a vision of academic sobriety in wire-rimmed glasses, a two-decade-old tweed suit, and a wing-collar shirt and black cravat that wouldn't have looked out of place at a party celebrating the end of the Civil War. It was quite too much a coincidence for Annabel, whose giggles broke out into strangled laughter.

Daisy, turning to the incomer, whose pale face was already starting to turn a blustery red, fought to keep her own grin from breaking out into laughter, asking pointedly if she could be of help, while behind her, Annabel had to bite her hand or succumb to her uncontrollable mirth.

"The, er…the…er, ladies…er…," Tompkins stammered.

"Yes, Mr. Tompkins, what was it?" Daisy stated as blandly as she could, biting her lip and folding her hands tightly in her lap.

"You…er, asked…er, when, er…the dean could see you… He's free, er…now."

"Thank you, Mr. Tompkins," Daisy managed with a straight face, as the now purple-faced man dumbfounded her by actually making a short bow before hurriedly leaving.

After the two women had managed to control their laughter, Annabel asked, dabbing a tear from her eye, "And just who was he?"

"Oh, just one of your many admirers it seems, who has his own job he should be doing right now that isn't errand boy, I might add," Daisy quipped. "Are you okay to hang around here for a little longer if I go see the dean about my impending absence from work?"

Annabel was serious again, her manner changing as if a switch had been tripped, "I am grateful, you know? Seriously, Daisy, I can't believe you've been so good to me, after all this time, and I've brought nothing but troubles to your door."

Daisy smiled. "Don't look at it that way. It was worth it to see you give that stuffed shirt a near heart attack any day of the week," she joked. "I'll be back as soon as I can and we'll be out of here."

Annabel held out her arms in mock jubilation. "At last, alone with the books; I'll try and contain my enthusiasm!"

Daisy couldn't help but smile as she shut the door behind her.

* * *

The ruined man's eyes snapped open and he inhaled sharply in a series of long, desperate breaths, like a drowning swimmer come up for air.

He rolled onto his side and doubled up convulsively, coughing raggedly and sucking in great gulps of air. Moments before, his lungs had been empty sacks of flesh, now they worked anew and were struggling to feed his blood and brain once more.

How long had he lain not breathing and dead? Had it been minutes, hours? Not more than that, surely, or he would never have managed to crawl back from that black abyss beyond life. The memory of the terrible emptiness was evaporating like a fever dream, and thankfully so.

His eyes focused again and, even as inured to horror as he was, he could not help but stare at the girl's shadow burned into the wall with a sickening feeling in his empty stomach and a macabre fascination for the details.

The shadow was all that was left of her, all anyone would ever find.

His mind replayed the events of the early morning with crystal clarity. His running game of stalk and hide had drained him utterly. After he had consumed the memories of the watcher, one of the things in the sky had almost seen him, drawn by his use of black geometry. The strain, coupled by the dread of what he had learned, had prompted him to venture another Aklo rite to keep him concealed, but it had been misjudged and had nearly destroyed him. His strength had fled him, forcing him to find refuge in a filthy tenement block. He had passed the night in a sea of dimly remembered torment, like a fever dream, until the worst had faded as the wan sun crept up over the vast and unfamiliar city.

Gathering what remained of his strength, he had slumped in the open window of the filthy stolen room, feeling the cold air of the morning cut through his threadbare coat and swathed face, offering some slight relief from the needle-legged things he felt crawling under his bloating, too-tight skin. A fit of coughing had wracked him then, bringing further pain like knives stabbing into his sides, and he could do nothing but feebly hold on to the rough brick window lintel and wait for the attack to pass, wait and hope that he didn't topple out of the tenement into the alleyway below—it would have been an ignominious end indeed for one such as he.

After the coughing agony faded, he remembered wiping bloody spittle away from his withered lips and cursing aloud, using a few choice words of gutter French and Souk Arabic to better convey his disgust to the winds.

How had he come to this? A swollen, poison-blooded dead man walking…he, who had once been feared and respected, now reduced to the status of a cursed leper cowering in a festering flophouse surrounded by gaudy ignorance and squalor in this ugly, infant city, in this uncouth child-nation. But he knew how he had been laid so low: he had been betrayed. His own arrogance in his abilities had brought him to the brink of extinction, a mistake he would not repeat when he found his betrayer.

But first he had to live long enough to extract his revenge.

The death that had taken hold of him would not be denied, but he knew of a way it might be delayed, however fleetingly—if he could fashion the Aklo well and he found a suitable subject—by daring to go beyond what he had ever attempted before and steal, not merely memory, but the spark of life itself.

The old man he had followed here from the soup kitchen would never have sufficed; the light of his life had been a mere guttering candle stub wasted away by the ravages of age and drink. Let the flies already crawling across the bathtub in which his body lay have the last of the wretch and be welcome to him.

No, the Voorish ritual was dangerous, and he could dare attempt it only sparingly. He was in truth no demon or god, but a man, a man who had gleaned a few secrets in his turbulent and dark-hued life. Before the hand of the traitor had delivered him up to the curse which had so brutally afflicted him, he had used his secrets sparingly, very sparingly, and so he had prospered, and even now, when desperation and the yawning grave beckoned, he still baulked, still had to be careful—for nothing was certain, and the abyss clutched at the tatters of his soul.

Stranded in the window like a dying spider, he had found himself laughing bitterly a few moments later, his black reverie dispelled when his eyes beheld a girl picking her way down the alleyway below him from the bustling city street beyond.

He would have believed her appearance a prayer answered by a dark god, but he had left such ignorance as belief in divinities that cared enough to answer men's prayers long behind him. Forcing his eyes to focus, he had seen that she was perhaps eighteen or nineteen, pretty and lithe. He marveled for a moment at her slim hips rolling as she walked under a short-hemmed flapper dress the color of faded lilacs, an old red jacket that had probably seen more years than she, draped over her shoulders. She swayed a little in her narrow heels, her blond pageboy hair tousled and out of place.

Beautiful and so young, he thought. Up all night and slinking her way home, then. Even though she was exhausted and likely hungover, he could smell the life on her from here, two stories above her—feel its warmth, its soft vibration. He was reminded absently of an old story he had once been told by a French slaver, who had operated out of the Street of the Sailmakers in Al Hamidiyah many years before, of another pretty girl in a red cloak, destined to be beset on the path.

"Alas, my dear, you are a perfect dinner for a wolf," he had whispered in his best book-learned English.

He'd raised his good arm and forced his bandaged fingers into the painful configurations of the worm-lord's sign, calling upon the sleepers of the desert to lend him an echo of their majesty, fresh blood spilling from his lips at the effort.

In the alleyway below, the girl staggered, her bare knees colliding with a trash can; she fell to the ground without making a sound. Gathering what remained of his strength, he'd considered her for a moment as she groped helplessly through the old newspapers and broken glass of the alley floor, her eyes blinking furiously, her pretty mouth working soundlessly in agonized shapes, soundless because he had taken her voice, sightless because he had blinded her.

He remembered thinking it would be a difficult climb for him down the back stairs to fetch her, but she would likely follow where he bid her once claimed; how could she not cleave to any help offered to her?

He took no pleasure in her suffering, but knew that it was needed for him to survive. Perhaps, he had thought, someone else will see her and she will be saved? The streets at both ends on the alleyway were busy after all, and all someone would have to do would be to turn their heads at the right moment as they passed by. Perhaps someone would rescue her in the time it took him to reach her side, but perhaps not.

He had already crossed a continent and defied a god to make it thus far; so close to his quarry he could almost smell it, he had little choice but to go on. But as for this nameless girl who had chanced to cross his path while taking a shortcut to a home she would never reach, she had no choices left at all.

Letting out a wracking, gasping sob, the ruined man crashed back from the realm of memory into the bitter present, moaning and vomiting blood, and was once again alone with the horror of the shadow on the wall—silent accusation of what he had become and an indelible mark that stood testament to a lost girl.

No matter how many times the stain was painted over, sooner or later the darkness would show through. Even if the plaster was replaced or the wall itself were ripped down, or indeed the whole building torn apart and another rose in its place, that screaming shadow would remain, not as a stain or after-image in any mundane sense, but an ugly scar on the skin of the world.

He had to get out, get moving, he knew; once again he must stay on the move, outrun his crimes. Aside from his own predicament, there was also no telling what other consequences might have attended the ritual's wake and the gate he had opened. Even now, every living thing within a hundred feet of the room in which he had lain was likely dead or wished it was, from the cockroaches in the walls to the rotgut-soaked tenants that called the dilapidated building home.

The room was not safe any longer, even for the likes of him, nor would it ever truly be safe again, even after the event faded. The gate had lasted mere seconds, but its effects were far more permanent; the barriers had been scraped thin like torn silk stockings in countless directions, and now there was no telling what might come or when.

Pity the fool who slept here now.

The girl was gone, too late now for her, too late forever.

There remained a fragile thread of hope for him, however, if not for survival perhaps, then at least for revenge.

The ruined man climbed up off the bed. He felt strong again, if clumsy, stronger than he had before. The jagged, crawling pain aching in his bones was still there but it was distant now, as if trapped for a time in a shuttered chamber within his body.

He was not saved; he had no delusions about that. He had merely succeeded in turning back the clock, three weeks, four, more? He could not be sure just how much time he had gained, and at what price.

He caught sight of his own face in the cracked and pitted mirror on the bathroom door and, despite himself, he shuddered. It was even worse than before, no man living would have recognized him now, no woman do anything but turn her face away in revulsion and horror. *What price?*

"I am…I am Henri Damascus. I…will…go…on," he growled in pain.

It was not the name he had been born with, but the one he had fashioned for himself, bled for, striven for.

I cannot have those whose paths I cross flee in terror, not when it is I who must go as unnoticed as I can, he thought, tearing up strips of the girl's discarded underskirt to freshly bandage his head, hiding his face once more and feeling the material become greasy and sodden almost instantly as it touched the atrocity visited on his flesh.

I must play the leper for real now.

He must move. He had his quarry's scent once more, but it was not enough, the spoor too old to yield a swift confrontation, and yet he needed to be swift. He must act while his dearly bought strength lasted and not squander it frivolously, for as he was the hunter, he was well aware that he was also hunted in turn, and by things far worse than he. Yes, the streets of the great city had fouler things crawling in its shadows and soaring unseen upon the hot air that rose above its canyons of concrete, brick, and steel, than the men and women that peopled it guessed at. Beyond them, he felt something else, something vast and terrible approaching, its time and place come around, a northward tugging that sent a terror into his bones.

Visions lurked on the edge of his mind, painted by the horrors he had committed to gain them: a white tower set against a black storm and a blacker sea, a bleak, green-choked valley populated only by the unburied dead and their screaming souls, a house of doors rent open, the face of his betrayer with an arrogant smile cracking into oozing corruption, a hill of dead idols, a tall, black figure upon a withered hill, the sky boiling like purple blood, the terrible figure turning, turning toward him—*No!*

Some things he must not allow himself to see too closely, or he would be lost—for to gaze upon the face of the Ancient Ones was to court annihilation.

Ah, that was the trap, the cage: caution to survive his enemies, speed to escape his fate, in wielding power he tempted death, and in searching, he must dread what he found. *What a dark, insane joke it is to be merely human in a universe where our place is no better than that of vermin scurrying in a trash heap,* he thought as he reached into the side of his mouth and pulled out a handful of splintered black teeth, letting them fall to the blood-stained floorboards.

Up, old fool, move!

* * *

"Ah, Miss Walker, please do come in and take a seat," Dean Price Wyngate gestured from where he was standing at his wide study window on the third floor of the Administration building and ushered her into the room.

"Thank you," she said clearly, and he held out her chair for her before crossing behind his own desk and taking a seat.

Perhaps the most urbane of the university's current crop of professors, Wyngate was a long, lean man in his fifties with an angular, hawkish face that wouldn't have been out of place on a marble bust of a Roman general—save for the neatly trimmed arc of moustache, of course. He had European manners and the kind of refined taste money alone couldn't buy.

Dean of Mathematics at Miskatonic University, technically he wasn't Daisy's direct superior, but with Dr. Armitage on extended sabbatical owing to health grounds for nearly a year now, Wyngate, by virtue of his cool intellect, competency, and political skill, had assumed a degree of charge over the entire library complex in the kind of polite, bloodless, ruthless, and bitter *coup d'état* that was the particular purview of old academic institutions.

Daisy didn't like him, although he had never given her any real cause for antipathy, and she made pains to keep her feelings about him concealed for the benefit of all concerned.

Moments later, the door opened behind her and Wyngate's secretary brought in hot tea on a silver Queen Anne service, which most assuredly did not belong to the university. Wyngate waited with cool patience for the tea to be served in quiet ritual and the door to close with a soft click before speaking directly to her; all the time, his calm and appraising gaze never wavered from Daisy, calculating and weighing up what, she didn't exactly know.

"I understand you wish to take a short leave of absence from your duties here at the library?"

"Yes, an old school friend has unexpectedly died and named me her executor...," Daisy found herself lying freely, the story as well rehearsed in her mind as if she'd memorized a role in a play; after all, the truth wouldn't exactly do. "Selma Nash, of Kingsport, she..."

With a polite cough, the dean interrupted her, "Yes, I'm sure that's quite in order. Take as much time as you feel is decent and appropriate." He picked up a sealed ivory-white envelope from his desk-blotter and handed it to her with almost theatrical grace, "Here is a formal note of written permission countersigned by the university president. I've ensured a duplicate has been entered into the record."

Daisy was left speechless for a moment and let the envelope drop to the desk as if it were a lead weight, taking hold of her tea to hide her sudden confusion. She'd expected to have to argue her case against the dean, lie through her teeth and, if need be, fight tooth and nail for the unplanned absence. Dean Wyngate was, after all, a noted upholder of orthodoxy, both scientific and administrational, and a stickler for form and procedure, who valued rigor and competency in others and little else. He had been known to drum out undergraduates whose interests strayed too far from what he believed was the right path, and had a reputation of quietly ridding the university of any staff member under his auspices who proved themselves "unreliable."

"Thank you, Dean Wyngate, I appreciate your understanding in this," she finally managed to say.

"Not at all, Miss Walker, if there is anything my office can do to assist you, you have only to ask. You have proven an invaluable asset to the university," he continued solicitously, "and I fear we, which is to say the senior faculty, have not made plain in the past how much we value your work here with us."

Now she really did feel like she had walked into a parallel world, and she found herself floundering for a response. "That's very kind of you to say; I really have, and do, enjoy my work here—it's my calling, so to speak."

"And it shows in your diligence and your skill," Wyngate said with an easy smile that never reached his calculating eyes. "There have been problems at the Orne Library, as we both know, given poor Armitage's condition, and the other, unrelated…incidents of a few years ago, of which I need not speak further to you. Both were sequences of events which, without the efforts of the faculty, and not least of all your good self, could well have resulted in terrible scandal and discredit, and perhaps worse for this institution."

Daisy sat bolt upright. It was as if cold water had been splashed on her face by his words. In her mind was a fleeting image resolving itself from the blank darkness in her memory: a deserted hallway, a heavy wooden door hanging open, scratch marks in the plasterwork of the wall, a crackling noise like dead leaves underfoot—and it was gone.

Daisy blinked and nodded slowly.

"Yes, and since then your diligence has seen the colonial archive and the restricted collection in better order than it has been for years, I'm told, and your work in admissions and donations has been exemplary. Yes, indeed, your work here has been of great value to the prestige and merit of Miskatonic University. We owe you a great deal."

Daisy fought to keep up with what the dean was saying, her mind still reeling, groping for hidden meaning in his words and the turn the increasingly strange conversation was taking. *Wait a minute; I hadn't anything to do with ordering the restricted collection—that was Armitage's private concern.* But Dean Wyngate wasn't the kind of man to make a mistake, at least not that kind of mistake.

Realizing a heavy silence had fallen between them, Daisy quickly recovered her composure and said, "Well thank you, again. I'm sorry," she forced a smile, "I'm never very good at receiving praise; I never quite know what to say."

"Your manners and decorum do you credit, Miss Walker. Do you plan to leave for Kingsport soon?"

On firmer ground again, she quickly replied, "Yes, on Saturday if it can be managed. I've a few things to sort out here first, work and such. I'm just off to the station shortly to obtain our tickets."

"Ah yes, your friend will be traveling with you, Miss Ryan, isn't it?"

"Yes," Daisy said, "another old friend from my college days, although I would have wished for better circumstances to bring us back together again."

Wyngate nodded in agreement. "I'm afraid I haven't had the chance to make her acquaintance personally, but she has been quite the talk of the halls for the last few days."

Daisy smiled again with effort. "Yes, she's gathered quite a few admirers; she's been a breath of glamour and novelty at a cold and dreary time of the year, I think."

The dean's eyebrow arched as if the thought had never occurred to him. "Of course, I'm sure everything will work out satisfactorily. Well, have a safe journey, Miss Walker, you and Miss Ryan both."

The interview over, Daisy found herself standing and retrieving the envelope from the table, and was nodding a goodbye when Wyngate spoke again suddenly, as if a matter had come unexpectedly to his recall or he had made an abrupt decision to tell her something. "I hesitate to mention it, but have you had any trouble recently on campus?"

"On campus? No," she replied cautiously.

"Well, as you are leaving I doubt it will affect you, but we have had reports of some uncouth sorts, indigents, where they ought not to be."

"Indigents?"

"Indigents: tramps, vagabonds, the homeless I suppose you might say—a sad indictment of the times. There is no cause for alarm, and no serious incidents, yet. Just a few disturbed trash cans and reports of trespassers near the dormitories, but as we want no trouble or repeats of past misfortunes, we are increasing campus security, just in case." He smiled. "If you should see anything untoward, please bring it to my attention."

"Of course," Daisy replied, far too occupied to pay the matter any real attention.

Daisy's mind raced as she paced through the wide foyer of the Administration building, her square heels clicking rapidly on the tiled floor. *What happened to me? Why is this blasted chunk of my memory missing, and why should such a commonplace thing as sorting out old books be the source of this dread I'm feeling?* The thoughts ran around in her head over and over, and each time there was no answer she could give.

She was certain she had never catalogued the restricted collection. The collection sat both within and apart from the famed rare books collection of the library, and was made up of the most valuable, or in some cases most controversial, of the Orne Library's texts—texts not for public display or access apart from the most exceptional cases. She'd been in there dozens of times over the last few years, and seen that the volumes and artifacts contained within were tucked up safe in a brand new vault, each book and object properly cased and bagged; she doubted many

provincial banks had so much security. But the collection's organization, that was Doctor Armitage's purview, with his assistant
Abigail Foreman running the day-to-day operations of the wider
publicly available rare books collection—or at least that's what
she'd thought.

Instead of returning to Annabel when she reached the library,
Daisy detoured quickly into the main rooms, and, without pausing to remove coat or hat, she stalked swiftly across the parquet
floor drawing askance looks and even a few *tuts* as she disturbed
the relative peace of the readers and students. Lifting the gate
of the rare books desk with a hard glare at the flustered Abigail
Foreman, the senior librarian, who rightly considered the area
her personal domain, Daisy brushed aside her breach of protocol
without a word. Instead of offering her colleague any word in
explanation and ignoring Abigail's blustering, she simply went
to the stacked drawers of index cards behind the counter and
methodically started rifling through them, referencing and cross-
referencing one to another.

Abigail looked aghast as Daisy's deft fingers plucked out cards
seemingly at random and laid them together on the low table
beside her.

"This is most irregular!" Abigail managed to squeak at last, as
Daisy all but slammed shut one of the lower drawers.

"Abigail, this is important, please," Daisy said, shuffling the
index cards into some order. "Look at these."

Abigail peered down at the titles laid out before her: *Dhol
Chants, Nameless Cults (Ab'd), A Discourse on Hieratic Amulets in
Sacrifice, Monstres and Their Kynde (folio), The Key Obsidian, Won-
ders of the Invisible World (annotated and expanded), The Last Will
& Testament of Israel Sutter, Livre D'ivon (incomplete),* and a dozen
unnamed but numbered manuscripts and literary fragments.

"Yes," Abigail said defensively, looking around at the library
where several sets of inquisitive eyes quickly looked away.

"These have all been marked as reassigned to the restricted collection from the rare books collection," Daisy said, watching her colleague's face carefully. She knew Abigail was a diligent and clever woman. They had never been friends, but rather no more than civil colleagues, just about able to make small talk at meetings and functions; there had always been a distance between them. It had been something she'd thought no more of than a simple misalignment of character between them, brought on by a difference in background, age, perhaps ambition, and maybe where they saw a woman's place in the world—it was something she'd encountered before—but all of a sudden she wasn't so sure that was it at all.

Abigail looked afraid.

"Yes," Abigail said carefully, choosing her words, "when the collection was reorganized, those books were taken off general access. They are still, of course, available, I mean here, with the proper authority… I…I'm sure you could see them if you wished, after all you're more than qualified and a member of the staff." Abigail laughed uncomfortably. "Although, I don't know quite why, the…," she trailed off as if not knowing what to say.

It was a matter of protocol and procedure; Abigail was a first-rate organizer with a wide erudition, but the specialist knowledge needed to judge and catalogue the rare books collection in this kind of qualitative way would have been well beyond her. There was something else, too.

"The pencil annotation here on the cards," Daisy asked, "is that your writing do you think?"

Abigail swept up the index cards, saying, "Must be, mustn't it… Here let me put those away for you, I can see you are in a terrible hurry, Daisy," and turned away to the index drawers.

"Yes, thank you," Daisy said, letting it go, already knowing that there was one more person she needed to talk to before leaving Arkham.

"I understand you're going away to Kingsport soon, you and…
Annabel is it?" Abigail asked with obviously forced bonhomie.

It seems everybody knows my business, Daisy thought acerbically.
"Yes," she repeated. "It's something of a sad occasion, but it will
be good to see the old place again. I haven't been back in over a
year."

"So glamorous, like a picture star, I was telling my husband—
and tall!"

"What…oh Annabel, yes."

"Prettier than Norma Shearer, but I prefer Mary Pickford myself," Abigail commented, her back turned, diligently replacing
the index cards in their slots. "I overheard some of the students
saying that she was on Broadway, your friend I mean, not Mary
Pickford, of course."

"No, nothing like that," Daisy replied, somewhat bemused by
the rapidly changing conversation. "Anyway, Carol's going to be
looking after admissions until I get back, which should be in a
fortnight or so at most, I think."

Abigail nodded and smiled enthusiastically as Daisy withdrew,
soon wrapped up again in her own thoughts.

A quick glance at her watch told her that she'd left Annabel
alone for over half an hour, and when she reached again the familiar refuge of her reading room door, she was ready to weather
a storm of good natured invective about her tardiness in returning, but when she opened the door, she found Annabel entirely
lost in her own thoughts and unaware of her prolonged absence.

She was sitting incongruously on top of Daisy's desk, her legs
swept up underneath her, knees bared, her left hand rested on her
booted calf and the right supporting her weight. Annabel's eyes
were fixed on one of the open books on the desk, and her face
had a serene, distant expression.

"Now," Daisy said, "if old Mr. Tompkins came in and saw you
like that he really would have a heart attack!"

Annabel looked up and with a scandalous chuckle said, "Well there are worse ways to go!" athletically swinging out her legs and dropping with catlike grace to the floor beside the desk, spoiling the display slightly by knocking over a couple of stacked books in the process. "Drat!" she said, and stooped to retrieve them.

Daisy came over and helped pick them up. "I'm sorry I kept you waiting—the wheels of academia don't exactly turn with speed, I'm afraid—but we are all clear for the day after tomorrow. I've one more call to pay this evening, then I'm free and easy; meanwhile, you can pop out into town and see if there's anything you need to buy for the trip."

"Thanks again, Spook, this means more to me than I can say," Annabel said, placing her hand on Daisy's arm. Annabel's quicksilver mood slipped into deadly earnestness with the unexpected speed of a cloud passing across the sun.

"Don't worry, Annabel, if he's there to find, we will find him," Daisy said, genuinely touched by Annabel's obvious emotion and gratitude. "Kingsport's not that big a town; besides, we'll get Claudia on the case, and I'm sure if any eligible young men with money have arrived, she'll know about it—the black widow poised to strike!"

Annabel's mood changed again in a flash and she wrinkled her nose comically. "*Eeeue!* That doesn't bear thinking about!"

"Get your coat and let's be off," Daisy said briskly, but smiling, wanting to be away.

As Annabel turned to the coat stand, Daisy looked down at the open pages of the book that had so captured her friend's attention. It was a large chapbook compiled from illuminated cuttings taken from a number of 18th century Psalters and works of poetry, annotated by an unknown hand who had penned their own ciphered notes in the marginalia. Rare it was, but hardly priceless or particularly noteworthy in itself. Nevertheless, its illustrations were often striking and contained a number of sup-

posedly "magical" alphabets, not one of which had sparked Annabel's recollections, she later shared. It was not any of those,
however, to which the book had been opened, but rather to one
of the poetic pieces in Italian beside a full page painting of a
trio of fallen knights, sleeping or dead on a barren plain—it was
hard to tell which. In the distance behind them was a lone dark
figure—a pilgrim, perhaps, by the grey, hooded robe—advancing
out of, or toward, a darkening horizon.

"Were you looking at this?" Daisy asked Annabel.

"Yes, I thought the composition of the picture was wonderful,
but it seems very sad. I couldn't read the Italian, though…"

The language was hardly Daisy's strong suit, either, and the
blotching of old stains that obscured part of the text wasn't a
help, but she could pick out some of it.

She translated haltingly out loud, her fingernail passing slowly
above the ornate calligraphy: "'In visions…summoned…walks
in dust with bloody feet…the fool's desire, met upon…without
end…who is this who comes?'"

"Not exactly cheerful, is it," Annabel said in reply.

Daisy shrugged and closed the book.

CHAPTER SIX

Morgan sat at his desk. The apartment room that served as his living space-cum-office was dark save for the muted glow of the battered desk lamp and the dim yellowish flare of the streetlights outside. He considered his chances of just running, getting the hell out of the city, out from under the coffin dirt he felt was being shoveled over him, and running before he was all the way buried.

Morgan felt alone, and far from help. It wasn't that unfamiliar a feeling, but he despised it all the same.

It was getting on two in the morning, and he was expecting company.

His apartment was on the edge of the city proper, a second-story corner at the edge of a little commercial block. It had been meant for the family that ran the store below, but they were long gone and the store all but disused, the elderly owner's health strong enough to keep him breathing but little else. It was spacious for one person, and had windows on both sides, private access from the street via a metal staircase and landing, and it was all but anonymous from the road—all reasons he'd taken to it, but now it felt dangerously exposed and as echoing as an open tomb. *A looted tomb at that,* he thought, looking at the mess the police had made during his sojourn at the city's pleasure, which he'd more or less piled up, rather than cleared away.

He'd righted his desk and replaced the lamp bulb, and that would do—*no sense in making long-term plans,* he'd thought with bitter humor.

After leaving Annabel's apartment building without looking back, he'd hailed a cab and bounced around the city a while, knowing he was likely being followed, determined to make Laski's interest in him work for his own plans, stopping by the public library to grab an atlas and almanac of New England to pass the time. He'd only been up that way once before, and the memory was far from a pleasant one. It was a gamble, he knew, but better Laski came to him than the other way around, and hopefully Sal's life spared would incline the mobster to talk, not just send in a crew of torpedoes with gats blazing.

So Morgan set himself up to wait, half a bottle of real vodka—straight off a Vladivostok boat—by the lamp, and next to it lay the big Enfield revolver from his shoulder rig, cleaned, oiled and primed, its little brother resting out of sight. Beside them sat two open books from the library; quite unexpectedly it had been these otherwise innocuous texts that had stopped him dead in his tracks and left him feeling like he was already dead and buried.

Kingsport, he'd found it all right: quaint little place by the sea, about as old as America gets, famed for its ocean mists, picturesque architecture, long-standing artist's colony, and genteel repose. Oh, the dusty almanac had been voluble in its praise. Yes, Kingsport, just a few hours' jaunt downriver from Arkham. *Damned, blood-haunted Arkham,* where he had sworn never to set foot again, and for nearly three years had kept that promise, and intended to keep it as long as he had strength to draw breath.

His chest cramped with phantom pain staring down at the mute ink on the map; just a trick of the mind he knew, a memory echo of agony gone by. He'd carried a bush knife in those days, trusted steel more than guns. The blade had been a gift from an old friend, back from his days in Rhodesia, back when he was still learning just how dark the corners of the world really were. He'd thought he'd learned all he could, but Arkham had taught him otherwise, and he'd left behind the blade in that godforsaken, "quiet little town," either sunk to the bottom of the river, or maybe still dug in the guts of the thing that had nearly killed him.

Now that he thought of it, it was amazing how much he'd put the whole mess, the whole horror, behind him. Amazing how much he'd pushed out of sight in the cold grey of memory, there to float in the deep with visions of veldt land piled high with bodies, burning Macau slums that screamed with human voices louder than the roar of the fires, the smell of his brother's sickroom, dead friends, and dead enemies—just another petty atrocity that had chased him around the world.

Except, of course, Arkham had been different; in Arkham he had brushed up against something more than just the indifferent slaughter of Mother Nature or "the evil that men do." Arkham had shown him something else entirely, something incomprehensible and insane, unearthly in every sense that mattered. It all started to fit in some ways: that had been what he'd caught the edge of when looking into Shawcross's lifeless eyes, the fear that seemed to have worked its way into the fabric of Annabel's apartment block like a cancerous rot, the figure in the picture walking the waves. It had been there all along, but he'd blinded himself to it, *out there waiting in the dark.*

Was it why Shawcross had singled him out? Because he'd already seen *something*, lived to tell the tale, however barely? How did Shawcross know? He'd told no one. And what did he know?

Suddenly all the hokum he'd heard digging around about Cormac and the occult didn't seem quite so funny at all.

"Tony, my boy, just when you think it doesn't get any worse," Morgan muttered to the dark as he took a slug of vodka and recapped the bottle; drinking any more would do his reflexes no damn good at all.

The windows were open to let him listen to the street outside, and even though the blinds were half-closed a cold, damp breeze permeated the room. He looked at his watch—a quarter past two—his company was late and his gut told him that wasn't a good sign.

The desk lamp flickered, and when it steadied again it seemed dimmer than before. There was a heavy, shuffling tread on the metal stairway outside, the tread mis-echoed and increased—there was more than one. He realized abruptly that he'd heard no car pull up, no footsteps on the sidewalk. Dark certainty settled in him that he'd gambled and lost.

This is not going to go down well. For a second he considered dowsing the desk light, but quickly dismissed the idea furiously, *I am not going to cower in the dark; I'm going to see their damn faces, whoever they are!* Instead he reached out and twisted the green glass oblong hood of the lamp back as far as it would go so the light spilled directly forward onto the doorway, and braced himself on the edge of his seat. With the light in their eyes, he might have a sliver of advantage.

Time to roll the dice again. "It's open," Morgan raised his voice, but didn't quite shout, the edgy calm that came with life or death decision enveloping him as it so often had before.

The door swung open and the hulking derelict stepped in from the night.

Morgan didn't let the surprise register on his face, even though he was fairly confident the reeking figure couldn't see him clearly. The derelict, however, was clear to him standing in the lamplight's circle. It was the same tall, feverish, wasted man he'd seen in Manhattan both before and after his visit to the Falling Angel; the gaunt, pockmarked face, the oily beard and mane of lank hair were the same, he was sure. The foul man held his head slightly to one side rather than look directly into the light, but Morgan saw the same glassy heat in his eyes as he'd witnessed before.

The derelict started forward, seeming uncertain as to what to do next, and Morgan saw that a meat hook hung limply in his left hand.

Morgan picked up his Enfield revolver, his fingers wrapping firmly around the pistol grip. "Don't!" he ordered.

The derelict stopped, but made no reply, instead sidestepping to the left of the door, coming no closer, and on his heels a second ragged figure entered, this one shorter and fat, his hanging belly misshapen and somehow lopsided, his upper face entirely obscured by a wrapped scarf of dirty oilcloth. Then a third entered as the fat man stepped to the right, this one a woman in her twenties, layer upon layer of dresses and coats obscuring an emaciated body that looked like a conglomeration of grey sticks, her too-wide eyes seeming milky white in the dim spotlight from the lamp.

Their distorted shadows danced across the ceiling as they fanned out with dreadful purpose and in utter silence; the light glinted malevolently from the jagged teeth of the broken wine bottle in the woman's hand, the fat man slumped sidewise dragging a chair leg behind him, the end wrapped in a tangle of barbed wire.

Morgan was caught between cold and unreasoning fear and the desire to gun each one of these ghoulish figures down in turn; it was fight-or-flight but he knew he had to hold his nerve. If they rushed him, he knew he wouldn't get them all—there was no more than a few steps between them and the desk, and part of his brain told him he should have fired as soon as he had seen there was more than one coming through the door with weapons, but their shocking appearance—the terrible solemnity of them—had knocked him off balance, and now he knew he had to regain the initiative quickly.

"One step forward, any of you, and it will be the last step you take," he declared loudly with more calm than he felt.

The three were completely, unnaturally still.

Morgan studied them as the moment stretched out into an eternity. Who were they? *What* were they? In all his travels he had never seen anybody possessed of such a dreadful, feverish *emptiness* as these three standing before him. They were as glassy-eyed and dead-faced as dolls, and yet in their stillness was a horrific humming vibration of barely restrained frenzy, the muscles in their faces and limbs not slack and limp, but drawn as tight as a steel hawser.

"What do you want?" Morgan asked, breaking the heavy silence.

He had not expected them to answer, but when they did, it sent an involuntary shudder through him to hear it, their voices strained, almost hysterical with force.

"Salvation," the tall derelict uttered, his lips convulsing around the word.

"Joy," the woman spat through gritted, bleeding teeth.

"An end…to suffering," came a wet stammer from beneath the cloth covering the fat man's face.

It took every ounce of self-control for Morgan not to pull the trigger there and then.

"The Legion of Rapture?" Morgan said, abruptly remembering the words on the pamphlet.

"Yes," came a new voice from the darkness beyond the door. "I must apologize," the voice's accent was thick with the southern states, the words slow and wrung out. Morgan immediately knew it was not a voice he recognized.

"I fear, perhaps, you were expecting other guests?" the newcomer continued with sly humor.

"Who are you? Show yourself," Morgan demanded.

"First, be so kind as to lower your firearm," the voice insisted sibilantly, almost sounding offended, "then we can discuss this matter like gentlemen."

"With these three clowns here? Forgive me, but that would seem like a very stupid thing to do," Morgan replied.

"My brothers and sisters are merely concerned for my well-being, *Mis-ta* Morgan. You are, they say, a very dangerous man. Death," the voice spat, "follows close behind you, isn't that so?"

Insult or warning? Perhaps both, but Morgan needed to know more, and almost felt the abyss open up beneath him as he walked the razor's edge.

Carefully, Morgan lowered the pistol to the desktop, but kept his hand close by it, easily visible in the spill of light from the angled desk lamp.

A wizened, almost scarecrow-like figure resolved itself between the darkened doorway to the street beyond and the pool of light from the lamp. He was an older man, the wrong side of sixty by Morgan's guess, thin-necked and bald-headed, with stained and unhealthy skin, a pinched, tiny mouth, and protuberant, sickly, bloodshot eyes. He wore layers of coats and shirts barely cleaner than the three that had preceded him, and at his throat the white and black dog collar of a preacher.

"Who are you?" Morgan demanded.

"The savior of the broken, the helpless, the beaten, the down-trodden, and the damned. I am a humble messenger of he who is to come: the Lord of Nightmares and Dreams of Wonder," he whispered urgently, his pinched mouth suddenly parting in an obscenely wide smile.

"A name? Your name?" Morgan returned.

"Oh, I doubt you heard'a me, friend——Marks, for what it's worth to you, the Reverend Eli Marks."

"Tell me, 'Reverend,' where exactly would I find your denomination if I looked you up?" Morgan asked with an edge of viciousness entering into his voice.

The wizened man threw back his head and laughed. "Oh, *Mis-ta* Morgan they did not tell me you had a sense of humor, I do appreciate that. My church is white sky and black earth, the darkness without and between, whither he walks."

The man growled deep in his throat, his voice dropping to a scattered whisper like gravel cast across a tombstone, "My congregation is the ignorant vermin that crawl across the face of this world, in abasement they come to know me, in hopelessness they find my truth shown to them, nightmares and ecstasies. And it is given to me to show them how to see and to tear the scales from their eyes, so that they shall revel in joy and know bliss—the only true bliss mankind can ever know. Dream much, *Mis-ta* Morgan?"

Morgan caught himself; for a moment, he felt as if he was falling, the dark room fading from view, but with a hard blink he brought himself back around to the terrible danger before him.

"No," Morgan growled.

The scarecrow-like man snarled for a moment, and continued, "You have an interest in one of my flock, *Mis-ta* Morgan, a stray sheep from my fold. You seek him, as do others."

"Maxwell Cormac."

"Yes," Marks hissed. "I would know what you intend and for whom you search?"

Now that's interesting—not where is he? But what do you want with him?

"I'm afraid my client's business is confidential, 'Reverend'—professional etiquette, you understand?" Morgan replied coldly.

Marks hissed again, brownish spittle dripping down his chin. "Do not mistake bravery for idiocy, *Mis-ta* Morgan. Yours is to dance for the pleasure of pipers you cannot see and powers you cannot understand—you are a puppet, a playing piece, a sack of meat born to die, and no more—remember that!"

Morgan said nothing, the strange lapse of vacancy that had stolen over his mind had burned away entirely, and his fear had gone with it, to be replaced by a cold and powerful hate. He found with sudden vehemence that he hated this man, this so-called "reverend" he had never met or heard of before. In what he had said and how he acted, unwittingly, Marks had put a face to everything cruel and mad that Morgan had ever encountered in the world, and Morgan wanted him dead.

"Now answer my question, *Mis-ta* Morgan: who sent you here to poke and prod and ask questions, who? Was it the bandaged man? Who is he? Is he one of them, come up from the hot south lands? Tell me!"

"How did you know I was expecting visitors?" Morgan asked evenly, answering the questions with one of his own.

"What?" Marks replied, angrily taken aback.

"How did you know I was expecting Laski or one of his boys here tonight? I doubt you're exactly a friend of…oh! Of course."

It fell into place suddenly in Morgan's mind: *Sal*—the hood had never made it to Laski to deliver his message. It was these bastards, this "Legion" that had been knocking off the mobster's crew, looking after their "flock," and Morgan had been the one who'd tied him up like a lamb for the slaughter, even took the bullets out of his gun. He'd been a fool, a damn fool, even after seeing them after him in the street, he hadn't added it up. The vagrants and the gin-swill bums—Prohibition's dead men walking, slaughtered by bad liquor and hard times—no one saw them, just walked right past. He'd been as blind as Laski's crew.

Morgan swore violently in self-recrimination. *Sal's blood is on my hands.*

"If you—," Marks began to hiss.

"Shut up!" Morgan cut in viciously and pulled the trigger again and again.

The .32 snub-nose Morgan had concealed under the desk

let out three hollow booms in rapid succession. He'd aimed for Marks, but the angle was bad and he wasn't sure if he'd hit him as the preacher fell from sight, but the woman toppled on her back with an unholy shriek as one of the soft-headed slugs bored into her stomach. Without pause to find whether he'd found his mark with the first volley, Morgan swept to his feet, grabbing the Enfield off the desk and smashing the lamp across the room with the same violent motion, diving to one side as a pandemonium of howling and sudden fury broke out in the room.

The light spun crazily through the air throwing kaleidoscopic shadows before smashing against the wall. In the momentary flashes Morgan saw the two hulking figures on either side of the door rush toward him, stumbling in the confusion, their weapons swinging wildly before them.

In the sudden darkness that followed, Morgan fired the three remaining rounds from the .32 at where he guessed the fat man had lunged. He was rewarded by a grunt, followed an instant later by the sound of a heavy mass crashing into the desk Morgan had vacated moments before.

Dodging toward the wan light from the open doorway, he raised the Enfield in his other hand and fired at where he hoped the second attacker was, the report from the revolver deafening in the confined room and the muzzle flash suddenly blinding. He heard the bullet only shatter window glass. Before the gunshot had faded, his enemy dove at him, half-seen in the dark, and Morgan ducked away from the roundhouse blow that came swinging in as the tall man howled like a tormented soul. A hot line of pain scored across Morgan's upper arm as the meat hook kissed him but didn't bite. Morgan pushed the big revolver into the tall man's side savagely and pulled the trigger—this time the thunder was muted by flesh.

The tall man collapsed abruptly to his knees, still flailing with the hook. Morgan parried the iron barb aside with a blow from the spent .32 and fired again into his attacker's chest with the Enfield. The muzzle flash lit up a freeze-frame of a gaunt, wild face contorted with utter hatred for a brief instant before the snarling madman toppled onto his back and was still, his heart shot through.

Morgan pulled himself through the doorway after Marks, but the preacher was gone, and there was no sign of him on the empty side street below. Breathing heavily, the night air felt like cold blades in his lungs, and as he looked down onto the metal staircase below him, something black and wet glistened on the railing. *I winged him at least.*

A low, keening groan washed up from the room behind him, the hellish sound sinking into his bones and sickening him suddenly, and his breath frosted cloudily in the air.

With monumental effort, Morgan turned his head slowly back to look into his apartment. The darkness there was impenetrable and hungry; it seemed to drink in all the light and heat from the world. He felt, rather than saw, that something moved within the darkness.

Wet crunching sounds echoed dimly from the black interior as the moaning gave way.

It felt like there was a vice tightening around Morgan's chest. He couldn't seem to draw breath into his lungs, and his ears roared as if he'd suddenly been plunged deep underwater.

The stench of blood and offal spilled from the darkened doorway, and there was a damp, flapping sound like wet cloth being snapped taut.

With every fiber of will in his being, Morgan fought against the burning agony that pressed down on his arm in order to raise his gun against the darkness.

A screech so loud and sharp it knifed through him but never registered as sound erupted as something from a twisted nightmare launched itself from the blackened doorway on tenebrous wings. Morgan pulled the trigger of the Enfield convulsively, and fire and thunder spat forth, granting him a glimpse of the thing from the darkness that was more than he could ever want to see.

Its body in size and crude shape was that of a famine-wracked child, leprously wet, and the glistening red-bronze of a cockroach's armor. Its limbs were many segmented spars of cancerous bone, and around it the air flickered grey with the suggestion of unseen, insectile wings. But its face, *its face,* was so much worse because it was draped in an all-too recognizable mask: it was the woman attacker's face, worn taut over an inhuman blankness like an overstretched glove, but where her wide eyes had been now were bloody, empty tunnels, and the mouth was no more than a lolling black smear without dimension or depth—a rip into fathomless blackness beyond.

With an agonized clenching of his hand, Morgan fired again an instant before the thing slammed into him, smashing him halfway over the iron railing. He heard himself scream as fresh pain burned like hot light across his upper chest and exploded in his left knee. His guns were torn from his hands and a moment later he found himself hopelessly clawing at the railing to prevent himself plunging to the sidewalk below, leaving him hanging in empty air by the tips of his fingers.

Morgan hauled himself painfully back over the rail and collapsed to the steel certainty of the landing, letting out a ragged cry of half pent-up fear and half visceral relief. The thing was gone into the night—he didn't know why or if it would return—and, as he stumbled over the threshold of his apartment, the carrion reek and the numbing sensation in his head faded. He looked around in the darkness where everything had been rendered into a foreign and unwholesome world by sudden massacre and unthinkable horror. He bent double, coughing, pain lancing into him now the shock was wearing off and he fought the urge to curl into a ball and await death or the dawn—whichever arrived first.

The darkness inside the charnel house that was his apartment was now a natural one, bled out at the edge by the glimmer of the street lights outside, and as Morgan staggered and limped to the edge of the room he stumbled. He righted himself, and retrieved a small battery flashlight from his overcoat pocket and swept it slowly across the scene, swearing under his breath.

The bodies of the two men he had killed lay where they had fallen, one on his back by the door and the other folded over the table looking more like a man in his cups than a corpse, save for a small wound at his temple. Of the woman, however, there was almost nothing left except a corona of blood shaped like a child's angel in the snow, shot through with a few tattered strips of sodden cloth.

Morgan fought down the shakes he knew were coming as the first flush of adrenaline ebbed out of him. His chest and shoulder were bleeding freely and he had no idea how deep the cuts were. It also felt like he'd cracked a rib at the back when he'd hit the railing, and he could already feel his knee starting to swell where it had been slammed; as soon as the shock and adrenaline wore all the way off, he was going to start hurting—a lot.

Morgan staggered out of his apartment, pulling the door shut behind him and limping down the clanging steps gracelessly. He could hear no bells or sirens and that was a minor miracle in itself. The neighborhood—largely commercial in nature—was silent, and perhaps what few tenants there were within earshot had decided whatever they had heard, they wanted no part of, but he couldn't ride that luck for long. He limped, bleeding and battered, a raincoat covering the worst of his injuries, carrying on for three blocks, until he found a call box under the sodium lights of an empty picture house lobby.

He hammered on the receiver until a blurry sounding operator responded.

"Copperhead Industries, Manhattan," he answered through gritted teeth when she asked how she might direct his call. He couldn't think of a single other damn thing to say.

* * *

Daisy Walker looked down at the over-large measure of cherry brandy in her hand and swallowed hard, not knowing whether to try and knock it down in one belt or surreptitiously hide it behind one of the many curios and bizarre *objet d'art* scattered about the over-stuffed room in Professor Walters's house in Arkham.

"Ah yes, sit here, this one's quite passing clean," her host ventured fussily, slapping dust from a padded dining chair quite out of place in the sprawling study.

Daisy sat, the chair making an amusing *humph* noise as she did so, causing her to blush slightly as she concealed her still-untouched glass behind a handy portmanteau on a cluttered church pew close to hand.

Unceremoniously dumping a stack of first editions atop an already teetering pile of manuscripts in a way that made the librarian in Daisy wince, Harvey Walters cleared a seat across from her and sat down with a satisfied smile.

Daisy couldn't help but smile to herself as she took the professor in, captured here in his sanctum sanctorum of crazily stacked books, over-filled pipe racks, fearsome tribal masks, and a somewhat sad-looking stuffed crocodile hovering precariously overhead.

"Now, Miss Walker, to what do I owe this singular honor, as late as the hour might be… Oh, ought you really to be here at all? I mean, a bachelor professor like myself entertaining a young female faculty member in his study after six o'clock? I must consider your reputation."

Daisy couldn't help but let out a little good-natured laugh. Harvey Walters had more than enough years under his belt to be her grandfather, and was the very model of old Yankee propriety, making the thought of any *im*propriety by anybody that knew him somewhat inconceivable. He was a spry old gent, to be sure, and with his fluffy mutton chop sideburns, monocle, and more than slightly eccentric beliefs, Daisy was very fond of him, and she respected his intelligence as one of the few genuine polymaths she'd ever met. In terms of habits and manners, he was stuck somewhere in the last century, but at least he was nothing like some of the faculty "old guard" like Tompkins, for whom a woman with her own opinions was about as shocking as a bicycling fish.

"That's all right, Professor Walters," she began brightly. "I won't stop long, and your secretary and housekeeper are in the next room to play chaperone if needed," she demurred.

"Well, if you're sure, Miss Walker," he said, nodding, his attention wandering slightly to the front page of an old newspaper his disturbance of the room's top layer of detritus had uncovered.

Notionally a visiting professor (although he'd been in residence at the Miskatonic longer than she had), Harvey Walters had enough academic clout to be left alone to do pretty much anything he liked, and was also *de jure* outside of university politics. Moreover, he had always shown her kindness and respect in their dealings, and been close friends with Professor Armitage, not to mention a benefactor of the library, all of which was why she was here, looking for answers.

"Professor Walters?" she asked, calling him back to the here and now.

"Oh, oh, yes, Miss Walker, what can I do for you? You said it was a library matter—at this late hour—oh, please don't tell me I've misplaced something important again!"

"No, nothing like that," she smiled. "I was wondering, well it's a bit of an odd question but…"

"Go on, m'dear."

"Well, it's about the restricted collection…"

Walters's expression shifted from one of mild distraction and companionable cheer to a deadly earnest and focus she had never seen or expected of him. For a moment, Daisy was quite taken aback and almost lost what she was about to say.

"Please continue," he prompted.

"You may remember when I first came here, to work at the library, back in '26, I became very ill—it was influenza, I think?"

"Yes, 1926…I remember it well… It wasn't a very good year in a lot of ways…a strange year, a year to be consigned to history, one of Arkham's worst perhaps…but it passed. Many died."

"The influenza outbreak?" she prompted.

"Yes, that was it," he replied distantly, as if recalling bad memories. "Why do you ask?"

"Well, you see, I just can't remember around that time very well, and I was wondering if you could help me out."

"Some amnesia is to be expected in cases where the patient has suffered a protracted period of delirium owing to fever. It bears no long-term adverse prognosis," Walters said as if reciting a lesson. "The Fern-Cooper studies are very illuminating in this regard. I…I have a copy of dear Carolyn's case notes here somewhere, I'm sure."

"No, no thank you, Professor Walters, that's not what I mean. I was wondering if you could help me out in recalling just what I was doing—here at the university—at the time I was taken ill, you see?"

"Oh," he said, and fell quiet.

"Well," she pressed on, "before today, I was under the impression I'd never had much to do with the restricted collection. I mean, Professor Armitage handled the books directly in the past, didn't he? But today, the dean mentioned what good work I'd done in cataloguing the restricted collection, and, well, I just don't remember what I did. I felt quite a fool," she forced a smile, "and yet when I checked the card catalogue later on, there was my handwriting on the index."

Walters seemed to look right through her, not seeing her at all. "There are two restricted collections now, quite apart from the rest of the rare books, wheels within wheels; not many know that of course, even on the faculty staff…"

Daisy blinked. *Two? Surely that couldn't be right?* But even as Walters spoke, she felt that cold numb feeling, just as she had felt in the dean's office, although no images came this time unbidden from the depths of her benighted memory, but there was a *familiarity*, as if she was being told something she already knew.

"The dean and I agreed, and Armitage complied with our wishes. There had been too many incidents, you see—most seriously back in late '25 and '26—one way or another that turned out to be a very bad time, and the university was threatened with scandal and worse—but such things are best left forgotten.

"The incident in 1926 was the last straw, you see. I helped pick up the pieces afterward, and I contended that the rare books collection, or at least parts of it, were a lightning rod of sorts, drawing in…well, let's just say a very unwelcome kind of storm.

"We divided it then, not once but twice. We took aside the more…unfortunate items and left the less…hazardous, esoteric items, or at least those we believed to be 'manageable'—the expurgated, adulterated, and incorrect, the incomplete, not to mention the outright harmless. Those—along with some works that simply had a very considerable monetary value—they became the Orne Library restricted collection. Still available to scholars, with permission, of course, and kept under lock and key, secured and overseen, more than enough to justify our reputation as a first-rate library, and to prying eyes that knew no better, Miskatonic's rare books remained the legend they had been. But some works, and there were some—the worst—well, those we put out of sight and out of mind."

It felt like her heart skipped a beat as the import of his words sank in. "Those books were dangerous," she heard herself say.

"Yes, as dangerous as any bacillus or wonder weapon that the sciences may dream of now or in days to come, mangled truths as they might be, or malign lies passed down through the ages. But we dared not be entirely rid of them, either, for like any knowledge, salvation might be found there as well as destruction; I've seen the proof of that myself."

"Sifting them one from the other sounds like quite a job?" she prompted in a quiet voice.

"Yes, it was difficult and not without cost—you did very admirable work."

A long silence fell between them.

Walters suddenly started, as if waking from a daydream. "Oh, do forgive me, Miss Walker, what rot am I talking about now! I really must watch my musings aloud from sounding too portentous! Rare things can bring out the worst in men, that's all I mean, greed…greed and folly, that's the problem! Avarice, fanaticism, irrationality—there's the danger!" he said getting to his feet and snapping open his pocket watch.

"Upon my soul, is that the time already," he said briskly, "and an attractive young lady in my quarters after hours to boot! Well, Mrs. Charlotte will have my guts for garters if I don't go and get ready for dinner soon! A treat to have you 'round, Miss Walker, always a pleasure to see you."

Catching hold of the sudden change in mood, Daisy stood, realizing that by bringing up his venerable battle-axe of a housekeeper and her punctilious rule, Walters had made a firm, if friendly, end to their talk.

"Thank you, Professor Walters, likewise," she said, still inwardly reeling from another revelation, in what had been a day filled with discoveries that had rocked the foundations of what she believed about herself and what she considered the truth.

He beamed back at her. "And that young chap of yours, very promising anthropologist I hear, Ted, isn't it? Keen mind, I'm told, gone up inside the Arctic Circle, I understand? Have you seen the aurorae yourself—quite wonderful! Well, I'd love to have you both to dinner when he's returned, probably nag you to death with questions, of course, must forgive me," he suggested, seeing her to the door. "You're going away tomorrow, somebody said?" he added suddenly, just as she was on the threshold.

"Yes, I'm taking my friend to Kingsport, but everybody makes it sound so final," she said without quite meaning to add the last statement.

Confusion and concern warred on Harvey Walters's careworn, age-lined face, and worry seemed to win. "Yes, yes of course, hang on," he said quickly. "You've forgotten your book," and dove back into his study with alarming speed.

"But I didn't bring a book," Daisy said to the empty hall, non-plussed by the unexpected aside.

A few minutes later Professor Walters reappeared carrying a modern-looking, well-thumbed black notebook held shut with a red elastic strap. "Here you are," he said with unexpected gravity, "I'm so sorry."

She reached out with what she found was an unexpected mixture of revulsion and familiarity and took the notebook with both hands. She opened the book at a random page and saw it densely covered with writing, her own writing—so like Annabel's, only smaller and neater—and spotted with shorthand notations of her own devising; there was no one else's it could have been.

Without thinking, she reached inside her jacket pocket, slipped her faculty absence letter inside the covers and shut the book. It felt right, complete, as it was meant to be, *like an avalanche tumbling downhill, the turning of a clock's gears, the long drop and the sudden stop of a hangman's noose,* she thought.

"I must be getting back," Daisy heard herself say. "Annabel will be wondering where I am."

"Of course," Harvey Walters said sadly, "the best of luck."

CHAPTER SEVEN

The Falling Angel was closed for business. Its exotic, emerald-draped interiors were echoingly empty and the darkness thick, save for a pool of white light over the empty main bar.

Where the hell is everyone? Haskell thought. Late afternoon it may be, but the place should still have been alive with the crew—the scrambling kids who worked as runners swabbing down and bottling up—the scattering of slouching gangsters, hardened drinkers, and the endless to-and-fro it took to keep a speakeasy this size in business; those he would have expected to see at this hour.

Instead of being let in on his arrival, he had had to bang repeatedly on the metal door before it had been unlocked, and the withered, silent old man in caretaker's overalls who'd dragged open the door without comment and locked it again after him was not a face he recognized.

Damn, I didn't believe it, but now I've seen it with my own eyes; Laski's all through.

To see the place like it was now—vacant and hollow, silent—to see it so damn *empty*, it was somehow shocking. It gave him the creeps, but as of recently, that was nothing new for Detective Burke Haskell, nothing new at all.

The sweat that even now coated Haskell's wrinkled brow, despite the cool, stagnant air that filled the empty nightclub, had nothing to do with how quickly he'd made it across town to answer Laski's summons, nor the three day hangover he was still nursing; instead, it had everything to do with fear.

After the ungodly mess he'd walked into at Emile Brothers, he had stupidly imagined that things couldn't have got much worse, and how wrong he had been. Aside from Devlin and a dozen other faces off the streets, a dozen of Laski's torpedoes and rumrunners had either turned up dead or vanished in the last month, leaving Laski boxing helplessly at shadows.

Stories had spread that most of the strange deaths and disappearances that had hit over the last few weeks, Laski, and the Falling Angel were somehow connected. The gin-soaks and the party set had very quickly found somewhere else to do their drinking—the word was out, Laski was a Jonah. Soon, Laski's crew had reached outcast status even with the street walkers and two-cent shills. The rest of the syndicate were already looking the other way and muttering about carving up his territory down the line, as if he were already dead.

It was just like the stories he'd heard about what had happened in Red Hook years ago, not that Haskell had believed a word of the drunken tales he'd heard from old beat bulls in their cups at Halloween—not until he'd seen what was left of Devlin, or worse, poor damn Sal Finny, spread about that Ryan woman's apartment like somebody had fed him through a threshing machine.

Laski's ship was sinking, and Haskell knew he had to extricate himself from the wreck of the mob boss's organization before he went to the bottom along with it.

Haskell looked around the empty bar, clutched the battered brown valise he was carrying to his side and felt with his free hand to ensure himself nervously his pistol was safe in his shoulder rig. The caretaker had already disappeared somewhere and he could see nobody else waiting for him. Had the rats already left the ship? Or had Laski turned on his own people and driven them off?

This is the last time, damn him. I don't care how much money he throws at me or what he threatens me with, I'm having nothing else to do with him. Maybe I'll take a spell of leave, and by the time I get back, Milo Laski will be nothing more than a bad memory.

As Haskell approached the bar, a door behind it opened and a thin figure stepped out, and Haskell found himself looking down the brutish black barrel of a Tommy gun. Cold panic clenched his stomach like a sickly vice.

"Woah, Jackie boy!" Haskell shouted. "It's me, Detective Haskell, enough!"

Jackie Loeb was one of Laski's right hand men and a stone killer, a hundred pounds soaking wet but as mean as a starving dog. Haskell had recognized him instantly by his narrow-shouldered frame and hard-angled face, but now that he'd stepped partly into the light, all Haskell could focus on was the stark lines of the submachine gun in his hands, from the hard metal of the vented muzzle to the fat drum clip that hid the killer's trigger hand.

Haskell hated the things, wouldn't even bring himself to touch one if he could help it; stock-in-trade of the city's gang warfare, he'd seen too many times just what they could do to a man's body.

Haskell himself, for all he played the hard man when he needed to, had pulled his own gun no more than a half dozen times in his life with the intention of using it, and pulled the trigger in earnest less than that. As far as Haskell was concerned, the gunplay was better left to the nutcases and the fools. Burke Haskell intended to see retirement fat and happy.

The gunman didn't move.

In Haskell's mind's eye he already saw himself all but cut in half on the floor of the bar, screaming out his last breath. He lifted up his hands slowly in surrender and licked the salty sweat trickling across his lips.

"Jackie," he managed to croak, dry-voiced, "it's me, Burke, Burke Haskell. Laski, the boss, he sent for me, I got the stuff from the evidence locker at central, just like he asked."

Jackie Loeb sidestepped stiffly behind the bar and, without a word, gestured sluggishly with the Tommy gun for Haskell to enter.

Haskell quickly complied, venturing a quick glance at the gunman as he passed—Jackie Loeb looked like hell, hopped-up and as if he hadn't slept in days, his skin an unhealthy yellow in the hard light. Haskell had just enough time to realize there was blood on the side of Loeb's suit jacket before he was through the door, which was shut quickly behind him.

Haskell didn't need to be told where to go next. He tramped along the corridor, breathing hard, acutely aware that his clothes were now plastered with cooling sweat. He went by vacant dressing rooms and closets—somehow it was even worse than the front house, it made his skin crawl.

At the end of the long corridor, he had only two drections to choose from, up or down. He glanced downward to the cellar door first. Through there, he knew (although he'd never seen it with his own eyes), was the trapdoor where the joint took in its deliveries, which meant another route out of the building, but with a heavy heart, he instead turned and mounted the short flight of narrow stairs upward to the windowless box room where he knew Laski held court when in residence at the club, and otherwise was used to cut dope and count the take.

He knocked at the heavy door, and, receiving a muffled answer in reply, gritted his teeth and stepped inside. The room was disturbingly heavy with shadows, lit only by a flickering overhead bulb which seemed on the verge of failing at any moment. Already on edge, Haskell began to silently panic, his heart starting to pound in his chest.

"Come in and shut the door," Milo Laski growled in a low undertone.

The darkness deepened as Haskell reluctantly shut the door behind him, multiplying his fear.

"Is that you, Mr. Laski?" he asked, peering at the squat, heavy figure seated in the high backed chair behind an old desk in the center of the room. It looked like Laski to Haskell, but the voice was somehow wrong, almost slurred, and much quieter than he would have expected from the loud, brash gangster he'd never known to do less than bark his words.

Haskell wanted to turn and run.

"Yes, Haskell, it's me." The reply came after some moments.

The figure behind the table leaned forward and put his hands closer to the light; they were brutish things jutting out from under immaculate white cuffs, with every finger sporting a ring of some kind. If that hadn't been enough for Haskell to recognize the mob boss, a moment later the wide ridge of Laski's bald head came into the light with its old knife scar as undeniable proof.

"You got it?" Laski asked.

With a start, Haskell realized there was another figure in the shadows behind the desk that he somehow hadn't noticed when he came in. A heavy, broad man dressed in a wide-brimmed hat and an overcoat with its collar turned up so that his face was hidden. Haskell guessed he was some hood of Laski's, a bodyguard maybe. Given all that had happened, he didn't wonder at the mobster's paranoia.

"You got it?" Laski repeated as the lights flittered into blackness and resumed again.

"What's happening to the lights?" Haskell ignored the question; unease at his surroundings had rapidly begun to overcome his deeper fear of Laski.

"Electrics," Laski growled. "Buck up, the dark…the dark ain't so bad."

"For you maybe…," Haskell murmured and looked up at the bulb. The light had stopped flickering, but instead began to pulse slowly between faint and bright.

"You got it?" Laski asked again like a broken record.

Haskell tossed the battered valise onto the table, but walked no further into the room. "Here, and you can keep the money, call it a parting gift."

Laski's right hand began to twitch spasmodically and then was abruptly still, the mobster said nothing and the moment stretched.

Haskell gritted his teeth and continued, "Whatever you got yourself mixed up in Laski, I don't want no part of, understand? This is me and you done."

Still the mobster said nothing in reply, and drawing fresh courage from his own bile and the remembered shame of how he'd felt when Loeb's gun had been leveled at his stomach, Haskell's anger and fear came out of him in a torrent. "You're poison now, Laski, Typhoid-goddamn-Mary—no one in the department's gonna touch you now, not me, not anybody, and if you make trouble we're gonna come down hard, and you got troubles enough already!"

A moth began to hammer repeatedly into the light bulb overhead with an insistent crackling-tapping sound almost as if it was trying to dash itself to oblivion. Haskell looked up and found himself blinking in pain as the bulb flared hot and white. He felt the air in the room become stifling and oppressive; the shadows seemed to thicken, and he badly wanted out of the confined space.

Laski made a strange choked series of noises and his shoulders shuddered.

"What? What did you say?" Haskell asked, unable to make out anything intelligible from Laski's groans.

Haskell's growing panic and sickly discomfort was reaching boiling point, but he felt like he couldn't move, like a fly trapped on a pin.

The mobster shuddered again and Haskell realized in shock that Milo Laski, the terror of Manhattan's speakeasies, was crying like a child.

The figure beside Laski's chair gave out a hollow sigh.

Behind Haskell, the door opened, causing the detective to back away and turn sharply, but he was too late reaching for his gun as Jackie Loeb came through the doorway, the Tommy gun braced on his hip. Loeb staggered uneasily inside and jerked the door shut, never taking his wavering aim far enough away from the trapped detective to make the chance of Haskell making a play anything but suicide.

Loeb staggered to a halt when his shoulder came into contact with the shadowed wall, and as he did so his suit jacket flapped open to reveal a pepper-marked shotgun wound in the gunman's side like a bloody stigmata through which Haskell could see broken rib bone.

Haskell's mouth worked open and shut silently as once again he raised his hands in surrender.

There was a strange wet cracking sound as the figure beside the chair withdrew his hand from inside Milo Laski's back, fingers unclenching stiffly from around the mobster's exposed spine. Laski whimpered and collapsed face-first onto the table, twitching as if an electric charge were passing through him.

Haskell barely noticed as his bladder voided, gushing hot urine down the inside of his legs as he watched the bandaged-faced man pluck the silk handkerchief from the collapsed Laski's top pocket and wipe greyish, red-flecked viscous matter from his freed right hand.

The man let out something between a racking cough and a chuckle. "Forgive me the…what is the word in English?… Melodrama, yes, that's it, melodrama.

"We have not been introduced, Detective Haskell; I am Henri Damascus. It appears our friend Laski was not as durable as I had hoped. A pity, I would have preferred to have had willing answers to my questions, and you would have answered this one more honestly. Sadly, time presses me so that I cannot employ other means as I might."

Haskell's teeth began to chatter uncontrollably as he stared at the stranger's stained, bandaged face and gloved hands as he leaned over the table and upended the valise, spilling its contents. Damascus's gloved fingers sifted urgently through the mess of folded pictures and carbon paper file copies of police records Haskell had been asked to steal, and through his shock, Haskell realized it had been for this *monster* he had taken them, not Laski.

"Yes," Damascus said in his ravaged, drawn-out voice, "Ryan, Cormac, but Morgan—where is Morgan's file? Ss-speak!"

Haskell jumped to answer. "No file, there was no file in the record. It's suppressed, I didn't know who by, some suit from the DA's office maybe, I don't know who has it! His place burned up in a fire, a couple of days ago, I heard." Hysteria made Haskell trip over his own words in haste.

"It is them, I can smell it, it is their doing—he is their plaything, their tool, their weapon, no, they don't want to dirty their own hands, they daren't! The Ancient One stirs and even they fear it," Damascus rattled in his ravaged, painful voice. "I have been watching, biding my time, I know."

"Look I just, I just want…," Haskell stammered.

Again came that awful coughing laughter. "What? What is it that you want? To live?"

"Yes," Haskell quaked.

"Oh, we all want to live, Detective, do we not? For there is nothing else—no heaven, no hell, nothing but the abyss yawning in the grave…this crawling, pathetic life is all." The ruined man reached up with one hand and parted the bandages covering his face. "See what I will endure to hang on to this pathetic life, for the alternative is so much worse…"

Haskell let out a short, broken scream and collapsed against the wall as his knees gave way beneath him; his teeth snapped shut and he tasted blood.

Damascus pulled his bandages aright. "The Curse," he said painfully, "the Curse of Yig, in one of its many vile forms, that is what you see—my reward for profaning the…sacred…fane, my trespass."

"I…I don't understand," Haskell whimpered, fighting back the urge to vomit. "What are you?"

"I am but a man, a thief, a sorcerer perhaps, but still a man," Damascus said with deep weariness. "A man spending the coin of stolen life; I should be dead, many times over. The curse, the curse should have had its way, but like a serpent myself, I twist and turn in its grasp. I shall not pass into the hungry abyss before I am avenged on the one who betrayed me, left me to suffer alone a fate that should have been their's as well."

Damascus unfolded a crinkled blood-stained picture. "Yes, I have seen this in dreams, this tower, this…lighthouse I believe you would call it…here I shall pursue my quarry, its name was in Laski's mind, as well, although he failed to realize its significance."

"Let me go, please, I've done nothing to you," Haskell pleaded. "I, I have a wife, and a son."

"Alas, Detective, we are all some mother's son, and all food for the worms of the earth—King…Kingsport, do you know of it?"

Haskell shook his head violently in reply, tears streaking his cheeks.

Damascus lunged across the room with frightening speed, putting his bandaged face inches from Haskell's own terrified one. The broken detective recoiled backward with a cry.

"It is unfortunate then, Detective, that you can be of no further assistance to me," Damascus coughed, "and I have no time to make use of your corpse, unlike our friend Loeb here. So, I am afraid you have only one last favor to give, something I must insist you do for me."

Damascus's gloved hands shot down and grabbed Haskell's legs in a vice-like grip.

"Unfortunately, I am a hunted man, and my handiwork I am sure, has not been…unnoticed," Damascus's voice dropped low to a cracked whisper. "Those who cursed me still would seek my life… I have evaded them—here on the streets of your city—but my enemy has allies of his own I never guessed at, allies with dangerous tools at their disposal. I must avoid them, if I am to reach my quarry."

"I don't, how I, what…?" Haskell stammered.

"There is an old saying in the lands of the Great Rift: 'If a man should needs outrun a lion, it is best he hobble his goat first.'"

The bandaged man began to mutter in an unnatural drone, the note of which seemed to penetrate Haskell's skull and reverberate hatefully like bees were crawling and hatching in his head. The note died, and Haskell screamed as a sensation ripped into him as if boiling acid had been poured over his legs.

As Haskell slumped unconscious to the floor, Henri Damascus rolled onto his side in a fit of terrible coughing which shook his ravaged body. Black blood stained the bandages around his nose and mouth and, as the fit subsided, he spat gobs of reddish matter onto the dirty floor.

The stricken sorcerer held up his arm and the enslaved carcass that had once been Jackie Loeb clumsily pulled him to his feet, head lolling.

"Too much," Damascus whispered, "too much, too soon."

He was sapping too much of his strength too quickly; even the inadequate bindings on the revenant he had raised using the Aklo would not hold long, and he had no materials or strength to make them fast. He must be away and soon; it was time for him to leave the city, the dance had moved on. He needed no augury to guess where this "Kingsport" would lay—northward, that was where his dreams were pulling him, dreams of green fire and white fog. The woman had gone there, following her own soul's calling, and he would do the same. *I have no choices left.*

Damascus reached down and smeared his own blackened blood on the unconscious Haskell's face, forcing more of the Aklo tongue incantation between his lips. It was a poor disguise, but he doubted the *thing* they would send would count for much by way of subtlety—they had shown none thus far.

"Guard this place," Damascus ordered the walking corpse, "kill anything that enters."

Damascus hurriedly gathered up the stolen papers back into the valise and fled as quickly as his tortured body would carry him.

* * *

The world died screaming.

The girl stumbled forward, her vision swimming, the corridor sliding erratically to the side, breaking apart like the grains inside the Kaleidoscope her brother had brought her for her birthday.

She had been walking for a long time; her dolls had fallen by the wayside some time back, choked with cobwebs and dust, she couldn't remember where.

She looked down at her shiny leather shoes with their silver side buckles, then beneath them to the light and dark tiles of the floor. The white shone like moonlit snow, the black fell away, falling forever.

Step on a crack, break your mother's back.

She walked-stumbled-tumbled-crawled. The screaming grew louder.

Where is father? I must tell him; why doesn't he come back? I have a fever; he must send for the doctor to make the medicine.

Empty pictures stared down from the walls, all the people in them stolen away.

Coming down with fever; couldn't play the stupid parlor game, but he promised, promised, Michael promised. I wasn't bad!

Half a face looked up at her, familiar, painted red; a hand grasped frantically at her stocking-clad shin, leaving crimson stains as the fingers failed to find purchase.

Lottie, is it Lottie?—She cannot be the one screaming; she has no mouth.

The maid was gone, sucked away into the narrow black tile like she had never been.

Stepped on a crack.

Onward and onward, she placed one foot in front of the other as the Kaleidoscope turned, the screams sounding a song without words, insistent, calling to her, louder, ever louder.

I'm not listening.

She turned away from the staircase where the shadows curled like ink in water, vines of thorns and mouths, slavering, the woodwork burning away to ash in a fire whose flames she could not see, but burned so very cold.

Not looking.

To the wide window she crept and ran, slid, and stood still.

Perhaps my father is coming, coming up the drive in his big motorcar; perhaps he has medicine for my fever.

The sky over the valley was violet and black; the trees thrashed in a hurricane without sound, splintering, falling. Down in the town, the houses toppled and dissolved in fires the girl could not see, and, in place of smoke, the screams of the people rose to the tortured skies. Only the blackened church steeple still stood high, but soon its pinnacle cross would crack and crumble to splinters as the ants swarmed around it, dying.

Kingdom come.

Something shapeless and vast swooped by, and on the driveway below, a running figure—she didn't have time to tell who—came apart in ribbons, their screams caught, trapped in the air long after the ribbons fell to the ground and soaked the gravel red.

I don't want to see!
But closing her eyes made no difference.
Darkness rose up behind her; its shadow blackened the glass.
Father! She turned.
It was not her father.

Annabel woke up convulsing on the bed, a silent scream caught in her mouth. Slowly, her heartbeat fell back from its stampede and she regained control of her twitching muscles, which now ached violently as if she'd been wrenched by ropes on a medieval wrack. She sobbed and caught her hand in her mouth in mute terror, but already the dream was fading, her memory of it unraveling, coming apart like tissue paper in her mind's eye, until only the echoes of her now nameless fear and the sheen of sweat that covered her skin stood testament to the fact it had ever been.

After some time staring fruitlessly into the dark, she gathered the strength to reach out feebly and switch on the electric lamp by her bed. Its light revealed the cozy little bedroom at Daisy's cottage and she sighed in sudden relief—she had dreaded, however irrationally, what it might have shown her instead.

The lids of her eyes grew heavy, so very heavy, and she closed them, her lips parting to let her breathe slow and deep, her hand flickering toward the pillow on which her head lay.

Her breath fogged the air, and her lips darkened to blue. The lamp guttered and failed, plunging the room again into darkness.

* * *

The old man's head snapped around suddenly from where he had been lost in dreamless study of the embers of the great hearth in his house on Water Street. The cat who had been curled up beside him shot up and arched its back, hissing in warning, its hackles raised and its blue eyes blazing. On the wide oak table by the window, the tiny lead chips suspended on cords inside their myriad of bottles shuddered and chinked as if a truck had thundered past at full tilt, but the night was silent and there had been nothing to disturb the house or its occupants, nothing, at least, that could be seen.

"Hush now, Foolishness, hush now, kith of mine. Quiet yourselves now," the old man ordered.

The old man reached for his stick and hobbled to the window and looked out across his tree-lined garden to the wall and the street beyond. The night was black as pitch and still as coffin air, but he did not doubt that few in Kingsport would sleep easily again this night. Somewhere nearby, blood had been spilled, and the threads of the world torn to allow that which was without entrance. So entreated, it had come, and propitiated with murder it had gone out—on what bloody business he did not know or care to know—but it passed now over the earth with the speed of thought and a hunger no mortal mind could encompass.

"What black folly is this, what madness, what foulness is done this night?" the old man muttered.

The wind was turning, the storm was coming. Soon he faced a decision: aid or hinder, take up arms, or flee to far and forgotten shores where he might hide again, at least for a time. But in his heart he knew his might was long past its zenith; yet he also knew that the *presumption* of those who worked such wanton arts riled him, the *insolence*, here in Kingsport. Hadn't he helped clear the place of that suicidal madness before with blood and fire?!

He sighed; other measures would have to be taken, measures he would have rather avoided.

He grunted as he sank back in his chair. "I have lived too long," he said and shook his head at the cat, who, having settled again on the rug by the skull-lined hearth, favored him with an inscrutable look.

On the roof of the old house on Water Street, black wings slowly unfurled.

* * *

Burke Haskell was awoken by the sound of gunfire somewhere close by. He screamed out in the memory of pain as he came around, but it was no more than a ghost; there was no pain, only numbness.

He tried to stand, but swiftly collapsed back to the floor. His hands groped for his legs—they were cold, unfeeling, like they weren't even connected to his body, but some horrible fabrication where his own limbs should be—they were dead. His mind reeled in confusion as he fought to sort out the jumble of horrors he had experienced into some coherent whole, but he recoiled from it, refused to believe; he felt trapped in a nightmare from which he couldn't awaken.

There was another dull roar of gunfire, and a surge of adrenaline brought him to some semblance of his senses. *Loeb's Tommy gun, but who's he firing at?*

There was a shuddering movement behind him, and Haskell cried out again in alarm. He fell over on his back and saw Laski, or what was left of him, juddering, still slumped at the table.

"You got it?… You got it?" what remained of the mobster grunted over and over again.

Oh god, it's not a nightmare, it's all real! The realization crushed him and left him drowning in fear.

Somewhere below, another burst of gunfire was abruptly stopped by a strange hammering-booming sound that ended in awful silence.

I've got to get out! God, he's hobbled me! That's what he meant—outrun the lion! Something's here!

Haskell still couldn't get his legs to move; frantically, he felt around his legs but couldn't see any kind of injury or hurt done to them, but they were useless! Whimpering, he dragged himself further into the shadows of the room, fingernails scraping against the rough floorboards.

Laski shuddered violently again, his heavy hands banging on

the table. "Immmmil…lo…lasss…," he groaned.

"Shut up!" Haskell let out in a helpless, frenzied whisper. "Shut up, they'll hear!" and with sudden remembered panic, Haskell dragged his revolver from its holster, hanging on to it with both hands, trembling uncontrollably no matter how hard he tried to remain still.

There was a deep, hollow boom followed by a violent rushing sound, as if a storm wind had been unleashed downstairs in the speakeasy's bar, and distantly Haskell could hear glass breaking and cloth tearing. The seconds stretched into an eternity, and Haskell fought against a scream that wanted to begin somewhere in his belly and rip out of him and never stop. Soon, the floor beneath him, the doors, everything began to creak and grind like the whole building was being twisted on its foundations by an enormous, violent hand trying to wrench it clear off the ground.

The room's only light bulb shattered, plunging Haskell into total darkness, but even robbed of sight, he both felt and heard the floorboards warping as if a rippling wave passed through them. Then came a great screeching crack as the heavy doorframe began to buckle, and agonized moments later an almighty booming crash resounded like caged thunder as the door was sundered explosively. Haskell cried out as he blindly tried to protect his face from a storm of flying splinters whirling unseen about him.

The nightmare blackness *breathed*, and something vast and terrible entered the room, and with it came an unholy, chilling reek as of rotten blood and befouled vinegar. Haskell's eyes and nostrils burned as an alien cold devoured darkness around him as if he had been plunged into icy water.

"Mmmmmil—," Laski's voice was cut off abruptly. The table splintered and Laski's body with it. The darkness was filled with a sudden cacophony of guttural screaming as if from a thousand hungry maws, and all was liquid movement and vast rushing of frigid air.

With the last sane impulse of his life, Burke Haskell jammed the barrel of his service revolver up against the roof of his mouth, and pulled the trigger.

* * *

Captain Carl Grissom waited with one foot up on the running board of his Ford, his elbow braced against the hardtop. He took a last drag on the third cigarette he'd smoked since he'd been standing waiting at the intersection and flicked it to hiss in the wet gutter.

He glanced at his watch. *The wretch is late, but at least the damn rain has finally stopped.*

Inside the automobile, he heard his driver, a sergeant named Burns who had been with him for years, shifting around, trying to get comfortable. His old partner wasn't his only backup, either; he had another two guys further along on each of the roads leading from the intersection, scoping out cars and passersby—not that there had been many of either. There was little likelihood of the meet going bad—after all, he'd called it, but Grissom hadn't lived so long in his trade without being careful.

A long black Mercedes-Benz slid out of the gloom, hooded headlamps shimmering, whitewall tires turning slowly as it coasted to a halt, metalwork grill grinning like a slavering wolf.

The motorcar came to a stop beside him and the passenger window slid smoothly down. Inside, a grey, round face turned to regard him with iron-cold eyes.

Grissom looked in with shocked recognition, but didn't let it show. *I called for the monkey, but got the organ grinder, damn.* "Mr. Shawcross, an unexpected honor," Grissom said, not quite able to moderate the resentment in his tone.

"I take it that your request to meet Mr. Dane at this particular location indicates a renewed interest in Anthony Morgan?" Shawcross asked flatly without preamble.

Grissom glanced over the car to the burned out hulk of the building across the intersection. The floor that had once housed Morgan's rented rooms had been obliterated. Nothing was left of it but a few charcoal-caked spurs, and the shop below was a hollowed out, scorched wreck.

If Shawcross wanted it straight with no middlemen, then that was fine by Grissom.

"Yeah, I know your pet warned us off, and we have been very cooperative," Grissom said, "but things have been getting real crazy down here—messy, public, everything we don't want—and word has it Morgan's mixed up to the top of it. The city fathers are concerned."

Something resembling a smile spread over Shawcross's features and Grissom felt his neck twitch involuntarily.

"Of course," Shawcross began with all the warmth of a viper. "Unfortunate things have occurred, but rest assured they were unavoidable given the circumstances, and nobody of any consequence has suffered; the city fathers need not trouble themselves further. As it is, the vermin have been flushed from the long grass and fled, and your fair city will be the better for it."

Grissom shifted uncomfortably despite his determination not to show that Shawcross was getting to him. It seemed as if an unwholesome heat was radiating out of the open car window, and Shawcross's low, powder-dry voice was grinding on his nerves more and more with every word he said.

"Well, so you say, but now they tell me I've got a dead detective looking like somebody fed him through a combine harvester and a landmark building in rubble to add to the pot!" Grissom spat.

"As I said, Captain Grissom, nobody of consequence," Shawcross replied coldly.

Grissom riled and clenched his fists. He wanted nothing more than to reach in and drag the scrawny grey man out of the car by his neck and smash his head against the sidewalk, but was kept in check by the knowledge that it was the last thing he'd ever do.

"You say it's over?" Grissom snarled through gritted teeth.

"As over as such things may be. Events have quickly moved on, and moved elsewhere to more troubled ground, as we expected they might," Shawcross said. "All here will now lapse back into its normal round of petty human vice and violence in its due course, the disturbance removed."

"And Morgan? Is he the one playing bloodhound for you?"

"He is no longer your concern, if he ever was; speak not of him again," Shawcross replied coldly, and waved his hand, indicating the interview was over. At this signal, his car's huge German engine roared into life.

Grissom stood there for a time watching the taillights of the Mercedes-Benz fade away into the gathering twilight and swore under his breath. He took a long, last look at the burnt out corner of the city block, muttering, "Goodbye, Killer, I did warn you the rope might have been the better way out."

CHAPTER EIGHT

The journey to Kingsport hit trouble right from the beginning for the two women. Daisy had planned a midmorning start for them and, given that the seaport was only half an hour or so away by rail, they'd elected to take the day's first connecting train at ten rather than risk the road after weeks of rain and more forecasted. She'd also telegrammed reservations ahead for an open-ended stay at the Lighthouse Inn. The inn was one of Kingsport's better respected establishments, catering to the upmarket summer tourists, but open the year around, and more than glad of the trade, it seemed, by the somewhat obsequious tone of the swift reply.

The day, the first Saturday of October, had been grey and overcast and Daisy had woken not long before the feeble dawn. Despite only a few hours' sleep and a nagging headache, she was filled with a nervous energy to be about their business. She let Annabel sleep, and made their final preparations as quietly as she could, reasoning that her friend deserved as much sleep as she could get.

Privately, Daisy felt the whole trip might still mean a colossal letdown for Annabel if there was neither hide-nor-hair of her Maxwell. Or, perhaps worse, if indeed they discovered that something terrible had happened, what then?

I'm a librarian; what exactly do I plan to do if confronted with some cult member or crazed bohemian drug addict, anyway? Harvey Walters had been right: she'd first-hand experience of some of the people they had turned away from the restricted collection, and one or two had made her genuinely shudder, beyond their furtive secrecy and sometimes deficiency of personal hygiene.

The truth was the strange beliefs of others didn't prevent them hurting you, she knew, if that was where their fanaticism led them to. Mulling on that realization was why she'd spent a portion of the early hours digging out an old wooden box from the top of the pantry (where she had finally found it) and parsing out quantities of brittle grey powder into cylinder loads, something she had not done more than once or twice since she had been first shown how while standing hip-high to her grandfather.

It was as Daisy had gone outside to retrieve her mail that she had seen the Saint Mary's Hospital ambulance rattle past, its bell sounding shrill and urgent despite the early hour and near-deserted streets. The sounds faded, and she turned back to go inside and was stopped dead in her tracks by what she saw: dozens of deep gouges and scratches on the heavy wood of her front door, cracking and chipping away at the dark blue paintwork, splintering deep into the wood. With her heart heavy in her chest, she willed herself to examine the markings more closely. They seemed almost nonsensical, patternless: in one place the paint was striped by slashes as if a lion's paw had struck it, while in another, a deep, single ragged cut like that from a heavy knife blow. Nor were they at the same height: some marks were low, others as high as the upper frame. But having paced the outside of the cottage, there was no other sign of any attempt to do damage or force entry; it was both baffling and profoundly disturbing.

She telephoned the police operator almost out of reflex, her mind still reeling. *Who…what attacked the door? Why did neither of us hear it?* She had expected confusion, maybe even derision or disbelief on the other end of the line, but not terse dismissal, and that was what she had received. The hostile voice on the crackling line had informed her that neither Sheriff Engle nor any of the deputies were currently available, and took a few tersc details before asking her to clear the line.

Putting the dead handset back on its cradle after the operator had severed the call, she immediately made the decision not to wait for the police to show up, and get going as soon as they could. With that in mind, and not wanting to be alone, she went to knock on her guest bedroom door to awaken Annabel. Her first knock met no reply, neither did her second, nor her much louder third. The marks on the front door rushed up before her mind, and she immediately imagined just what such a savage assault could do to an unprotected sleeper, and threw open the door, half-expecting it to be barred against her or to be greeted by a spray of scarlet. Instead, Annabel lay in the center of the old brass bed, curled up in a fetal position, comforter drawn up tight around her, only one milk-white shoulder exposed, raven-black hair covering her face.

Daisy, her nerves already on edge, went to wake her friend, but could not. With a rising note of panic she pulled back the comforter, and shook Annabel with more force than she had intended. Annabel's head lolled back alarmingly, her eyes flickering open but only showing the whites.

"Annabel!" Daisy shouted in alarm.

"Not looking," Annabel whispered.

"Oh, thank God! Annabel, Annabel?" Daisy prompted, gently tapping her face.

Annabel's lips moved and she let out a moan which carried with it the most dreadful sense of fear Daisy had ever heard.

Without an instant of conscious thought, Daisy slapped her friend hard across the face, leaving a stinging red handprint on her cheek. Daisy took a sharp intake of breath at what she had done, but moments later was trying to hold onto Annabel's pale shoulders in an effort to stop her from hurting herself as she began to thrash and whimper terribly and not, Daisy realized quickly, as one having a seizure, but in frightened helpless panic. Daisy clung to her friend as the thrashing slowly subsided.

Good Lord, am I like this when there's nobody here to see me? Daisy thought as she caught her own breath, and pushed aside a sudden wild thought that somehow she had passed on her dreams like a contagion, for since Annabel had been here, she had not experienced a single nightmare of her own.

Annabel seemed now to be calmer, more in a faint than actually sleeping, and the flickering of her eyes had ceased. Huffing with effort, Daisy was thankful that she'd never been particularly weak of limb as she managed to bodily heave the taller Annabel to the upper edge of the bed and prop her in a sitting position. She then proceeded to splash water from the jug on the nightstand onto Annabel's face and neck, and continued to gently shake her, eventually drenching her camisole and much of the bedding before being rewarded by a spluttering, half-sleepy voice.

"Spook, Spook…why am I so wet, is the window open?"

Daisy burst out with a short laugh in undisguised relief as the tension that had closed around her chest like a vice suddenly broke loose.

"It's okay, Annabel, you were having a really bad dream and I couldn't wake you… I might have overdone it with the water," Daisy said.

"Oh…," Annabel sighed in an exhausted voice, running the fingers of one hand shakily through her damp hair, "and how."

Getting Annabel up on her feet took the better part of an hour and a half, and included several pots of strong coffee and a heavyweight fried breakfast that Daisy had to stand over Annabel like a mother hen to make her eat. She was lucid, but seemingly exhausted as if she hadn't slept in days. Annabel was more than a little cranky to begin with, but taking note of Daisy's unusually somber mood, she reined herself in and slowly realized something else was wrong. Once Daisy had been persuaded to tell her what had happened to the front door (something Daisy had found herself curiously reluctant to do), Annabel's mood became one of deadly earnestness and angry self-reflection.

"It's followed me here… I'm so sorry, I've put you in terrible danger, I know I have," Annabel said desolately as Daisy began making final preparations for their departure. "I am a stupid, selfish fool, and I can't believe I've done this to you!" she said, shaking her head angrily. "Stay, Spook, I'll go on my own, I can't…"

"Don't you dare, Annabel Ryan!" Daisy cut in, hands on her hips, in her best chilly *what are you doing with that* voice she used with those taking too many liberties with the library's books. "You've gone and got me mixed up in this, but I invited you here. I said the first night you came I'd help you, come what may, and I'm not backing out now. I wouldn't do that to anybody in trouble, least of all an old friend—at least I'd like to think so."

Annabel looked up at her and smiled tentatively. "You are the real McCoy, Miss Daisy Walker, you know that?"

"Nonsense," Daisy said briskly, "I'm the mousy, bookish one remember? You're meant to be the beautiful, fearless adventuress. Come on, snap out of it, at this rate we are going to miss our train."

Annabel laughed warmly. "Maybe once I was. Oh all right then, I'll go get some war paint on." She stood up, set her shoulders, and went off to finish getting ready.

By the time Annabel returned to the front parlor, the taxi had arrived and their luggage was already being loaded. True to her word, her poise had returned, and she was every inch the pale princess of mystery again, her face subtly powdered and her eyes tinted with a hint of midnight blue shadow concealing her fatigue. Daisy spared herself a moment of mild indignity that Annabel looked better composed than she did, particularly when she had to cough loudly to get the taxi driver's attention to inform him they were ready to go once Annabel had made an appearance outside.

Leaving her defaced front door behind her, and pinning a small note of explanation—should the police actually arrive at any point—she couldn't help but feel a chill creep up her spine as her eyes were drawn to the gouges and cuts scaring its surface. But she pressed on regardless. *"Half a league, half a league, half a league onward,"* she found herself reciting in her mind as she climbed into the back of the rickety, disreputable-looking taxi as the driver cranked the ignition handle. The Tennyson poem wasn't exactly comforting; it seemed appropriate, but hopefully not too much so, she thought as they started off, Annabel's gloved fingers curling around her upper arm for support.

Arkham brooded. The day was drab and colorless, and the streets seemed sparsely peopled, and those they saw had an unwonted hurry to them, shoulders hunched, hats drawn down low. As they crossed over the river, an ambulance rattled by them in the opposite direction, its bell ringing in alarm, their taxi pulling a wide berth to one side in order to let it pass.

"That's the second time I've seen that ambulance today, and I heard it again while making breakfast," Daisy said. To see the ambulance running to or from an emergency once a day in a town of Arkham's size was a rarity, three times separately in a morning was all but unheard of.

"Do you think…anything's happened?" Annabel replied.

"I don't know. Driver, has there been an accident of some kind?"

"I wouldn't know, ma'am," the driver said in an entirely un-convincing tone and hunkered down in his seat.

As the taxi puttered through Independence Square—which seemed almost entirely deserted, except for the police wagon parked near Founder's Rock, two constables looking solemn and almost furtive beside it—and onward toward the station, the streets became all but empty, and several stores and busi-nesses seemed closed where they should have been open. Nei-ther woman had to tell the other that something was wrong.

They pulled into the station parkway, and Daisy felt Anna-bel's grip on her arm suddenly increase to a painful clutch dig-ging into her. She glanced at her friend to see her eyes were wide with shock. Following her gaze, she saw the old stationmaster Bill Washington standing talking animatedly to another man, a small, wizened, scarecrow-like figure with a bald round head perched on a long, scrawny neck like a vulture. The stranger wore a long, tattered brown overcoat and his left arm was wrapped up in a dirty-looking sling.

"What's the matter, Annabel? What do you see?"

"Him!" Annabel hissed. "That old man! I know him—from New York—that awful man, that preacher—it was horrible, Spook, no! We can't stop here!"

"What? Slow down, what are you saying?"

"On the street—he's a monster—he was making it all worse!" Annabel spoke at breathless speed. "It can't be a coincidence— it's him I'm sure of it! Outside on the street corner I saw him, as well, around the fire pail with the drunks and wrecks, I remem-ber now, I never made the connection before—how could I have missed it, the way he would look at me?"

The taxi was pulling to a stop and Annabel was on the verge of panic. "Drive on! Take us back!" Daisy shouted to the driver.

"What? But we—," he began.

"Back to my house, *now*, we've changed our minds—do it!"

Daisy demanded in a voice hard enough to make the man flinch involuntarily.

Muttering under his breath, the driver complied; Daisy made out the word "women" somewhere in his quiet diatribe, but didn't give a damn what he thought of her or her gender.

Annabel calmed down quickly as they made their way back. "I'm sorry, but there's no way I'm getting on that train if that *man* is anywhere near it—not after last time… But we have to get to Kingsport, I feel sure—maybe he's looking for Maxwell, too, one of the ones he warned me about; surely that means he might be in the area, Maxwell, I mean?" she whispered urgently, her thoughts running at high speed.

Daisy, calmer now that the moment had passed, thought quickly on the problem. If the man was who Annabel claimed, and it was more than just a coincidence he was here—and how could it be anything else but true?—then here at last was something flesh and blood, not some nebulous, nameless fear— something *real* that could be dealt with, a problem to solve.

"Ted's motorcar," Daisy whispered back, "we'll use that, go as soon as we can, today."

"Do you think it will make it that far?" Annabel asked seriously; having ridden in it a few times, she'd already had a taste of how unreliable it could be.

"It'll have to," Daisy replied. "We'll fill her up, and take the back road out to the Aylesbury Pike, just in case they are watching the road south, then loop all the way around to Clark's Corners and take the long route to Kingsport; if we're lucky, we can still be there before dark."

"Now who's being paranoid?" Annabel asked, and her tone was more one of relief than reproach.

Daisy sighed a little. "I hope so," she replied nervously.

* * *

The sea had passed the point of high tide, but still sat high against the harbor wall and drowned the beach, spreading out before Kingsport in the sun in a turning blanket of glittering iron and fathomless thunderhead blue. By the wharf, a small, expectant crowd had gathered, restive and murmuring solemnly as if awaiting a service in church. Behind them, in the shadows where the narrow streets and alleyways of the town came down to meet the docks, and under veiled store awnings overlooking the scene more furtively, solitary figures looked on.

The old man stood apart from either set of watchers, leaning against the high sea wall above and away from the crowd, looking out on the expectant tableau below. With one hand he rested on the salt-stained stone barrier, the other braced on his gnarled walking stick, impassive and still. His colorless eyes took in all, while the sea breeze carried the murmured voices of the crowd to him as clearly as if he had been standing among them.

Now and again, the glances of those below flickered nervously from the object of their attention to the old man's vantage point, warily lingering on him as if to assure themselves he was still there and no closer.

Out in the bay, the small white boat drew steadily closer, the single living figure that occupied it propelling it along with sure, rhythmic strokes against the swell, and the old man silently approved the skill and economy with which the pilot, the keeper of the North Point Lighthouse, handled his craft.

As the boat closed to the dock, a surge-swell suddenly pitched the deck forward, and for a lingering moment, the tarpaulin-covered cargo lashed in the small boat's bow was clearly visible to the onlookers, sending a fresh murmur that rose and subsided like the waves below. Sheriff Claiborne, as if startled into action by the sight, ordered his two deputies to try and disperse the small crowd with little enthusiasm or success. Claiborne himself singled out young, half-witted Marni Sawyer and scolded her for bringing her knee-high, and doubtlessly sharp-eyed, daughter to see such a spectacle, and was greeted by muted stubbornness for his trouble. Foolishness—*What child of the world isn't birthed astride the grave?*

The old man looked on in silence, knowing that Claiborne didn't understand—he was not of the old Kingsport blood, nor, as an immigrant, was he truly part of the slow influx of wandering dreamers, searchers, and outcasts that, down the years, had found this town of mists at the edge of the world. No, Claiborne—a political appointee by the great and good of the town—was formerly of the Boston Police Department, and the easy charm and discretion with which he dealt with Kingsport's wealthy families could not make up for the fact that he had neither salt nor sky in his veins.

He won't last.

These were dark days come 'round again for Kingsport, and rumors already circulated that the new sheriff was losing his grip on the town. There had been trouble with strangers abroad, discord and violence, even some disappearances, it was whispered, and the sleep of the wealthy in their high houses on Central Hill was as troubled as that of the battered old seamen who rented the dilapidated stone and shingle shacks tucked out of sight behind the cannery and the old shipyard. This, however, was the first body that had been found, a new and frightening development, which served only to give shape to the town's fears and provide more questions than answers.

The keeper's stern face, blank with concentration, was now clearly visible as he guided the boat in against the heavy swell, and the harbormaster, Kreel, letting none stand for him in so onerous a task as this, went down the green-slick stone steps to the very edge of where they disappeared in the high waters, there to throw the line and tie off the keeper's boat. This maneuver achieved, Sheriff Claiborne, visibly nervous and impatient, descended unsteadily to the landing beside Kreel, much to the consternation of the harbormaster and the handful of sailors who had been drafted to help carry the cargo ashore. Unconcerned, Claiborne reached out to the boat, nearly slipping on the stones and dragging better men with him into the water, but the sure-footed harbormaster hauled him back, the tarp covering the cargo caught in Claiborne's grasping hand.

Shock rippled through the crowd. Marni Sawyer cried out and fainted, her fall to the cobbles thankfully slowed by the quick hands of her daughter, who nevertheless went down with her. *"Who is he?"*—*"his face!"*—*"God save us"*—*"What could do that?"*—*"Never in my days"*; the jumbled cries came up to the old man on the wind as the tarp was hurriedly lashed back in place, and the keeper moved to rid himself of his fell cargo.

The keeper's cargo was—or rather had been—a man. The body's identity unknown to any present and the remains mutilated perhaps enough to remain unknowable. The corpse had washed up on the landward side of the North Point rocks earlier that morning, and the knowledge of its discovery had quickly spread through the already fearful town like a plague.

Soon enough, the body was taken ashore and bundled into a waiting hearse, and afterward, while the men folk of the harbor returned to the Rope and Anchor, carrying along with them Marni Sawyer for the solace of rough brandy and a warm fire, the crowd broke up and shadowed figures slunk back silently into the alleyways of the town.

For a time, Claiborne remained, questioning the keeper, who would not leave his boat, and received only terse and unsatisfactory answers in reply. Eventually, the harbormaster cast off the line and the keeper turned his craft back, well-rid of his unwanted jetsam, and headed out over the increasing swell of the turning tide, sensing, just as the old man had, bad weather rolling in fast, and mindful of his duty.

Looking sick and uncertain, Claiborne clambered back up the slick steps with some assistance, and back down the now deserted dockside. The sheriff found himself staring up at the old man who watched him grimly from his vantage point, silently judging him and finding him wanting.

Claiborne's mouth began to move uncertainly, but he said nothing as the harbormaster joined him and, venturing a respectful nod at the figure he had known since boyhood simply as "the terrible old man," Kreel put his calloused hand on the sheriff's shoulder and turned him gently away. Claiborne forced himself to regain some measure of composure and shook off the grip, walking back angrily to his waiting motorcar.

No, he won't last—Claiborne has seen…but seen nothing, the old man mused. The body pulled from the rocks had not been in the water more than a few hours at best, nor was it mangled enough to have fallen from Kingsport Head. Any old salt could have told Claiborne that, to wash up where it had, the corpse's origins lay on land, not sea, but he had not asked. This stranger had been taken, disfigured, and slain; then he had been given to the waters and the waters had spat him back out, unclean thing as it was, reeking of malignancy.

What troubles had come to Kingsport had grown worse, and unlike those gathered here, the old man knew them for what they were; he knew what was coming, just as he knew there would be blood yet aplenty. But to him, it was but another storm to ride out as he had so many in his long and shadowed life.

The old man remained at his vantage point long after the others left, watching the keeper's boat dwindle into the shadows of the North Point rocks, and none too soon. The waters of the sea grew ever more restless, the skies on the horizon were darkening to an ugly slate-black, and the wind rose with the promise of violence. Beyond, the old man felt worse things than lightning and rain stirring, and the dim echoes of the whispers that called them, urgent, fearful, and angry. It was time he was home.

The old man turned and began his slow walk home ahead of the coming storm, aware that one pair of eyes watched him still. The watcher looked out from a darkened doorway on the edge of the waterfront, looked through eyes with which the old man had himself once seen—in dreams.

* * *

Balked at the railroad station by the appearance of the fearful preacher and Annabel's panic, their luck had not exactly taken a turn for the better as they attempted to get out of Arkham—or at least so Daisy judged—but they had persevered and refused to bow before whatever turn of fate that seemed determined to keep them in Arkham.

After paying off the grumbling taxi driver at the house so she could calm Annabel down and dig out the keys, Daisy had almost run the three streets to Ted's empty lodgings to pick up his battered motorcar. Along the way, she had seen no one she cared to stop or talk to in the unnaturally quiet town, glad that a good portion of her working life spent on her feet had shown her the wisdom of erring toward common sense over fashion as far as shoes were concerned. It had taken five hard goes at the crank handle and a little unladylike language to get the engine started, and after hurriedly jamming their cases into the trunk and back seat, it was past eleven when they were finally on their way.

The car rattled its way northwest, as planned, up the Aylesbury Pike, and the farmland on either side very quickly grew sparse and forlorn, with much of what they could see swallowed by thickets of woodland and dense underbrush. The road was ill-used and ill-maintained, with nothing along it save a few scattered farms and hamlets right the way up to Dunwich, to which Daisy had never had occasion to go, and given its unwholesome reputation as a paragon of decay and the worst things that could happen in an isolated, old town, she had no intention of ever doing so.

For more than an hour they traveled, and never saw a single other traveler on the road—on foot, horse-drawn, or motorized—and the conversation between the two women ranged from bouts of trivialities to terse discussions of what had happened earlier in the day—during which Daisy got a better idea of who Annabel believed the preacher to be, and her friend's new-made mental connection between him and the menacing vagrants she had seen near her New York apartment. Daisy had made a connection with the dean's inquiries to her about "indigents" in Arkham causing trouble, which had led to Daisy asking a slew of direct and pointed questions to Annabel, perhaps more harshly than she had meant to, leading to a long brooding silence between them. They were both very much on edge.

It was early afternoon when they spotted the overturned truck, half upended in the ditch by the side of the road.

Daisy brought the car to a stop and insisted, against Annabel's vocal resistance, that they see if anyone had been hurt.

"But what if it's a trap?" Annabel had said.

"Now it's you being paranoid," Daisy had replied, as light-heartedly as she could manage. "This isn't a dime novel, and somebody might be hurt in there." But she'd taken the Ford's crank handle with her in case.

Daisy walked over to the wreck, displaying more confidence than she genuinely felt, and Annabel, her curiosity getting the better of her, trailed uncertainly behind. The truck was a very early model, clearly owned by some farm hereabouts from its condition, and its bodywork was coated more in rust than paint. There was nobody inside the empty cab and the side door hung open, trailing in the standing water of the nearly overflowing drainage ditch.

The scene was desolate and empty, and nothing moved but for

the slowly gathering wind rippling the long grass and scrub that ran up to the woods beyond.

"Do you think the driver fell in the water?" Daisy whispered doubtfully.

"No," Annabel replied softly, "I don't think so; we'd see him floating if he were dead."

Daisy nodded; it was a sobering thought.

"I'd say this came off the road in the storm last night, the skid marks on the road are filled with water and the inside of the cab's soaked through, as well."

Daisy looked around. Annabel was right; the truck seemed "settled" somehow and partly sunk into the ditch mud, as if it had been there for some time.

"Hello! Is there anybody here? Is anybody hurt?" Annabel shouted suddenly, and Daisy nearly jumped out of her skin.

A flock of whippoorwills suddenly broke from the trees in a fury of beating wings and eerie screams, and both women stepped back startled.

"Annabel!" Daisy almost growled.

Annabel smiled ruefully at her with a familiar, wild sparkle in her eye. "Well, you were the one who thought somebody might be lying injured," she shot back.

The silence descended again, and Daisy began to shiver slightly as the cold wind teased at her, feeling uncomfortably like they were being watched.

"Well, we're not exactly dressed for it, but do you want to find a place to cross the ditch and take a look?" Annabel asked with a distinct lack of enthusiasm.

"No, best not, we have a long way to go yet. We have to fill up at Clark's Corners anyway. We'll let them know about the truck and be on our way."

After another few miles back on the road, they at last turned southward at Gallow's Crossing, and put the brooding, bleak country that lay to Arkham's west behind them. They made Clark's Corners—a little town that was not much more than a main street and farmers' market—just after three in the afternoon, making Kingsport by nightfall increasingly unlikely.

The town was well-kept and showed signs of being prosperous, but was more than a little unwelcoming, and the sight of two unfamiliar and young "city" women driving alone together in a motorcar drew uncomfortable stares and a strained civility behind which something ugly lurked. The tension dropped away slightly after Annabel tactfully managed to hedge that they were from "the university" into the strained conversation at the general store, and "soon expected elsewhere." Blatantly overcharged for a few late-season apples and some bread and cheese, as well as for gas, they nevertheless didn't complain, nor by silent consent did they pause to mention the overturned truck they had seen. They were very glad to be on their way again.

Annabel half-expected them to be followed and said as much, repeatedly looking out of the rear window and offering a few choice words about the "charm" of New England's rustic locals, but they were not pursued, and the road behind them remained as empty as ever. As for Daisy, she soon had enough on her hands just keeping the car on the road. The country south of Arkham gave the overall impression of being better tended and more wholesome than that to its west, and consisted largely of smallholdings and farms tucked away amid gently rolling hills interspersed with dense orchards and the stubborn remnants of thicker, darker forests that could have stood in for a hundred other vistas in New England.

However, the rain and the storms had bitten hard here, and the roads had been washed with mud and run-off. The thin tires slid and spat stones, and more than once Daisy was forced to swerve around a fallen branch or waterlogged pothole big enough to bust an axel in. The motor juddered and shook, the engine coughed and hacked, and the jolting suspension—hardly worth the name to begin with—soon had them both feeling sick, and quite beyond eating the food they'd picked up at Clark's Corners. Daisy in particular was having a hard time of it, the drive a constant physical struggle with the steering wheel, breaks, and gears which soon had her wrists and ankles aching. Annabel openly and honestly praised her strength, although Daisy avowed it was more to do with "sheer bloody-minded stubbornness."

Their progress was slow but steady, the overcast day darkening into full twilight, but by Annabel's map reading they were at last approaching the fork in the road which would lead them down to the coastal plain and either to Kingsport or Marten's Beach depending on which fork was taken. It was the last leg of their journey so they allowed themselves a small outpouring of relief and a little fantasizing about the pleasures of hot drinks and hotter baths, and Annabel, not for the first time, offered to trade Daisy as driver, and was just as before politely rebuffed on grounds of the motor's temperament, and, as Daisy pointed out, "a few laps 'round a country park in a Daimler" wasn't the same as learning to drive.

It was not long after that last exchange that heavy, fat drops of rain began to fall, a few at first, then increasing in frequency, the sky ahead darkening rapidly to the color of soot. Soon, the rain was coming down in sheets, hammering against the hardtop and leaking in at the window edges, filling the car with a damp cold as the asthmatic windshield wiper failed to do much beyond render the world a blur. Daisy pursed her lips and murmured a curse as the wheels started to lose traction and Annabel was forced to wind down a window, holding an emptied bag above her head as an improvised umbrella, so she could navigate.

They made it as far as the crest of the hill where the road forked before Annabel and Daisy finally agreed on stopping— they could see the down-slope was already awash, and the nearby creek was full with rushing water. Annabel spotted a patch of stony ground by the roadside, regular enough to once have been the foundations of some sort of house and yard, on which they could park without sinking in the mud or blocking the road and there, with very little choice, they hunkered down to sit out the storm.

Sensing they were stuck for the duration, they ate their meager dinner and Annabel clambered into the back seat and atop the bags to get as comfortable as she could. Daisy, being half-a-head or so shorter, opted for the more precarious bed of two front seats. They bundled up under car blankets and coats, but it was thoroughly cold and miserable as the wind rose, shaking the windows, and the rain hammered down like the end of the world.

Annabel began a half-unfocused monolog of the places she'd been, of the thunder and lightning rolling down from the mountains where the Greeks of old once thought Olympus stood on high, of getting scandalously drenched at an open-air party in a Parisian courtyard, and subsequently having to fend off the attentions of an over-amorous Swiss dignitary. Half-listening, Daisy started to nod off with a curious warm sense of nostalgia—years ago at the Hall School when they had shared a dormitory, Daisy would sometimes fall asleep listening to Annabel recount the imaginary stories of all the adventures she would have when she was older, and now the circle seemed to close and those adventures were both real and memory to her, a decade later.

Despite the cold and the discomfort, Daisy slept, dreamless and deep.

It was fully night by the time Daisy woke, but she couldn't have said which had brought her back to the world, the dull rumble of distant thunder or Annabel's cries. It took her a few moments to get her bearings properly and overcome the sudden painful twinge in her lower back from the hunched-up posture she'd slept in.

"Annabel, are you all right?" she asked the dark.

An inarticulate murmur, heavy with something like panic, reached her from the back seat, but from where she was lying, Daisy couldn't see her friend.

Grabbing the seat back, she pulled herself up and looked about her. Outside, the rain was still falling, but nowhere as heavily as it had been before, and out on the seaward horizon she could see flashes of lightning pulsing dimly, long seconds passing before the sound of thunder reached them.

Fumbling in the glove box, Daisy found Ted's small electric lantern and turned it on, blinking in the sudden light. Annabel moaned and thrashed her head away from the light, spitting out a jumble of tortured words, slurred and painful to hear. Daisy realized immediately that Annabel was still dreaming, caught up in some terror of her mind she couldn't escape; her struggles had already thrown off her blankets, and quickly seemed to get worse, her wrists and knees banging painfully against the confines of the back seat.

"Annabel, Annabel, wake up! You'll hurt yourself!" Daisy shouted with mounting panic, reaching out to shake her nightmare-webbed friend.

At Daisy's merest touch, Annabel shuddered and convulsed with terrible violence, nearly leaping off the seat and screaming loud enough to rattle the window panes. "I won't see!" she cried out hoarsely, and her booted feet began to kick at the door, shaking the car, her eyes rolled back in her head showing only the whites.

Frantic, Daisy flung open the driver's side door and threw herself out of the car, leaving the lantern jammed unceremoniously on the dashboard, shouting out painfully and nearly slipping as she realized she'd removed her shoes to sleep and left them in the car. Panting for breath, Daisy clambered to the side door where her friend's head lay, not wanting to risk being kicked half to death, as the car continued to rock with Annabel's violent thrashings and her cries pierced the night. Daisy managed to open the slippery door handle on the second try and was immediately knocked painfully onto her rear as the door shot open and Annabel flew out as if she had been catapulted forth.

Annabel cried out again, but this time in pain as she rolled on her side from the stony patch of ground to the muddy road.

"Ahh! That hurts!" Annabel shouted, and Daisy almost wept in relief at hearing the very conscious, if pained, stream of invective that followed.

Daisy hauled herself up by the car door and thought of a few choice words of her own as she swept her wet hair from her face and pulled her dress—the seat of which now muddy and soaked through—straight.

"Annabel," she shouted, "have you hurt yourself?" She was still alarmed by the speed and force with which her friend had leapt from the motorcar.

"Spook? Help me, would you?" came the breathy reply. "It feels like my leg's on fire!"

Daisy peered out into the half dark to where she could see Annabel was doubled up, her fingers scrabbling, trying to work the buttonhooks of one of her high boots.

"Hang on, I'm coming!"

Silently dreading her friend had broken her ankle in the tumble, she set out gingerly across the stony ground, wiping the rain from her face and flinching as a stone bit into her heel and she felt her stockings rip. *Marvelous!* she couldn't help but think with mild outrage. *Today just keeps getting better!*

As she reached Annabel at the very edge of the pool of light from the car, she could see her friend was in a worse state than she, her dress disheveled and torn, and a trickle of blood running down from her upper arm where she'd hit the ground, smeared and diluted by the rain. Annabel's only concern, however, seemed to be struggling with her left boot, which she almost clawed at with her fingers, letting out a suppressed whimper of pain an she did so.

"Be careful, Annabel," Daisy chided. "You'll make it worse if you've fractured something."

"It's not broken; it feels like it's burning! I have to get it off!" Annabel spat through gritted teeth.

"Calm down, let me look," Daisy replied, kneeling beside her, but as soon as her own hands closed around Annabel's boot she froze in shock; the wet leather was heavy with a terrible coldness, as if she had grasped a frost-covered iron railing with her bare hands.

Thunk—

The sudden and unexpected sound stilled the both of them. It was the sound of a weighted object dropping down hard onto sheet metal, deforming it.

The two women's heads turned together to the source of the noise and their eyes widened, almost hypnotized by the shock of what they saw.

The black-winged, nebulous shape sat perched on the roof of the motorcar like a stone gargoyle come to life. In the dim, rain-swept light they could see little of its detail, but what they could see was enough to fill the nightmares of a madman's slumber: obscenely long finger-claws shuddering restlessly like the spear-tipped legs of a monstrous spider, sharp shoulder blades, long, back, curling projections like horns jutting away from an impossibly featureless blank curve of a head, and furled, bat-like, membranous black wings on which the rain pattered and shone as if on wet rubber.

Daisy's mouth fell open, but she couldn't say anything, couldn't stop staring at the *thing* that had descended from the night. It was as if the thunderstorm had concentrated itself inside her head, and her mind was filled with an endless, reverberated roar: half her own scream and half a blizzard of static. She could do nothing as the creature took flight and leapt toward them, its great shadowy wings swallowing the distance between them in a single, almost contemptuous, beat. Daisy dimly heard Annabel cry out in alarm as the thing reached out for them, and an instant later Daisy felt the thing strike her as it swept by, the impact of its wing-beat shunting the air from her lungs and sending her flying onto her back.

Annabel saw the nightmare's glistening spindle-claws reaching out for her with appalling clarity as it swept in, the awful void of swirling darkness where its face should have been following swiftly behind. At the last moment, her mind's desperate demands to her body telling her to move were answered, aided in some part by the burning, fiery pain that ate into her leg and spiked into her mind, distracting attention even from the horror before her. She rolled aside and the claws snapped wetly in the air above her, but the respite was momentary, as she felt the clawing, groping fingers wrap around her narrow waist and begin to tighten. Her mind blank of anything but the need to escape, she kicked and struggled and spat like a fury, and the fingers began to loosen again and she was thrown onto her back as the nightmare's wings beat the air and a tail whiplashed, sending up wet spray around her.

It hovered just above her, blotting out the light, its terrible void-face arcing down like a lover in search of an embrace. Annabel screamed out for help, and with every ounce of her strength, she shot out her hands like claws, her manicured nails sinking immediately into the tenebrous mass of the thing's face, the skin like wet, ice-cold cobweb. Utter revulsion drowned her, and she fought the urge to vomit. She clenched shut her hands in the mass of the thing's head and raked them clear again with all the force she could manage.

The nightmare incarnate reeled back in the air, screaming

without sound, fresh pain like broken glass grinding down a blackboard stabbing into Annabel's head; distantly she was aware of the sound of a car windowpane shattering. Momentarily free, Annabel drew in a short ragged breath and struggled to her feet, crying out with the agony in her leg; stumbling, one foot then the other, she found purchase and began to run, head down like an athlete, her boots skidding in the mud, rain lashing at her. A cold claw caressed her back, finding purchase on the hem of her dress. Panic like she had never known raced through her, spurring her on, her heart hammering in her chest; the claw grasped, her dress tore, and the black ground slipped away beneath her. She was falling, tumbling, sliding down a muddy slope. After a jarring, whirling moment she was still again, left spread-eagled and in tatters in a muddy pool, as the shockingly chill water bled the last reserves of energy from her exhausted limbs in an instant.

A claw clicked shut around her booted left ankle and cold fire lurched into her veins, dragging the breath from her in a ragged scream.

Annabel had no strength left in her to fight as she was drawn up off the ground by her leg, her face turned into the pool, causing her to splutter for air. Her skin crawled as the long fingers fastened around her leg and ripped away at the leather, but she could do nothing but moan in revulsion. Thunder sounded close by, the grip suddenly let go, and her shoulders hit the soft ground with bruising force; her boot came free and instantly the agony in her leg subsided into a chill echo of itself.

The thunder roared again and something whip-cracked by above her. Annabel's eyes flickered open and she saw the nightmare thing still hovered above her, its wings flapping angrily as it spun around in the air, sending up sprays of rain. The thunder peeled again, and light flashed, but it was wrong. The nightmare creature jerked backward suddenly, and Annabel realized it was not thunder she was hearing, but gunfire!

Another shot sounded and Annabel managed to roll unsteadily onto her side. There she saw Daisy standing side on, her back ram-rod straight against the night, the electric lantern clutched in her left hand, angled upward, and in her right an enormous antique-looking pistol wavered at arm's length. Daisy's face was a mask of determination and anger the likes of which Annabel had never known in her friend, and she could see Daisy's lips moving rapidly, but couldn't understand what she was saying. Daisy worked the pistol again and it spat a tongue of flame into the dark, and with a snap and rush of chill air, the nightmare turned in the sky and was gone, black fading into blackness like a smoke ghost.

Daisy staggered over to where Annabel half-sat-half-laid, and sank to her knees beside her, dropping the heavy pistol into her lap and flexing the fingers of her right hand painfully.

"Good… Good Lord," Daisy stammered, and let out a sigh.

Despite herself, Annabel let out an abrupt spurt of laughter, and hugged her friend fiercely to her chest, tears mixing with rain on her face.

After a few moments, Daisy struggled to her feet, pulling up Annabel with her. "Come on, we need to get out of here; that…*thing*… I'm not sure I even hurt it—it might be back at any moment."

"Do you think we can m-make King-Kingsport tonight?" Annabel asked, starting to suddenly and violently shiver from the cold, her exhaustion, and the quickly fading adrenaline.

"We'll have to! I'm not staying out here in the dark, and you're in a worse state to rough it than I am. I'd rather crash than stay out here, besides. We'll both perish from pneumonia if we don't get carried off by—," Daisy stopped herself short, *"monsters"* she had been about to say, the reality of what had just happened crashing in on her and taking her breath away.

Annabel plucked the electric lantern from Daisy's grip and

wrapped her fingers gently in her friend's hand. Annabel shone the lantern across the muddy roadside until she found what she was after. There, half-submerged in a small puddle, lay a hard-edged, shard-like black object. It reflected the lantern light, glittering with a strange, unnatural emerald sheen. Daisy gasped.

"I-I'm, s-sorry, Spook," Annabel shivered, "I have a c-ca-confession to make."

CHAPTER NINE

Daisy Walker reached out for the blue bone china coffee cup on its gilt-edged saucer and noticed her hand was shaking slightly. She curled and uncurled her fingers slowly and deliberately, dispelling the involuntary tremor. She knew it was a sign that no matter how calmly she appeared to be carrying on with things, no matter how much she overrode her feelings by force of will, deep down, she was still to some extent in shock.

The world is not how I believed it to be.

Daisy sat alone at an old circular table in one of the four Victorian bay windows that fronted the picturesque ground floor of the Lighthouse Inn in Kingsport. Its square panels of antique glass offered an unobstructed view down the hill, across the cobbled harborside to the sea wall and the grey rolling ocean beyond, and even though the day was a cold and overcast one, she could clearly see both the pale lance of the North Point Lighthouse rising up from distant sea rocks to one side, and the brooding titan bulk of Kingsport Head on the other. From her high-backed leather chair by the window in the hotel's all but deserted restaurant-cum-lounge, Daisy had time to contemplate a vista that had fascinated many artists down the years, a panorama at once salt-sprayed, rugged, and strangely ethereal—like a fragment of a dream. It was a view she was familiar with, having lived a part of her life in Kingsport, but it had not lost its power to draw her inside herself, and set her mind adrift.

It was her second morning in Kingsport, and in what quiet moments she'd allowed herself since her arrival, she had done a considerable deal of hard thinking about her and Annabel's current situation, what had happened to them on the road, what the events of recent days meant, and what they implied, not only for the future, but for all she knew. Annabel's letter had started a slow but devastating chain reaction for Daisy that altered the way she saw her life. It was, she reflected, in the manner of a stone on the path that, once kicked loose, could displace others of its kind, and those yet more, until an avalanche was birthed that left a mountainside forever afterward changed.

She smiled sadly at the thought. *A bit melodramatic, old girl; a simile worthy of Walpole or Poe maybe, and not usually applied to librarians at provincial universities—but not far wrong in my case.*

The letter, no…before that: the chunk of her memory gone missing…Annabel's story, her conversation with Professor Walters, the evidence in the card catalogue at the Orne Library, the scratch marks on her door, and finally, the impossible, nightmare *thing* that had attacked them on the road and tried to drag Annabel away in the night to who knew what terrible fate—they were all like puzzle pieces slotting themselves together in her mind, configuring in odd and awful ways to suggest other truths too strange and unspeakable for the light of day. If she were a winsome virgin bride in a gothic novel, she might have dramatically dropped dead of fright, or if some closeted poet in a pulp magazine's weird tale then she ought to have been driven mad or had her hair turn white at the very least.

She smiled to herself and turned a lock of her hair around her fingers, *still blond.*

She allowed that she was bearing up surprisingly well, a chip off the old Maine block, even though she was not without her doubts. *Do the insane know the truth of their condition?* she asked herself, and not for the first time over the last day and a half. *Can they know? Would I know?*

But such a comforting thought as mere lunacy wasn't something her own all too analytical brain let her get away with; there was too much very real damage to ignore—to the roof of her car, her front door, not to mention the state poor Annabel had been in afterward. She herself had three long, parallel bruises across her shoulder blades to prove it, marks where the wing-spars (or claws or whatever they could rightly be called) had swatted her aside as easily as a grown man might have a child. Strangest of all, these ideas, these events, somehow did not come to her as revelation, but with the familiarity of something once known, but long forgotten, like visiting a wood walked once in childhood or hearing a song lost down the years, like returning to Kingsport itself, in fact.

I am afraid, but why shouldn't I be? I am not mad, and such things exist.

Although prone to ignoring her surroundings while in deep thought, Daisy was far too jittery and uneasy to fail to notice the cautious approach of Albert Dukes, the proprietor of the Lighthouse Inn, across the well-varnished floorboards of the lounge. At his approach, she casually picked up the copy of the *Arkham Advertiser* by her hand and covered up the notebook and loose papers on the table before her in the pretense of scanning the front page.

"I'm frightfully sorry to disturb you, Miss Walker," Dukes began in his usual faintly cringing and overly oily tone, "but I was wondering if I might inquire as to you and your friend's health and condition, and see if there is anything else we at the Lighthouse Inn could do to make your stay a more comfortable one?"

Daisy looked up and forced herself to smile politely at the nervous little man. At around five feet and skinny as a rail, with big watery eyes and one of the most unconvincing toupees she'd ever seen, Daisy at once found Dukes to be both comical and more than a little unctuous, and couldn't bring herself to think well of him, even though she knew he had been the soul of consideration and discretion since their arrival.

"Much better, Mr. Dukes," she replied. "Miss Ryan is raring to be up and around again, but I've made her rest in this morning, so as not to overtax her recovery."

"Oh, I am glad to hear that, ma'am," he said, wringing his hands theatrically. "It's a marvel, the way she's recovered, after being thrown from the car like that. Why, I'm sure it would have been the death of me, a jolt like that in a rainstorm, I can't imagine what you two young ladies went through!"

The truth being clearly out of the question, the story they had decided on had been a simple one: the motorcar, caught in a mudslide in the storm, had gone spinning and sliding down the hill, Annabel had been thrown out into a water-logged ditch, and Daisy had somehow regained control before the auto flipped and crashed. There was enough circumstantial evidence to back them up and nobody to gainsay them on their battered arrival at the hotel in the small hours of the morning, and so the story had gone unchallenged. Furthermore, Kingsport, it turned out, had other more pressing matters to concern it than the fates of two women caught in a storm on the road.

"Has the sheriff called again at all?"

The decidedly middle-aged Dukes blushed somewhat before replying, "Why no, ma'am, nor am I surprised after the talking to you gave him the morning you arrived—you sent him off with quite a flea in the ear, and it was no more than he deserved."

It was Daisy's turn to blush slightly; after her experience on the road and an inability to sleep despite her exhaustion afterward, the bullying sheriff—who clearly had as little respect for woman as he had for thieves and malcontents—had been more than she could take.

He'd come barging in demanding to know about the "accident" and their business in the town and a lot of other fool questions to which she couldn't conceive of answers, and for a moment she'd wavered on the edge of tears, but instead she'd gotten angry, very angry, almost Imperial, in fact, in her wrath. Without conscious thought of what she was saying, she had called on her own standing and the constraints of civilized behavior, and threatened him with old and respected family names in the area and the influence and offices of the Miskatonic University as her recourse, and by the end of it she had found herself sounding like her father in his most apocalyptically framed sermons. By the time she had finished, it had been the sheriff, not Daisy, stammering over replies to her equally nonsensical questions about the state of the roads in his county and *"What better he had to do than accosting lady travelers"* and he had fled in full retreat, promising to locate a mechanic in due course to *"see to the safety of her motorcar."* The mechanic had appeared later in the day, but of the sheriff there had been no sign, for which Daisy was more than grateful as she was more than a little shocked and embarrassed by her behavior toward him. It was not like her, not like her at all, she thought.

"Perhaps that's just as well," she offered the hotel manager.

Agreeing to another pot of coffee and a slice of Madeira cake just to get Dukes on his way again, Daisy sighed and put aside the newspaper. *The Advertiser* had been full of nothing but banal articles, out-of-date syndicated columns, some notices of storm damage, and a strangely stilted report on the unexpected death of a boarding house guest, and offered no real answers to the commotion they had witnessed the day they had left Arkham.

Alone again, Daisy returned to the work with which she had been trying to occupy her mind. The notebook was undoubtedly her own, filled with page upon page of her own tiny and meticulously neat shorthand interspersed with book references, ciphers, strange lexicons, and copied passages and diagrams from what she could only assume were books from the Miskatonic University's restricted collection. The loose leaves scattered about it were the product of snatched hours from the last day and a half; they were notes she had taken, cross-references and tentative concordances she had created in trying to understand a book she could not remember writing in the first place, but which so patently had been the product of her own mind and her own past studies. But what had she been attempting and why?

Daisy yawned and rubbed her eyes as a wave of fatigue stole over her. She hadn't slept well since Arkham, and had spent most of the previous night fitfully watching over Annabel as she slept, almost death-fully deep and dreamless, utterly exhausted by what had happened.

She forced her eyes to focus on the last page she had transcribed in full from the shorthand, the section chosen for one reason only: the word "Kingsport" written clearly in the upper margin in red ink.

"...Although one of the first trading settlements of the early Mass. colony, King's Port's founding population was by no means heterogeneous, and in addition to the common merchant folk and puritan stock as may be expected, other moneyed families came from England, and most notably from the Channel Islands, to escape religious conformism and oppression in their mother country...divisions which were to bear bloody fruit during the witch craze of the late 1600s when the town turned upon its own and condemned many in their midst as worshippers of an 'ungodly sect'... Four were hanged after trial as witches, and diary evidence from noted sources in nearby Arkham at the time suggests that many more deaths may have occurred whose *details went unrecorded, perhaps deliberately, as they were carried out by mob 'justice' and blood feud… Rancor and discord indeed seems to carry on in the town until the Revolutionary War… sixteen dead in the burning of the church on Central Hill, provoking questions in Boston at the highest level about the role of the ill-rumored sea captain Abraham Carver and the town's 'Citizen's Watch' in the fatal fire which destroyed the building…in local magnate and town magistrate Eben Hall's actions in staunching outrage and investigation in the aftermath, the conduct of seizure of goods and in driving several old and renowned families from the region under pain of legal sanction and veiled threats of further 'accidents.'"*

This condensed passage was taken (if she decoded her own references correctly) from a history of the early colonies privately produced in an interminable number of volumes in the late 1870s—which she dimly remembered and which was long out of print; she had clearly felt the need to summarize its dealings with Kingsport, but why? As curious as it was, appended to it on the opposite page was a transcription of something older and far stranger, a copied fragment of something she guessed from its tone and timbre to perhaps have been evidence or a statement from a court record from the self-same witch trial named before.

"Ask you why I and my kind bide here? Fool, have we not the right as much as you? More I say, more and bequeathed by powers and principalities older and mightier than thy prating Nazarene and worthless Crown!

"Know thee not the ground upon which you stand? This place betwixt earth and sea, life and death, endless sky and blackest depths, dream and waking. Betwixt that which is of man and that which is more than man can ever be? Drawn I am, my kin, and drawn shall those likened to us ever be—here to the cusp of the abyss to gaze beyond this petty sphere and its empty laws. Here to whither titans walk with earthly gait, their hour come around…"

And below this: *"I.S. is condemned by his own testament to be hanged unto death for the crimes of malefic sorcery, for blasphemous utterances in the ears of this court, and for the calling forth from the dark earth and starless sky, gaunt wing-ed shades and other foul spirits to plague men's sleep, do them murder, and bear off their children most dreadfully."*

"'Gaunt wing-ed shades'…'drawn ever be,'" Daisy whispered as she tapped her fingernail across the page. That would be one way of putting it. It was more than pause for thought, but not something to which she could affix any firm answers.

"Then there's you," she sighed to herself.

Daisy gathered up the sheaf of papers leaving only one. On it, she had carefully copied a line of strange, complex-looking glyphs and symbols made up of curling lines and interlocking spade-like shapes, many only barely, fractionally different and yet so configured as to make the head almost swim looking at them. Daisy had copied them from the black glass shard Annabel had been concealing from her—concealed from everybody—at her lost lover's request. The symbols were a kind of writing, of that she was sure—not letters as such, she thought, but abstracts—representative symbols—and she hadn't a clue what they were or where they came from. She was no archaeologist by profession, but had widely read on the subject and knew more than enough to realize that they were certainly not something to be found commonly upon the walls of Egypt, Babylon, or even Yucatán, and felt a quick pang of desire for her fiancé Ted, who, as well as maybe pointing her in the right direction, would have made for a very handy and welcome shoulder to lean on.

No, she had enough trouble and danger here for her and Annabel without getting anybody else she cared about involved.

But still they nagged at her memory, as if she had seen them somewhere before, or something very like them.

With growing dread, she had scoured her own notebook for

mention of the glass fragments or examples of the writing itself, but had found no definite match. The only thing had been several pages toward the empty back section of the notebook where she had filled the space with other, cruder, but no less strange symbols, which matched the first only in their ability to make her eyes ache and her head swim if she spent too long looking at them. The meaning of these equally disconcerting and mysterious symbols was likewise opaque to her, and her memory refused to jar them loose, the only explanations being the seemingly nonsense words "Gharne F" and "Ak-klo" in the marginalia.

And for such as this, men go on the run, go missing, get killed? Annabel is tormented, and we are attacked...and by what?—say it—a monster.

It was all riddles, gibberish, and more questions unanswered, as if she was looking at a tiny part of a picture but was unable to make out the whole.

Daisy yawned, folded up the papers, and put them, along with the notebook, in her small leather book satchel, the bag already heavy with the antique revolver lying at the bottom wrapped in newspaper, its single un-fired chamber giving her more reassurance than she'd admit.

But she had to put such things from her mind, at least for the time being. Soon Annabel would be up and around again properly, and would want to be on the hunt for her man, her Maxwell Cormac, and what if they found him, what then? Daisy had also arranged for them to meet their former school roommate, Claudia Cabot, for dinner, an ordeal for which she would need all her wits about her.

Daisy had never really liked Claudia beyond a friendship born of close proximity and need, and from the few meetings they'd had since graduation, as cordial as they had been, she knew that Claudia had matured from a viper-ish, snobbish girl to a fully developed, viper-ish, snobbish society matron, widowed more than once already, though not even thirty. Claudia was, however, as she had never failed to make known, of "old Kingsport blood," and as a long-term resident of the town and a fixture of what passed for its "high society," she might be invaluable to Annabel's search.

Daisy wrapped the satchel's strap around her arm and let her eyelids fall a moment, listening to the sea wind brush the old window glass. She could perhaps go and check some things at the library of the Hall School—she should be welcome there still, as she had parted on good terms, and Eben Hall's collection was still there under lock and key—and then the town records…if…soon…

The winds whispered and Daisy slept.

* * *

Annabel was going stir-crazy in the hotel room where she'd been more-or-less confined for a day and a half—or at least that was how it felt. In truth she couldn't remember much of the proceeding day; it had passed by in a blue of dead and thankfully dreamless sleep punctuated by hazy wakefulness in which she had been as weak as a new-born kitten and unable to hold a string of thoughts together, but she felt the frustration of inaction all the same.

This morning had been a different matter, however, and despite feeling battered and bruised, Annabel nursed a nervous energy that wanted to find some release. She wanted to be *doing* something rather than sitting cooped up in bed with last month's *Life* magazine and listening to the wind tease the curtains and the mantle clock tick on with infuriating slowness. She was conscious of her promise to Daisy that she would rest, and a great part of her didn't want to let Daisy down; after all, Spook had proven herself to be the best friend Annabel could ever have hoped for over the last few days, and she'd saved her life in the bargain. As long as she lived, she would not forget the sight of her standing there like an avenging angel in the dark, the old cavalry pistol glinting in the light from the lantern—the nightmare thing wheeling blackly in the air above her, the icy, cloying touch of its spidery claws—*No!* Annabel rubbed her fingers around her temples and willed the image and the fear it brought with it from her mind. *I mustn't think about it. I have to find Max. All it means is that he was right; the danger was so very real all along, every strange word and unbelievable hint of powers and forces beyond natural laws, all of it—he wasn't mad and he wasn't lying. He loved me, he was trying to save me from it by keeping us apart, save me from the dark.* And that proof was to her worth all the horrors she had seen, the danger, all the fears she had nursed over the weeks past. *He loves me and I love him.*

Annabel threw back the satin comforter impetuously and drew up her bare leg to where she could see it better. The narrow, dark line, almost like a shadow, where the shard had been against her skin that last night, was still there, standing out against her smooth white skin. It wasn't at all like a bruise or a burn. It didn't hurt; in fact, when she put her fingers to it, it felt cool to the touch, but she had no sensation from it at all—she felt nothing, as if that part of her body were somehow…not there. She tried not to dwell on what it meant, whether it would always be like that, but instead she clung to the fact that she no longer had to lie to Daisy about it; her promises to Max to keep it close to her and secret from anyone else, and bring it to him when he called, were not voided by the fact she had broken her word willfully, but by fate that had spilled the damned thing out into the mud.

Daisy had it now. She'd hidden it somewhere and Annabel was glad—she didn't want to touch the thing again, the memory of the cold agony it had caused her worse in some ways than even the thought of the creature.

The two of them had talked the broken shard over and around and around, first frantically in the nervous exhaustion of their break-neck journey into the town after the attack—Daisy driving like the very devil was on their heels—and later the following night after Annabel's oblivion of sleep. Had the thing come for it or for her? Neither of them could be sure. Had the broken shard called the thing out of the dark, or attracted it somehow, like a moth to the flame? Had it been sent for them? Had it been the storm? There were no answers. Annabel nursed the belief—more hope for hope's sake, she realized—that the shard had worked some power which had grown ever greater the closer she had come to the rest of the fragments that made the thing whole, and that maybe it meant the closer she came to Max, as well.

He could be no more than minutes away… He's got to be here, I know it.

Annabel had never been a conventionally religious person, and while she felt a nebulous faith in the spiritual, particularly in her art, and held true that there were perhaps things beyond common conception of the world and what was in it (proof-positive of that she now had, and of the most dreadful kind), she could find no solace in prayer or the trappings of the Christianity she had been notionally brought up in—which had been cold comfort after the death of her dimly remembered parents—only in her own desire to make things right. Against strange horrors and strange fates, she knew she had only her faith in herself, faith in Daisy who had already done so much, and her faith in Max.

Annabel swung her legs out of the bed and winced as a twinge of pain shot up from a pulled muscle in the small of her back.

"Well," she said to the empty room, "I'm done sitting here like an invalid, anyway."

After all, she added mentally, *I did promise to stay in bed until I feel better, and aches and pains aside, I do feel better; I've certainly slept better away from that damned thing than I have in weeks.* She felt propelled by different forces all to the same end: she needed to be out and looking for Max, she needed to get out of the damn bedroom, and there was something else, too—a faint calling almost—from outside, from Kingsport, a place she hadn't seen in years, waiting beyond the door, whispering at the windows, the sea, and the sky.

Having resolved to go out, Annabel steeled herself, got up, washed, and then dressed slowly and methodically, carefully stretching her numbed muscles and easing her aching joints into action. She selected a dark burgundy wraparound dress, cinched with a wide belt, and opaque black stockings—which, she reflected, was about as inconspicuous as her wardrobe got. She hid the more visible bruises on her face (which thankfully had not been heavy) and a livid scratch on her neck with some fairly expert use of makeup and a grey velvet choker, respectively.

Considering herself more-or-less ready to face the world, Annabel opened the door to Daisy's adjoining room and wore her best smile, bracing herself for the argument about her getting up too soon, but found herself strangely disappointed that Daisy wasn't there. She glanced at the clock on the wall—it was a quarter to eleven, and there was a whole afternoon before they were due to dine early with Claudia at six. Looking around, she quickly spotted a brown paper-wrapped parcel at the foot of the bed, inside which she found a pair of perfectly ugly but entirely sensible walking shoes in her size, and a lady's black raincoat with a slightly inflated price tag still attached.

Bless you, Spook! she thought, marveling at just how frighteningly well-organized Daisy's brain was, even in a crisis. The bookish introvert she had spent her adolescent years with really had grown into a formidably minded woman, there was no mistaking that, and she wondered with a rueful smile if the unseen "Ted" knew what he was letting himself in for. In her experience, there were a great many men who didn't have enough strength to cope with a woman their equal, let alone better, and she hoped for Daisy's sake he was one of the pearls.

It looked like Daisy had been gone for some time, and had

probably felt as cooped up as she had. Annabel recalled her friend had talked about looking up some records at the Hall School, and had no real urge to join her there. Instead, she penned a quick note on the thin hotel stationary to the effect that she was going out to get a breath of air and to have a quick look around town, and would be back by mid-afternoon, signing off with an admission "not to worry."

A momentary doubt crossed her mind about what she was doing, but it was swept quickly away by her desire to be free of the oppression of her room's four walls and the urge to be out looking, however vaguely, for Maxwell on Kingsport's streets. The decision to leave the hotel alone was arrived at in a moment and with only a faint pang of fear. The thought of taking some weapon crossed her mind, but she dismissed that as absurd; she had no weapon and had never stabbed or shot anybody in her life, and hadn't the first idea about how to go about it. She resolved to stay to the main streets, where there were people, and if she encountered anything dangerous or untoward, she would run—and that was all there was to it.

Annabel slipped out of the room quietly and made it all the way to the reception lobby without being observed once, a fact made considerably easier by the fact that it was off-season and less than a third of the hotel seemed to be occupied, and even the staff seemed thin on the ground. At the foot of the wide spiral staircase, she paused, self-consciously furtive, and observed that a flabby, vacant-looking man in a grey porter's coat was at the front desk, his attention focused on something he was reading under the counter. She wasn't quite sure why she felt the need to leave unobserved, but was thankful it wasn't the pompous manager out front—he would at least have tried to ply her with questions. Instead she strode out purposely through the great mahogany and colored glass-paneled revolving door that fronted the Victorian building without so much as a look back and heard no calls from behind her.

The sea air flooded her lungs and tasted salty and clean, and Annabel felt immediately vindicated in stepping out. The day was one of shifting skies and hurrying clouds, overcast one minute and bright the next, and with an equally restless wind that seemed directionless and searching. As Annabel began her walk, old memories of the town's layout fitted into place like a comfortably worn glove, and she found herself almost skipping down the paved sidewalk to where it met the cobbled harborside square. Feeling better than she had in weeks, she walked along the sea wall, letting the gathering wind buffet her back and push her on as it willed. The sounds of the gulls' cries and the distant rough talk of the fishermen down on the shingles below heralded memories of the past that came and went like phantoms. The sight of the looming colossus of Kingsport Head reared up before her like a titan in a dream.

She blinked. Her lips were numb, and she found she was standing looking out to sea. She had come all the way up to the edge of the path up the rock, a quarter of an hour's walk if it was a minute, but she didn't remember any of it, nor did she remember how long she had been standing there, looking out to sea, she realized with a start. Her legs were stiff and she stamped her feet to be rid of the cold, and was immediately rewarded by a twinge of pain from her wrenched back.

"Ow," she muttered softly.

The North Point Lighthouse seemed to shimmer and flicker in the distance like a mirage, and for a moment it was as if she could (quite impossibly at this distance) see a lone dark figure waver there beside it, as if walking along the waves. She shuddered, and not entirely from the cold.

"Best go now, missy," a gravelly voice spoke from behind her.

She turned, surprising herself by not being startled, to see the old man with his straight back, wild eyes, and thick grey mane of hair and beard. He was just as she remembered him: the same twisted walking stick, and the same wing-shouldered Yankee trader greatcoat like something out of Melville.

"Oh," Annabel said, smiling in recognition, "it's you. I don't suppose you remember me; I used to go to school here?"

She remembered him; he was a legend in the town, and the source of a dozen and more late night ghost tales of sunken pirate ships and murder on the high seas in the dormitories of the Hall School. "The terrible old man" they called him; it was a name the girls had not made up themselves, but instead something they had taken from the local-born staff of the kitchens and the cleaners, who had more than enough tales of their own centered on him. She hadn't thought about him in years, and here he was, just as she remembered seeing him about the town, haunting the dockside, just as he did now, no doubt just some old sailor who'd outlived his shipmates and to whom stories attached themselves for his grim manner and solitary ways.

"Aye," he said, his hard flinty eyes fixing on her, "I remember you. Come Halloween, the others wouldn't dare so much as cross my gate, but you'd go up to the door and knock afore running." He grunted with what might have been a chuckle.

"Well, I'll be!" Annabel remembered with a sudden flash. She couldn't have been more than fifteen; she had quite forgotten pushing the old iron gate open, picking her way up the overgrown path, her breath catching as she looked around the wild garden and its strange painted stones with trepidation, before rapping on the door and fleeing again to where the other girls cowered behind the wall. She had forgotten it completely. "However did you remember—"

"Best be going now," his grim voice spoke over hers, silencing her. "There's brave and then there's foolish, missy, remember that, so you best be on your way."

Annabel felt a frisson of fear on hearing the old man's words, not quite directed at him, but at suddenly being so exposed here on the edge of the town, where Kingsport's cobblestones met bare rock and dark sea.

She shook her hair and said goodbye nervously, and the old man bowed his head in a curiously formal manner as she turned and hurried, refusing to let herself run, back along the sea wall and into the town. As soon as she had got back within earshot of the bustle of work on the beach and in sight of a handful of folk moving about on their own business in the harborside square, she felt safer again, and paused. Turning, she looked back for the old man where she had left him, but he was not there.

But there was another figure, further off, vague and indistinct—had he walked on in the opposite direction, up the path into the rocky heights? *No, no, it's not him, it's somebody else.* The figure was tall, thin, somehow ragged and hazy. She turned away.

Determined not to let the old man and her own memories spoil her sense of purpose, she gathered herself up and set off at a brisk pace southward along the curve of the bay, making for the web of small stores, cafés, galleries, and small tourist-oriented guesthouses and cottages that dotted the less "working" reach of the bay. It was far from "carefree" and "gently bustling," as her memories of high summer here recalled it, and many of the smaller establishments were closed for the oncoming winter, but there were enough people around to make the town feel anything but desolate, and while most she passed seemed intent on hurrying about and keeping to themselves, some offered her nods of acknowledgement, a few gents raised their hats as she passed by, and one or two rougher types looked at her wolfishly in a manner which, if not exactly welcome, at least seemed part of a normal and familiar world.

After a few more minutes, she moved inland, coming to what was commonly known (perhaps a little pretentiously) as Kingsport's Artists' Colony: a crisscross of narrow streets and courtyards that had been more or less taken over by a small but thriving bohemian set of artists, poets, and aesthetes whose number waxed and waned with the season, living off the summer tourists as patrons and as tourists themselves to the locals. Filled primarily with harmless castoffs from New England colleges and vaguely wayward scions of "good families" drawn to Kingsport for its vistas and its artistically "conducive" atmosphere.

In her latter, rebellious days at the Hall School, this tangle of streets had seemed the height of sophistication and decadence, and was the destination for several truanting jaunts and evenings out of bounds. Later spells in Paris and London had shown her just what decadent had really meant, not that the naïve eyes of her latter school years had known the difference back then. She'd never gotten into any real trouble here, and had nothing but bittersweet and fond memories of the place, despite her own attempts at art, spurred by what she had seen, being quickly suppressed by the school, and the resulting curfew and opprobrium she'd had to endure. She had been distraught at the time, as tame as it all now seemed, and walking here brought it all back.

She had an inkling that if Max was hiding in Kingsport, then it would be here, where strangers bore little cause for comment unless they deliberately made waves, particularly if they seemed a little fey or blue-blooded, and Max fitted the second category if not the first.

She café hopped and breezed a circuit through what small galleries remained open this late in the season for the next few hours, but could not have related a word about the work she saw, or at least appeared to look at; instead she studied faces, passersby, even photographic studies in search of him and, warily she admitted, other, less welcome individuals she might recognize, but no one she knew. More than once she caught herself looking for tall, thin, and fearful shadows at the edge of sight, but fortunately, those too were absent. She also listened, and where it seemed appropri-

ate, made small talk with strangers although her heart was hardly
in it. The locals were tight-lipped, but the artists and bohemians
were in a mood to talk, and what she heard (or rather overheard
in most cases) filled her with a slowly mounting dread. Kingsport
feared, and when it slept, its dreams were troubled.

There had been disappearances, unaccounted absences, flaring
tempers, and gathering ire, and the storms had come and gone
again without rhyme or reason. An unknown body had washed
up in the bay, its face mutilated beyond recognition—the sheriff
named it an accident, a sailor lost overboard on some passing
ship and carried into the harbor, but the town's old salts scoffed
openly at that, and even the moneyed families behind their high
old walls on Central Hill didn't believe a word of it. The body,
however, had not been the first strange event or the last, and the
artists talked of one of their own number driven to suicide by
what he could not capture on canvas, and another carried away
the previous morning by the ambulance for Arkham, trapped in
an opium fever from which he could not break free.

There were other, stranger tales of dead birds covering the
sands of Marten's Beach a little ways up the coast, and of strange
fires lit high up on Kingsport Head in the small hours, but these
stories were more stilted that the others, as if speaking of them
out loud, however vaguely, might bring some ill-fortune down
on the teller. Annabel, it seemed, had not escaped or outrun the
darkness that she had fled first New York, and then Arkham,
to avoid, despite the relative peace of her stay at the hotel—the
shadow had been here waiting for them all along, and she feared
now more than ever for Maxwell, and dread about what might
have happened to him dug into her heart.

Torn now between keeping up her so far fruitless search for
Maxwell and the urgency of telling Daisy of what she had learned,
she set out again, working further into the town to the inner,
landward edge of the Artists' Colony, to where the oldest tene-

ments of the town grew up against the hillside. Worse even than the old sections near the sea dock, these were tangled warrens and narrow alleyways of old colonial housing left behind by progress and cut off from the prosperity of the upper part of Central Hill by the trolley car line like a castle moat. Here the electric lights were few, and she knew from one dimly remembered experience of her youth, when the mist came up and night fell, it was like stepping into the dark age of another, fearful world.

At the edge of the shadowy district, and acutely aware that it was well past four, she stalled, uncertain whether to carry on or retreat to the hotel and whatever haranguing she was due from Daisy, when her eyes suddenly caught the figures of two men talking to each other in the distance on one of the narrow alleyways that snaked almost vertically up the hill. They were both of good height and build, and wearing ragged and dirty outdoor clothes; both were disheveled, but young, and both looked somehow familiar—

It's him!

Her heart caught in her throat: one of them was Max! The realization thundered into her brain like a derailing train. He looked like hell: gaunt, sick, and pale, his always immaculate hair long and disheveled, with unaccustomed stubble darkening his hollowed cheeks, but it was him!

She started running blindly forward, almost stumbling, and shouting his name over and over again, but the men did not see her—they turned and walked on briskly, and were out of sight in seconds around the twist of the alleyway. Annabel ran on, soon panting for breath, tired out from her exertions of the day, with all her aches and pains returning to her with a vengeance, but still determined, she pressed ahead until confronted by a junction where she was sure there shouldn't be one. Confused and desperate at the sight of her lover, only to be denied him again, she picked the turning that seemed to lead most directly upward to where she believed she had seen him and the other man, and after being confronted by a dead end that terminated in a sagging, boarded up house, turned again, and almost screamed out her frustration. An old woman in a shawl gazed at her from a doorway as if she was an alien form of life, but as Annabel started to ask her if she had seen the men, she darted back inside and slammed the door fast, and Annabel heard the sound of bolts being shot fast.

"Great, that's just great!" she muttered and bent forward, putting her hands on her hips while she caught her breath again.

She heard erratic footsteps on the cobblestone behind her, slipping and scuffing in their hurry, getting closer. She was suddenly acutely aware that she had done just what she had promised herself not to do: strayed from the people and the beaten path, not just once but twice. *"There's brave and then there's foolish,"* the old man had said, and she had a sudden, deathly sinking feeling he was about to be proven right. She looked around herself; what few doors she could see were shut tight, the windows shuttered or boarded over. There were a few narrow stairwells down to basement level rooms in some of the tightly packed buildings, but if she went down one of those it would be a bad gamble, because if her hiding place was discovered there would be no way out.

Run then. She breathed deep and steadied her aching body to do just that when, from the alleyway up ahead, a young man in a ragged overcoat and a shapeless brown sweater walked into view. Her heart leapt and crashed in almost the same moment—it was not Max—but she was suddenly sure it was the man he had been talking to.

The young man saw her, his jaw dropping in shock; quickly recovering, he raised up his dirt-stained hands in a gesture of peace. "It's you!" he breathed in seeming awe. "You must…you must come with me!" he said, edging forward.

Instinctively, Annabel took a step backward. He was somehow

familiar, a face known, but naggingly forgotten, and the strange luminosity of his yellowing eyes alarmed her; they gleamed as round as saucers, the pupils no more than black pinpricks.

"Who are you?" she demanded, sounding a good deal more in control than she felt. Behind her, the scuffling footsteps had stopped, but she dared not turn away from the feverish-looking man. *I'm trapped!*

The man's mouth moved unevenly, and Annabel winced as he slavered suddenly, foamy spittle running down his mouth in a torrent as he struggled to talk. "Please, please come, pleeesssse," he whined as he slowly advanced on her, his fingers starting to jerk spasmodically toward her, imploring almost, pawing at the air.

"Where's Max? What have you done to him?" she heard herself shout.

"Joo-ooy and rapture," the feverish man moaned and lunged at her.

She was ready for him, and his grasping hands found nothing but air as she ducked lithely to one side, ignoring the ache that shot up her back. As he partly overbalanced, his arms flailing, she seized her moment and turned to run downhill, but was immediately checked by the presence of another man hurtling toward her. She got a flashing impression of a dark overcoat flapping and a square fist hurtling toward her, and let out an involuntary shriek, but the fist sailed by and slammed into the cheek of her first attacker. The feverish man fell and his grabbing hands, claw-like, dragged the newcomer down on top of him, while Annabel's shoe turned and skidded on the cobbles, the air rushing out of her lungs as she landed on her back. All three were down.

The newcomer was up first, his booted foot smashing into her attacker's jaw with an audible crack, spinning the ragged man across the cobbles, where he shuddered and lay still.

She was still struggling to her feet when the man's grip tightened like an iron cuff around her upper arm.

"Come on!" he growled. "There's always more of them."

She was jerked unceremoniously to her feet, and suddenly they were running again, pell-mell down the hill. He skidded from time to time, and he swore, but his grip on her arm never wavered, and she was dragged along as much as ran with him. Breathless minutes later, they had reached the trolley car tracks and were out of the warrens, and he swung her into a yard behind a laundry, white sheets flapping on the lines and the smell of lye soap pungent in the air.

"Sit down," he said, and pushed her, not un-gently, onto a packing crate where she gratefully sat for a moment panting. He had an accent, she realized—*English?*

"Thanks, I think?" she managed to say after a few gasping breaths.

She looked up and studied her rescuer—he was a big man, broad shouldered and solidly built, hardly out of breath it seemed, with an angular, thoughtful face that betrayed little, and searching, cold eyes. In a midnight blue suit and black tie with a white, wing-collar shirt, he certainly didn't look like the ragged man who'd attacked her, but he might well be one of Laski's killers she realized with a shock. He put one hand to his knee and grimaced, while glancing at the yard entrance from which they had come.

Annabel looked at him, and calculated the distance to the street. *If his leg's hurt, maybe I can outrun him?*

"I'd rather you didn't, Miss Ryan. I've come a long way to find you, and I've done quite enough running today," he said as if he had read her mind.

She looked back at him and blinked in shock at the black automatic pistol held casually in his hand. It was not exactly pointing at her, but the message was clear. She had seen one like it before, *German,* the thought floated unbidden into her mind.

"You seem to have me at a disadvantage," she sighed.

"Well," he said with a flicker of a genuine smile, "that makes a change, at least. My name is Morgan, and I believe you have something I want."

CHAPTER TEN

Anxious fear and vexed temper were warring for control of Daisy's mind. It was nearly five o'clock, and still Annabel hadn't returned. Mostly, she blamed herself for dozing off downstairs, but the rational part of her mind said that had been more or less inevitable given how exhausted she'd been, and there was no cause yet to definitely worry. Annabel's note had said she would be "back in time for dinner" and that time hadn't yet elapsed.

It's so like her, Daisy thought angrily, *running off whenever the spirit moves her. She was always the same, couldn't sit still, no thought for anybody else as long as there was something more interesting to do elsewhere!*

Daisy sighed and checked herself, she was being unfair; she was deep down afraid for what might happen, even in a town in broad daylight, when anything "wrong" that had happened to them so far seemed centered on the night, at least to a great degree. *Daylight,* a cruel corner of her mind quickly pointed out, *that wouldn't last long even if you weren't clutching at straws and seeing a pattern where there is only circumstance.*

She had refused to wait; after a few hours fretting over her missing friend she'd left a strongly worded note of her own, and gone out herself, half-hoping to bump into Annabel on the street. She'd been to the garage to pick up the repaired (at least to the stage where it was road-worthy again) motorcar, which brought more than a twinge of guilt at what Ted was going to say when he saw it. Then, to the library of the Hall School, where she had been cordially greeted by the friendly, if somewhat distracted, staff, many of whom were old colleagues. She had returned a little after four, and here she was, fretting again, and still no Annabel.

She didn't want to think about what had happened or what she would do if Annabel did not return and was silently regretting how she had dealt with the town sheriff who she might very-well soon need.

There was a voice in the hall—*Annabel!*

The door opened and Daisy got to her feet, the barbed comment she had chosen dying in her mouth as her friend was pushed into the room ahead of a tall, powerful-looking man in an overcoat and a fedora.

Annabel looked sheepish, if anything, and Daisy blinked as Annabel mouthed a silent "Sorry!" as she stepped inside and the man shut the hotel room door behind him.

Daisy gathered herself up to her full height and set her shoulders. "Who are you, and what are you doing here?" she exclaimed in a tone that brooked little refusal.

The man seemed momentarily taken aback by the authority in her voice, and then smiled, saying, "Listen, sister, I don't know you from Eve, but you need to keep your voice down and do just as I say, and we can avoid any unpleasantness. Now please, remain still and don't do anything stupid, the both of you."

Daisy bridled at the man's order, but there was a dark edge to that voice that said he meant every word, and a wary, barely restrained violence to the man that somehow put Daisy in mind of a tiger she'd once seen sitting perfectly still in a cage in the Boston Zoo—still, but one hair's breadth from murder if only the steel bars hadn't been between him and the sluggish meat outside the cage, and there was no cage between her and this particular animal.

"He's got a gun, Daisy," Annabel whispered in a soft, desperate voice as she came to stand beside her.

To Daisy, the comment seemed oddly superfluous.

"He's come here after me, after Maxwell," Annabel continued.

Daisy nodded, her eyes never leaving the man who stood, seemingly relaxed, his hands by his sides in front of the door. There was no sign of a gun, but she had no doubt it was in easy reach.

"More to the point, I want what Cormac stole," Morgan said flatly.

"We don't have it," Daisy replied coolly.

"That's what she said; she lied. So are you, although I admit you're making a better job of it."

Beside her, Annabel let out a snort of indignation. "And he searched me very thoroughly too," she muttered, looking daggers at the man.

"You didn't have it on you—that you weren't lying about, but that doesn't answer my question: where is it? You don't want me to ask again."

Daisy took a deep breath and let it out before saying, "We don't have all of it, only a small piece. Maxwell Cormac has the rest, but we don't know where he is."

"Daisy!" Annabel cried out in alarm.

"Do you have it here?" There was no triumph in the man's accented voice, Daisy noticed, only something like resignation.

"Yes," she said, her throat suddenly dry. She knew what she was about to do was a terrible risk, but what other choice was there? "I have it here," she said and turned toward her book satchel on the dressing table by the window.

"Don't!" she heard him say, but even though Daisy felt that her stomach had turned to acid and her heart was pounding like a hammer, the die had been cast and she kept moving, gripping the satchel with one hand and ripping the straps open with the other. She felt rather than saw him moving across the room with frightening speed as she grasped the heavy pistol in her hand and turned, yanking it free, her thumb struggling to work the hammer. The man was almost on top of her—a dark moving mass. She pulled the trigger, there was a sharp *clack* and…nothing happened, no thunder, no shot.

Misfire! she thought with sudden, sharp clarity. *The rain!* She cried out and fell back against the dresser, her wrist burning in pain as if her hand had been torn off, the heavy pistol falling to the floor with a thud.

Daisy reeled and looked down; her hand was still there, it just ached like all hell from where the man had viciously twisted the gun from her hand. She gritted her teeth, panic fought with anger, and anger won—she wasn't beaten; with her left hand she grabbed a pair of scissors from the dressing table and she turned around, prepared to go down fighting, not just for her own life, but Annabel's as well. The scene that confronted her could have even been comical, if her friend wasn't moments from death.

Annabel stood frozen like a still life, a table lamp raised up in her hands to strike, the torn electrical wire still swinging, an inch from her forehead, the black barrel of a skeletal pistol. In the man's other hand was her grandfather's cavalry revolver, held by the heavy barrel like a club.

"Sit down!" Morgan growled at Annabel.

With a grimace, she did what she was told, letting the lamp slump to the bed beside her. "Can't blame a girl for trying," she replied with barely concealed scorn.

He turned the gun on Daisy.

"Put that down," he ordered coldly.

"No," she whispered. It was as if she was looking at herself—at him at the end of a long tunnel—and she could hear the beating of her own heart far louder than any words that were said.

"Daisy!" she distantly was aware of Annabel saying.

"Damn it all, don't make me kill you."

She just shook her head slowly from side to side, vaguely feeling her hair swish against her cheeks where it had come undone.

The moment stretched forever.

Morgan sighed, and seemed to deflate. As the two women looked on with shock, he gently tossed the old revolver on the bed beside Annabel, who looked at it as if it was a poisonous spider, ejected the chambered round from the automatic and put the pistol back in his shoulder holster, swearing violently.

Despite herself, Daisy blushed as Morgan righted a ladder-backed chair that had been knocked over in the struggle and sank down with the air of an exhausted man at the end of his strength.

"Who the hell am I kidding," he said at last, running both hands through his hair, dislodging his fedora. "Damn wildcats, the pair of you. You'd have made me do it, as well, damn you."

As her heart slowed down, Daisy realized she wasn't about to die and came shakily back to her senses. Her knees felt like water and she had a sudden urge to visit the bathroom, but instead she forced herself to sit down on the padded dressing table stool and open the hand she'd blanched white with the death grip she'd had on the scissors.

"Wasn't lying," Daisy said weakly.

"No, no you weren't," Morgan conceded. "Look, let's try this a different way—truce."

"Oh and how does that work, you kill us later? Kill Max?" Annabel demanded angrily.

"I'm not…," he began, caught himself and sighed, "I'm not an assassin, understand. If I were, your blond friend here would be very much dead now, all right? No, no, that's not a threat, that's not what I mean...ah—"

Annabel cut in, "I don't know you; I'm sure I've never seen you before, so how do you know me?" Since the start of the conversation, her eyes hadn't left Morgan for an instant.

Morgan turned to her and gave her an appraising look. "No, we've never met before today—I've been too many steps behind you since you left New York—but I've been tracking you down to get ahold of your beau, Cormac; I assume that's what he is?"

Annabel nodded.

"And you, where do you fit in all this?" he asked, looking at Daisy.

"I'm Daisy Walker. I'm not 'that blond' or 'sister'—Miss Walker will do fine from you," she said as calmly as she could manage.

He smiled again. "A fair point. My name's Morgan, Tony Morgan."

"And what are you, Mr. Morgan, if not an assassin?" Daisy responded.

"Well, that's kind of complicated in some ways, but I imagine 'bounty hunter' is as good a title as any. I hunt people down— but not to kill them, not as a rule," he qualified. "I got tangled up in this mess back in New York. Let's just say I got in trouble and got my marker bought out by the people Maxwell Cormac stole from, and they seemed to think I should be the one to play bloodhound for them.

"What, may I ask, do *you* do, Miss Walker, and how did you get involved?" he added with a slightly exaggerated civility to match Daisy's.

Daisy was taken aback a little by the question. "Why, I'm a librarian, at a university," she replied as if that was perfectly obvious. "I'm Annabel's friend; she came to me for help, and so I'm here."

Morgan's smile widened. "And here's me betting on Amazon warrior complete with Civil War-era hand cannon—a librarian? Well, I don't bet you get many late returns."

Daisy forced the shadow of a smile from her own lips, and said, "Well, now we've been properly introduced, let's get down to business—you said 'truce,' and that's fine, I don't want to hurt anybody or for anybody to get hurt. Now, just what are you about, Mr. Morgan?"

"First," he said, "level with me: do you know where Maxwell Cormac is? Are you two hiding him?"

"No, we don't know where he is, I…I mean we are looking for him ourselves; as to hiding him, I only wish it was so," Annabel said emphatically. Morgan looked at Daisy, who confirmed this with a shake of her head.

"But you expected to find him here, right, in Kingsport?"

"Yes—at least I'd hoped to," Annabel began in a careful voice. "We had arranged to meet here once…once he knew how to get rid of the *thing* properly… Look, I know this sounds crazy, and I don't really understand it myself, but he said you couldn't just smash it or anything normal like that. Certain 'conditions,' he called them, had to be met, or that would have made an even worse mess, or at least that's what he said. But it was too danger-ous for him to carry the whole thing around together, he said, and so he gave me a piece of it, the smallest bit, to keep safe for him.

"I know it sounds like something conjured up by an opium pipe or a lunatic in a cell, but I believe him, now more than ever, I…we, we've had the evidence of our own experiences to know something's terribly wrong with the fragment of the thing he gave me. Something unnatural, something powerful in a way I just don't understand, and I don't want to understand.

"There's been a shadow hanging over me, stalking me, some-thing terrible out of the corner of my eye, ever since I've had the fragment of…of whatever it really is… It's gotten inside my head and I've seen things in my nightmares you couldn't imagine: monstrous, horrific things, the world eaten away by invisible fires, people torn—," Annabel choked on sudden emotion and put her hand to her mouth a moment before recovering from her brief loss of composure, and came back more forcefully than ever. "You asked us to level with you, Mr. Morgan, very well, here you are: I want Max back. I want him alive and well and the rest can go back to the hell it came from; so you can have the fragment or whatever it is, have the whole damn thing for all I care, as long as giving it to you gets Max back for me!"

"Agreed," Morgan said without hesitation. "If Copperhead wanted a murder done, they hired the wrong man; they want their artifact, and that's what I'll give them, and if Cormac gets found and gives it up, I'll have no further beef with him. That's as much as I can promise. Help me, and I'll help you: simple."

Annabel looked at Daisy for reassurance, and she nodded her agreement. The danger around them was very real and closing in; they would be fools not to take Morgan's help, and perhaps protection, if he was on the level, and really, what choice did they have?

Annabel started her story, the words coming out in a rush, and as he listened, Daisy watched Morgan. His face betrayed little, but she could nevertheless tell he was absorbing every word of what he was being told, slotting pieces together in place, aligning clues into some pattern he had up till now only had part of, and guessed silently that she had uncovered more strange dimensions to the matter than even he imagined, but that could wait. For now, she was content to watch and listen as Annabel went on to explain her own involvement with Maxwell Cormac.

Prompted by Morgan's clipped, but apposite questions, Annabel explained what Max had told her about the organization he had found himself working for, his involvement with it and the occult, what he'd felt compelled to carry out to prevent some looming catastrophe in the future, and went on to detail his desperate attempt to cover his tracks and flee unnoticed from New York. She noticed grimly that even when Annabel's story strayed into regions that most would have considered fantastical or mere hysteria (even though she kept details about their attack on the road to a bare minimum), Morgan took these revelations as calmly as he might have hearing about a change of weather, which in itself spoke volumes about the scope of what they faced.

Much of Annabel's account was familiar to her, but hearing it again end-to-end, as before, she got the sense that it was not the whole story. Annabel had withheld the truth from her once; was she doing it again? Or was it merely that Annabel's love was blinding her to something darker about her missing lover? Reading between the lines of Morgan's questioning, that was what Morgan seemed to suspect...

"So you're saying that the man who attacked me in the alleyway today and that awful preacher have nothing to do with this Copperhead organization?" Annabel asked Morgan.

"No, far from it; I'm not saying Copperhead isn't involved, but as far as I know, I'm their only man in the firing line. They are powerful, they have money, and a hell of a lot of political clout, and I don't doubt they are more than capable of as much mayhem and murder as you might wish for, but this isn't their turf, and they're loathe to step on it directly as far as I can tell. Something about this part of the world they want nothing to do with, at least not directly. If I didn't know better, I'd say they're scared of the place."

"But who are they? Lask—"

"Milo Laski's dead," Morgan interrupted her flatly. "As far as I can make out, your man Cormac made some kind of deal with him, used his connections as a bootlegger to get on a boat back to New York with his stolen goods. Once that fact was found out, it was enough to make him and anybody that worked for him marked for death."

"Who by? I don't understand, I was sure his men were tailing me, that he was mixed up in Maxwell's disappearance somehow…," Annabel said in shock.

"I think they *were* tailing you—somebody got to Laski before I could at the finish, so I don't know for sure—but if you were to ask me for a hypothesis, then I'd say Laski saw hell coming down on him and realized Cormac was the only thing that could save him, maybe, and was using you as bait to find him, until you skipped town and he ran all out of options."

Annabel lapsed into silence and it was left for Daisy to ask for an explanation. "What happened to him, in New York, after Annabel ran away?"

"Someone started taking apart Laski's organization bit by bit; his crew suddenly starts turning up missing or dead, but it doesn't go down like another mob staging a gang war—more like a nasty little boy tearing the wings off a helpless fly. This goes on until there's just Laski and his inner circle left going crazy and shooting at shadows. Lucky me, I manage to walk into the middle of this mess, asking the wrong questions, at the wrong time." Morgan let his story peter out, as if distracted by some unpleasant memory.

"Go on," Daisy prompted.

"I nearly paid for my blundering about with my life," he replied coolly. "I got a bit busted up and I ended up taking a few night's rest in a private hospital, courtesy of my so-called employer, and missed the final act of our mobster Laski's sordid career—you remember the Falling Angel?" he threw the question to Annabel, who seemed lost in thought herself, and she nodded in reply. "Well, it really did—fall, I mean." Morgan continued, "The whole building somehow collapsed with Laski and three other men inside. Two of them were unknown, though one was older than the other; the known one was a corrupt cop named Burke Haskell." Annabel blinked hard. "So you'd heard of him, as well?"

"By reputation mainly," she replied, "but I know that he was one of the men who had been tailing me in the city before I left."

"Well, there's one more face you don't have to worry about seeing in a crowd anymore. They were all crushed near beyond recognition: they IDed Laski from his jewelry and Haskell from his badge number."

They lapsed into quiet for a time, and it was Annabel who spoke first. "How did you make it up here so fast?" she asked, piecing together a timeline in her head from the events they had spoken of.

"Oh, Shawcross—he's the man in charge of Copperhead at their business office in Manhattan—he doesn't spare any expense, I'll give him that. No sooner had they bandaged me up, stuck some needles in my arm, and transfused me with a pint of blood or so, they pushed me out of the door and onto a private plane to an airdrome north of Boston somewhere, and a waiting car hell-for-leathers me here and dumps me off to fend for myself," Morgan said ruefully.

"Lucky you," Annabel retorted. "You should have been on the road with us."

"Clearly, you believe someone is directly responsible for this man Laski's death," Daisy said pointedly, changing the subject, "but if not Copperhead as you claim, then who? What has this strange preacher and these tramps or maniacs or whatever they are you have both spoken about, what have they to do with things?"

As if in reply, Morgan got up and handed her a folded piece of paper. On opening it, Daisy read the name of the Legion of Rapture and studied the strange not-quite-cross, not-quite-sun-burst symbol that dominated the thin scrap of paper in alarmed recognition.

"They're some kind of nomadic mission or church, or at least that's what they appear to be, anyway, but no legitimate church or charity—Christian or otherwise—will have anything to do with them, and with good reason.

"I have it on good authority that you'll find advertisements like that in scores of towns and cities along the east coast, from New York to Bangor, and plenty of out-of-the-way stops in between. They 'tend'—if it can be called that—to a flock drawn from the homeless and the hopeless—people with nothing to lose—and peddle them a line in the glory hereafter and heaven on earth, after the End Times have come, of course. But if you start to look into that, it gets considerably more sinister.

"It seems nobody knows just how many of them there are, or where exactly they are based. But they've been linked to sudden violence and bouts of lunacy and homicidal madness among those that have attended their services. Piecing things together, it seems they show up from nowhere, blow into town, and set up their 'mission' in the worst slums and ghettos. Sometimes they take over a disused church or a flophouse. They choose places where a hot meal and a hand to help are most needed, and, if you ask me, places where their victims are least likely to be missed. Sooner or later, before the law pays too much attention to the dead, the mad, and the vanished, they blow away again on the wind, and find themselves a new town, and more desperate souls eager for their poisoned snake oil—whatever it really is."

"'Beware you of false prophets,'" Daisy quoted quietly, "'for they shall come unto you in the raiment of sheep, but they shall be in truth as ravening wolves.'"

"Very succinctly put," Morgan said, considering her thoughtfully.

"My father's take on the Sermon on the Mount, one of his favorite lessons; he was a minister, and it seemed an apt quotation. But where do they fit into all this—this 'cult' or 'mission' or whatever they are?"

"I met their leader—or one of them at any rate—called himself the Reverend Eli Marks. He claimed Maxwell Cormac as one of his flock, and wanted very much to know why I wanted to find him. That and if I'd seen a 'bandaged man,' but I don't know if they were one in the same or if he was speaking of someone else on Cormac's trail. That, in all honesty, was the part where I nearly lost my life and things got more than a little crazy.

"And not to frighten you ladies unduly, but they are here, now, in Kingsport. That advertisement I found stuck to the wall of the Rope and Anchor down by the waterfront, and I came across its duplicate in New York myself. On top of that—this town's afraid."

"Yes," Annabel ventured, still half lost in thought. "I found that much out this afternoon; dreams and madness, just like you said, and that man who attacked me, was he one of them—he seemed to know me?"

"I think that's likely. I saw you in the Artists' quarter, and tailed you from there."

"I didn't see you!" Annabel replied hurriedly.

Morgan shrugged. "I've managed to stay alive this long in my trade for a reason, Miss Ryan. Anyway, when I saw you start kicking up a storm and shouting Cormac's name at the top of your voice, it seemed the right thing to break cover and chase after you when you ran," he said wryly, "and I think, on reflection, it was a good thing I did."

"You think they baited me on purpose, got me to run up into that warren of alleyways so they could grab me?"

Morgan nodded. "To play on *Miss* Walker's wolf analogy, that's what predator's do: separate their prey from the pack before gobbling them up."

"But it was Max, I'm sure of it, somehow…it didn't just look like him, it *was* him," Annabel said, pulling herself up to her full height and glaring directly at each of them in turn as if daring either one to contradict her. "Oh, I know desperation can make you see things, but I'm not some hysterical girl, and I know what I saw—it was him, and I'd stake my life on it again. You're thinking perhaps he's one of them, or perhaps he's been drugged or mesmerized or something, but I don't care. I want him away from those awful people and back with me, no matter what."

"I believe you, Annabel," Daisy said.

After a thoughtful pause, Morgan also replied, "So do I, for whatever that's worth. But what that actually means, what it implies, that's something else."

Morgan was about to continue when there was a knock on the hotel room door, and in an instant, he was on his feet by the door with his pistol in his hand.

"You're not taking any chances are you?" Daisy whispered to him and calmly went to open the door. It was one of the porters inquiring if they needed any additional places set for dinner. Daisy demurred and turned back into the room with a start and checked her watch; it was already twenty-to-six.

Daisy hurriedly explained their dinner engagement, and Morgan agreed it should be kept. The interval would give him the time to recover his things from the Rope and Anchor where he'd been staying, and check into the hotel, as well, and they hurriedly arranged a meeting after dinner in the hotel lounge to further compare notes and plan what they should do next to find Maxwell Cormac and the rest of the artifact. In this rushed and perfunctory manner, they sealed their alliance, the tacit understanding between them that Annabel and Daisy wanted only to find Annabel's missing love, and Morgan, satisfied with the artifact, would depart without trouble. That left a whole lot still unsaid, and although Daisy was still uneasy in her mind, she conceded it would have to do for now, and was the best course of action for them, particularly in the light of her own unspoken desire: that she uncover the truth of what she now suspected about the world and about her own past, no matter how dreadful that revelation proved to be.

Just as he was leaving, Morgan turned and asked, "One last thing, the fragment, where is it?"

Annabel looked at Daisy questioningly, as well.

Daisy felt suddenly uncomfortable at the center of their attention. "It's hidden as safe as I can manage," she answered flatly.

"You don't trust me, do you?" Morgan asked not unkindly with a flicker of a smile crossing his face.

"I'm sorry, no, not fully," she replied, unable to meet his eyes.

"I don't blame you," he said, "I just wish we knew what the damn thing really was."

"Oh," Daisy said, looking up at him with a surprised expression, "I didn't say did I? I was checking certain texts at the Hall School library this afternoon: it's a calendar, or at least part of one, a very old astrological calendar—I'm mostly sure of that now. It tells you when the stars are right."

* * *

Night had come swiftly to Kingsport, the sky had grown overcast in twilight, and the wind had fallen away as softly as a dying breath. With the darkening of the day, the mists had come up again from the sea to slowly swallow the town.

From his vantage point at the window of a garret room overlooking the harborside, Henri Damascus watched and felt the night descend on the town. His stolen life was ebbing away, drip by drip, and if he attempted to conduct another ritual, what would be left afterward would no longer be remotely human, and anything that remained of his selfhood would be little more than an insane echo of what was once a man. Soon, in hours perhaps, in days at most, the power sustaining him would fail for the last time; his tortured flesh would succumb finally to the curse he had brought upon himself by taking the tablet from its fane, the curse which by rights should have belonged to the architect of that crime—to Maxwell Cormac.

I am dead already; a phantom, a ghost left nothing but shadows and dark vigils, decrying my fate.

As if to prove him a liar, the pain came again—a fist of agony closing in his chest as his heart stopped beating for long seconds. He grabbed helplessly at the windowsill, struggling to remain standing, his fingertips, fleshless now to the bone, digging furrows into the painted wood. With a violent spasm which shook his whole body, his withered heart beat again, slow and sluggish; like an animal drowning in tar, it struggled fruitlessly on.

He had come here to die, to this dark and accursed place, where every street echoed with the footsteps of other places, other worlds, and the miasma of horrors uncounted settled on the dreams of men. Well had his enemy chosen this place, for lurking beneath its calm exterior were countless fractures and gateways to the beyond, sunk into the flesh of the land and sea like the veins of a living body, pumping with the black blood of nightmares.

He would weep, but he had no tears left in him.

Below the window, a figure hurried by with swift caution, dark overcoat flapping at the swirling mist, his head turning slowly as he went, alert for danger.

Morgan! Immediately, the embers of his hatred fanned into roaring flame, pushing aside all thoughts of dissolution and death, denying fate until vengeance had been claimed.

Damascus flung up the sash of the window, his joints creaking audibly in their sockets. Once he had been a well-fleshed man, one who enjoyed the pleasures of table and worked to maintain his strength; when the curse had first come upon him, his flesh had tightened and begun to bloat, and then to wither unevenly, leaving him a shapeless, mangled form, but the awful, agonizing affliction and the steps he had taken to remedy it over time had not been without certain side effects to his advantage.

With his fleshless fingers clinging to the window frame, he half-swung, half-tumbled out into the night air, letting his body drop, his creaking arm taking his weight for a moment before he let go and dropped like a fat black spider into the misty street far below.

He staggered swiftly to his feet, pausing only to snap his left shoulder back into its socket soundlessly before he began his pursuit. Once his breathing had been a tormented gasp; now, unless he wished to speak, he did not breathe at all, and to his eyes, cataract-white as they were, the night was naked before him.

* * *

Morgan pressed on as quickly as he dared. Things were moving fast, too fast in some ways, and the cold itch in the back of his brain told him he was being played—*but what's new?* he asked himself.

The women, though, that had been a surprise, and picking up Annabel in the street was a stroke of fortune he'd needed. Some might have said it had been dumb luck, a one-in-a-million shot, but they'd be wrong. Right place at the right time—the trick was in knowing which was which in advance, and so he'd staked out the Artists' Colony, as it spoke to the facts he knew about the Ryan woman, and his gamble had paid off.

She was everything that had been said about her: beautiful, smart, and with something almost wild about her. He'd caught sight of her the second she'd turned the corner in a crowd at a hundred paces; there was something about her beyond the looks—a fire. She really was in love, though—either that or she was the best liar he'd ever crossed paths with—and he knew from experience the old adage was true: love was blind, and he found himself hoping that Annabel was somehow right about her "Max," even though Morgan knew in his gut, as well as from the evidence, she was dead wrong.

But the other one, she'd been a bolt from the blue—Miss Daisy Walker, *damn.*

Just beyond the radiant pool cast by a wrought iron lamp-post's trio of gaslights, Morgan paused on a street corner to get his bearings. It was getting on past eight and there were still a few passersby, rendered almost shapeless by the gathering mists, and here at the corner of Drake Street at the foot of Central Hill, a handful of motorcars still coughed and grumbled, moving almost painfully slow, their headlamps sweeping a path before them, while further up the hill toward the small town hospital, he could hear the bell and rattle of the trolley car on one of its last rounds of the evening. He knew, though, that within an hour or two, even this sparse traffic would cease, and the streets would belong to the mists.

His departure from the Rope and Anchor hadn't been the most cordial of affairs, but then he hadn't expected it to be. Jonas Riggs, the bartender (whether he actually owned the place had never been clear), had been more than happy to take his money, both for information and for the woefully overpriced re-bottled liquor he touted, but he'd also been quick to show him the .45 he habitually carried and made plain his willingness to use it, if the need arose, and made mention of just how handily close the sea was.

Riggs had been content to get Morgan out from under his roof; a stranger, particularly one with Morgan's look, was trouble he didn't need, but even the hard-eyed barkeep had cautioned Morgan about wandering about the backstreets and docks of the town at night when the fog was up— *"People get lost,"* he had said, *"when the mists come."*

Had Morgan been some rube from out-of-town, he'd have thought maybe the barkeep was trying to scare him for kicks, and if he had been on an ordinary manhunt, he'd have reckoned on rum-runners, smugglers, or some other local trouble who had business in the dark they didn't want overlooking—and that could still be true—but now, after the thing in New York, after Arkham, he took the warning in a different and far more dreadful light.

This would be Morgan's third night in Kingsport, and although the last evening had been spent hunkered down in the bar slowly making his way through a bottle of Canadian Club that was nothing of the sort, while the mother of all tempests raged outside, the night previously—his first in the port town—had been enough to convince him that Riggs's belated warning had been anything but local superstition.

It had been gone midnight when he had picked up the man's trail from beside the docks. Having excused himself from the bar for some "air," he'd taken his own turn around the town, getting the lay of the land, and with his own key to the courtyard door of the room he'd rented in the converted stable out the back of the Rope and Anchor, he'd anticipated an extended tour, if warranted, wouldn't cause any particular problems. Riggs's guests, it seemed, had common needs for privacy in coming and going and were routinely obliged.

The man had been furtive, suspect in the way he moved, too jittery to make much of the stealth he affected as he cleaved to the shadows away from the street lamps. Morgan, his skill aided by darkness and the rising mist, had gotten close enough to make him out: dressed in a shapeless overcoat and a fisherman's slouched hat, he had a young, unkempt face that managed to look feverishly sick, even cloaked in the shadows as he was. He'd followed the man through the dark with an increasing sense of being led on and a deepened misgiving, which only intensified when the man suddenly disappeared, as if swallowed whole by the night.

A familiar, dark instinct settled upon him then, warning him of danger, and instead of going either forward into the unknown or retreating directly back the way he had come, he had ascended rapidly up into the body of the town. Instead of mere minutes, his journey seemed to take hours, the roads and alleyways twisting back on themselves impossibly, the paved sidewalks giving way to cobbles and dirt, the spill of the gas lamps fading to be replaced by fewer, weakling palls cast by candles left on high window ledges, and the mute flickering of hearth fires bleeding from the edges of closed doorways and the chinks of shuttered windows. Morgan had steeled himself against rising panic, and did his best to move systematically through the almost pitch black streets, despite strange rustling-whistling noises in the air he could not place, and the acute feeling of being hunted down.

When he had found himself suddenly out of the dark, claustrophobic alleyways, and in an open square on the upper part of Central Hill, his relief had been palpable and he had almost laughed out loud, but was checked by the sight before him.

Morgan looked down at the slumbering town in the shadow of the great rocky mass of Kingsport Head. Here, the air had been chill and clean, and the rain-slick roofs of the houses nestled by the harbor glittered like pale glass in the moonlight; beneath them the insidious fingers of sea mist crawled like low and hungry serpents through the alleyways and tangled streets of the lower town—a town as in a dream of olden days, devoid of any semblance of modern civilization. It had been a strange, eerie, and almost spectral sight—the peaked roofs and steeples utterly unfamiliar from the town in daylight. The view brought with it long-slumbering memories for Morgan of far older seaside villages he'd seen in Cornwall on his one boyhood trip to England to see his relations—little places of timeworn stone, forgotten by the centuries and heavy with the weight of neglect. It was like he had walked into another time.

Then the slow, pale lance of the lighthouse lamp out in the bay had swung around across the town like a ghostly blade, and the shadowy outlines of clusters of modern buildings, the thin silhouettes of overhead trolley car lines, parked automobiles, and the like—all had been laid suddenly bare like a conjurer's trick, dispelling the illusion.

Illusion? A trick of the night and the fog? Was that all it was? Morgan wasn't so sure anymore; he wasn't sure of anything.

He had almost run headlong back to the courtyard of the Rope and Anchor, every sting of recent injury and stress flaring hot, his lungs raw as if he had run a marathon. His watch had shown that no more than an hour had passed since he'd picked up the man's tail, but his body and his mind vehemently disagreed with that assessment.

No, he thought, breaking his reverie, suddenly aware he'd been standing by the streetlight for some minutes and the traffic was already thinning out, *I'm not getting caught out here again in the mist without a damn good reason.*

As Morgan hurried toward the waterfront, he was pleased to see the welcoming lights of the Lighthouse Inn rear up ahead of him, noticing for the first time how the bright gas lamps on either side of the hotel's main doors were fashioned to imitate a lighthouse lamp, right down to the expensive glass lens that amplified them, and paused a second to wonder.

Inside was warm and welcoming, with murmured conversation and soft violin music drifting from within. No sooner had he stepped through the revolving door from the street, than the obsequious manager, Dukes, was out from behind the carven oak reception desk and offering to take his overcoat; Morgan deferred.

"Is my room ready?" he asked.

"Of course, sir, fourth floor, by the stairs, as you requested," Dukes replied submissively with a greasy smile.

Morgan nodded and held his hand out for the key.

Dukes ferreted off and swiftly returned, handing the old-fashioned key and its small brass number fob to Morgan, and looked quizzically at the single large briefcase he was carrying.

"My other baggage will be brought 'round in the morning," Morgan answered the unspoken question.

"Very good, sir; will you dine? We are still serving for another quarter hour, but of course we can make an exception for a valued guest such as yourself, if needed, and the lounge restaurant always remains open as long as needed for our clientele. Our dinners are among the finest in the town, and our chef well-regarded," Dukes offered with clear pride.

Morgan thought for a moment before answering. "A sandwich sent up to my room would be fine. I'll be back downstairs in a short while after I've settled in for coffee—that, I assume, I can get late?"

"Of course, sir."

"Did a call come through from New York?"

"Yes, sir, I was just about to mention that. A young lady called about eight, I'm afraid she wouldn't leave a name or message, but insisted she would ring back, which she as of yet has not done. But alas, lines of communication to Kingsport are somewhat unreliable, even with the new Wireless Station, but I digress, I'm sorry," Dukes said, wringing his hands.

Morgan shook his head. "That's fine. If she calls, at any time, you come find me, regardless of the hour."

Without waiting for a reply, Morgan turned his back on Dukes and limped up the stairs.

* * *

A blacker shadow than the night detached itself from the outer wall of the hotel as Damascus swung his head around to the edge of the window to watch Morgan's assent up the stairs until he was out of view.

Weakness overcame him and he experienced a horrific, empty moment of oblivion before he again came to his senses. He was running out of time.

Creeping around the gravel outside the building, he looked in at the brightly lit interior—the fat porter, the guests dining, some in tuxedo and black tie, the women with their bright, painted faces and lush, shear dresses, tables replete with food and gleaming silverware, the haze of tobacco smoke, the drift of music through the glass—all lost to him now, no more than dim, painful memories of joys that were now denied him.

As he passed them by, finger bones gently scraping the glass, conversations grew stilted, fine meats lost their flavor, and one ruddy-faced old woman turned to stare at the glass window, perfectly featureless and black from her perspective, with barely concealed horror. They could not see him, of course, but the more sensitive among them could feel his presence near them, like someone walking over their grave.

He pulled back from the window and they returned soon to normality, although one or two couldn't help glancing back to the glass warily from time to time, without knowing why.

He saw the three women at the corner table, and beneath the stained bandages that covered his face, what remained of his mouth twisted into something resembling a smile. To his accursed eyes—now already half-seeing the nightmares that lay beyond as readily as he saw the bricks and mortar of the inconsequential human world—all three of the women burned brightly, far more brightly than any others present, but all in differing ways and degrees. It was, however, the tall, raven-haired beauty that interested him most, and the forces that circled around her were terrible indeed, for he had seen her face in dark dreams of destruction and in the fragments of plundered memories. Suddenly, so much made sense, and the black configuration of events became clearer to him than ever.

Oh, but how they had all been played, every one of them—sorcerers, devils, killers, prophets, and a queen. Even now, he sensed the servants of the enemy drawing close, moving in the fog with designs they thought their own, but they had all danced to the Lord of Nightmares's tune, and through their actions would he walk the earth again to grant his monstrous boons and wreak havoc on the sanity and flesh of men—or at least so his enemy hoped. *But, perhaps there is time yet for a discord of my own.*

Departing from the window, and casting about to ensure he remained unseen, even from those that flew invisible on the night wind, the thing that had once been Henri Damascus crept around the grey stone flanks of the hotel and into the lee of its chimney stacks.

With patient, deliberate movements, he scaled the wall like an ungodly, huge spider, slowly and with malignant purpose. While his strength remained, he might yet have his vengeance at least in thwarting his treacherous enemy, if he could not slay him. He had time yet to stir the embers of the slumbering fire, and perhaps set the master's house aflame.

* * *

The dinner had transpired to be just as civilized, polite, and ghastly as Daisy had feared, despite the good food and pleasant surroundings and the hotel's faded elegance. But for her, at least, after the events of the last few days, the evening had an air of normality to it that had its own charm.

Claudia Cabot (once more having reverted to her maiden name, and formerly Mrs. Simmons, and then until recently Mrs. Albright) had proved to be a mine of information, although, sadly, much of it seemed of no use at all as far as their situation and Maxwell Cormac.

Still wearing mourning black (although in this case the ensemble was a glamorous one of French couture with a décolletage of lace roses), she was every inch the well-heeled Yankee blue-blood, but she couldn't hold a candle to Annabel, who, even given the time she'd had over the last few weeks, was both immaculately turned out and poised, seeming almost to shine like silver flame in a silk gown.

Claudia was a woman satisfied with the sound of her own voice, and was more than happy to hold forth on any conceivable topic concerning Kingsport's small but well-established elite, as well as the principle families of nearby Arkham and Salem.

In response, Annabel, despite all, had been a triumph, and had taken the lead in holding up their end of the small talk with subtlety and humor. Daisy had marveled at the ease with which she had gotten on with the oft-times brittle Claudia—clearly she'd learned a trick or two on her travels when it came to dealing with salon vipers and social climbers.

Daisy spoke only to interject on a few points related to the university and those few faculty members who intersected with what passed for New England high society. For the main, she was happy to merely listen in, the food being excellent and her own thoughts more than enough to occupy her. As the courses drifted by, topics such as the prospects for the forthcoming presidential election and the scandal of the recent feuding over the Collins estate were laid bare. Each was treated with Claudia's customary mixture of holier-than-thou opprobrium and cattish scorn. One topic, however, caught Daisy and Annabel's attention more than most: Claudia's opinion on the general inadequacy of Kingsport's newly appointed sheriff in dealing with the growing problem of tramps and vagrants in the county, although Claudia knew little by way of actual "fact" on the matter of what she called "the filthy scourge." When pressed, she only alluded to certain "undesirable types" loitering during the town's off-season and causing concern, and further mentioned the danger of them squatting in one of the disused fallen manses that dotted the surrounding countryside between Kingsport and Arkham, which set Daisy thinking afresh.

As the evening wore on, Daisy noticed Annabel was beginning to flag at last, and as a result, she interposed herself and spoke of the fog gathering outside the windows, and the growing chill that came up from the sea that even the banked fire in the restaurant's marble hearth could not dispel. Taking the hint in part, and genuinely disliking the prospect of the encircling mists tightening around her any place but her home, Claudia had the maître-d' call for her car, and with a parting shot of social one-upmanship, loudly had the evening's check placed on her account. This, with a repressed smile, Daisy was more than happy to allow.

Afterward, as Daisy and Annabel retired to the adjoining lounge for coffee after seeing Claudia to the door, Annabel visibly deflated as she slumped into the padded booth seat.

"Oh my, I thought that would never end," Annabel sighed, letting her head loll against the backrest.

Daisy laughed. "You were marvelous."

Annabel looked sidelong at her friend and gave a conspiratorial wink. "Do you think she fell for it?"

"Fell for it? You about charmed her out of her family silver. I had no idea you could be such a scoundrel, Annabel," she replied with mock admonishment.

"Oh, that," she smirked. "That kind of film-flam only works on the vain and the greedy for approval, not the stout-of-heart and virtuous like you, Spook. But, then, if you'd met some of the people I did in my travels, you'd soon see I'm a rank amateur when it comes to flattery and corruption!"

Daisy found herself blushing self-consciously by the unexpected compliment. Changing tack, she said, "No sign of our intrepid Mr. Morgan."

Daisy looked around. The lounge was empty but for a bespectacled old gent with a soup strainer moustache working his way through a stack of periodicals at a table by the door. Huffing occasionally to himself, he hadn't even looked up when they entered.

"No," Annabel agreed, "perhaps he's out playing bloodhound again, or sleuthing or whatever he does other than threatening women with guns and frog-marching them across town."

Daisy caught the note of concern concealed within her friend's flippant remark. "Do you trust him, Annabel, really?"

"I don't know, do you?"

"Maybe…that's not the most definite answer is it?" Daisy replied uncertainly.

"I think we can trust he is who he says he is somehow—he saved me from that maniac, and he certainly could have killed me himself if he wanted to, or you for that matter, I've no doubt of that, and I don't believe he'd have needed to shoot us, either."

"Yes, my wrist's still aching for proof of that one. I don't think I've ever met anybody that felt so dangerous just to be in a room with."

"It's his motives that worry me; will he really help us, or just himself?" Annabel said with a sigh.

"Well, as long as we get to the bottom of this, and he keeps his word, I don't suppose it matters that much whether his motives are entirely as he's told us."

"Handsome, though," Annabel quipped.

"Annabel!" Daisy shot back with mock outrage.

"What? Don't tell me you didn't notice?"

"He was holding a gun on us!"

"All the more reason to pay attention!" Annabel giggled.

"I'm spoken for!"

"No harm in window shopping. You need to spend some time outside your cloister, 'Sister' Daisy."

"Annabel Ryan, you are too much." Daisy laughed quietly and Annabel with her, feeling some of the tension drain away. She smiled warmly; she had needed that.

Coffee was served, and they sat in a comfortable silence for a few minutes.

"Oh, Spook, it's all a bit beyond me—nightmares, creatures, madmen, and all. I just want Max in my arms again. The rest can go hang," Annabel offered, rubbing her fingers around her temples.

Daisy saw then just how fatigued her friend really was, and almost kicked herself for not sending her to rest sooner. "Go on up to bed, Annabel—you're done in." She glanced at her watch. "It's nearly ten already. I'll give Morgan another hour or so, and then call it a night."

Annabel was uncertain. "I'm not sure I should leave you here alone…"

"Look, I'm sure I'm as safe here as I am, well, anywhere," Daisy said with a smile she hoped conveyed more confidence than she actually felt. "There will be people around for a while yet, and the porter at the desk all night."

"Well, if you're sure—I am boiling up a headache you could strip paint with," Annabel said with a wince.

"You want me to walk up with you—safety in numbers?"

"No," Annabel replied, "who'd walk you back down? Besides, if I see so much as a thimbleful of shadow where it shouldn't be or hear a single flappy noise, I'm going to scream so loud they'll hear me in Arkham."

"You do that, and I'll come running," Daisy said earnestly.

Annabel looked at her seriously, and quite unexpectedly reached out and took Daisy's hand in her own and squeezed it for a moment before letting go. "What on earth did I do to deserve a friend as good as you, Spook? You're a real peach—you know that?"

"So I'm phantom fruit now?" Daisy replied quizzically with a grin.

Annabel got to her feet tiredly, smiling, and shook her head. "Less time in libraries, remember!"

Daisy smiled back as she watched Annabel leave, then looked glumly into the shiny black surface of her half-drunk china cup of coffee. She was feeling a little twinge of conscience. It wasn't as if she had actually lied to Annabel, or even Morgan for that matter, she just hadn't told them everything. After all, she wasn't certain herself, and she had to be sure.

She reached down to the book satchel she'd been dragging around all evening and took out her notebook to occupy her while she waited for the bounty hunter to put in an appearance.

I have to be sure, she thought, and turned to the trial transcripts.

CHAPTER ELEVEN

Morgan snapped suddenly awake, snatching up the bowie knife from the bed beside him. There was nothing but stillness in the room as he looked around, nothing out of place. No sound from the corridor outside, either, and yet the instinct for danger that had awoken him was one he'd long learned to respect.

He'd been dreaming, and less than pleasantly. *Was that what woke me?*

He looked at the clock he'd set by the bed. It was still, the dial frozen at five minutes to ten, while his wristwatch read quarter to midnight. Still fully dressed, he'd meant only to shut his eyes for a spell, guessing he'd have late business tonight, and now he was late. He swung his legs out of bed with the intention of heading immediately downstairs on the chance the two women were still waiting, but paused again, utterly still, listening, his senses completely alert. *There's something wrong.*

With deliberate caution and speed, Morgan threw on his overcoat, double-checked and loaded both the serial numberless

Luger pistols that had been a gift from Copperhead, put them out of sight in his shoulder rig, tucked his knife into the sheath at the small of his back, and proceeded as if he was in enemy territory as he left his room. Scoping the corridor before stepping out, Morgan moved slowly and quietly, alert to any hint of danger. The hotel was deathly silent.

Morgan reached the staircase and was struck by a sudden strange feeling, not exactly déjà vu, but something like it—a cold familiarity with the moment in which he found himself—as if it was meant to be. In its way, the sensation was more unnerving than anything else about his current situation.

What the hell are you doing here, Tony? That vaunted luck of yours is going to run out and you're going to get yourself killed! The thought came to him suddenly, unbidden, and along with it the realization that he'd been dreaming of Arkham, only minutes ago, dreaming of the night he should have died in the waters of the Miskatonic with his chest ripped open.

So if I get killed, so what? I've been courting death my whole life, he fought back savagely in his mind. *Maybe it's about time I quit delaying the wedding. What else do I really have, except tilting at windmills and slaying dragons, pretending I have some kind of damn life other than this?*

Sternly, he put one foot on the first stair and started downward.

A woman's footsteps rushed up toward him. He recognized Daisy immediately from her well-proportioned build and the semi-restrained tumble of blond locks framing her pale, serious face; her expression, however, was one of intent concentration and worry.

"Miss Walker," he brought her up to a halt with an urgent whisper, "what's happened?"

She looked at him with a measure of relief, but with a wariness that didn't leave her clear blue eyes, which took him in and weighed up the situation immediately.

Morgan stopped himself from smiling at her like an idiot. *I am going to have to watch myself around you, Daisy Walker. I'm going to get far too smitten if I'm not careful, and I need a clear head if I am going to live through this.*

"Annabel's gone, disappeared from her room," Daisy said in a clipped, over self-controlled manner that let him know she was keeping herself firmly in hand, despite her emotions running to the contrary. "She went up to her room to sleep just before ten, while I stayed downstairs," she continued without prompting, preempting his need for explanation. "I stayed reading in the lounge, waiting for you. I somehow lost track of time—which seems strangely easy to do here," bitter self-recrimination crept into her voice. "By the time I realized what time it was, the whole hotel seemed empty. I went to check on her and she wasn't in her room and her bed didn't even look slept in, and she hasn't even taken her coat. It's my fault: I shouldn't have left her alone."

Morgan took her by the arm and started them both back downstairs. "Damn, that's almost two hours she could be missing. Did the night porter see her leave the hotel?"

"That's the thing: I couldn't find him by the desk, I even called in the back, but there's *nobody*. I got what your room number was from the register. I was coming to find you—I didn't know what else to do." She looked at Morgan's face, and brought them up short before they reached the lobby. "There's something very wrong here isn't there, beyond Annabel going missing?"

"I'm afraid so," he replied without turning to her, "and don't beat yourself up about losing track of time, I did as well, and that's not something I'm famed for, believe me. It's something about this damn town—you're right about that—like you're half-way caught in a dream you can't wake up from half the time."

Daisy shook her head and murmured, "It used to have its moments, and the place has a reputation with the artists, of course… some have even called it 'the Kingsport fugue,' but I can't remember it being, well, this bad. I thought it was just me, after what happened on the road."

"Yeah," Morgan replied, "I kind of guessed I wasn't getting the full story on that one."

"Strange you should mention that; I thought that about your story, as well," she returned.

Morgan smiled and pulled out one of his Lugers and held it out to her barrel first. "You know how to work one of these things? It'll be a deal handier than that antique."

Daisy set her jaw and took the black pistol off him without hesitation. "I'm sure I'll work it out."

Morgan shook his head and smiled again, quickly showing her how to work the automatic. "You really are a piece of work, Miss Walker."

"I'll take that as a compliment. Now what are we going to *do*?" she whispered fiercely.

"That's how I meant it," he shot back, drawing his second automatic. "To answer your question: what we are going to do is check this place out and look for our missing porter for a start. Based on the last few weeks of my life, I'd lay money on him not just having slithered off somewhere to catch up on his beauty sleep."

She nodded. "But what about Annabel?"

"She's either still here, in which case all is well and good and we'll find her in due course, or she's long gone into the fog. And, unless you have some idea of where, careering off into the night after her isn't exactly a sane plan, or a healthy one. Now, keep that gun out of sight, watch my back, and try not to shoot me, Miss Librarian."

"I'll try," she murmured earnestly.

They reached the lobby and found it as empty as Daisy had said. Outside the glass of the hotel front, the mist had thickened into a sea of fog which mutely rolled, desolate and almost glowing, seeming to still and deaden the air, even inside the hotel's stout walls.

Morgan took the measure of the deserted lobby, lounge, and restaurant with quick, efficient movements, Daisy trailing behind him. Again he had that strange sense of something dangerous and alien at work, like watching a predatory animal stalking prey.

"Can you feel that?" he asked quietly.

Daisy shook her head in reply.

"Cold air—there's a door open to the outside." He paused a moment and then indicated the swing doors to the kitchen. "Through there."

Morgan carefully pushed open the doors, and Daisy heard the asthmatic hum of an open refrigerator from within. Following him inside, she caught her breath when she saw the body outlined under the pool of the electric bulb. It was a man, all but unrecognizable, his upper body and face a mass of open red wounds, rendering him into little more than butchered meat. Beside him, one of a trio of powder-blue enameled refrigerators hung open, jars and plates of food smashed on the floor before it. Beyond the body, on the other side of the large, cluttered kitchen, a back door stood ajar, letting wisps of mist filter in.

The smell of blood hit her and Daisy gagged reflexively; she felt the grip of the pistol grow slick in her grasp.

Morgan scanned the room before kneeling by the body. "The porter—looks like somebody came up behind him while he was fixing himself a snack, slit his throat. The rest of this…was unnecessary," he whispered warily.

"Good Lord," she replied weakly.

Morgan looked back at her. "You okay?"

"I think so." She waved a hand at him dismissively and coughed. "Not exactly something I've seen before, or smelled. I'll cope; don't worry about me."

"Well, I don't think this was Annabel's doing. Somebody came in and surprised him from through that door. Does that back onto the street, do you know?"

"What? Of course it wasn't her…," Daisy replied hurriedly. "There's a courtyard first, and the hotel garage—*oh good God*." With sudden evident shock she started toward the outside door as fast as she could, weaving around the kitchen tables away from the body on her way to get there.

"Wait, Daisy, what's wrong?"

"The fragment—the glass!" she exclaimed. "I hid it in the car!"

"What?" Morgan shot back, jumping to his feet.

Just at that moment, the darkened wall behind Daisy seemed to erupt as the meat locker's double doors were violently flung open. Two hulking figures covered in layers of coats and ragged clothes burst into the room, moaning and keening like tortured animals. One of the flying doors struck Daisy in the side, knocking her from her feet and saving her life as a fire axe, swung at head height, cut the air where moments before she had stood.

Morgan calmly took aim and fired three times in rapid succession, his Luger barking thunderously loud in the enclosed space; one of the ragged figures toppled midstride. The axe-wielder—Daisy seemingly forgotten, and oblivious to his friend's fate—charged onward and swung again before Morgan could target him, sparks flying as the axe blade struck the gun in Morgan's outstretched hand, sweeping it away. Morgan jumped back, dodging a backswing with the axe's spike as the maniac spat garbled and incoherent curses at him.

Morgan, backed up against the refrigerators and rapidly running out of room, jumped back over the porter's body and nearly slipped in the dead man's blood as the axe swung again, smashing a deep gash in the metal refrigerator door, nearly tearing it from its hinges. Morgan closed in and lashed several short-punched body-blows into his attacker in hopes of gaining some space as much as inflicting harm, and was rewarded with nothing more than a dull grunt for his efforts. *It's like punching a damn tree!*

On the other side of the kitchen, Daisy, winded but otherwise unharmed, staggered to her feet and recovered her own pistol from the floor, but as she turned toward the ongoing fight, she froze in her tracks as the other ragged figure dragged itself up spasmodically, its gnarled hands gripping one of the heavy tables as it hauled itself unsteadily upright.

"Hold it...don't!" Daisy shouted as she clutched the pistol in both hands, uncertain of what to do, her mind rebelling at the idea of shooting anyone in cold blood.

The figure gurgled and slavered as it turned toward her, and as she caught sight of its face, Daisy felt her knees turn to water and she rocked unsteadily on her heels, the air seeming to rush by her. The man's jaw was hanging off to one side where Morgan's bullets had smashed it, and the red hanging mass beneath the bared ivory upper teeth was seething with a thick, ropy, black fluid, which gathered and knotted itself into tendrils as she watched in horror, dumbstruck by what she was seeing.

Morgan grappled with his enemy, his hands now wrapped around the axe haft, matching his skill and leverage against the seemingly inhuman strength and fury of his enemy, which easily outmatched his own considerable muscle power. His back slammed into the wall, but he managed to roll with the impact and spun his opponent into a rack of pots and pans which crashed to the floor, but his enemy's grip on the axe never wavered. Foul breath with the strength of an open grave washed over him, and Morgan realized in a shocking instant of clarity that the maniac's left eye was entirely missing, leaving a gaping reddish tunnel at the back of which something horrific and wormlike pulsed. Morgan sprang back, and, suddenly unopposed, the maniac was thrown forward by his own strength. Morgan sidestepped as he crashed past, the axe swinging wildly, and as he went by, Morgan leapt on the maniac's back, drawing his bowie knife and ripping the heavy blade up and under his enemy's ribs toward the heart, crashing down on top of the ragged man as he fell to the bloody ground.

The thick black tendrils probed the air obscenely toward Daisy from the ruin that had once been a human face as the thing dragged itself toward her along the kitchen table, grunting pig-like snorts. Finding her reason at last from the riot of terror and disbelief that warred in her mind, Daisy pulled the Luger's trigger again and again, the bullets jerking the half-human body this way and that, and causing the tendrils to lash the air frenziedly. Slowly, it collapsed backward, howling mournfully as Daisy fired all eight rounds and kept on pulling the trigger, the pistol clicking empty as the maniac broke apart into a black, frothing, gushing mass which bubbled and spat on the kitchen floor, and she backed away as the rank liquid inched closer to the toes of her shoes.

Blinking slowly as she fully came back to her wits, she looked up at last and found Morgan standing over the other attacker—now dismembered but with some of the body parts still twitching nightmarishly on the floor—the fire axe in his hand.

Morgan caught his panting breath. "You hurt?"

"No," Daisy said in a faint, distant voice. "You're covered in blood."

"Occupational hazard," he replied, still breathless.

"They won't die. It's all true…not human…were human once, but not now…," she murmured.

"What's that? Come on," Morgan replied. He quickly checked all the doors and, peeking out into the courtyard for a moment, assured himself that the danger, at least for now, was over.

Daisy let her arm fall limply to her side. "I wanted to forget, my mind made itself forget, but it's real, all real…the books, the creatures, all of it. I remember. Oh, dear God, what *are* we?"

Morgan skirted around looking for his lost handgun, finding it in the sink, the barrel dented and bent. He cursed briefly and made his way back to Daisy, who, sweeping her hair out of her eyes with the back of her hand, held out the empty pistol to him.

Morgan took it, changed the magazine and gave it back to her.

She frowned in confusion. "Hadn't you best take it?"

Morgan shook his head and held up the bloody fire axe. "This seems a bit more effective in keeping the bastards down…pardon my language…whatever they are, and you're doing fine with the pistol as far as I can see. Come on, we need to check on your car."

She followed behind him as he retrieved a flashlight from a nearby shelf and cautiously pulled open the rear door of the kitchen with the axe held at arm's length. Outside, the night mist curled in the cold air, dissipating somewhat under the hotel's lights. Morgan snapped on the flashlight and swept its beam across the small walled courtyard. Everything was still, with a half a dozen automobiles and a small motor van parked in silent rows like sentries.

"I don't understand," Daisy whispered urgently as they stepped outside together. "Why hasn't anybody come out to see—the noise, the struggle. Where is everybody from the hotel?" she said looking upward. Aside from the windows that overlooked the main staircase and landings, almost every window was dark.

"I don't know, but you're right: the racket should have shaken somebody loose from up there," he said, advancing cautiously into the cold courtyard.

The chill air with its salt-sea tang was a blessing for them both after the rotted, abattoir stench of the kitchen.

"That's it!" Daisy shot back, and dashed over to Ted's battered Ford.

"Be careful," Morgan said as he kept a lookout, holding the flashlight high to shine on the motor as Daisy leaned in and opened the door.

"No!" she shouted, and backed out looking sick and desolate. "It's gone! There's a space under the dashboard where the lining has come away. Ted, my fiancé, it's where he hides his spare keys because he was always losing his. I wrapped the glass in a handkerchief and wedged it in there before I went out this afternoon. I don't understand—nobody knows about it but me!"

"You're sure, not even Annabel?"

"Damn it, Morgan, no!" she said angrily. "What are we going to do now? Even if we *can* find her, I'd hoped…," her voiced cracked with emotion, but she quickly regained her composure. "If we still had the fragment, we might have been able to trade it for Annabel somehow, but now what?"

Morgan kept the flashlight trained on her, offering no reply as the tendrils of mist curled around them.

"Well, what now?" Daisy spoke firmly, her head held high, taking his silence for accusation. "Are you cutting your losses and running, Morgan? Or have you decided I'm not to be trusted, or lying about where I put it?"

Morgan watched her standing there in the night, cold, fraught, and scared, but under it pure guts and intellect—refusing to give in, whatever came. There was something glorious about Miss Daisy Walker. He let out a long slow sigh and lowered the light. *So much for not getting personally involved.* "No, Miss Walker. I don't doubt you for a minute, but your friend Annabel—her I'm not so sure of. This whole mess stinks to high heaven—look." Morgan swung the flashlight beam toward the wrought iron gate that led from the courtyard to the fogbound street beyond. "The padlock's open, not busted—somebody let them in. They got what they came for and left a surprise party for whoever came down to check, that is, unless the fragment was on either of those two back there, which I somehow doubt."

"They were waiting for us," Daisy replied.

"Us or somebody, hell I don't know what's going on here, but whatever the game is, we're losing. Come on back inside," he said, sweeping the flashlight back and forth around the mute courtyard. "I need a drink, and it looks like you do, too."

* * *

Am I dreaming? I must be dreaming… Annabel's mind was a confused jumble of images and expressions and sensations. She was cold, bone-gnawing cold, and yet she did not shiver; she could feel a slight breeze tug at her evening gown and flutter at her exposed skin with brittle fingertips. Far, far away she could hear the waves as they crashed against the rocks, the sound softened into somber melody by the distance.

Where am I?

She stumbled, her ankle almost turning under her, and was suddenly aware that she was walking, putting one front in front of the other, and the ground waxed alternately grass soft and stone hard.

Am I blind? she asked herself, the strange numbness in her head drowning any sense of fear or panic. *No, not blind…fog, darkness and fog.* She raised up her hand, almost drunkenly, and grabbed at faintly luminous wisps. To her dimly felt surprise there was a palpable sensation as they slithered through her grasp, like chill, damp cobwebs.

Cobwebs—memories tumbled through her mind at the word and its association, images and feelings sliding into a configuration of meaning.

She remembered dinner, Claudia's petty jealousy and easily played vanity, Daisy's intent stare, that brain of hers working nineteen to the dozen on every word she heard, Max, so close, so unreachable. She remembered being in her room.

She looked down at her feet, moving as if of their own accord, carrying her along inexorably to a destination she had no choice but to pursue. She was descending, the rocky ground steeply sloping beneath her, the fog thickening, the breeze dying away. *Kingsport Head? How did I get up here?*

The man—there had been a man waiting for her in her room, by the side of the window, wide open, curtains fluttering—a man with a bandaged face.

Strange, so strange, like a nightmare memory unraveling itself with the dawn light… She had been about to scream, but he had made no move toward her; he had said Maxwell's name, offered to take her to him—the words holding her in place like a spell. He had asked for the fragment, she had told him she didn't know where it was, and he had doubled up, shuddering, and she had realized he was weeping—weeping without tears and without breath. Then there had been the sensation of being carried on someone's back, of being high off the ground, the fear of falling, of smashing into the ground into a thousand pieces, of motorcar roofs like cigarette cases laid out on a table.

Then, a struggle of black wings beating in the dark, the bandaged man crying out in his hollow voice, the sound fading into the distance. Falling, spinning, the stars and the cold air, spidery fingers wrapped around her flesh like cords, biting into her skin, the moon huge in the night sky, the thundering sea and the lonely high house, the white scimitar of light slashing through the dark.

A dream, all a dream—only ever a dream.

She stumbled again, and this time she fell onto her hands and knees, but instead of the uneven, stony earth, she felt instead something infinitely colder, hard and smooth to the touch. Her eyes flickered open and focused; the black and white tiles rose up to meet her and were gone as she closed her eyes again.

Not looking; where is father?

Someone was beside her, a strong, rough hand lifting her not un-gently to her feet.

"Father?" she whispered.

"No, child," the old man said. "Alas, no, and alas that it has come to this, but I have no choice. It's you they want. I tried to warn you, but that time is past."

"Daisy!" she cried out weakly, finding her voice again. "Max, help me!" She wanted to run but her legs would not obey her. Instead, she stumbled on against her will, with the old man to guide her and the distant crashing of the waves and the snap and flutter of black wings high overhead.

It felt as if she had been walking for hours, but perhaps it was only minutes, when at last the old man let go of her arm. Ahead, the fog was thick, and deep within it were strange greenish lights and the insidious, guttural rhythm of an ugly chanting she did not understand.

Annabel fought to clear her head; it was as if she were deep under water, looking out at the world on the surface, tears streaming down her face as she tried desperately to think straight.

A lean, dark figure resolved from the fog before her.

"Have her, then, and be damned," the terrible old man said from behind her. "Take your tribute and be gone from Kingsport," he spat with scorn.

There was laughter in the darkness. "Oh, we have one final rapture to enjoy first, my dear Captain, now everything is in place and the stars are right."

That voice, I know that voice! "Max!" she shouted.

He stepped forward, gaunt and feverish-looking, but still him, still her Maxwell, and he was smiling at her.

"Yes, my darling, I'm here, Max is here!" he shouted, his arms open wide.

She rushed to him, a wordless cry of happiness and relief escaping her lips, but before she could reach him—mere inches from his embrace—a dozen strong hands seized her, lifting her off the ground, and no matter how she kicked and screamed, they would not let go.

Maxwell Cormac laughed. "Behold!" he shouted. "As my father foretold, she has come of her own free will, and what was shall be again!"

The black winged shadows flapped and danced around the terrible old man who was their master, and Cormac recoiled from them.

"Enough—get thee gone," the old man said harshly.

"The bargain is done," Cormac quickly offered, "and through her, the key shall be turned and the gate opened. In her suffering we will bear witness to the true face of creation and know joy everlasting!"

Annabel's screams were cut off by a filthy, smothering hand. The darkness took her.

* * *

Daisy and Morgan went through the kitchen without a word. Daisy kept her head straight, refusing to look down as she stuck to the edge of the room and avoided the bodies, picking up her book satchel from where she had dropped it in the fight. She knew what lay at her feet and didn't need to see it again. Morgan waited for her at the inner door without comment. As she reached him, he held a finger to his lips for silence and then tapped his ear.

Listening carefully, she heard a whiny, almost hysterical voice in the distance.

"Dukes?" she mouthed silently, and after a second, Morgan nodded in agreement and pushed his way back into the hotel restaurant.

They found the hotel manager behind the lobby desk, dressed incongruously in a purple smoking jacket over powder blue pajamas, frantically trying to raise the operator on the hotel telephone. He almost had a heart attack on the spot when he saw the state of them both, and shrieked at the sight of the bloody axe held casually in Morgan's hand. It was all Daisy could do to calm him down, ordering him to be quiet at the finish in her most inflexible tone and sitting him back behind the desk where he proceeded to hug himself and shiver, staring at them both as if they were some unknown and savage species.

"You got anything to drink?" Morgan demanded, laying the fire axe on the counter top.

Dukes shook his head. "This is a law-abiding establishment," he managed to stammer.

Daisy tutted impatiently—as if they didn't have a lot worse things to contend with than a Prohibition citation. "There's a bottle behind the register; I saw it when I was looking for your room."

"That must be Bartholomew's. I never touch liquor: I signed the pledge in '22!" Dukes squealed nervously.

"Bully for you. Well, I don't think Bart's going to be needing it anymore," Morgan said scornfully, reaching over and grabbing the bottle before stalking off to find a pair of glasses for them.

"Who were you calling?" Daisy asked, folding her arms defensively.

"The sheriff," Dukes quickly replied, "but the operator couldn't put me through. She said there was no answer, then I couldn't reach her, either…I couldn't reach anyone! I saw…I saw…"

"Who else is here in the hotel? Why aren't more people down here?"

Dukes looked sick as he tried to reply, shifting uncomfortably in his seat. "I don't know. I thought that, but I was afraid to go and look after seeing…"

"You weren't asleep, were you, Dukes? I mean tonight?" Morgan demanded as he returned, pouring two highball glasses each with a stiff measure of whiskey from the bottle.

"No, no, I have trouble sleeping. I have a delicate constitution," Dukes replied sheepishly. "I was reading in my room on the first floor when I heard the shots and saw…"

"You think they are all still asleep? That's it? The others—deep asleep?" Daisy asked Morgan.

"What did you call it earlier?"

"'The Kingsport fugue'—but that's just what the artists call the atmosphere of the place." Daisy's voice held little conviction.

Morgan shook his head. "I'm saying I wouldn't be surprised

if half the damn town is sleeping like the dead awaiting the last blast on judgment day, and the other half is too scared to so much as twitch the curtains in case of what they might see. Welcome to bloody Kingsport." Morgan snapped his head around to Dukes, who was staring at them open-mouthed. "Keep trying the damn phone," he ordered.

Daisy took her drink and went and sat, head down in thought, on the blue-cushioned couch by the door, laying the pistol on the low table in front of her. Morgan walked over and stood in front of her.

"Listen, Miss Walker, if you want any chance at all of getting your friend back alive, if she is still alive, you need to level with me now."

"About what specifically?" she replied, looking up at him tiredly.

"How about what just happened for a start," he said, dragging up a chair to sit by her. "Look, you're a strong woman, I can see that, I happen to like strong women, but when that—whatever he was—dissolved into black slime, you didn't exactly seem that surprised—shocked, yes, but not surprised."

She stared into space, slowly quoting, "'Good things of day do droop and drowse, whilst night's black agents to their preys do rouse.'"

Morgan sat quietly for a moment before asking, "That's Shakespeare isn't it? Macbeth?"

Daisy, pleasantly surprised, smiled a little. "You surprise me, Mr. Morgan; you have hidden depths, it would seem."

"Not really, just a wasted education," he replied, returning her smile.

Daisy sighed. "It's a quote that's been running around my head since Annabel and I were attacked the other night. There was this, well…let's just say 'night's black agent' fit it very well. I thought it was just after the fragment, but it wasn't; it was after

Annabel, as well—I was irrelevant to it. I think I realized the truth even then, I just wouldn't let myself believe until I thought it all through, until I was going crazy with it."

Despite the shadow hanging over them both, Morgan realized Daisy needed time; thinking the unthinkable was one thing, saying it out loud to a stranger was another.

Daisy pulled her book satchel to her chest, propped her chin on it and looked at Morgan with fathomless eyes. "It's too insane," she said simply, "too insane to even think about."

"Try me. After what just happened, I'm a very receptive audience."

"What do you believe in, Mr. Morgan?"

"Call me Tony."

She smiled a little and asked again, "What do you believe in, Tony?"

"That's a complicated question," he replied, and looking at her he realized the question was in deadly earnest. "Myself—right and wrong, as trite as that might sound, and that your word is all you have, I suppose. The rest? The rest I haven't been so sure of for a long time."

Daisy toyed with her drink. "You're different to most people, you know that? But then I suppose you need to be. You're a loner, Tony, and I doubt there are many things you can afford to trust on blind faith. Most people believe what they are told, they don't question. They see the world through the filter of human civilization: religion, tradition, ideology, state, nature, science—what if that, all of it, was wrong? Could we live with that? Could we go on, get married, have children? Build for a future—if there was no future?"

Daisy closed her eyes before continuing in as bleak a voice as Morgan had ever heard, "What if everything we are, everything we can be, what if it's all just a sandcastle on the beach waiting to be annihilated by the next tide?"

"Daisy, I don't understand," he spoke quietly. "What do you mean? I don't want to push you, but if you know what we are facing, I need to know, no matter how crazy it sounds—I don't think we have much time."

Daisy smiled sadly. "I told you, it's too strange to contemplate really—as a thesis acceptable in the abstract, but quite different in the flesh." She drew in a deep breath and went on, "Look, let me tell you how it came to me, how I lost my beautiful ignorance.

"I was raised in a very religious household, puritan you might almost say, but for as long as I could remember my true faith was knowledge, I guess—reason, curiosity, finding out things—I could never know enough, never get enough stories. Does that make sense?"

Morgan nodded.

"As soon as I could read, I read everything I could lay my hands on, and not just facts and figures, I loved books of all kinds, I loved stories, and I particularly loved things that would transport me elsewhere, let me escape from what was a loving home, but also a very austere one—haunted castles and dispossessed princesses and family curses, that sort of thing was my favorite, and it stayed with me all the way past college. So, much later, when I came across old books with bad reputations and stories more outlandish than anything in Poe, I was hooked. That was my trap, and I walked right into it—after all, how could it be real?

"First here at the Hall School and later at the Miskatonic, I'd become a librarian by then and a researcher, a pretty damn good one, too—my job was my life and that was what nearly destroyed me. I read things, and began to see patterns, began to put things together, in here," she said, taking out her notebook from the satchel and handing it to him to leaf through.

"Things that couldn't possibly be true, about not only our

world, but all those beyond it. Things beyond anything our modern oh-so rational and self-satisfied minds and our childish science can reach or understand—not truly."

He was about to interject, but she held up her hand to stop him; she knew that if she didn't say it all now, she never would. "I found out, to my cost, that there are secrets that lay behind certain ancient cults and are the origin of even the oldest myths—secrets too insane to be true—but I didn't realize that, couldn't believe. I called something up, attracted its attention, quite by accident.

"Magic is too prosaic and foolish a word, and misleading, in a way. It is an alien science trapped in symbols and sounds, triggering patterns, cause and effect. I may as well have been playing with matches while I sat in a pool of gasoline. Somebody died, I think…I nearly died…but my brain shut down, made me forget. It's still unclear to me, but it's starting to come back, all of this has brought it back.

"I had the evidence of my own eyes, and I found out that some things were perilous to know, things that destroy the reason and sicken the soul, things from which the brain's only solace is utter madness or blissful ignorance." Daisy shook her head. "I'm still not making much sense, am I? Well, put it this way: I believe in learning and science and the physical world around me. I believe in those things because I have the evidence of my reason and my senses to know they are true. I also believe in monsters, and that the world is not as we think it is—for just the same reason."

Daisy was on the verge of tears as she finished, but drew in a deep breath and composed herself. *There,* she thought, *I've said it out loud. No more running from it, no more forgetting.*

Morgan sat back and refilled his glass in silence for a moment before speaking. "Miss Walker, I've been a lawman, a mercenary, and a bounty hunter. I have a kind of talent that finds trouble and doesn't make a man friends, not the kind he can keep," he said solemnly. "I am a loner—you're right about that. I've drifted from one job to another on three continents and always found the same things: greed, corruption, petty-mindedness, and the evil that men do.

"I'd heard stories, of course, everybody does, especially out in the colonies—the supernatural, I suppose you'd call it, but I chalked them up to superstition and self-deceit—I knew better. Then, a couple of years back, I was here in the States, tracking down a man—a murderer on the run—a bad piece of work. I tracked him up from the Bayou country all the way to Arkham, and when I caught up with him—well, I had a good long spell in the hospital afterward in which to conclude my worldview: I had to cope with believing in monsters.

"I've a feeling that's why my 'employer' singled me out for this fun parade in the first place. Somehow, they knew I'd faced it before and survived. Oh, and the fact they might very well qualify as part of that 'world not as advertised' theory of yours themselves.

"So this Legion of Rapture," he continued thoughtfully, pouring another measure of whiskey for himself, "this mess that your friend's hooked up in, even that thing Cormac stole, it's all bound up with horrors most people don't even suspect exist; we can agree on that. But where does that get us both?—Aside from tickets to the funny farm if we make it out of this?—I have a feeling, Miss Walker, that you have some kind of answer to that?"

Daisy drank a sip from her own whiskey, coughed suddenly, and flushed, and despite everything, they both smiled.

She took the book back from him and opened it to her notes on the Kingsport trial transcripts. "Let's assume, for the moment, that all we have said is all too real," she began, affecting a brisk, business-like manner, "and that Kingsport is a place, well, let us just say a place that has long been touched by forces older and stranger than mankind knows.

"At the end of the Revolutionary War, a strange religious sect that had long flourished here was prosecuted and scattered. There were deaths and witchcraft trials, and those that survived were driven out of Kingsport. This secret cult that had made Kingsport its home, it was said to have worshipped things they called down from the stars, and from the deep places of the seas and the earth…and from out of time. They conducted a reign of terror before they were attacked and broken up, and much that was theirs was lost and scattered.

"But the cult had been drawn here in the first place because they believed Kingsport, the very land on which it stood, was special—that the barriers between worlds were thin here, and at certain times, when the cosmos aligned, there was no barrier at all. They held that Kingsport was a precipice that looked out into the beyond, and that anybody could step off, and fall." Daisy paused to look at him, trying to see if he followed her reasoning—if he believed her.

"And you think that's why this modern-day cult came here, why they seemed to have drawn Annabel here, and dragged us along for the ride?" Morgan asked.

"Yes. Yes, I think so. There are parallels, but they aren't the same thing; this Legion of Rapture seems more like a ravening band of madmen and murderers from what we've seen, rather than secret astrologers and seekers after wealth and occult power, handing down their hidden ways from generation to generation—as Sutter's followers were said to be. But they may be after the same thing…" Her own train of thought led her into silence.

"And what's that?" he prompted, seeing the tension in her face.

"To commune with beings they thought of as gods, true gods—not some medieval painted devil or benign savior, but horribly real entities of unbelievable malign power." It came out in a rush, as if saying it out loud unleashed a dam inside her. "Things in dimensions as far beyond human as humanity is above something you might see squirming on a microscope slide. They called them the 'Ancient Ones.' Some said Israel Sutter even called one, or at least tried to, and caused the great storm of 1781, nearly destroying the town in doing so."

"And toppled the lighthouse…," Morgan said, remembering the print he'd found in Annabel's room.

"Yes," Daisy said, letting out a sigh of relief that he hadn't called her crazy, despite everything they'd seen.

"The monsters—these creatures—where do they fit into this?" Morgan said, trying to get a handle on what she was telling him.

"There are lesser entities, as well, not just the Ancient Ones, and 'monster' is a very good word for them, for they are inimical to life as we know it. I assume they are things like we have encountered; some are like mindless predators, if the ancient books are right, others congealed dream stuff, servants of greater beings, or relics of intelligences other than man, things born of other stars and other times. They are what we've faced, I believe, and been lucky to live through meeting.

"Those madmen that attacked us, my guess is they were just men once, like you said—the detritus of the world, the lost, the ruined, swept up by that preacher's snake oil. I think he makes them see things, rends the veil, and the more they see, the more infected they get—the more the outside becomes part of them; some likely die or go mad, others become 'tainted' I suppose you'd call it, no longer really human at all."

Morgan sat back and ran his hands down his face. "Damn," he said, "that's quite a story to take in, and I guess it means this has all been, what? Some sort of madman's game?"

"A ritual, I think. Even us coming here: looking at it now, it was like Annabel was left to follow the trail of breadcrumbs… maybe we all were. It all may have been part of it somehow, maybe even her coming to me, the old friend from her past, with a head full of bad wiring and secrets she needed to forget."

Morgan looked at her and again was struck by her quality—her strength of character and intelligence were rare indeed—she'd put the pieces together, and had the courage to face their conclusion, and stared down her own demons in the process.

"I think Annabel was led here, first and foremost," Daisy continued, "and that we were shepherded, almost, watched. She's a willing sacrifice, or at least a deluded one, I fear—but I don't know why." Daisy slapped her hand down on the table in frustration. "I cannot see *why*—what's it been for? Nothing but horror and death can come of it, if this is to do with an Ancient One, and that makes everything we've seen pale into insignificance. I don't pretend to know what they really are, Morgan, but bullets and axes won't stop them. I'm not sure anything on earth can. As for poor Annabel, I don't want to imagine…" Her voice cracked with desperation.

Morgan got to his feet slowly, having reached his decision. "Stay here, I'm going up to my room for something with a bit more clout than a pocket pistol, and then I'm going out after Annabel."

Daisy started from her seat. "But we have no idea where she is. You can't just walk out into that fog. I want Annabel safe more than anything, but it's suicide—you said so yourself!"

Morgan smiled lopsidedly. "Which is why you're staying here, Miss Walker, and if pajama boy here can raise some help on the telephone, you send them right after me. Besides, I think my goose is cooked either way, and I said I'd help, and like you, I don't go back on my word."

"But where are you going to start?"

"Kingsport Head," he said decisively. "That damn hunk of rock seems to have something to do with this—that friend of yours had been painting it, seeing it in her sleep, as well, I wouldn't wonder, and what's more, I trailed one of those maniacs up near there and lost him, so it seems as good a place to start as any I can think of. But this time, I'll be ready."

Daisy looked furious, and Morgan wanted to say something flippant and offhand funny, just to hide how touched he felt, but couldn't think of anything. He certainly couldn't tell her what he really thought—that if he took the fight to them he might just buy some time before they realized the clean-up crew they had left hadn't done its job. Maybe he could even inflict enough damage before they took him out—if he was as lucky as people seemed to think—that they might very well overlook Daisy Walker, and give her a small chance to see another dawn.

"Look," he said at last, "if I can't find anything or get hopelessly turned around, I'll make my way back, but I'm going to try and get ahead of these monsters for a change, Miss Walker."

"You can call me Daisy," she said forlornly.

"Daisy," he said, reaching out and putting a hand on her shoulder. "If Annabel's still out there, I've got to try and get her back, and if I get all torn up for the trouble, you can say 'I told you so' afterward, all right?"

There was no dissuading him, and he retreated back to his room to make hurried preparations. Daisy was left pacing the lobby in frustration and fear for Morgan and Annabel's safety, the Luger jammed in her belt, and her notebook swinging in her hand like a talisman as the interminable minutes dragged by.

Dukes had given up trying to call out some time before, and had since lapsed into staring into space, worrying at his fingernails, so when the telephone rang, the hotel manager let out an involuntary shriek of panic before grabbing the earphone from the receiver set.

"What, who?" Dukes whined. "Morgan, he's…"

Daisy shunted Dukes out of the way and grabbed the earphone. "Hello, who is this?"

"Hello?" came the voice on the end of the crackly line. "I need to speak to Tony Morgan; it's extremely urgent!"

"Hello, my name is Walker, Daisy Walker, I'm Tony's friend; can I help?"

"Tony's friend? I didn't know he had any, well any up north anyway." The woman on the other end of the line seemed taken aback.

Daisy struggled with something to say to make the woman trust her. "I'm a librarian, with the Miskatonic University, I'm… urm…helping out with the Cormac case."

"Oh, right, that makes sense at any rate, well I hope you're on the level, lady, because I've been trying to get ahold of Tony all day, and this is real urgent. I'm Greta, Greta Thorson, by the way; Tony and me go back some, but I bet he didn't mention me, did he? Not that you have to worry, you know, nothing biblical, you understand?"

Daisy wasn't sure she did. "No, no, he didn't mention you. You said it was important, what you had to say to him?"

"And how! Well, I've been doing some deep digging in the federal records, and I hit pay dirt. It's about Cormac and the Ryan girl, both."

Daisy felt a sudden chill descend down her spine. "Go on."

"Well, he asked me to find out what I could about them, particularly if there was any connection beyond them meeting in New York, and bingo, I found it."

"What connection?" Daisy heard herself ask.

"Would you believe they are both from the same hometown, born five years apart, but in the same place—Sutter's Well.

"It was so hard to pin down because both ended up having their surnames altered after some disaster that hit the place back in 1913, some big fire killed more than a hundred people, all hushed up—more than likely bad practice on the part of the mill owners started the damn fire in the first place. It looks like half the town burned up. It never recovered, pretty much a ghost town now by all accounts."

"Sutter's Well?" Daisy echoed. *Sutter!* The text of the trial commentary ran through her head.

"Yes, it turns out our boy Cormac was put out to a very well-heeled foster family in his teens after his own people died in the fire. His father looks to have been the town minister of all things—a man named Marks—Cormac is the name of the foster family. The real kicker is the girl, though."

Daisy felt weak; she dropped her notebook on the lobby counter and held onto it for support. "Go on," she managed to say again.

"She's a Sutter, properly Annabel Regina Sutter, *the* Sutter you might say, the last one; there's a brother, apparently, but he's locked up in a madhouse somewhere, *non compos mentis* and burnt to a crisp, etc. She had only just turned nine when it happened—from what I can tell, the family lawyers changed her name to avoid the scandal and packed her off to a sanatorium abroad to recuperate afterward. She wasn't burned, but was found wandering in severe shock afterward. After that, she goes through a succession of boarding schools back in New England—I don't even think she knows who she is."

Annabel, oh Annabel, they've brought you home! The last of the line of the old Kingsport cult, Israel Sutter's long lost blood. Sutter, who called up the formless beasts of the stars to do his bidding and destroy his enemies. Sutter, who, when the stars were right, communed with the Ancient Ones to gain nightmarish wisdom on certain black and hidden solstices.

On the other end of the crackling phone line, Greta was struggling to make herself heard, but Daisy was no longer listening. She let the handset slip from her fingers. "Thank you," she whispered, and broke the connection.

Oh, poor Annabel, you've been betrayed, running half way around the world and you never knew from what, but they brought you back again, and I know where they've taken you.

Her thoughts running away from her, Daisy was oblivious to

her surroundings until Dukes started shaking her frantically by the arm. She looked up, suddenly aware of a cold waft of air and a metallic crumbling sound as the revolving door at the front of the lobby turned, its lock simply falling apart. A squat, dark figure came in from the night. A withered, claw-like hand rose up to doff a shapeless hat from a misshaped, bandage-wrapped head.

"Mam'selle Walker." The voice was paper-thin and drawn, almost beyond hearing, whispering like the winds through dead leaves. "We have not been introduced, I am Henri Damascus."

CHAPTER TWELVE

Morgan's knee still pained him some, and he could feel the stitches in his side itch—no doubt he'd busted a few loose in the fight—but he put the discomfort from his mind, focusing instead on the matter at hand. With methodical precision, Morgan finished priming and reassembling the four Mills bombs and moved on to putting together the cut-down Browning Auto-5 shotgun from inside the velvet-lined briefcase.

Both had been provided by Copperhead when he'd demanded portable firepower after what had happened at his apartment, and the fact they had the weapons to him within hours spoke volumes about the organization he had been blackmailed into working for. Even if what Daisy had implied about the world was untrue, there had to be a reckoning.

But it *was* true—he knew it in his gut—every damn thing he'd grown to suspect. There really were monsters waiting in the dark. In some ways, that didn't even matter anymore; his mind was clear. *It's all come down to this, and I know what I have to do.* Back in the prison in New York, Captain Grissom had told him that he may have preferred the rope, but Morgan knew the answer, the same as then: *if death wants me, it can come drag me down,* added to which he had two young women depending on him, one of them very fine indeed, and he'd signed on to fight for far less worthy causes in his time.

He finished loading the shotgun with its five 12-gauge slugs and stuffed another dozen in his overcoat pockets for good measure. Then, he checked his spare pistol, cleaned and sheathed his knife, and hung the four Mills bombs on his shoulder rig.

He caught sight of himself in the mirror on the way to the door and smiled. "You look like you're running late for a war, Tony," he said to his reflection. *It's a strange feeling,* he thought suddenly, *going to your end.*

He hefted the heavy shotgun onto his shoulder. Pausing to turn the light off, he cursed once and left it. *Better to light a candle, as they say.*

The hotel was as dark and silent as ever, and beyond the window glass, Kingsport slumbered uneasily in its shroud of mist, its people lost deep in the arms of nightmares which their waking minds would not let them remember. The white beam of the North Point Lighthouse flashed its ghostly arc out in the bay. Morgan checked his watch; it was near half past one and he couldn't afford to dawdle—there was no telling when they would attack again—but priming the fuses in the notoriously temperamental hand grenades wasn't exactly the kind of thing you rushed.

He was almost to the lobby when he heard Daisy speaking in a serious, flat tone, and somebody answering in a half-heard whisper. He slowly advanced down the stairs, shotgun at the ready, and was greeted with a strange sight indeed: slumped in the chair he himself had vacated was a stocky, misshapen figure with a cloth-swathed head, swamped by a stained-looking great-coat, one tattered sleeve hanging empty. Standing some distance away by the lobby counter, Daisy held her gun on the newcomer warily, her expression fixed and angry, while Dukes was nowhere to be seen.

The bandaged man, Morgan recalled suddenly. *So this is him, just sitting there?*

The man's face turned toward him as Morgan advanced down into the hotel lobby. "Ah," the seated figure whispered hollowly, "the warrior returns."

Daisy turned to him in obvious relief. "Morgan, this...this 'man' claims to know what's happening and wants to help us."

"He says his name is Damascus, and Maxwell Cormac hired him in San Salvador to steal the bar relief the fragment is from before Cormac betrayed him."

Damascus nodded in greeting as Morgan quickly scanned the lobby for trouble before standing beside Daisy, his gun never wavering. "You all right?" he shot quickly to Daisy.

"Yes," she replied quickly. "He gave us a shock, just walked in off the street—the lock on the door seems to have rusted to bits," she added with exasperation.

"Dukes?"

"Well, first he fainted, then he ran off to his room crying— quite the man, that one," she said scornfully.

"The hell with him anyway."

"Alone at last," Damascus whispered, cutting across them both, "and time is running very short for your beautiful Annabel."

"What do you know about that?" Morgan asked, leveling the shotgun at Damascus's head.

The bandaged man made a wheezing, rustling sound that might have been laughter. "And this is why I waited to talk to the inestimable Mam'selle Walker first—you have only one answer to anything, friend, and not a terribly effective one at that; I am already dead," he rasped, almost silently, "and fear nothing you can do to me."

The pieces fell into place in Morgan's mind. "You were in New York, stirring up trouble between the Mob and the madmen from the Rapture, weren't you?"

Again that dusty, laughing sound. "Yes, I was hunting, hunting for him that betrayed me, for my vengeance on him. Yes, and I saw you, as well—servant of vipers—you I steered well clear of, although I did not learn of Mam'selle Annabel's involvement until very late in my enterprise. But enough of that, we have so little time; they almost have what they want now, all of it, and very soon...very soon, the time will be right."

"Right for what?" Daisy demanded.

"Why, to show your Annabel the truth; they will make her remember, and if they do that, she is lost. They will also have forced a breach that will be almost impossible to close, and our world will be a step closer to the grave—not that it matters much now to me," Damascus offered and held up his remaining hand, flexing fingers that ended in blackened bone before them.

"Dear God," Daisy whispered. "What happened to you?"

"The Curse," Damascus whispered like a soft wind through a graveyard, "of Yig, the price of defiling the fane of your employers, Morgan—for they are less human even than your foes, or did you believe otherwise? The curse that should have been Cormac's, but instead is mine, as the thief who first laid his hands upon their ancient map of days. But he underestimated me—he believed I would die—but I have defied the grave for my vengeance, although the consequences for me have been less than favorable...and it was mine, nearly mine..."

"What happened?" Morgan asked.

"He abducted Annabel!" Daisy cut in angrily.

"Yes," Damascus, "as I was explaining to the mam'selle: I wished to thwart Cormac, even if I could not kill him, and so I took the woman before his creatures tired of their game. I hoped to learn her secrets for myself, perhaps retrieve the artifact, barter for my worthless life—but it was not to be. Other powers interfered," Damascus jerked the stump of his left arm, "most forcefully." Damascus slumped again in the chair. "But you do not have it, they have all now… They were watching you ever since you came here, mam'selle. As for me, I am spent, I shall not see the sunrise; I came here only to see if you might yet be triumphant—a vain hope, I know."

"Damn it all, this isn't getting us anywhere," Morgan raged. "I have to go and search for Annabel, and I can't leave you here with this…monster." Morgan's finger tightened on the shotgun's trigger.

"Wait!" Daisy shouted. "I know where she is, or at least I think I do!"

Both Morgan and Damascus looked at her in shock.

"The ruins of the old Sutter mansion," she explained quickly. "It's along the causeway on the other side of Kingsport Head— that's why you couldn't find them in town… Dear lord, we even went there on a school trip when we were younger, to sketch and do a nature ramble… I remember now, Annabel got sick afterward—had nightmares for weeks—the school nurse thought she'd eaten something she shouldn't have. She was always getting into trouble, running away…" Daisy's voice trailed off.

Morgan looked at her, lost, and she shook her head clear and went on. "Annabel isn't Annabel Ryan; she's Annabel Sutter— your friend from New York called with the information. The Sutters were among the key families in the old Kingsport mystery cult. They did terrible things in service to the entity they called the Lord of Nightmares—that must be what they want from her: to call on the cult's hungry god! She may even have done it before—there was a disaster when she was little; it almost wiped out the town she was born in. That insane preacher Marks was the town minister."

"Yes," Damascus rasped, "with the Valusian Book of Days they could pick the most auspicious hour, and with her blood they could open the way, close the circle, and perhaps murder the world."

Morgan shook his head savagely. "I don't pretend to understand any of this, but I've got to go—now. From what you two are saying, it's likely already too late."

"I'm going with you," Daisy said firmly. "I know where it is— you'll never find it in time in the fog."

"Based on the memory of a school trip? Now who's being crazy?" Morgan retorted angrily.

"I'm coming with you and that's final."

Morgan just stared at her for a long moment, his face a mask of controlled emotion, and said, "Very well, but you do what I say, when I say it, understand?"

Daisy looked him squarely in the eye and nodded, intending to do no such thing.

Morgan pointed to Damascus with the shotgun. "You're coming along, as well, but don't imagine we're friends."

Damascus issued another of his papery laughs, staggered uncertainly to his feet, and sketched a bow.

* * *

Annabel looked around her with a mixture of disbelief and terror, but deep down the horror didn't touch her; where her heart had been, there was now only desolate emptiness.

She knelt upon weather-worn flagstones of what once long ago may have been a garden terrace and stone-pillared arbor, its outlines sketched still by a few broken statues and low, half-overgrown boundary walls of a formal garden long choked with weeds and wild thorns. Some hundred yards behind her were the larger, vine-clad ruins of the great house which the garden had formerly accompanied, and ahead in the far distance, the sundering night sea and the looming dark colossus of Kingsport Head.

She was not bound, but she did not try to run—she had nowhere to go, and no chance to escape the score or more of ragged figures that staggered and circled in a strange, drunken, jerking reel around the four great bonfires, burning with eerie emerald flames, that circumscribed the area in a diamond shape with her and the fallen stone arbor at its center.

The figures' droning, ugly chants and insane cries filled the night air, and three times already they had brought someone before her, a captive, pleading and screaming. She had seen each in turn butchered before her eyes by the man she had loved, their spilled blood steaming on the flagstones while the twisted preacher capered and shouted to the stars, their bodies then torn apart and cast into the hungry flames.

Her nightmares had at last come to her wide awake.

The Reverend Eli Marks dropped to his knees in front of her and took her face in his hands, his feverish eyes boring into hers, his rank breath spilling over her.

"Do you see, child, do you see?" he pleaded.

She tried to drag her head from his hands. "You're a murderer and insane—you all are!" she screamed, dragging up defiance from the depths of her sorrow and despair.

"Oh, blessed child," Marks spoke reverently, "it was you that showed me the way, don't you remember? You tore the scales from my eyes and showed me the truth, burned me with the invisible fire of the Ancient Ones, showed me the terrible beauty of the slaughter and the black, limitless gulfs beyond."

Annabel slapped and tore at his hands and face, leaving red scratches with her fingernails, but her tormentor didn't even flinch.

"You saw him," Marks whispered urgently as she struggled to break free, "the herald of his coming, the Treader in the Dust, the Lord of Nightmares! You held him in your eyes, and you will do so again."

He released her face and clasped his hand over his heart, his grin splitting open his face.

"No, I can't, no…," Annabel whispered, feeling something dark and cold steal across her mind.

"I lost you for so long, and long was I broken and blinded," Marks crooned, "but we have been with you, watched you, protected you—in New York, Arkham, we have killed over and over again, all for you—and now here at last you have found us again; of your own free will you deliver yourself up to us."

"The glass…," she sobbed.

"Trash!" Marks shouted and laughed. "Worthless to us once its secrets had been read, but to you—to you it was all—it sang to you in your dreams, it drew you on, whispered, called his name."

Annabel sobbed, the enormity of what he was saying too terrible to take in.

Marks flung himself to his feet and threw his arms up skyward, roaring, "The gate shall open and the Feaster from the Stars will come to my call! Kingsport will suffer this night for defying our will, and your friends will be as dust!"

"No!" Annabel screamed.

"His hour comes around, but first this night, you will see, you will know rapture! And then you shall lead us in glory—tonight is only the start!"

A hideous keening sound drowned out everything, cutting through Annabel's mind like a razor blade scraping glass. Between the cracked stone pillars of the arbor, the world ripped open.

* * *

They had taken Dukes's showroom-new, soft-topped sedan over her Ford, both for its speed, and because, as Morgan put it, "He deserved no better than to lose the damn thing."

Morgan was behind the wheel with Damascus slumped beside him. Daisy was perched in the back with the fire axe propped between her knees and her pistol trained on the back of Damascus's seat, her finger well away from the trigger in anticipation of a bumpy road. Not that she imagined it would do much good to shoot him; the man—or whatever it was he had become—was walking around with an arm torn from his socket seemingly unphased despite his protestations of near death; he didn't bleed, and he didn't breathe.

I'm sitting in a car with a walking, talking, corpse! Daisy thought in shocked realization, *and heaven help me if that isn't the strangest thing that happens tonight!*

The car engine coughed and rumbled, and the flash of its headlamps speared through the coiling mists as the sedan swept through the fog on its way to Kingsport Head. The sedan had no side windows, just a windshield, and the cold, damp air tingled on the skin of Daisy's face as she pulled down the dark cloche hat she wore more firmly on the pin that spiked her bunched-up blond hair. She wore her satchel over her raincoat, despite Morgan's suggestion she leave it behind, and held onto it tightly with her free hand, gripping her notebook through the leather, the solid shape of it comforting her in some way.

Once they were underway, Daisy's mind was focused on giving Morgan directions, and the stress of that helped keep her thoughts off the strange feeling of utter unreality that washed over her; a sensation somewhere between delayed shock and a waking dream overtook her as they drove on through the town.

Kingsport seemed more unreal than ever to her, as empty and mute as a lifeless painting or a vast succession of benighted dollhouses. Nothing moved, save the uneven, shifting mist, and they saw no living soul, not even a dog or a wharf rat scurrying by. Adding to the strange vista were the muted orbs of the streetlights of the main thoroughfares, which hovered as ethereally as marsh phantoms, and they saw almost no lighted windows in the houses and buildings, which became no more than black silhouettes, painted backdrops in the mist.

"It's like something from a dream," she whispered.

Morgan only nodded in reply, trying not to let on just how much difficulty he was having in following the road. The mist seemed to resist the headlamps unnaturally, gathering into thick, coiling tendrils where the light was strongest. Worse still was how what his lights revealed seemed to shift fantastically, glistening wet asphalt suddenly giving way—to his eyesight at least—to cobblestones, or even hard packed dirt for a few seconds before the mist thickened again, and when it parted once more, the modern world had again regained its grip. Morgan simply gritted his teeth and carried on driving as fast as the mist and Daisy's clipped directions would allow.

Damascus, for his part, sat in utter silence, speaking only once to indicate a turn that somehow neither Daisy nor Morgan could see in the dark. Morgan, despite seeing nothing but blackness, had spun the wheel at the last moment anyway and suddenly they were climbing upward, away from the town and away from the mist's grip, although tendrils of the stuff seemed determined to grip clammily onto the sedan, following behind them for a time in pale streamers.

The motorcar rumbled up the narrow, winding road around the flank of Kingsport Head, and as Daisy looked behind them at the bay below, the sight stole her breath away. The town was shrouded under the strangely glowing fog, and bordered on all sides by deepest night; it was not the town she thought she knew, but a city in the mists, vast and labyrinthine. The dark shadows of the buildings seemed to shift and wan, suggesting spires, and even minarets, she knew could not be real. Out in the glittering black waters of the bay, the lighthouse flashed its scimitar of light, impossibly bright and powerful, like a beacon perched on the edge of eternity.

The sedan shuddered, its hard-rimmed tires spitting gravel chips as the road grew rougher, and Daisy turned from the view of Kingsport, unexpectedly wiping tears from her eyes.

The mist gone at this height, they negotiated the rear flank of Kingsport Head, and the road was as empty as if it had been made for them alone. Morgan hammered the sedan into giving him every ounce of power it possessed, and the motor jerked and rattled in protest. Daisy braced herself in her seat and clung on for dear life as they crested the height and started to plunge downward at speed, the left side wheels leaving the ground for a few moments during one bend in the road.

"Sorry," Morgan murmured apologetically from the driver's seat as he battled with the gearshift and decelerated slightly. With Daisy directing them to the right side path, they began to traverse a series of roughly stepped descents down toward the seaward end of the Miskatonic Valley and their destination.

Although Daisy could see little on the darkened hillside, she knew from memory that the area was dotted with the tumbledown remains of cottages and small holdings dating back to colonial days, deserted when settlers had moved on to far easier pastures inland as the country had been opened up. Neglected and desolate, the old bridle pathway down which they sped was storm-washed and ill-repaired, and the sedan had to slow down further to avoid a broken axel or sliding into catastrophe entirely. As they approached sea level, patchy mists began to come up again, but these seemed to have a far more natural quality to them than those they had left behind.

Spotting a withered old tree almost bent back on itself beside the road, Daisy called out, "Here, there should be a fork that takes us parallel to the water for a few minutes and then there's a hollow at the end of a steep slope, that's where the old Sutter manse stood, I'm sure of it; just ruins now, but all the land on this side of the Head was theirs once."

Daisy could see the old colonial county map in her head as plain as day, her own memories overlaying it like a projector slide. "I'm right, I know I am," she said quietly to herself.

The pathway began to rise again for a few minutes when Morgan abruptly killed the headlamps and applied the brakes hard, skidding them to a halt. Daisy, righting herself in the back seat after being thrown by the sudden stop, peered out of the front windshield. "Oh my!" she exclaimed in shock.

"That's one way of putting it," Morgan muttered back, opening the driver's side door and clambering out.

He was quickly followed by his companions, Damascus leaning against the hood of the car, as they looked out on the strange and nightmarish scene below.

Emerald fires burned in the night. The ugly sounds of guttural, clotted chanting and agonized death screams rose up in the chill air. Perhaps two hundred yards away at the foot of the steeply inclined slope, down which the rutted road continued at an angle, lay an undergrowth-fringed area of flattened, landscaped ground on which a great manse and its gardens had once stood.

The house's ruins stood out blackly in the eerie green firelight, and sheltering within them, Morgan could see the outlines of tents and ramshackle vehicles. Scores of dark figures staggered and cavorted—seemingly without purpose or aim—around the four great blazing bonfires, their distorted shadows playing monstrous patterns against the hillside. There was something utterly terrifying in what they saw, something offensive to reason and heavy with evil. To Daisy, it was the infectious, sickening madness she could hear in the chanting, worming into her like the droning of an insect trapped inside her skull, that was the worst of it; while for Morgan, who had seen his share of massacres and horrors in the forgotten places of the world, the scene was like some distillation of inhuman cruelty and self-willed savagery, and the movement of the figures held the likeness of maggots seething in a corpse. There was something weirdly familiar about the flickering green light, but he could not place it in his mind.

"The Legion of Rapture, I presume," Morgan offered, struggling to keep the shock from his voice.

"There are so many," Daisy said, equally shocked by the nightmarish sight before them. "How…how are the fires green?"

"I don't know… I'm not sure I want to," Morgan replied in a low voice as he racked the bolt on the shotgun. "They haven't seen us. At least their own fires will blind them; that's something, not much, but something."

"There is your friend, at the center of the broken pillars! Can you not see it? We are too late!" Damascus hissed angrily, gesturing with his claw-like hand. "The gate is already open—can you not see it—there before her!"

Daisy stared intently at where Damascus was pointing, forcing her eyes to focus on the spot at the dead center of the space bounded by the strange bonfires. It was as if something blurred the night air like a heat haze, almost as if it was actively resisting her seeing clearly, and then, with a snap in her mind, the view resolved; she saw Annabel and cried out. Her lost friend was kneeling on the ground, her hands raking furiously at her head, staring into, into *what?*

Daisy's stomach lurched and she gagged, a feeling of absolute vertigo taking her, as if she teetered on the precipice of some vast abyss and the ground was giving way at her feet. It was only Morgan's quick grasp of her arm that stopped her from falling.

How did I not see it before? There was something, something terrible, hanging in the air above the broken stone pillars, a swirling black vortex of a size she couldn't guess at, something at once so thin as to be two-dimensional and so deep it could swallow the world. It was a negative light, an anti-light—it ate her vision and left an afterimage of itself as if she had stared into a blinding sun.

Damascus might have chuckled. "Ah, mam'selle, you see it now? Yes?"

"What is it?" Daisy said, finding her voice again.

"Why, the truth, of course, the darkness beyond our pitiful existence. It is a gate, you might say, to a place more terrible than any of us can imagine, a place to which the drab hells of scripture and fantasy pale to nothingness—a wound in the face of the world," Damascus replied.

"I can't see anything in there," Morgan said alarmed. To him, the area at the center of the bonfires was a blur of flickering shadows that suggested form and movement, but no more.

"Closer you will—not that you might wish to. Something comes," Damascus hissed.

Coughing and regaining her composure, Daisy tugged her coat straight and said firmly, "Annabel's down there, I have to get her out, she's looking right into that thing!"

"Too late," Damascus whispered.

"I'm damned if it is," Morgan said coldly and flung open the car door, holding up a warding hand as Daisy tried to join him. "You're staying here!"

"Damn it, Morgan, don't do this."

Morgan laughed, somewhere between bitterness and triumph. "Miss Daisy Walker, it has been a pleasure," he said, first tipping his hat to her and then throwing it away. He turned to Damascus. "You're so keen on dying, monster, how about taking a few with you; can you drive with that one claw of yours?"

Damascus nodded haltingly, and was pushed by Daisy into the car muttering something she took to be in Arabic. Morgan opened the passenger side door, shoved the shotgun inside the seat well, and climbed up on the running board as the engine turned over. The headlamps stabbed into the night and the sedan growled into life and began to plummet down the hill, leaving Daisy shouting after them at the top of her lungs.

She stood there for a moment, her heart warring with her head. She knew she would not be able to live with herself if she ran, despite the fear that pounded her heart; but she also could not stand by while others died—she just couldn't. Knowing full well that she was likely willing her own destruction, pistol ready in hand, she began to half-run, half-clamber down the hill after them, not headlong, but with as much direction as she could manage, toward where her friend was prostrated in torment.

I don't believe I'm doing this! Hang on, Annabel, I'm coming!

The air split as by a thousand gutted animals, crying out for blood.

* * *

Annabel's mind came apart. The world shuddered and flickered like a cinema reel breaking down, slowing, snapping, the darkness between the movie frames going on forever.

Blood ran down her face; she felt it, sticky-hot, and tasted its copper-sharp tang on her lips, but there was no pain, only exquisite emptiness.

She let her head loll languorously from side to side; there to help her was the old scarecrow preacher on his knees, hands raised up, screaming to the heavens—she remembered him now. He used to be so much more handsome when he was young; she had stared at him every Sunday in the pulpit of the little white church as she daydreamed through the sermon—handsome, just like his son. She turned away and beheld her lost lover, her deceiver; fever-sick and murder-drunk, he staggered insensate, butcher knife loose in his hand.

Fools.

Weaklings.

Liars.

The voice in her head pounded, at once alien and familiar.

Step on a crack, break your mother's back.

The cold ground before her was a checkerboard of light and dark, fathomless without floor or sky, and in the distance, a dark, harrow-thin shape was drawing closer, famine-hungry, made of night.

Before it, something wavered, traveling fast, spiraling toward her, eager to be free—a living whirlwind of stars, as empty as she, beautiful and athirst, as cold as the ashes of dead worlds.

She laughed and held up her hands as it passed over her, felt the blood freeze in her fingers at it slipped through them like water.

Michael promised I could play, she thought petulantly, *I found the book, not him—it whispered to me.*

The ground shook and something pushed against her from behind, a flash of light and the beat of an immense drum. Boundlessly, she fell sideways, the stones rushing up to meet her. Her eyes fixed again on cold eternity and the black pilgrim drew ever closer. Her lips parted and she grinned.

Looking now, listening now.

Father was long gone, but she was still going home.

* * *

The rattling sedan bucked like an angry horse as Damascus threw the car into a tight turn. Morgan clung on desperately, the third Mills bomb bouncing from his hands somewhere behind him, the pin still in his teeth.

He spat it out and swore, and had just enough time to wonder in panic if it had bounced back into the car when a dull boom sounded someway behind him and the back of the car was showered with earth and shreds of their pursuers.

Morgan had no real idea how much damage they had done, or what the next move was, except to blast and scatter enough of the maniac things to give them room enough to rescue the girl and drive the hell out—there was no time to think, just act. The road had hooked them by the ruins of the house and toward the diamond-shaped space bathed in flickering green light. The first grenade Morgan had thrown into a dense clutch of ragged figures

near the first bonfire, and the effect had been devastating, toppling them like pins, but the second went wide thanks to the sedan plowing into a hulking body that actively flung itself in their
path. For a moment, he feared he'd caught Annabel in the blast,
but couldn't see clearly as the sedan turned away in a tight circle.

Everything was chaos. Up close, the ragged figures leered and
screamed; some seemed not to even notice they were there, muttering and shuddering, trapped in a mania none but they could
see, while others came at them like devils, savage and uncaring
of their own fates. The abused engine of the sedan coughed and
stalled at the outer edge of the diamond of fires, and Morgan
pulled out his back-up revolver, mercilessly pumping shots into
anything that came close.

"Get it moving!" he shouted at Damascus. "We're too far
away!"

A trio of ragged figures surged toward the driver's side as
Morgan's revolver clicked empty. Frantic that all was about to
be lost, adrenaline singing in his veins, Morgan jumped off the
passenger-side running board and scrabbled for the shotgun he'd
pushed into the seat well. Claiming his prize, he backed up, about
to fire through the vehicle at the madmen, but saw Damascus's
hand sweep out and obliterate the face of the first ragged attacker
to reach him, scooping it away like wet clay. Morgan's stomach
kicked and he staggered backward away from the car, his brain
refusing for a shocked moment to accept what he had seen.

A blade pierced his back, burning pain flaring as its point
glanced off his shoulder blade. Morgan whirled around and
brought the shotgun up, smashing the sawn-down stock into
the chin of a filthy man old enough to be his grandfather, who
spun away sideways, spraying teeth. An instant later, a ravaged-
looking man, stripped to the waist and covered in lacerations, ran
at him from the emerald-shot darkness, a railroad spike raised
high. Morgan pulled the trigger, blasting him from his feet, and

followed his shot with a second as more distorted forms came out of the flickering nightmare light.

Hissing, vile words spat out behind him, and Morgan swayed, light-headed, as a cacophony of screams rang out from the other side of the sedan, its engine shuddering again into life. Recovering his wits queasily, Morgan turned and jumped up on the sedan's running board, just as several of the ragged figures fell away from the other side of the car, and even in the weird green half-light he could see their flesh bubbling and sloughing off.

Damascus—dear God, what is he?

The sedan juddered forward, and began again to pick up speed and to turn inward. To Morgan's horror, he could see a few of the men they had struck down begin to stagger to their feet in their wake, their black silhouettes distorting, shifting. *"Tainted,"* Daisy had said, *"the outside gets inside the weakest ones,"* hollowing them out—like the two at the hotel—they must have been among the two farthest gone, set to kill or be killed.

The headlamps swept across the broken stones of the arbor, and he saw Annabel, laying there on her side—*Am I too late?*—while above her, the air wavered and shimmered blackly like a heat haze in the desert, stabbing needles into his eyes. With effort, he tore his gaze away from the spinning darkness, and saw—*Cormac!* A shiver of raw unadulterated hate shot through Morgan at that moment. He had started all this, this death and madness, and he would pay if no one else did. Morgan raised up the shotgun one-handed as Maxwell Cormac, his dress shirt blackly wet in the weird light, looked on at them and laughed ecstatically, and behind him Morgan saw Eli Marks, the false prophet, with his head-splitting grin. Snarling, Morgan pulled the trigger and held on, pain lancing up his arm as he tried to keep the shotgun on target as it spat out its remaining three shells in rapid succession, the muzzle flash a clean, blinding white.

The screaming howl of a thousand voices rent the air, immeasurably louder than before, and the sedan swerved erratically, forcing Morgan to drop the shotgun in order to cling on, pain shooting from his thigh as something struck him.

Damascus howled something in a language Morgan couldn't understand as the sedan tried to accelerate, kicking up dirt and slewing wildly. Something vast and all but invisible was in the air above them—a coiling, grey shadow without substance, its rippling bulk filled with pale stars.

Morgan heard himself scream as the air froze around him and he was kicked free, falling into the night.

* * *

Daisy pulled the trigger and ran. The Luger barked and flashed, and the chattering, faceless thing in the dark screeched and toppled backward as she fled away from it.

She was dodging and weaving, running for her life between black shapes that leapt from the green-painted darkness like specters from a nightmare. Her legs were burning with the effort and her breath came in panting gasps. She was trying to get close to Annabel, weaving in and out of danger, desperately trying to get near. Daisy could hear the sedan churning up the ground and the roar of gunfire, and from the corner of her eye she caught glimpses of the motorcar drawing on the madmen like moths to a flame. She could not let the chance to save her friend slip by—it was as if her whole life had been ground down to a single desire, a single instant of action, and there was nothing else but to run and dodge and shoot when she had to.

Daisy cried out in shock and terror as she tripped over something in the dark, dropping onto her side; desperately, she clung to the gun as she backpedalled across the wet ground, sliding away from something alive—moving. The great screaming came again, ripping into her brain, and she screamed with it as the emerald bonfires flamed up like furnace blasts. In the sudden vivid light she saw what it was she had struck in the dark: a terrified middle-aged man in a ripped tuxedo and a deranged white dress-collar, his hands and feet bound, his face set in a rictus of terror. Some part of her brain that was still reasoning recognized him dimly—*the hotel restaurant, he was there! Was that tonight? How could this be the same night?* And then another thought stole across her mind. *How many didn't make it home in the fog? Is Claudia here somewhere?*

Coldly, she fought down her panic and clambered to her knees—*Annabel first!* The blazing light of the fires burned from green to blinding white and she saw, as clear as day, the sedan swerve for a final time with *something* distorting the air above it, as it slammed into a low, moss-covered wall with a sharp explosive crack and rocked to a halt. The darkness descended as she watched and the sedan's soft top was shredded like tissue paper, and, in a moment, the whole car was jerked violently into the air like a child playing with a toy.

"No!" she screamed involuntarily as the sedan came apart, torn by some ungodly invisible force, shredded body work and hot engine metal showering down. Daisy watched in horror as Damascus's squat figure was plucked mid-air from the wreckage like the meat from an oyster. The night coiled around him and he began to spasm and jerk as if struck by spears from every angle; he started to collapse in on himself, deflating and withering as the air around him thickened into brownish-black tentacle-like coils.

Daisy, her heart beating in her chest, looked on in appalled fascination at the terrible sight before her. An awful, hateful moan of countless tortured voices reverberated about the space, sickening to hear, and in its wake, a great, swirling wind struck up, battering her almost off her knees.

In the sky above, the Feaster from the Stars lashed in agony; it whirled and moaned from countless shadowy mouths, and beneath it the ragged men staggered and screamed. In a sudden, inhuman frenzy of rushing motion, half-visible tendrils lashed down and struck at any living thing they could reach with hungry, lamprey maws sharper than splintered glass.

Daisy cried out and rolled aside as one of the maws shot toward her across the sky like a shadowy harpoon, bringing with it a flood of blizzard-cold air. The tendril speared into the unfortunate captive behind her, and she could do nothing but watch aghast as his flesh collapsed in on itself and he was sucked dry, the shadowy tendril suddenly flashing a livid, blood red as it drank.

"Mad," she whispered as she continued to backpedal away, glancing wildly around. "It's gone mad! The Curse of Yig..."

She had no way of knowing if it was true, but the thought cannoned into her mind. Damascus had been poisoned by the curse, and by some dark art had kept his body working even though long past death, and the thing, whatever it was, had drank him dry, *drank in the poison!* Now it was gorging itself, feeding as fast as it could to rid itself of that taint!

In his death, Damascus had had some measure of his revenge.

Daisy clambered to her feet again as all around her the Legion of Rapture was slaughtered by a horror of their own conjuration—jerked into the air or crushed like insects by the maddened thing from beyond. Some fought, some fled, some merely cackled insanely as they were swept to their deaths. The bonfires began to smother and scatter into sparks in the sudden rushing turbulence, while the sky above the garden turned a livid, viscous crimson—moving and coiling like a blanket of immense goredipped worms blotting out the stars.

Something rattled and slavered beside her, and Daisy's breath caught in her throat as a woman's torso dragged itself toward her on boneless limbs, the collapsed flesh of its head splitting open vertically, revealing white, glassy teeth. Daisy fired three times at point-blank range, flipping the hateful thing onto its back, and it spilled apart into yellowish ammonia-reeking foulness.

Annabel!—It was her one thought, her anchor to sanity.

Daisy ran.

* * *

Annabel got to her feet slowly, and stretched as if awaking from a deep slumber, before straightening her hair with her fingers.

It's all so very clear now.

She looked down, smelling blood. The Reverend Marks lay dead at her feet, a hole the size of a fist punched clean through his shallow chest. She studied him for a moment, fascinated.

Beside her, somebody giggled. She turned—it was Max.

"He missed me!" Max giggled again, fingering a ragged hole in his shirttails, and then flinching as something whipped overhead.

She looked at him, her head to the side, and frowned sadly. "I remember you—you broke my heart."

Confusion stole across Cormac's stupefied, once handsome features. He was about to say something in reply, but instead screamed soundlessly as his flesh began to crack and blacken. Cormac dropped to his knees, cinders flying up from his crumbling body like burning shreds of paper into the night.

The unrecognizable, ashen mass crashed to the ground, forgotten, as Annabel Sutter smiled, and turned to greet her friend Daisy as she ran out of the dark.

* * *

Daisy refused to look at the dreadful, looming vortex above them, no matter how it nagged at her insistently and whispered longingly in her head—instead, she focused only on her friend. It was not until she was almost at touching distance that Daisy realized that something was dreadfully, nightmarishly wrong.

Annabel had no eyes.

Daisy fell backward as if struck, landing on her backside on the cold, wet stones.

Annabel smiled down at her. It was the most awful thing she had ever seen, and with it something deep down inside Daisy, a spark of vitality and sanity, died.

"Spook, little Spook," Annabel said, in a strange double-echoing voice—both woman and child, "you came, I knew you would, always such a good friend."

"Annabel!" Daisy gasped desolately, her hand to her mouth. "I'm sorry, I'm so sorry."

"Oh, Spook, don't you see? You must see, you'll be so much happier when you do."

As Daisy watched, something like a shadow flickered around Annabel—a double-image fashioned of terror and night, impossibly thin and tattered, hungry and endless. Daisy whimpered and tried to raise the Luger in her shaking hand.

"He's coming, he's coming soon, and nobody can stop it," Annabel whispered.

Daisy screamed as the gun in her hand withered and crumbled into black splinters, agony blazing cold in her hand for a brief instant before she felt nothing there at all but the echo of pain too great for her mind to encompass. Daisy rolled onto her side weeping, clutching her icy-cold hand to her chest.

Annabel turned to face the carnage and the devastation that had been wrought, the writhing red beast in the sky, and the cries of the dying. She laughed, throwing her arms wide. "Isn't it marvelous?"

Annabel turned and looked down at Daisy with her empty gaze and smiled again her terrible smile. "But it's nothing to what will be when they come back, Spook—oh, we'll have a fine time then."

Daisy recoiled and cried out as Annabel reached down and ripped off her cloche hat, and then made a handful of Daisy's hair to drag her by.

"Come along now, Spook, it's time we were going home," Annabel said and turned toward the rippling darkness, dragging Daisy behind her.

"Pray...god," Daisy stammered.

"What's that?" Annabel asked. "Oh, Spook, ever the strait-laced minster's daughter with her books and her stories—pray if you want—it will do you no good, and be forgotten soon."

Annabel had misunderstood. Her grip was like ice, shooting pins and needles of pain into Daisy's head, making it hard to think straight, but with her good hand Daisy reached down and clasped the notebook inside her satchel. She didn't need to see it, she remembered it all now, as well as she remembered anything— all locked in her famous memory—the forbidden history, the sigils and diagrams, the burning words and what they meant.

"*IÄ, IÄ,*" Daisy began, "*YOG-SOTHOTH,*" who is the Key and the Gate.

Annabel staggered. Her grip on Daisy's hair slackened.

"No...not fair...," the child's voice said softly.

The terrible alien words continued to tumble out of Daisy's mouth, again and again. *Will the change. Trip the pattern. Turn the key. Shut the gate. Look into the abyss.*

Annabel staggered and let go, and something cried out *through her* as if trapped far, far away, in utter loneliness and everlasting despair.

Daisy fell as the ground heaved and shook like a storm-wracked sea. The sky split asunder and was filled with a bellowing red-mist rain, but still Daisy went on, chanting the rite to call on the echo of an entity older than the stars themselves—although her teeth bled and her ears were filled by a maddening piping that made her want to start screaming and never stop. There was thunder and darkness...

Until everything was still, and the only sound was the waves crashing forlornly along the rocks of Kingsport Head.

...Daisy flickered in and out of consciousness, caught between living and dying.

In her deathly dreaming, she saw a terrible, lean, dark pilgrim walking, ever closer, across the cold and fathomless gulfs of eternity, never stopping, and behind him, mournfully, went a little girl in a dress as black as the night.

The girl looked back across the depths of nightmare to Daisy with empty, hungry eyes.

EPILOGUE

He sat in the dusty, deserted lobby and sweltered, gripping a cheap secondhand briefcase to his chest like a life preserver. Outside, the streets of Boston in late November were rain-swept and cold, but inside, the nameless building was as hot as a Turkish Bathhouse, and the effect had been to turn his last good suit into a sodden rag.

He fidgeted nervously; he didn't want to be here, but he had no choice, not after Kingsport, not after his world came apart. He needed the money, and nobody was going to help him; the papers where still full of the Crash and catastrophe.

For the fifth time that day, he silently swore to quit drinking and pull himself together. Gladys wouldn't have him back the way he was, but with the money, maybe he had a chance. He was terrified.

A door opened and he fought the urge to leap up and reach for a gun that was no longer there, a gun he'd already pawned a week back.

He blinked rapidly, not quite believing his own eyes: it was a beautiful, austere woman who looked utterly out of place in the dim, disused building.

"Sheriff Claiborne?" she asked before he could gather his wits.

"Yes, I mean, I used to be," he stammered in reply.

"Come with me," she said coldly, and turned away.

His questions died on his lips and he made himself follow her along a corridor and down a spiral staircase, her back turned to him; she seemed deaf to his voice as he tried to keep up.

The basement room was dark and infernally hot. Claiborne found himself standing in the pool of light cast by a single feeble bulb at the foot of the staircase, unwilling to follow the woman into the darkness. He wrung his hands and called out to her, but was answered only by the hissing of pipe steam somewhere close by.

He fidgeted and began to whine under his breath, caught between fear and desperation. Fear won, but as he began to turn and reach out a trembling hand to the stair rail, a dry, rasping voice froze him to stone.

"Mr. Claiborne, thank you for coming to see me."

He turned, trembling, toward the voice in the darkness. "Mr. Shawcross?"

"Yes," the paper-thin voice answered. "You have the papers?"

Claiborne clutched at the briefcase he was holding, as if suddenly remembering its existence. "It's all here. You said you would pay—," he began, but was cut short by Shawcross.

"Yes, yes, you will be amply rewarded. I have no time for pleasantries, Mr. Claiborne; tell me what you have brought."

"It's—it's all here—the report I tried to file on the murders and the disappearances last month, everything I could salvage and keep from being burned, even a picture of the wreck at the old Sutter ruin; it's gone now, the ground all heaved up like a plowed field, nothing but scraps and rubble now. You can't see much, but the whole place stank of blood, and there was a damn car axel poking out of the ground half-buried with the tire still on it! I wanted to dig it up, but they wouldn't let me. They said I was a troublemaker, a drunk—they threatened, they—"

"Calm yourself. Who threatened you?"

"The mayor, the city treasurer, all of them, the Kingsport people, they hounded me out of my job—they know something—they all do! The old man, that terrible old man, watching me wherever I went—"

Something *hissed* in the dark, and it was not the steam pipes, but something larger and infinitely more malign. Claiborne began to tremble as it dawned on him that he had made a terrible mistake in coming here, in answering Shawcross's letter with its folded green bills and promise of many more to come.

"Speak not again of him," the paper-dry voice insisted. "What of Morgan? Tell us of Morgan."

Claiborne's head darted from one side to the other; there were things moving in the darkness beyond the feeble light, and he was no longer sure which direction Shawcross's voice was coming from.

"I—I—I don't know," he said with rising panic. "I spoke to people that had seen him around town the days before, before it happened, but there was no sign of him afterward. I don't know what happened to him. They covered it all up, went on like it never happened. It was the woman, that Walker woman from Miskatonic—she was the only one that showed up again, maybe a week later, the only one of the missing that was found, and she wouldn't talk, she…she frightened me."

There was a broken hissing noise from somewhere to his left; it sounded like mocking laughter.

The briefcase slipped from Claiborne's fingers and hit the cement floor with a thud. He had meant to throw it, but he didn't have the strength; he was feeling dizzy with the heat, terrified and nauseous, suddenly conscious of a bitter musky smell in the basement room. His legs were like rubber and he couldn't will them to move.

"Look, I'll just go. You can…you can have the papers, I just need a little money; you can send it to me if you—"

"One more question, Mr. Claiborne, and you will have your reward: where are the fragments made of black glass I spoke of in my letter, did you see them?"

"She, she had them, took them away…a car came, from Arkham," he whispered, the words slipping out without thought.

The hissing in the dark grew louder and more urgent, and then fell away to silence.

Claiborne fell to his knees. "So hot, so hot," he moaned, struggling uselessly at his collar.

"Yes, yes," the dry voice came again, twisting, growing more sibilant. "We dislike it here; the chill and the dampness are not to our taste—nor is this place—too close to danger, and worsening every day. Calamity and nightmare, these are the signs."

"I don't…understand…," Claiborne sobbed.

"*Your wife will be paid handsomely for your offering; fear not, we always honor our debts, as Morgan and those who have aided him will find out soon enough.*" Shawcross's voice had lost all hint of humanity now—it was a vile exhalation of serpentine breath, a twisted mockery of language.

Claiborne tried to scream as alien, golden eyes hovered on the edge of the darkness.

End of Book One

About the Author

Alan Bligh is a full-time writer and game designer
from Nottingham, England. His credits have included
radio scripts, various roleplaying games, such as *Dark
Heresy*, *Rogue Trader*, and *Cthulhu Britannia*, and
the *Imperial Armour* book series of sci-fi wargaming
expansions for Forge World.

Dance of the Damned is his first published full-length
novel. It has let him bring together his long-time
loves of cosmic horror, noir, and dangerous old books.
He has a fondness for tea and cats, at least one of
these tendencies which he shares with H.P. Lovecraft.